A
CHRISTMAS
HOPE

BOOKS BY JOSEPH PITTMAN

A CHRISTMAS HOPE

A Linden Corners Novel

JOSEPH PITTMAN

Kensington Books
www.kensingtonbooks.com

KENSINGTON BOOKS are published by

Kensington Publishing Corp.
119 West 40th Street
New York, NY 10018

All Kensington titles, imprints, and distributed lines are available at special quantity discounts for bulk purchases for sales promotion, premiums, fundraising, educational or institutional use.

Special book excerpts or customized printings can also be created to fit specific needs. For details, write or phone the office of the Kensington Special Sales Manager: Kensington Publishing Corp., 119 West 40th Street, New York, NY 10018. Attn. Special Sales Department. Phone: 1-800-221-2647.

Kensington and the K logo Reg. U.S. Pat. & TM Off.

ISBN-13: 978-0-7582-8880-6
ISBN-10: 0-7582-8880-8
First Kensington Trade Paperback Edition: October 2012
First Kensington Mass Market Edition: October 2013

eISBN-13: 978-0-7582-9169-1
eISBN-10: 0-7582-9169-8
Kensington Electronic Edition: October 2013

10 9 8 7 6 5 4 3 2

Printed in the United States of America

This one's for . . .

The Keene Family

I will honor Christmas in my heart,
and try to keep it all the year.
I will live in the Past, the Present, and the Future.

—Charles Dickens, *A Christmas Carol*

AUTHOR'S NOTE

Welcome home to Linden Corners. I certainly feel that way, even though the village exists only in our minds. Many years ago I created the world of the windmill, populated with characters such as Brian and Janey and Annie and Gerta, as well as an assortment of local residents like Martha, Chuck, Marla and Darla, all of whom have become real over the course of two books.

Writing again about the magical world of Linden Corners was not without its challenges. First, to tell a third story of the windmill—after *Tilting at Windmills* and *A Christmas Wish*—was worrisome to me; I didn't want readers to suffer from overkill when it came to the village's landmark . . . yet how I could not write about it when immersed in the world it enveloped? Second, I had already written about how special the Christmas season is to Brian and Janey, so what new traditions were there to discover during the holidays?

Turns out, plenty. By opening up the story to include some characters new to Linden Corners—at least, the present-day village—the wealth of story and opportunity started to come together. In these pages you'll meet new friends and get reacquainted with old ones, and rediscover that storytelling is endless, just like the revolutions of the windmill.

So yes, welcome back; we may just meet again.

A
CHRISTMAS
HOPE

$\mathscr{P}$ROLOGUE

YESTERDAY

Just as nobody knows the future, nobody need fear the past. So the only choice left was to live in the present, with a guiding light called hope leading you through your days. That's how I see it, my dear, but of course that's hardly news, not to you. You who knows me so well.

Speaking of this elusive thing called hope, let me tell you about the place I've found . . . or is that rediscovered? A sense of promise lives here, inside waiting dreams, unwritten tomorrows. Powered by love and family and by the wintery whims of the wind, we called this magical little village Linden Corners. It's a place that some are born to and never leave, while newcomers accidentally stumble upon its borders, soon charmed by its welcoming brand of community. And others, like me, we return to the land after many years away, looking for something that may no longer exist.

But that's getting ahead of myself. To understand now, you need to know about then.

I remember that time of my life like it was yesterday, the details bright and colorful in my mind even as the photographs from those cherished moments were awash in sepia-

faded tones. Nostalgia always seems steeped in the colors of black and white, silent and evocative, like an old film. Of course those memories were now decades old—as, inevitably, was I. So many years have passed, and while the world may have changed, the only constant in life as far I've discovered comes from the endless revolutions of the great windmill's sails, standing proud against blue skies when I was a boy, remaining so in the same location all these years later, a piece of history alive today making fresh memories. I can hardly forget how those latticed sails spun in breezes both gentle and fierce, my young self imagining the turns of the old mill acting as the beating heart of Linden Corners, its blood flowing, inhabiting our souls.

I was a red-faced newborn when I came home to live inside the warm farmhouse on the outskirts of Linden Corners. It had been in the Van Diver family for at least four generations, dating back more than one hundred fifty years, more time than any of us really chose to count. No one liked to acknowledge the passing of years, we are loathe to admit time's continuous ticktock, all the while knowing it was never in our favor. All of this I knew, from the passage of the years, from a life mostly behind me.

Now I have returned to this place I once called home, but somehow it appeared time had come to a complete halt. I am decidedly older, two months shy of my eighty-fifth birthday. It is a cool, late October night and Halloween will fast be upon us, the first of the holidays that will dot the calendar's final push toward the New Year. The fruitful banquet that is Thanksgiving lurks just weeks later, a difficult time, as it is a celebration of family and I have none. And before long arrives the day folks endlessly prepare for, one so rich with spirit and yes, with hope, with gifts sealed, surprises hidden beneath bright shiny paper to await a child's wide-eyed discovery. It is the day called Christmas, that special time of year when we acknowledge the birth of Christ. But also a day of joy for me, as it was to this sleepy village of Linden Corners where I was born, on a blustery, snowy, early Christmas morning, my parents receiving the one and only gift they ever truly desired—a child, a son. From the start I was a boisterous, wailing child who, as snowy drifts grew deep and white blankets coated the sidewalks, sent his echoing cry out over the land, down to the spinning sails of the windmill and beyond, into the frigid air, one more voice heard from in a world seeking the hope of tomorrow.

I had been deemed the future of our tiny family, the first-born male of a new generation, but as history would come to dictate I would remain the one and only. Here I was, Thomas Van Diver, an infant with a big name and big expectations, draped in swaddling clothes and brought to the farmhouse and its neighboring, spinning windmill. Home to Linden Corners and into the loving arms of two people who lived to share love and laughter. There would be many happy times inside the close comfort of our farmhouse, I do remember those, but there were troubled times and sad ones, too, and it was this lingering sense of sorrow that led to my family's eventual departure from Linden Corners. Only now have I found my unsteady feet back on its rich soil all these decades later, in an effort to bring my life full circle. An effort to remember my past and embrace today, even as I seek answers to what the mysteries of tomorrow may bring. Life is filled with uncertainty, you can choose to embrace it or run in fear of it, and in the end you can only hope for the best.

There's that word again: hope.

Once upon a time I knew the meaning of that word.

Then once upon another time life took it away from me, leaving a hole in my heart.

My mind suddenly drifts to a simpler time. To my last Christmas in Linden Corners.

* * *

"Thomas," I heard my mother call to me, *"where have you gotten off to?"*

She wasn't really looking for an answer, as my all-knowing mother knew just where her mischievous son had hidden himself. Our harmless game of hide-and-seek always ended with the same result, me stashed behind cardboard boxes in the musty old attic. As her booming voice enveloped the strong walls of the farmhouse, I was busy climbing the steep wooden steps that led upstairs, where we stored all the memories of our little life. Her voice could stop an elephant, and for a moment I was brought to a stop on the third step, my destination just within my grasp.

"What did I tell you about going into the attic—not today."

"I won't peek, I promise," I called back, my voice meek.

No reply was forthcoming and I assumed I was in the clear to complete the final steps to my desired destination. But as I took that next step, I heard the sound of a throat clearing behind me. I turned, guilt coloring my face as red as Santa Claus's suit. How had she gotten up here so fast, and without me even sensing her presence? Mothers, I had come to learn, were not unlike superheroes, gifted with their own powers of deduction, their own stealth approach.

"Thomas, not today," she said, her voice weary, almost tired.

That was rare for Lisbeth Van Diver, a woman with an easy smile and a genial nature. Which is what gave me pause today, the lack of such poise. For a five-year-old boy whose world revolved around his parents and his isolated life inside this village, the idea that something was wrong sent a wave of worry over me. My lips began to tremble and I fought hard to keep tears at bay.

"I'm sorry . . ." I started to say.

"Shush now, just come down and help me in the kitchen,

you can help ice the cookies," she said. "You know, the ones your father so likes."

I quickly agreed to her request, making my way not only down the attic stairs but those that led to the ground floor, my stubby little legs trailing so close after my mother as though I'd been tethered to her. But I did sneak a look back upstairs, wondering about the attic's secrets. With tomorrow being Christmas Day—and my birthday—it could be anything, a new bike or perhaps a set of model trains that I'd seen in the Sears catalog last month. Papa had let me cut out the colorful picture and it still hung over my bed, the bright red engine blowing its whistle only in my dreams. For a boy who lived a quiet existence, the idea of the unknown discoveries of the world called to me, set my heart beating. Wanderlust, I would later learn it was called, but at five I could barely pronounce such a big word much less understand its meaning.

So I joined my mother in the kitchen and I spread sweet, sticky red icing on the sugar cookies, topping them off with a chunk of homemade white chocolate. My mother loved to bake, and she could often be heard singing as she worked to feed her family, lately Christmas carols. I loved the sound of her voice, a high soprano that was lilting and soothing, a memory that drew me back to the crib. But today she was quiet, and again I felt fear stab at me while looking up to observe her mood. She just kept working, decidedly focused. I took in the scene around me—Papa's favorite cookies, Papa's favorite meal of pot roast and roasted potatoes with gravy and boiling carrots, its scent filling the big kitchen.

Wait a minute, my young mind protested, isn't this my birthday, and as such, shouldn't I be making my choice of cake and ice cream, deciding upon my favorite meal? Suddenly the room felt smaller, like our family had shrunk.

"Mama, where's Papa?" I asked hesitantly.

"He'll be home soon," she said. And then, matter-of-factly, she said, "He has news."

Her tone told me everything I needed to know, even at that young age.

News was shorthand for bad news.

Papa arrived home an hour later, just shy of six o'clock that night. When he walked in, the cold air breezed in with him, and ordinarily Mama would tell him to close the door, we're not heating all of Linden Corners. But tonight she was silent as that mouse in that old Christmas story as she accepted a tender kiss from him, one that lingered, as though each were savoring it. He tousled my hair, attempting a smile.

"How's my boy?" he asked.

I looked up at him and like always, he seemed like a blond giant. Lars Van Diver was six feet two with a shock of thick hair that some might have called white, and tonight he loomed even larger, as though the distance between us had grown since last I'd seen him, just this morning. His coloring made him blend into the backdrop of the pale wallpaper in the dining room, the notion that he was gradually slipping away crawling inside myself. Instinct is a funny thing, it knows things before your mind does, and by the end of dinner, where I'd barely touched my pot roast, my fears were confirmed. Papa was going away.

"Your father has been drafted, Thomas," Mama said. "Do you know what that means?"

"He has to fight in the war."

The year was 1942 and America had been thrust into the Second World War over a year ago, with the Japanese surprise attack on Pearl Harbor. I was too young to fully understand, but I saw the pictures and bold headlines in the newspaper and heard the president talk on the radio, and if *his meaning didn't exactly sink in, his tone did. Dedicated men from all over the country were leaving behind their families to fight an enemy who seemed to dislike us overnight. Like a friend at school, now just a bully you wanted to avoid.*

There was no avoiding this, the war.

"When do you have to leave?" I asked, my eyes reflecting the sadness present in my parents' expressions. I was feeling selfish now, having been jealous of all of Papa's favorite things, food and desserts, being served. Even my attempt to sneak into the attic had me feeling like I'd betrayed a trust. Was his leaving somehow my fault?

"Tomorrow," Papa said, "but not till the night. So I can report first thing on the morning of the twenty-sixth. Oh-six-hundred."

Mama explained that was military talk for six o'clock in the morning, but it didn't sink in, my little self trying to process the sooner concept of "tomorrow." Christmas Day, my birthday, perhaps the one day on the calendar set aside for family unity, a time for us to celebrate all we'd been blessed with. And now it came tinged with deeper meaning.

"Thomas, why don't you go play, let your father and I talk."

I agreed with a fair amount of reluctance and left the table, my dinner half-eaten. Even the sugary goodness of the cookies had lost their appeal. As I climbed upstairs to my room, I heard murmurs emanating from the dining room, Papa and Mama having a serious discussion. Finding my way to my bedroom, I closed the door and fell to the bed. I didn't cry, I didn't pout. I just lay there, thinking like I'd never done before, maturing as the minutes ticked away toward midnight, when Christmas would arrive, Santa bringing gifts, but taking Papa from me.

Just then I clambered out of bed, running to the window. I stared up at the star-glistened sky, looking for Santa's magical sleigh, led by its eight reindeer, listening for the familiar jingle of bells. But I heard nothing, just the wind. Across our expansive lawn, I looked down at the windmill as its sails turned. I thought I could hear them creak in the wind, so old and forgotten was the once-heralded windmill, an icon to a different time. We no longer farmed on the land, and as a result the windmill had lost its purpose, standing there against the landscape as though waiting to be rediscovered by someone else, a new family.

That awful fear hit me again. With Papa going off to war, would Mama and I continue to live here, just she and I against the world? If we had to leave, would we travel by train, thus ensuring I'd be granted my wish of wanderlust? I thought about where Papa was going, very far away, to the other side of the world. I'd have to look at it on the globe we kept in the attic . . . and so that's what my mind quickly decided to do—against all common sense and previous warnings from Mama. I snuck out of my room and climbed the steps to the attic, just as I'd attempted only hours ago.

How time can change your life.

Earlier this afternoon I was blindly happy in my own innocence, the idea of brightly wrapped gifts dominating my thoughts as my birthday neared. Now, as the cold evening fell and darkness enveloped the farmhouse, life felt blacker, as though I'd just discovered that you don't always get what you want, a hard lesson to learn at age five. Because in that attic I discovered not a new bicycle or that desired model train set. What I found was a thinly wrapped package. I picked it up, shook it. It made no sound, and why should it. I knew what it was: a book.

"So, you found it anyway," I heard.

I looked up and there was Papa, on the top step.

"I'm sorry . . ."

"I was just coming up for it," he said.

"Is this for me?"

"It's for all of us, the three of us," he said, "it's for our family."

For a time that night, the Van Diver family was one, the troubles of tomorrow forgotten for one special moment. Fluffy white snowflakes fell outside, coating the frozen land, and the cold wind impotently blew past our farmhouse, the three of us impervious to the elements as we sat around a crackling orange-tinged fire. Papa had made warm cider with cinnamon, and we drank from ceramic mugs and we ate Papa's favorite sugar cookies, that last chunk of white chocolate the final morsel we would pop into our mouths. That's how Papa preferred to eat them, and so of course that's how I ate them. Our fresh Christmas tree smelled of pine and sparkled with lights and tinsel, giving the room a warm glow, a festive feeling. I knew it was just make-believe, like a stage set. But sitting in Papa's lap, Mama close at our side, I felt the loving embrace of my parents and for one night I was assured all would be right.

I'd been allowed to unwrap the book, my face aglow with what I saw.

"But why is Santa wearing a green suit?" I asked with surprise, starting at the unusual illustration on the front cover.

"It's an antique, Thomas, a rare book that almost no one else in the world owns," Mama explained with clarity. "And that means it's very old and very special. Back before you were born there were many legends about Santa Claus, who is also called Saint Nicholas. Your papa found this, picked it out himself."

"Enough of the history lesson," Papa said. "Let's tell the story."

I settled in, joy widespread on my cherubic face as he

began to read the familiar words: "Twas the night before Christmas, and all through the house, not a creature was stirring, not even a mouse . . ."

It wasn't the rhyming words I was concentrating on, but rather the deep, masculine tones coming from Papa as he read to me Clement Clarke Moore's famous Christmas poem, finding security in his confident voice. As he read each line and as he turned the pages, all of which were filled with colorful images of Santa (still green-suited), his flying reindeer, a cavalcade of holiday scenes came vividly to life. For a moment it felt like magic spun inside our house, and I settled in as I asked Papa to read it again, and then a third time, and finally during the fourth time I fell asleep, dreaming of my own sugar plums and dancing fairies.

It was a Christmas Eve I would remember forever.

Mostly because our family would never again spend Christmas in Linden Corners, and though I took many memories with me, what I left behind . . . was the book. Youth are foolish, not knowing what they have when they have it. With age grows a certain wisdom. You realize what you have lost, and you miss it dearly. You want it back.

And so here I am. That's the reason I've returned to Linden Corners, to rediscover the lost magic of Christmas all over again, to be able to revel in its joyful spirit. While the early steps of my journey were done so at your urging, it is just mine now to complete. Only when I hold that antique book in my embrace again will I consider my mission complete, not only for me but for you, for us. The last gift I ever received from my father, a gift that needs to be rediscovered and shared with the world, it is that which I must find. For me, but most especially for you, my dear.

PART 1

RETURNING HOME

CHAPTER 1

NORA

"How come it's snowing . . . it's only October."

"Because, honey, we're in the thick of Upstate New York and in this neck of the woods they only have two seasons, winter and August."

"That makes no sense, one's a month and the other is a season."

No argument there. She nodded agreeably. "Welcome to Linden Corners."

The boy looked dubiously at his mother. "Am I going to like living here?"

Good question, she thought. Was she? Did she ever like it?

The drifting snowflakes falling all around the fire-red Mustang were only the first hint that she was nearing the tiny village of Linden Corners, but it wasn't until she crested over the rise in the highway and came upon the spinning sails of the old windmill that she knew she was truly home. Home, she thought, afraid to taste the flavor of the word on her bitter tongue. What other notion instilled such a juxtaposed sense of both comfort and failure? Being back here was reason enough to sigh, and not in a relaxed way. Her name was Nora Connors Rainer, and she wasn't pleased by any of this, not the snow and not the sight of that windmill, not to mention the idea of Linden Corners itself. Returning to the place of her childhood meant only one thing: Her adult life was an utter disaster, and given the fact that her car was overstuffed with her belongings—what some might call "baggage"—a jury would render a verdict within minutes of deliberating. Guilty, Your Honor, of grossly mismanaging her life, as well as that of her twelve-year-old son. She was a lawyer by trade, unable to even win her own case. How she wished she could just continue driving through the village, it was small enough it would only take a minute or so. A one-blink-and-you-miss-it kind of town.

There was also a sense of claustrophobia about the town, too, or so thought the worldly Nora, who had traveled the globe and seen many beautiful sights, now seeing the world spit her out from whence she originated. Just when she needed her street smarts the most, home was calling, the comfort and security and understanding that you could only find inside the walls of your parents' house, now just a mile away and creeping ever closer. No doubt a couple pieces of her mother's famed strawberry pie awaited them both. With the windmill now fading to small in her rearview mirror, Nora felt her heart beating with nervous anticipation. Home meant many things to many people, but at this moment Nora needed its sense of reassurance. Knowing those old walls came complete with a supportive mother to hold you tight and tell you everything was going to be just fine, her mind told her maybe all would be okay.

But then she knew it wouldn't be, not initially.

Her homecoming would no doubt be seen as an occasion for her mother. So she had to assume the house would not be empty, since the sweet-natured Gerta Connors enjoyed having company. And said company would ask questions, and said company would expect answers. Suddenly Nora saw a houseful of guests, all of them stuffing their faces with pie, their smiles sweeter than sugar, but digesting gossip at her expense.

"Please, do me this one favor and don't let her have anyone over, I can't deal with . . . this, not now," Nora said aloud. "Don't let her think my homecoming is a celebration."

"Uh, Mom, are you talking to me?"

"Sorry, honey, Mom's weirding out."

"No kidding."

Her son's sarcasm, which had been coming on strong in the past six months, actually produced a rare smile on her tight face. Normally she'd reprimand him for his tone, but not today. He'd earned the right to vent as much as she deserved its wrath, she'd turned his life upside down. Still, Nora knew her mother, just as much as she recognized the friendly confines of Linden Corners, both the good and the bad. Having grown up here, she was well acquainted with the village's quirky tendency toward parties and parades, the happiest of holidays and heart-spun happenings, her mother, Gerta, oftentimes at the center of planning the numerous, joyous celebrations. Heck, it was only the end of October and the fallen snow already had a layer of ice beneath this fresh coating of snow, no doubt the residents had a name for such an occasion. "Second Snowfall" or something cheekily homespun like that. Winter in this region came early, stayed often, and you needed the patience of a saint and good driving skills to navigate its literal slippery slope. This year, Nora herself would be like the ever-present season, setting up roost for some time to come, though even she didn't know for how long. She could one day decide to leave, then a storm inside her could erupt and she'd be trapped. Again. Nestled in the lush Hudson River Valley, cocooned from the outside world, she could easily lose herself.

That part she liked.

Of course cocooned was just a nice word for hiding.

Nora Connors Rainer and her one son, Travis, had left the flatlands of Nebraska five days ago, enjoying the long drive and each other's company, if not necessarily looking forward to their final destination. They could have easily flown to Albany, had the car shipped or just sold it and bought a new one when they arrived, but Nora wasn't ready to sell off everything from her past life. Call her shallow, but she'd worked too hard to buy her sporty red Mustang. Too bad she hadn't worked as hard at her marriage. But hey, a car allows you to just turn on the engine and steer it to where you wanted to go. A husband tended to have his own ignition, liked to drive by himself, go off on his own, embracing the unexpected surprises around winding curves. So then why was she the one on the open road, heading into the tiny downtown of a village whose future best existed in a rearview mirror?

Not that the village was all that empty at four o'clock in the afternoon. She recognized several stores like Marla and Darla's Trading Post—twins she'd gone to school with, inseparable then, business partners now, sisters forever—and guarding the storefront, under the porch and seemingly oblivious to the snow, were two golden retrievers who lay quietly, sleeping the afternoon away in that lazy, entwined way shared only by our canine friends. Of course, too, there was the Five O'Clock Diner, run by the sharp-tongued, quick-witted Martha Martinson, plus the reliable Ackroyd's Hardware Emporium and George's Tavern, which she had known her entire life as Connors' Corners. It was where her father had happily toiled for much of his adult life. She'd heard about the renaming in e-mails and phone calls and how that wonderful Brian Duncan continued to honor George Connors's traditions and she'd seen pictures of the new sign, but the sight of it now made her heart ache for the loss of her father, for her still-living mother who had to live with the daily memories of her late husband.

But the store that most caught Nora's attention was darkened, a CLOSED sign posted on the locked front door. The building was in need of a paint job, flakes peeling off its sides. Elsie's Antiques it was called and had been for the better part of her life. But that was about to change.

Even in Linden Corners, change occasionally happened.

"Hey, Mom?"

"Yeah, baby?" Nora said, her eyes drifting away from Elsie's shop with reluctance.

"You know what today is?"

"It's Thursday, I think. Wait, what day did we leave . . . ?"

"No, not day. Today. It's Halloween."

Nora looked out her driver's side window and wondered how she had missed them. Too focused on seeing the village her way, she failed to notice how her son's eyes would view it. Seemed the sidewalks of the village were currently peopled with tiny ghosts and goblins, witches with straw brooms, vampires with fangs and tight abs, bums (though, truth be known, that last one might have not been a disguise), all of them carrying orange plastic pumpkins, winter coats unfortunately partly covering their clever costumes. Adults accompanied them to ensure nothing untoward happened to their ghoulish charges, or that they got too cold while out trick-or-treating. The allure of Halloween had lost its appeal years ago, just another foolish pseudo-holiday. She remembered dressing up as a ballerina when she was a kid; but heck, it's not like she played the part of a ballerina. People today, they tended to embody their costume rather than just simply wear it. As though everyone was starring in their own movie, stopping at makeup before stepping before the camera. While Nora may not like it, Travis always enjoyed planning his costume.

"Sorry. You were gonna be Batman this year, right?"

"Nah. Robin."

"How can you have Robin without Batman?"

"Dad was going to play Batman."

Well, that comment shut her up but good. And she felt worse than before, a sharp pain stabbing at her empty gut. Not only was Travis missing out on one of his favorite holidays, but he was missing it along with his father. She hated disappointing her only child—taking him from his home and school and friends, all he'd ever known, to return to . . . here. She looked again at the kids dressed in costume, one in particular covered in a white sheet with two eyelets. Ghosts indeed, they were all around, and not just on the sidewalks, but in the trunk of her car and inside her mind. Oh yes, those phantoms never left, did they? They never needed the arrival of a single day of celebration to come out and haunt.

"I'll make it up to you," she said.

"What, you'll be Batgirl?"

She smiled over at him, relieved to see he still had a streak of sweetness underneath all that almost-teenage sarcasm. "I promise to make the next holiday real special, okay, sweetie? I know how much you like Christmas, too."

"Uh, Mom?"

"Yeah, honey."

"The next holiday is Thanksgiving."

She actually laughed, loud enough to rattle the windows inside the car. The sudden release felt good, and at last she allowed her shoulders to drop. For Nora Connors Rainer, this new life they were starting here in Linden Corners, it was going to be harder than she envisioned. Good thing her mother was there to help, and not just with Travis's expected adjustment. Nora knew she needed all the help she could get.

"Oh, and one other thing?" Travis asked.

She was concentrating on the snowy roads ahead, yet she managed to sneak a quick look at her young son. She felt an overwhelming sense of love, knowing she would do anything to ensure a happy childhood for him. She knew how lucky she was to have him at her side. It might have been different.

"Sure, love, what's that?"

"Can you just call me Travis from now on? All that baby, honey, sweetie stuff," he said, "it doesn't suit the man of the house."

Nora's easy laughter from moments ago dissipated, like she'd opened the window and let her joy grow brittle in the cold air. Now she just wanted to cry.

How was it that her son was growing up when she wasn't?

She turned off Route 20, which served as the village's main artery, and wound her way up Green Pine Lane, remembering each curve of the road as well as she knew herself. When she caught sight of the old house, Nora felt herself retreat back to Travis's age, a helpless twelve-year-old girl with brown pigtails and hand-me-down clothes from her three older sisters and a sour, uncertain expression on her face. Only the hairstyle and clothes had changed. Oh, and her age.

Forty and moving back in with Mom.

Good job, Nora, she thought.

"Mom, I know you're still talking to yourself . . . even if I can't hear it."

"This is hard, Travis. Just give me a moment."

She pulled to the side of the road, tires crunching in the fresh snow. The house looked small, even though it had three floors, four bedrooms, and lots of space in the basement and attic. After all, her parents had raised four girls there—she the youngest, along with older sisters Victoria, Melanie, and Lindsay, so clearly the house had been big enough to accommodate them, big enough that if you wanted to hide you could. And Nora was a hider, even back then. Down in the basement or cuddled up on the old sofa, she could easily get lost in the fantastical world of whatever book she was reading, or the drama found in the pretend lives of her dolls. She wondered if her mother would insist that she take back her old room. Nora wasn't sure she could handle that, but also questioned where else she would hide. This was the first time she'd been back to the house since her father, George, had died, almost a year and a half ago. She took a deep breath. Yup, this was hard, harder than she'd anticipated.

"Okay, kiddo, you ready?"

"That's a new one."

"What is?"

"Uh, hello, kiddo?"

"Sorry, mother's instinct," she said. "Ready, Mr. Rainer?"

Travis just rolled his eyes.

"Got it, sorry, let's go," she said with another laugh; her emotions were a jumbled mess, there was no telling how fast her mood could turn. She guided them back onto the slick, snow-covered road, steeling herself for the final steps. It was just another three hundred feet before she would turn into the short driveway, their journey complete yet somehow also just beginning.

A blaring horn from behind caused her to slam on the brakes and that's when a loud smack jolted them forward.

"Shit," Nora called out, tossing the car into PARK.

They had been rear-ended.

"Mom!"

"Sorry, honey. Are you okay?"

"Yeah. Just surprised me is all."

"Okay, wait here, let me see what happened."

Nora unclenched her seat belt, not her teeth, as she made her way out of her prized car to assess the damage and to confront the dumb idiot who had crashed into her. What she saw was a battered old farm truck, two people up inside the high cabin. As she made her way toward the driver's side door, she stole a look at the back of her prized Mustang. The fool had taken out a brake light, left a small gash on the side bumper. She could see the bright red paint on the grille of the truck.

"Hey, look what you did," she said, pointing to the damage.

The man behind the wheel stepped out, closing the door behind him.

"What I did? You just pulled out, didn't even look to see if there was traffic."

"Traffic? In Linden Corners? Not exactly two concepts that go together."

"Nora?"

"Excuse me?"

"You're Nora, aren't you? Gerta's daughter."

Nora blinked away the snow that was falling in her face, clearing her eyes. Who was this farmer and why did he know who she was? She looked over at the other passenger in the truck, saw a young girl with a scrunched-up nose peering over the high dashboard, and that's when she knew who he was, knew who the girl was, and what they were doing here just a short distance from Gerta Connors's house.

"Brian Duncan," she said, placing her hands on her hips for effect.

"You recognize me?"

"No. But one and one in this case still equals four. I'm guessing that's Janey Sullivan in the truck. My mom talks about the two of you all the time."

"Small world, huh? She talks of you often, too, especially lately," he said. "We were just heading to your mother's house to pick her up to take her to the annual village Halloween party over at the community center. We call it the Spooktacular."

Nora allowed a knowing smile to cross her lips despite herself; she'd guessed it right. Linden Corners would never let a holiday pass by without some kind of celebration; like its middle name was "annual." "How nice. But I don't get your costume," she said, assessing his faded jeans, scuffed boots, and red flannel shirt. "You some kind of farmer?"

"Ha ha, no, I haven't changed yet. Janey in there, she's a windmill."

Of course she was, Nora thought.

"I'm sorry about your car," Brian said, "but you did just pull out without warning. I tried to warn you, but . . . you know, crunch."

"Yeah, crunch," Nora said.

Silence hovered between them, snow beginning to coat their shoulders.

Brian broke the quiet before it became deafening. "What do you say we get the kids inside where it's warm, then we can figure out what to do . . . about this." He spread his hands before the damage to her car. The truck appeared fine, just old and apparently indestructible.

Nora had other ideas about what she wanted to do, high on the list was wringing this guy's neck. Her car! But she knew Brian was right, get the kids out of the cold, deal with things then. Mother mode before lawyer, she told herself. She could hear her mother's words ring inside her mind, telling her that Brian is very practical and wise, and he had an easy, calming nature to his six-foot frame. No wonder Gerta liked to be around him, he had soothed her during a difficult transition period. Now it was Nora facing one, but she didn't need his bit of calm. She had no need for the services of Brian Duncan.

She gave him one last look. Even after an accident he had an affable way about him, from the gee-whiz smile to the thick brown hair where snowflakes were making him gray. Then she couldn't resist taking one last look at the damage to her car, wondering if it could be repaired. She wondered if the same applied to her.

"What's that they say?" Brian was asking.

Nora realized Brian was still talking to her. "I'm sorry, I must have zoned out. What did you say?"

"They say most car accidents occur when you're almost home."

Words failed Nora. What he'd said, she knew it was just another of those homespun adages courtesy of the quaint village of Linden Corners, yet the words rang deep inside her. She craned her neck to look over at her childhood home, so close she could almost touch it.

Yup, almost home. And it was no accident she was here.

CHAPTER 2

BRIAN

Before his unexpected move to Linden Corners, Brian Duncan was never a leader, as he was always content to be a follower. He had a tendency, sometimes annoyingly, to wait for others to plan the big events in life, happy to embrace the group dynamic. How things had changed in the nearly two years since this place had become home. Surrounded by a town full of residents, all of them dressed up in an array of crazy costumes and all seemingly having a good time, he had to admit he'd done a good job with the turnout. He'd been skeptical at first when Martha Martinson approached him about planning the village's annual Halloween party: "It will be good for you to get to know the longtime residents more, those who don't come to your tavern and drink their lives away."

"Oh, the boring people," Brian had remarked.

Still, it wasn't difficult to book the space, hire the DJ, ask a few of the local moms to help him decorate—many of them he knew thanks to Janey—and there you have it, the Eckert's Landing Halloween Spooktacular, now in full, gory swing. It was just after seven o'clock at night and much of the trick-or-treating was over, as least for the younger kids like nine-year-old Janey. The parents were happy to let their kids run around now in their costumes while under the protective cover of the auditorium at the Corner Community Center, known locally as the CCC, located just down the street from Edgestone, the local retirement center. Brian had been sure to pass along invites to the folks over there, thinking they would enjoy watching the children acting out their costumes with the enthusiasm only sugar produced. The party was scheduled to end at eight, when the kids and probably the seniors would go home and any of the remaining adults who wanted to continue the night's festivities could do so down at George's Tavern. Brian was expected at his business after the final prizes for best costume had been given out.

For now, he sipped at a glass of too-sweet fruit punch, watching as Janey interacted with her friends and classmates, running around the perimeter of the auditorium with a willowy grace as though the wind had taken control of her. She looked adorable dressed up as the windmill, her arms and legs serving as the four sails, countless Popsicle sticks glued to an old bedsheet with white lights brightening not just her mood but the room. Right now she was spinning her arms as she ran, and the effect was kind of cool, Brian had to admit.

"She looks happy."

Brian turned to see his friend Cynthia Knight standing beside him.

"Hey, hi, wasn't sure if you were going to make it," Brian said, giving her a quick peck on the cheek.

"What, and have Jake miss his first Halloween party? I don't think so."

Jacob Knight was the little miracle boy, a bundle of blue eyes and blond hair, who was hanging out in a pouch that clung to Cyn's shoulders. He was born back in July in the middle of the night, healthy, happy, a gift to parents who had long ago given up on ever having a child. He'd given new life to the residents of Linden Corners, a symbol that even in the face of tragedy inspiration was always around the block.

"What's he supposed to be?" Brian asked.

"He's an angel," Cynthia said. "No costume necessary."

"And you?"

"I'm the Goddess of Sleep Deprivation," she said. "See these bags under my eyes?"

"Ha ha," Brian said. "Where's Bradley?"

"Parking the car. Ever the good husband and doting father, he dropped us off at the front entrance," she said. "Don't worry, he'll be here, he wouldn't miss out on your lame attempt at a costume."

As if on cue, the usually buttoned-up corporate tax lawyer Bradley Knight appeared, dressed in blue jeans and an unusual-for-him blue-checked flannel shirt. He made his way through the crowd, kissed his wife and the head of his sweet baby before shaking Brian's hand. Standing together, both men looked like twins.

"Really, guys, farmers? Those are the best costumes you could come up with?" asked Martha Martinson, coming up from behind the small group. She was the proprietor of the Five O' Diner, and she knew of what she spoke. The diner opened at five in the morning, catered to the local farmers who didn't feel like cooking for themselves.

"Brian was supposed to wear a suit," Bradley said. "See, he was supposed to be me, I was supposed to be him."

"I just can't wear suits anymore," Brian admitted with a noticeable shudder. "Not since I left behind my old life in New York. I wore them every day for nearly ten years and I nearly strangled myself with those horrible ties. I know Halloween is about pretending to be someone else, but the idea of playing my old self . . . no thanks. I didn't like it then and I won't like it now. Sometimes even Brian Duncan doesn't compromise."

"You got to be careful of someone who refers to themselves in the third person," Cynthia said. "A sleep-deprived Cynthia should know."

"Look over there, you see that? You guys are dressed just like Marla and Darla," Martha said, pointing to a far corner where the notorious Linden Corners twins were huddling together over slices of pepperoni pizza. Indeed, Martha was right, both ladies wore simple blue jeans and thick flannel shirts, straw hats completing the image.

"Great, so now when people ask who we are, we'll say Marla and Darla."

"Now that's funny, we can say they're Brian and Bradley," Martha said, slapping Brian's arm before moving off, no doubt to spread the word to everyone assembled. She wouldn't miss a soul. Humor in Linden Corners didn't go very deep.

"All right you three, go have fun," Brian said, "and, Bradley, no need to stick so close to me, you know?"

"Sure thing, Darla."

"Hey, why am I her and not Marla?"

They all laughed before the Knight family went off to join in the festivities of the spooky celebration, leaving Brian to himself for a few moments of needed peace. He looked at his handiwork, the auditorium all aglow with orange and black lights, streamers, the "Monster Mash" song playing for like the eighth time already tonight, with the kids dancing and giggling at the silly, ghoulish-sounding lyrics each and every time. He was glad everyone was having a good time, even if he himself wasn't fully embracing the event. The party was missing one of its chief organizers. Gerta Connors, who had, of course, supplied the party with plenty of pumpkin pies. She was still back home helping her daughter and grandson get settled. But she had promised to make an appearance, "and hopefully coax them to join me, I think it would be good for them."

"For Travis," Nora had said.

"See you soon," Gerta said to Brian before he left them to their homecoming.

Brian recalled Gerta mentioning that Nora was coming for a visit, but from what he'd seen in the backseat of her now-banged-up Mustang it looked like more like Nora and her son were making Linden Corners their new home. It wasn't his place to pry, and while Gerta was usually very forthcoming with details about the lives of her daughters, so much so that when she didn't say anything she spoke volumes, this was one of the rare cases when she hadn't gone into details. Brian had to wonder if she even knew the whole story. The arrival of Nora Rainer was indeed a curious case. From the sour expression he saw upon her face, she didn't appear happy to have returned home, and him smashing into the rear of her car was not exactly getting their homecoming off on the right foot. If he were Nora, the last place he'd want to be was at a party full of people who considered gossip a sport.

Brian continued to absorb the party's antics, noticing a table of older men and women, most of them not dressed in costumes but enjoying the atmosphere nonetheless. At the center of attention was the white-haired ball of fire known as Elsie Masters, the longtime proprietor of her own antique shop located down the street from the tavern. She'd hit her seventieth birthday two months ago and, widowed more years than she'd been married, word was she had opted to sell the building and business when she moved into Edgestone. Her laughter dominating the small circle of people, she appeared to have made the transition to Linden Corners' retirement community all too well. Presently she was engaged in conversation with an older, silver-haired gentleman, his face undecipherable behind a plastic phantom mask. Elsie appeared to be flirting with a man whose presence was ghostly at best.

Brian, in his usual state of worry, sometimes wondered if

the retirement home might be a good place for Gerta Connors as well. How he worried about her living alone in that big house, especially during the long winter months, which, in this town, could mean most of the year. He supposed he should let the issue rest for now, what with Nora and her son, Travis, back in the village and living with her. Brian felt a pang of jealousy; he didn't come from much family—parents, a sister, a nephew—and what he did have, well, distance was a word that came to mind, even during hugs. Gerta Connors had become a combination of mother figure and grandmother, to him and to Janey, and he was forever grateful to have her as part of their lives.

In fact, the plan had been for her to join them tonight for the party, their makeshift family as tight as any blood relations in town. Gerta loved nothing more, outside of her family, than the strong community bond that existed in Linden Corners. And then, as if Brian had willed it, there she was coming down the stairs from the main entrance, and she wasn't alone. Brian couldn't help it, his heart swelled.

Nora was escorting her mother inside, the sturdy Travis at their side. Two of them wore eager smiles as well as costumes. Gerta was dressed, hysterically, as Queen Elizabeth herself, complete with crown and a scepter made from aluminum foil, and as the residents of the village began to notice her entrance they curtsied. Gerta played the role to the hilt with a final, royal wave that had them all clapping. Travis had apparently found some odd assemblage of clothes in the attic that helped transform him into a pirate, his mother's eye makeup completing the look. Nora wore sensible slacks and a sweater.

"Glad you could make it," Brian said. "Are you Betty Crocker?"

"No, I'm an accident victim," Nora stated rather defensively. "You didn't leave me much choice in coming. I wasn't about to let my mother drive herself in this snow. Seriously,

Brian, there's like six inches out there on the ground already and it's not even November."

Brian checked his watch. "Got less than five hours to go."

"Gee, can't wait."

"You can't turn back the clock, Nora, dear," Gerta said. "And you can't wish it forward, either, what's the point of that? All you do is lose precious time worrying about things you can't control rather than enjoying what time you have. Please, dear, just try and relax for once. My daughter here, Brian, she was always the uptight one of all my girls."

"Thanks, Mom, I'm so feeling the love in this room," Nora said. "So, Brian, how about you act the role of a gentleman and get me a drink. Wine will do, beer if I have to."

"Party's dry," Brian said.

"Excuse me?"

"It's a party for the kids, we agreed there'd be no booze."

"Don't you run my dad's tavern?"

Not exactly true, but for now he went with it. Truth was, he owned the building and the bar, a Christmas gift last year from her mother, but Nora didn't know that detail. "Sure," he said, "and when this party is over, you're more than welcome to stop by and I'll get you that wine you want. Though I have to warn you . . ."

"Yeah, I know, Dad never was any good at picking wines. Called it firewater, you were better off with water and a shot of prayer," she said, a hint of nostalgia crossing her pretty face. Like she was reaching back to remember her beloved father, the affable George Connors. "You know, Brian, the cheap wine is one tradition you could lose."

Brian nodded. "So, fruit punch or cider?"

"Cider, I'll pretend."

Brian started off toward the refreshment table, only to return moments later with plastic tumblers for them all. Along the way he'd found Janey and asked her to join them, suggesting perhaps she could invite Travis to join her and her friends, her nose scrunching up when he said it. A typical Janey look, though Brian had to be glad the idea of boys was still unappealing to his daughter. She'd only just turned nine a couple weeks ago and he was more than happy to keep her entrenched in the relative innocence of single digits. What would he do next year, or even three years from now when those dreaded teenage years reared their ugly head? He stole a look back at Cynthia and Bradley, happily showing off their gurgling little guy and he realized he'd missed out on all that infant stuff. How he and Janey had come together to form their family, it had been a long road, one tinged with much sadness but intermixed with enough happy moments to get them this far. They were a team, and they looked out for each other.

So, protest giving way to the generosity that embodied this town, Janey took hold of Travis's hand. He looked nervous as she led him toward a group of kids who were dancing up a storm. Some hip-hop song began and the kids squealed with delight, moving suddenly in a jerky motion that was lost on Brian. But Travis joined in, soon swallowed up by the group of kids. Travis was a nice-looking kid, and even if Janey was too young to see it, a couple of the older girls happily took the new boy into their mix.

"So, Nora, your mom says you're here for . . . what did you call it, Gerta . . ."

"An extended visit," Gerta said, almost on automatic pilot.

"Mom, that's what you've been telling people?" Nora asked, almost choking on her soft cider. "What will you tell them when they see that I've opened up a business here? That it's just a hobby?"

"You're staying here?" Brian asked, surprise in his voice. "I mean, living here?"

"Brilliant deduction, Sherlock."

"Now that would have been a good idea for a costume," Brian remarked.

Nora looked less than amused by his flippant remark.

Gerta clucked her tongue. "Nora, now don't get upset with Brian, he's just having a bit of fun, and quite frankly, you could stand to have some as well. Wound tighter than a toy mouse. Maybe you should join Travis over there on the dance floor, he seems to be having . . . what do the kids call it, a blast?"

"I'd take a blast right about now," Nora said. "Travis is a kid, he should be having fun. He doesn't know any better. Okay, Brian Duncan, just so we can get this over and done with and move on to . . . whatever, yes, I've moved back to Linden Corners, just me and my son, we'll be living with my mother. Travis has already been pre-enrolled—don't you just love that kind of lingo, 'pre'—at Linden Corners' Middle School, and starting tomorrow I'm the proud new proprietor of the former Elsie's Antiques, name change to come, thank you very much. Oh, and I'm five seven. Have I left anything out?"

The boisterous party around them continued to swirl, but for Brian it was like he was living in the exhaust of a vacuum, Nora's words swirling in his mind. She was apparently going through a major life change and wasn't happy about it, and as Brian knew firsthand, it wasn't an easy adjustment. But unlike him, who had started over in a town he didn't know and with people who easily, crazily, accepted him almost from the moment he arrived, Nora was returning to the place in which she'd grown up. So many people here knew her backstory, her situation, her family, and so she would have to endure the nervous stares, the long looks, the unasked questions . . . but what about the husband? Brian knew enough not to ask, not now. She'd only returned an hour ago, cut her some slack.

"Regardless of the circumstances behind your return, Nora," he said, "I hope you can find a bit of happiness in Linden Corners. I know I did; it was as unexpected as everything else about my journey. I didn't ask for it, but I embraced it. I just had to open myself up to the concept that tomorrow would be better than yesterday, and so forth. Look, if you need help getting the new business up and running, I can usually be found right down the street at your dad's old tavern. You're welcome to stop in anytime. No questions, no judgments—I should know. Folks here used to call me Brian Duncan Just Passing Through. Now I've let the moss grow under my feet, means I'm here for the duration, and I wouldn't have it any other way. If you'll excuse me, there are some people I need to see."

He realized his departure was abrupt, but if the once-named Brian Duncan Just Passing Through had learned anything about this life in Linden Corners, you made it what you wanted. You either took to its wondrous eccentricities, playing along with whatever the villagers were whispering about, or you lived life looking from the inside out. It was one of the reasons Brian continued to accept offers like planning and hosting events such as the Halloween party. Linden Corners might only have been his home for the past two years, but the way he'd ingratiated himself into the fabric of the community you'd think he'd been born here.

A woman named Annie Sullivan had done that, instilled in him that appreciation for this tiny town. She was still instructing him, even in spirit, and through the boundless joy of her daughter, Janey. It was Janey who had fulfilled the promise made by her mother.

And the majestic windmill, it kept them all spinning toward tomorrow.

Gazing lovingly at Janey as she laughed and danced with crazy abandon, her arms sliced through the air, and he imagined her taking to the wind, soaring to new heights. Her birthday month would come to an end in a matter of hours, and soon it would be time to unwrap the fresh traditions they had established last year while celebrating their first holiday together. Hopefully this year their Christmas could be free of the drama that had plagued them. But as he snuck a look over at Gerta, he realized such a wish might not be possible, she would have her own things to deal with. Her daughter Nora was a handful, a woman who seemed to have lost her way in life and who needed an infusion of hope. Brian wanted to help, if not the woman herself, then Gerta, who, usually so much a part of the Linden Corners community, was quickly reduced to a monarch with only one subject.

Gerta, the Queen, ended up winning best costume.

Janey came in a close second.

Which meant the windmill had taken a backseat to another story, and Brian Duncan was curious to see how it would all play out.

Ten o'clock that same night found Brian returning to George's Tavern to check on his business. Janey was staying overnight with Cynthia and Bradley, which really meant she was staying with the tyke Jake, who had quickly become the center of her small world. All summer long she had helped Cynthia with the new baby, heating up formula, learning to change diapers, anything else Cyn could entice her to do if only to catch a moment's rest. Janey loved to watch the baby sleep or to just hold him, and now that school had started again she had less time with them and often remarked that she was missing the best days of Jake's life. "Dad, it's like he grew an inch while I was in math class," she had said after the first day of the new school year. An exaggeration for sure, but Brian understood the separation anxiety.

So after the Halloween Spooktacular, Brian was fine with

having his little girl spend time with their best friends' little boy; they needed their bonding time as much as Brian needed to see about his work. Business had been slow since the start of the fall, and Brian often wondered how much more he could make ends meet with such an existence.

It was Mark Ravens's night to tend bar—he the handsome relief bartender who drove up receipts—and the cedar-scented room was hopping with the younger adult crowd, those who would have found the Spooktacular a total bore. Seeing all the cars in the parking lot, hearing the raucous activity coming from inside the tavern and the sounds of the jukebox wafting out into the night sky, Brian had to admit that his relief bartender definitely brought out a different mix, some of them from town, some from as far away as Hudson, where Mark also worked as a waiter at a resort hotel. Brian had been skeptical about paying someone else to help run the bar, but with his responsibilities to Janey, he'd had no choice, and Mark had proved to be the ideal hire.

Brian walked inside, immediately making his way to the long, oak bar.

"Hey, boss," Mark said with an easy grin, pulling on the tap to refill some goblin's beer. "How was the kiddie party?"

"The kids enjoyed it," Brian said.

"That's why they call it a kiddie party," he said.

"Funny."

"You, my friend, need a drink."

"Seltzer."

"One of these days, man, I'm gonna get you to loosen up," Mark said.

Brian didn't drink alcohol, not since a bout with hepatitis that had inadvertently sent him off on a personal journey that eventually landed him in Linden Corners. In an ironic twist, he'd become owner of this bar near about the time he'd been given the guardianship of young Janey Sullivan, and he'd made a vow that a clear head was needed to keep both running successfully. Health-wise, he was fine, it was just easier this way.

"Speaking of, you're certainly, uh, loose," Brian said, taking in Mark's almost-costume.

"Oh yeah, Sara's idea. You should see what she's wearing."

Sara was his fiancée, a waitress from the Five O' Diner across the street who had started spending a lot of her spare time at the local tavern, happy to be in the company of a certain bartender. They started dating and before long got engaged last Christmas, moved upstairs into the spare apartment, and had been blissfully happy ever since, even if they hadn't actually settled on a wedding date. You had to earn a living first, save some cash for such an expensive event, that was Mark's oft-repeated rationale. Thinking his costume was one approach toward earning the big bucks, Brian gave Mark a closer inspection. He was dressed in a loincloth and really, little else. Not many guys could pull off such an edgy look, but Mark wore his self-consciousness well. He clearly had a good body, muscular where it should be, lacking any flab. His chest and arms were coated with a blanket of dark hair.

"So, Mark, will a fifteen-minute phone call really save me fifteen percent or more on my car insurance?" Brian asked him.

"Funny, Brian," he said, "but no, I'm not a caveman. I'm Tarzan."

"And where is your Jane?"

He indicated the chatty crowd situated near the blaring jukebox, pointing out Sara in the middle of it. She was dressed in a tight-fitting outfit of leopard print, one of her shoulders the only bit of skin she revealed. Brian turned back to look at the near-naked Mark Ravens, words about to spill from his lips.

"Shut up," Mark said.

Brian laughed, then announced he was going to take charge of the bar. "Take a break, put some clothes on, have a drink if you need one." Mark happily accepted the chance to slip away from the busy action at the bar, but not before telling Brian the tips had been amazing that night, he might want to consider a costume other than the farmer look.

"My shirt stays on," Brian remarked.

Alone behind his bar, he felt oddly comfortable in a way he knew Nora didn't feel inside the borders of Linden Corners, though why he was thinking of her, he wasn't sure. Brian headed to the far end of the bar, wrapping an apron around his waist. Ready to settle in for a long night of serving drinks to thirsty patrons, he turned back at the presence of a new customer and found himself faced with none other than the aforethought Nora Rainer. Well, speak of the devil, he thought but didn't say.

"You promised me a drink," she said, hands tapping against the bar.

"So I did," he said. "White wine? Red?"

"Make it a shot, whiskey," she said. "After the day I've had, I think I need it."

Brian grabbed a bottle of Maker's Mark from the top shelf, poured her a double. "It's on me. Least I can do, you know . . . your car."

"Can we not talk about that?"

"Sure. We cannot talk about anything you want," Brian said, taking a sip of his seltzer. "You know, if I'm going to avoid pissing you off, I might need a cheat sheet of safe topics. Can you write that up for me? I've got a cocktail napkin if you've got a pen."

"Keep away from family and my life and you'll be golden."

"Nice talking to you," Brian said.

She knocked back her shot and Brian refilled it.

"Oh, is that how it's going to be? You getting me drunk, Brian Duncan?"

"Hardly my style," he said. "Okay, no nosy, intrusive questions about family, that's your personal business. But I do want to know, Nora Connors Rainer, about this new business venture of yours. Since we're going to be neighbors and all, I could send some business your way. You say you're taking over Elsie's antique shop, but something tells me you've got something else up your sleeve."

"Yes, I do," she said.

"Care to share?"

"Hey, I'm supporting your business, you'll have to stop by my store and support me."

"Uh, your drinks are on the house," Brian reminded her.

She laughed, and to Brian it actually sounded genuine.

"Don't expect the same treatment at A Doll's Attic."

CHAPTER 3

THOMAS

A Doll's Attic.

An intriguing name for a store for certain, and one he was curious to learn more about. If his hunch was correct—and he'd lived his life on his hunches, that's how he ended up back in Linden Corners—the owner of the re-jiggered antique business might just be able to provide the service he'd come looking for. So on this first morning of November, the snow having stopped and the roads freshly plowed, he felt brave enough to venture from his room, Elsie kind enough to drive him downtown after breakfast. So he dressed in his natty best, ironed slacks and a clean shirt, his blazer emblazoned with patches on the elbows that gave him that professorial look he'd worn his entire adult life, and just to put a finer touch on his outfit, he donned a bow tie of solid navy blue. He stole a look at himself in the mirror in his small bathroom, tried to pat down one of his stray, willowy gray hairs and failed. He shrugged. At eighty-four years old, he had to be content with what he could achieve.

He'd been a resident at the Edgestone Retirement Home for just over three months now, keeping mostly to himself as he adjusted to his new life in his old village. Certainly much had changed, the shops and the people, none of whom he knew, yet when he mentioned his surname a look of surprise lit up the faces of those long-timers. Thomas Van Diver, he would say with a polite nod, the reaction from the older folks immediate: "Of the Linden Corners Van Divers of long ago?"; it was both surprising to him and not. His ancestors had toiled on this fertile land for generations, and even if not for the last couple, memories stretched back far. History was the natural friend of the elderly. "One and the same," he would respond with a bit of pride when folks recognized the Van Diver name, not sure where that even came from. He wasn't a prideful man by nature, he was who he was, a man who had lived his life as best he could, quietly, thoughtfully, intellectually. Like that stray hair on his head, it wasn't the result but the effort.

He lived on the first floor of The Edge—as the locals called the old folks' home—which was a good thing. No stairs or creaky elevator, he could just step out from his one-bedroom apartment and into the corridor, sure to run into one of his neighbors on their way to the dining hall. It was nine o'clock on this cool autumn morning and late for Thomas to be eating, probably too late for most of the residents. This was an early-to-bed, early-to-rise kind of place, so he was taking his chances with whatever remnants of breakfast might be had.

"Morning," he said with a polite nod to an elderly couple who lived down the hall from him. Edna and Jack Something Or Other, darned if he could recall their last name right now. They were walking in the opposite direction, obviously having dined already.

"They're taking the dishes back to the kitchen," Edna said, her voice almost accusatory.

Thomas wasn't sure whom she was accusing, the staff for taking it or him for not waking for the worm.

He continued his slow shuffle down the long corridor,

turning from the main lobby still decorated for Halloween, and toward the dining room that doubled as their recreation room when meals weren't on the menu. Only five of the residents remained, none of them eating, content to sit quietly with their second cup of coffee of the day. One of them caught sight of him the moment he walked through the door, almost as though she were scouting him out. And she was. Elsie Masters, his new friend, was also new to life at Edgestone, though not to Linden Corners. She'd made a life change, just as he had, and he supposed they had bonded a bit over that while sharing a piece of pound cake. As the previous owner of Elsie's Antiques down on Route 20, she had retired, sold the business, taken up quick residence, immediately ingratiating herself into the social network here.

"Thomas, over here!"

"Yes, yes, Elsie, I see you, my eyesight hasn't left me yet."

These were the kind of predictable jokes you heard at Edgestone, it was all about aging when it wasn't about dying.

"We saved you some eggs and bacon, a heaping pile of greasy home fries, you need your strength," she said as he settled down beside her. "You know Myra, Judy, Fred, yes?"

"Good morning all," Thomas said.

"Now that you're here, let me warm this plate up for you."

"Not necessary, Elsie. I'm not hungry."

"Nonsense," she announced to the group, "such a typical male, so stubborn in his ways."

"I am eighty-four, hard to change me now."

"You don't know Elsie," remarked Judy, to the amusement of the others.

Elsie dismissed her combative comment with a wave of her liver-spotted hand, then grabbed the plate and marched headlong into the kitchen. She returned moments later, the plate warm, a cup of hot coffee in her other hand. She set the former in front of Thomas, staring at him with expectation. Her mix of moxie and mothering gave Thomas pause; it had been awhile since a woman had looked after him with such . . . vigor. For a moment he thought of his beloved Missy.

"Well, eat."

"She went to that effort, you don't eat your name is mud," Fred said like he knew.

Thomas readily agreed, thankful to have another male peer setting him straight amidst the complicated language issued from the ladies of the manor. He lifted his fork, scooping up a bit of the scrambled eggs. Slowly, with effort, the fork made its way to his open mouth, his hand shaking ever so slightly. He repeated the routine several times before finally setting the fork down, reaching more easily for a piece of crispy bacon. He happily chomped away, realizing the four of them were watching him intently.

Elsie, her eyes wide behind thick glasses, her gray hair tucked in a tight bun, gave him a curious look.

"Are you okay, Thomas?"

"Never better," he said. "Why would you ask?"

"Your hand, it quivered . . . you know, as you ate."

"Elsie, I'm eighty-four and not a day younger than I was yesterday. Eventually your parts start to break down and you just deal with it. Though truth be told, perhaps after that Halloween party last night I had one more Manhattan than my body is accustomed to. So perhaps that explains my waking so late," he said.

"I should have joined you," Fred said. "Sounds tasty."

"You shouldn't drink," Elsie advised.

Now it was Thomas's turn to wave away her comment, his hand steady now, assured. "Now, now, enough worrying over me. I'll have my Manhattans and enjoy them to the end. For now, though, you promised to take me over to your former store to meet the new owner. Tell me again her name, I'm afraid I've forgotten." Names were evading him of late, just another part of living so long. Your brain could only retain so much.

"Nora Connors," Elsie said.

"Rainer," Myra said. "She's married, that's what Gerta told me."

"Hmm, moves back to town, son in tow, but no husband," Elsie said. "I say Connors."

"I say none of that is any of our business," Fred said.

So that's how the battle of sexes came down, the women wanting to know more, the men content to sip their coffee and let the world work out its own issues. Regardless of this lady Nora's situation, she was now the owner of the antique shop downtown and for Thomas Van Diver that meant she might be useful to him. He hadn't come home to Linden Corners to sit and listen to idle gossip about who had what last name and why all day long. He was a man on a mission, and at eighty-four, he knew he had to act fast.

"So, Elsie," he said, finishing his coffee. "Shall we check out A Doll's Attic?"

"You know, I just don't like that name, it sounds a bit pretentious if you ask me," Elsie said. "I just don't know what was wrong with the previous name, served me well all these years, and look, we're both still standing, me and the building."

Judy, Fred, and Myra all exchanged knowing looks, words unnecessary. With Elsie a part of their lives now, that second cup of coffee in the morning wasn't going to be so quiet anymore.

Thomas, still new to how they did things at The Edge, rose to the bait. "Well, for starters, Elsie is not her name, so why would she wish to keep such a business name?" he asked logically. "She's got a perfectly fine name in Nora, and as far as I'm concerned, she could name the store whatever she wants, long as she gets me what I want."

Elsie tossed him a hard look through those thick glasses. "I thought you weren't so good with remembering names."

"At my age, selective hearing gets me through the day."

That shut her up, if only for now.

*　*　*

There was no new sign posted on the building to indicate a change of ownership, no hung shingle to sway in the wind, though the weather-beaten ELSIE'S ANTIQUES placard had already been removed. So the store wore a barren, empty feeling, at least from the outside, and Thomas had to wonder if perhaps he was jumping the gun a bit, poor woman had just arrived to town yesterday, or so Elsie had informed him on the drive over. Maybe she wasn't even open for business.

"Her lease starts today, first of the month," Elsie said. "She's a smart businesswoman, I'm sure she's open. Way she scooped up my business with barely a night's sleep, she's a woman on a mission."

Thomas could relate.

Edgestone Retirement Home was a half-mile drive off the main drag in town, too long for a man of his age to walk and he'd long given up on driving, not with his shaky hands, his unsteady feet. Not that he was necessarily afraid of hurting himself, it was the others on the road he had to be careful of. He'd shipped all of his belongings from his last home north of San Francisco, flown across the country and arranged for a car service to take him the final leg of his trip, to the blocky brick structure that was Edgestone. His new home, in a town that recalled an earlier time in his life.

Now, as Elsie concentrated on the wet conditions on the road, he was able to gaze out the window at the small village, see how it had changed and how it had not. Sure, he'd been nearly six when he and his mother had left town permanently, it was any wonder he could recall any of the details. The white-painted gazebo with the gabled black roof that stood in the center of the village park he recalled, some of the other buildings, too, had a familiar, yet faraway look. A place like Linden Corners, history was on its side, so it was a good place for an old man to come to, something they had in common.

The newly named A Doll's Attic store was situated in a

Victorian-style house along Main Street—that's what the locals called it, though the map just indicated Route 20—the lower floor used for business, the upper floors for many years Elsie's home. Thomas knew her story well, she'd been widowed seventeen years ago, her business becoming her life, but eventually the work and that winding staircase up to her apartment became more than she wanted to deal with, so, upon turning seventy, she made the difficult decision: sell the business, rent the house, move to Edgestone, and preserve her aching knees.

"Of course, it didn't all happen in that order," she said. "I moved first, Nora took over the business second, but even as I tried, I couldn't convince her—yet—to rent the apartment upstairs. Still looking for a tenant . . . interested?"

"Not the way you describe those stairs," Thomas stated.

"Guess Nora Connors Rainer or whatever her name is this week is not ready for a total makeover yet, but who can blame her with her life in such disarray. She's living with Gerta Connors, that's her mother, and it's probably a good thing, too, for both of them. Gerta's been alone in her big house for over a year, she, too, is widowed."

Lot of that going around, Thomas thought.

With all that history relegated to where it belonged, Thomas was ready to concentrate on today. He was looking forward to his meeting with Nora Connors Rainer, he would tell her his situation and see if she had the wherewithal to help him. And time was of the essence, and not just because of his advanced age. As he looked around, at the snow, at the icicles hanging from pointed roofs, crisp, cold air filling his lungs, he realized that Christmas was coming faster than spring, so the time to spring into action was now.

As Elsie pulled into the empty lot, Thomas looked over at her.

"If you wouldn't mind, Elsie, I do need to do this on my own," he said. "I very much appreciate the ride. As always."

"You're a very mysterious man, Thomas Van Diver."

"So does that mean you're not going to put up an argument?"

She patted his knee. "You'll tell me eventually," she said with knowing confidence. "I'll pick you up later, say in about an hour?"

"That's not necessary . . ."

"How else will you get back to The Edge?"

"May I call you? I may be longer than an hour."

She pursed her lips. "Mysterious indeed."

Surprisingly, Elsie had nothing further to say on the matter, allowing Thomas to make his slow escape from her car. As he hit the outside, the air was bracing, and as he exhaled he could see his breath turn to mist. It had been some time since his body had been subjected to a Northeast winter, this attack on his creaky bones might take some getting used to. He bustled as quickly as he could up the shoveled sidewalk, grabbing on to the railing to help guide him up the three steps to the storefront. He pushed on the door and it opened easily, the ringing of bells overhead announcing his presence.

He heard voices further inside the expansive rooms of the downstairs. Clearly he wasn't her first customer, as the strong baritone of a man's voice pervaded the open space.

"You're right, Nora, this place, it's gonna need some repair work. A fresh coat of paint for starters, and of course you'll need a new sign outside. Something catchy and bright, you don't want to miss the casual passerby, all those antique-seeking people who drive through town, got to give them a reason to stop, shop, and most importantly, spend." Then came a pause before Thomas heard, "I'm sure I can get you a good discount."

"Thanks, Chuck, I appreciate it," he heard, this time a woman's voice.

Thomas sauntered around the overstuffed room, checking out the sundry items that were on display, assorted styles of lamps and vases made of ceramic and glass, old dishes and other such knickknacks, all things he expected to find in such a place. What he was seeking, he was certain was not to be found on these messy, cramped shelves. Not meaning to hover, he didn't wish to disturb whatever transaction was taking place, but when things got decidedly personal, Thomas had to alert the owner that he was here. Clearly neither of them had heard the bell.

"Maybe you and I, you know, can grab a drink sometime."

"Oh thanks, Chuck, that's kind of you to offer, but I'm just getting settled," she said, trying to sound lighthearted even as Thomas could hear the edge in her voice. "I'm barely back in town twenty-four hours."

"I'm a patient guy, maybe next week."

There was a frosty pause before she said, "You do know I'm married, right?"

"I don't see no husband."

"You see this ring?"

"Yeah?"

"It's attached to my fist."

Stifling a laugh, that's when Thomas cleared his throat loudly and stepped into their line of vision. The two other people turned with wide eyes.

"Pardon me, I wonder, are you Nora Connors?"

"Rainer," she said. "Nora Rainer. Yes. And you are?"

Thomas paused, his expression falling to the man she had called Chuck, and if he had his way, chuck him out was what he would do. He was fortysomething, a slight paunch to his belly, a graying mustache and uncombed hair both in bad need of some fresh maintenance. A messy man indeed; even an unmarried, available woman would be rejecting his cheesy overture. Guy was probably a bully, and not a very good one, as he easily backed down, not just from Nora's offer of a fist sandwich but from Thomas's withering glance. Chuck bid a hasty retreat, though not before adding, "Hardware supplies, paint, they can be expensive. Just you think about it."

He left, the bell sounding again.

"Unpleasant man," Thomas said.

"He's harmless. I knew him back in high school, he was two classes ahead of me," she said, "and he hasn't aged well in any respect. Unlike you, Mr. . . ."

"Van Diver. Thomas Van Diver."

"You don't see many bow ties these days," she remarked. "So nice."

"My sole mark of distinction. If you'd believe it, I have a drawer full," he said, with a slight nod of his head. "Dress well, you feel well."

"I couldn't agree more, Mr. Van Diver, it's the mark of a gentleman," she said, extending her hand warmly. He shook it with a grip as strong as he could muster. A slight pause passed between them before their hands separated, strangers when they connected and now new friends as they parted. "A pleasure to meet you, my good sir, welcome to A Doll's Attic. Not counting Chuck, and I don't, you are my very first customer. Or so I hope—is there something I can help you with?"

With a sudden twinkle in his eye, Thomas said, "If you can, my dear, you may just make these final days the most special of my life."

CHAPTER 4

NORA

While his words may have shaken her, it was his subsequent request that had her mind spinning, with possibilities and with surprise, and with the thought that maybe she had bitten off more than she could chew with this impulsive new venture. There were no rules suddenly, no easy place to start. Unlike life as an attorney, which had you so attuned to strict schedules. There was safety in the law, procedure to follow, dates to adhere to, and ultimately a judge and jury to tell you whether you did well or not. Going out on your own with the winsome wish of trying to fulfill the dreams of complete strangers, it came with a different responsibility, one that you could not foist off on the system. Nora, though, had made the conscious decision that if she couldn't satisfy her own dreams, she might as well try and help others achieve theirs. And so A Doll's Attic was created, a place for her to crawl into, lost in the safety of the past.

"Before we get started, tell me your favorite Christmas memory," Thomas asked.

"I'm sorry . . . Christmas?"

"Surely a lovely woman such as yourself has some treasured moment from childhood?"

"I'd have to think about it," she said.

"Then it's not truly memorable," Thomas said, with a weary shake of his head.

Was that disapproval over her reluctance to play along, or the result of some condition he was suffering from? Nora was not having an easy time getting a read on her curious customer, he was all wisdom and age, with a certain air of mystery, a rare case of intimidation insinuating itself into her soul.

"Mrs. Rainer, the kind of moment I'm talking about should pop into your mind instantly. It should be ingrained like knots in wood, part of its fabric."

"I'm sorry, it's just . . . you surprised me. We only just got through Halloween and already you're putting visions of sugar plums dancing into my head. Like a department store eager to get the holiday shopping season going."

"Sugar plums," he said. "Is that a memory?"

"No, just a cliché."

"Oh Mrs. Rainer, we'll have to do better than that if we're to find what I wish."

She looked away, red-faced at her lack of professionalism. This would take some getting used to, controlling her tongue. When she had composed herself, reminding herself this was business, a retail one, and part of its success would lie with her interaction—and indulgences—with her customers. She dropped the defense she'd raised when the word *Christmas* was floated in the air and said, "Please, call me Nora."

"I could call you stalling."

At Nora's suggestion, they were sitting in a pair of wicker rockers, soft cushions helping to relax them, or at least, him. Situated by the large bay window that looked out over Main Street, she saw snow covering the ground and folks walking by all bundled up against the cold. Because of the weather, this talk of Christmas seemed wholly appropriate, even if it was only November first. All Saints' Day, a holy day of obligation in the Connors family, her mother had always insisted they go to church before coming home for a tasty feast. She could smell the pot roast in her mind.

"Baked Virginia ham," Nora suddenly said, her body leaning forward eagerly, as though ready to pop out of her seat. "I'm thinking of those meals my mother made every Christmas, we could smell it cooking all day long while we played with our new toys, Dad sitting in his chair smoking his pipe, the burning tobacco melding well with the smoky flavors coming from the kitchen. It was the one day of the year he wasn't telling us girls to quiet down. He just let us play. With our dolls and their houses."

Nora paused, looking over at Thomas. He just nodded politely.

"Wow, you're good," she said. "I haven't thought about that stuff in years."

"You're home now, it's only natural such memories will come to you."

"And you, Mr. Van Diver? Are you home?"

"As a matter of fact, I am," he said. "And what brings me here—because I know that will be your next question—has everything to do with home and with memories, with Christmases past and, God willing, Christmases present and future."

"If you don't mind my forthrightness, you mentioned 'final days,' " Nora said, feeling like she was intruding even as she posed the question. "Are you sick, Mr. Van Diver?"

"Not that kind of sick, no. It's just . . . well, let's say I am a long way from my youth."

"With each passing day, even today's youth can say that."

He nodded again. "Very astute, Nora. You have an appreciation for the past."

She gazed around at her new store, a mix of the old junk

that Elsie's Antiques still called inventory and ethereal ideas that existed in her mind of what she wanted to sell. "So, Mr. Van Diver, tell me about this past you wish me to find for you."

"It's appropriate that your store is called A Doll's Attic— a nod to your childhood and those aforementioned dolls you once played with," he said. "Not to mention a rather subtle nod to Ibsen and his own *Doll's House.*"

"Not for nothing was I named Nora," she said. "Just ask my mother."

"Ah yes, a heroine who is forceful, loyal, but at times foolhardy."

"Got me this far in life," she said.

He pursed his thin lips, not saying anything when others might have a stinging retort. Not from Thomas Van Diver, this man was a true gentleman. Others would have pounced on such a pronouncement, especially in her vulnerable state.

Then he resumed the conversation, diving into the deep end. "I want you to find a book for me," he said, getting to the point quickly. "When I was a young boy, five years old to be exact, I accidentally stumbled upon a gift that my parents had hidden in the attic of our farmhouse. It was Christmas Eve, and the curious boy in me was rather impatient when it came to waiting for his gifts. Rather than scold me for my behavior, my forgiving father whisked me downstairs and allowed me to unwrap the gift . . . which turned out to be a book. It was a hardbound, illustrated version of Clement Clarke Moore's *Twas the Night before Christmas.* With my mother at my side, and with our tree so beautifully decorated and the snow falling lightly outside, you couldn't have pictured a more perfect scene, Rockwell at his finest, eh? Oh, I won't bore you with all the details now, but I lost that lovely volume. I want you to find it for me."

"Mr. Van Diver, there are probably hundreds of editions

of that book around," she said. "Finding yours would be like finding the proverbial needle in the haystack."

"And are you not in the business of locating those needles?"

She considered his words before finally admitting he was right. "Touché."

"I can pay handsomely, an hourly rate, plus the cost of the book when you find it."

"If I find it."

"Doubt should never enter the picture when you have a mystery to solve."

"Okay, when I find it," she said agreeably. "But don't expect miracles right away. Might take me a few months. I'm just getting my business open and getting myself up to speed and so I have many contacts to establish; this is a new world for me. But of course I can do some early digging, put out some feelers to out-of-print bookstores and antiquarian book dealers . . . oh, you'll have to get me as many specifics about the volume . . . wait, let me get a notepad, I want to jot down some ideas . . ."

Thomas had raised his hand, asking for a stop to her flow of words. "Please, wait."

"Is something wrong?"

"Indeed, there is," he said, clearing his throat in an attempt to gather his thoughts. "You see, Nora, I may not have as much time as I've previously indicated. You need to do all you can to get that rare edition into my hands by this Christmas. No, wait, correction. By this Christmas Eve. The book is not called, after all, *Twas the Night after Christmas*. It's *before*. And it would make not only the most wonderful Christmas present for this old man, it would also be the ultimate birthday present."

"Birthday?"

"Yes. I wasn't quite five years old yet when I found the

book, but may as well have been. I was born on Christmas Day, so many cold winter nights ago," he said, "and I wish to celebrate what could possibly be my last one by reliving the most special moment of my childhood."

"You like to pile on the pressure, don't you?" she said. "And the guilt."

"I understand you were once a lawyer," Thomas Van Diver said, straightening his bow tie for effect, heightening the drama escalating between them. "That means you've got the drive inside you. You never back down from a fight. You like to win. It's in your blood."

"You really know how to win a girl's heart," she said, her sarcasm biting.

"Unlike the so-called gentleman from before."

For a moment she didn't know who he meant, was that some veiled reference to her husband? But then she recalled the unwanted attentions of Chuck Ackroyd, local hardware store owner and unhappy grump. "Oh, him, he's harmless," she offered, "but as for the rest of Linden Corners, I'm not so sure. It's the last place I ever wanted to live again."

"And yet here you are. Oh, how I beg to differ, Ms. Nora Connors Rainer," said the all-knowing, all-seeing gentleman with the fancy bow tie and the sparkling blue eyes that twinkled like those of the fantastical Santa Claus who populated the book he sought. "Like me, I think you are exactly where you are supposed to be, and at just the right time."

She allowed herself a surprise grin. He was good.

"So, do we have a deal, Nora?"

She shook his hand and said, "Let's get to work, Christmas Eve has a way of sneaking up on you."

"Just like the past," Thomas said enigmatically.

"I guess that's where *A Doll's House* comes in."

"Almost like a portal to our dreams," Thomas said. "Finding things we lost, even people."

Another enigmatic remark from him, one that left Nora

feeling like she wasn't getting the entire picture here. "Okay, Thomas, the past, I'm ready to go back if you are. Tell me about the book, what was so special about it?"

"Well, for starters, Santa Claus . . . jolly old Saint Nicholas, he wore a green suit."

The first full day of her new life was under her belt. It was five o'clock and outside the sun had already gone down, night settling over the tiny burg of Linden Corners. Down the street the Five O' Diner was doing a bustling business, hence its name; George's Tavern had just turned on the outside lights and a few cars sat in its now illuminated parking lot. She considered dropping over for a glass of wine, then thought better of it. She wasn't in the mood for conversation, not from Brian Duncan or any of his regular barflies. Like Thomas had said, the past was everywhere, especially inside the walls of the business her father had once owned, now run by a stranger her mother treated like a son.

Nora flicked off the lights, and in the darkness of her store she let out a heavy sigh, alone now with just shadows for company. It felt like her first exhalation since her arrival just over twenty-four hours ago, and the release felt good. She took up a seat on the bench inside the bay window, her back against one wall, her feet stretching far to the other wall, allowing thoughts to come to her. How odd she felt, like she was living inside a dream and one not her own; perhaps it was one she'd imagined for her dolls from years ago. So innocent they were, tall, leggy, and blue-eyed, so beautiful, changing clothes based on the whims of their owner. Her older sisters were more the fashionistas, always asking for new dresses and outfits for their blond beauties, while Nora was content to ground her girls in a more practical approach to life. She never heard a complaint from the dolls, just her sisters.

"Why am I thinking about those dolls all of a sudden?" she asked aloud.

The overstuffed store, filled only with inanimate objects, remained silent save for her own echo. She had to be content with an answer only her mind could conjure: it was the old man's fault. His presence had been unexpected, surprising, and intriguing, all of the things she had assumed this new job of hers would offer, sneak peeks into people and their lives, into what motivated them and kept their hearts beating. You get a sense of their hopes and dreams, of the things they have lost and want back. For Thomas Van Diver, it was a book, and not just any book but perhaps the most over-published title in the Western hemisphere not counting the Bible. There was more to learn about this specific volume, just as there was more to discover about the enigmatic Thomas himself. Was he really fearing that his final days were upon him, or was this just a ploy of his to produce faster results on Nora's part? She hardly thought a man of such refinement would play the death card with such callous disregard, which led her to believe that there was a nugget of truth in his words.

She had to help him, that much she knew. Wasn't this why she had made the big decision to move back home? To change lives, and maybe along the way help hers?

She was born Nora Connors and for the first twenty-one years of her life she'd spent her days carefully planning every aspect about her world: school, major, lovers, marriage, children, all of them and in that order, almost like a checklist of life experiences, to be marked off first before pursing the next one. Each Christmas she looked forward to receiving a wall calendar as a gift, thinking about those coming days and all she could accomplish. Her sisters, who were not so tightly wound, had it easy, good marriages with responsible husbands, cute kids, jobs if they wanted, able to coast through the days with few cares other than who would pick up Sammy after soccer practice or Lucy after dance class. And that was fine for them, just not for Nora. How simpler things would have been if she'd gone that route. How miserable she would have been if she had. But wasn't she miserable now?

Sometimes she felt like two people.

Nora Connors, high-powered defense attorney.

Nora Rainer, wife and mother, ready to attend the PTA and cook dinner.

Conflicted over being both, she'd buried herself in her work.

She'd married at twenty-six, two years after graduating from law school, one year almost to the date that she met businessman Dave Rainer. Travis had come two years after that, and as much as she adored her son and would drop everything for him, the fact that she was a successful trial lawyer meant she didn't have to. She could pay other people to drop everything for him. Isn't that how it was done these days for the woman who had—or wanted—it all? Dave had come to resent her time at the office, even when she reminded him he had known who she was when they met, when he popped the question in between court appearances, and after Travis was born. The only one of them who seemed to adapt well to whatever was thrown their way was Travis himself, a good-natured kid she considered the luckiest thing to have ever happened to her.

"And this is how I repay him, by moving him to Linden Corners."

Her voice echoed longer, as though winding its way up the staircase to the large upstairs, where Elsie Masters had lived most of her life. The elderly lady had offered the apartment to Nora and Travis, but she couldn't commit. Not when she could live with her mother, not when she and Travis could be there to help her. Staring upward, imagining the spacious rooms inside this old Victorian, Nora wondered

what it would be like to have her own place again, just she
and Travis. They would not always be underfoot, interrupting Gerta's routine, living close enough that they could
check on her anytime, day or night. Only problem with that
situation, Gerta would have none of it. To not live with her
would be to insult her, and Nora had enough family issues to
deal with without causing her mother any more pain.

Pain, now that was definitely a four-letter word, sharp and
biting. Nora knew that Gerta was upset about her daughter's
situation, even as she had refused to ask details over what
had happened. Why move back after all these years, where
was Dave, and just what was the status of their marriage? All
questions she could answer if asked, none of which she had.
Nora would have responded: good questions, all of them.
She supposed you could call it taking a break, or maybe a
trial separation, though the word *trial* made her laugh, because those she preferred to win and in this case, well, there
were no winners. Just lots of legal fees and a lot of hurt.

"Okay, kid, enough wallowing, bet Mom's got dinner
ready," she said, lifting herself off the cushions, bringing
down the curtains on the bay window until the morning sun
would beckon them again to rise. It was good advice, she
thought, turn in for the night, curl up in the darkness until
the brightness of a new day called to you, issuing forth its
daily change. Nora had never been one to shy away from life's
challenges, and she wasn't prepared to start now.

Gathering up her coat and keys, she made her way to the
front door, opening it up.

The jangle of bells above her brought Thomas Van Diver to
mind.

"I'll have to replace those," she said, knowing the last
thing she needed was a reminder each time a customer
stopped in of the challenge ahead of her. Because those jangling bells rang like the jolly sound of Christmas, Santa and
his magic sleigh flying through the night, bestowing gifts

upon deserving children the world over. With each ring of the bell, Christmas would feel ever closer and she still had one huge gift to secure for under the tree.

Would Santa remember to come to Linden Corners?

Would he remember the wide-eyed, impatient five-year-old boy from so many years ago, so besotted with family and with memories and with a certain edition of a book that somehow meant the world to him? She hadn't asked for details, and Thomas hadn't offered them. Not yet, they would meet again, more clues would be revealed that would help Nora on her search.

Nora wondered if the book really did still exist, and if so, where in the world it was. Had it been a rare edition, or something mass produced? It was a big world out there, the book just a thin slice of it, a story detailing one day of the year. She returned her thoughts to Linden Corners, imagining her world had just grown smaller, and instead, what she had found within the dreams of her new store, was a world of possibilities.

November first and her thoughts were all about Christmas.

She was reminded of her promise to Travis, that she wouldn't screw up Christmas.

Now that promise had been doubled, both youth and the aged were counting on her.

CHAPTER 5

BRIAN

For reasons known only to the universe, the endless evolutions of the clock tended to move more quickly the last couple months of the year, as though time was eager for its big celebration before turning the page to a brand-new calendar. November would feed fast into December, and before you knew it the holidays would have come and gone in a blink of an eye, the sky over Times Square suddenly awash with bright streamers and confetti, ushering in for all that resolute sense of tomorrow, a fresh start. For Brian Duncan, one-time New Yorker and now permanent resident of laid-back Linden Corners, he remembered the strains of last Christmas—his and Janey's first as a family, the struggles they endured over wishing to give the other the best possible holiday—and he was determined that this year was going to be free of drama. In fact, he was planning on perfection.

Of course, the concept of perfection and the reality of a nine-year-old girl seldom went together. Square peg, round hole. You didn't need the holiday season to tell you that.

"Janey, come on, you're going to be late."

"I know, I know, but I can't find it."

"Can't find what?"

"If I knew, I'd know where it was," she said with her famous exasperation.

Brian Duncan was standing at the base of the stairs, the grandfather clock in the hall signaling the advancement of time, calling up to the second floor of the farmhouse; hearing her response, he felt his brain hurt, a nagging, pulsing headache. He shook it, afraid his brain would rattle inside his skull. Had she really just said what his ears heard?

"Janey, I didn't ask where you put it, I asked what you were looking for."

The tiny, determined force of nature appeared at the top of the stairs, hands on her hips in that special way patented by pre-teenagers, the child inside that body already outgrowing its youth. "Dad, I wanted to bring something to school, but I forgot what that something was. Once I remember, I'll know where I put it and then I can go."

She made her roundabout way of thinking sound so methodical, it almost made sense. He looked at the big clock, then back upstairs. "You better remember in the next two minutes, the bus is probably already turning up the road, our driveway is the next stop. And I'm not driving you to school, I've got way too much to get done today."

"Well, you'll have all afternoon to yourself, I'm going over to see baby Jake after school."

If that was news, it was old.

Brian left Janey to her search-and-rescue exploration, returning to a messy kitchen to finish washing up the breakfast dishes. It was Monday morning, an early November day, and the sun was shining down on a mild day, with temperatures rising in the mid-forties. Some of the snow from last week had already melted, as though the taste of the holiday spirit was draining from the town, a mere appetizer to the larger meal of winter. Even though Christmas was still seven weeks away, Brian pondered the idea of the village not being covered in a white blanket of snow—unlike last year, when a powerful storm had left them nearly isolated from the world, and happily so. No snow on Christmas seemed as unlikely as Janey getting to school on time.

"Janey!"

"Yay! I found it, I remembered exactly where I put it," she said, galloping down the stairs, her book bag bouncing against her back. "Bye, Dad, see you whenever."

"Whoa, whoa, hold up, young lady."

Janey stopped short at the front door, spinning on her heels, again with hands on her hips. If her stance didn't say it all, the rolling of her eyes sealed the deal. "You said it, I'm gonna be late."

"What did you remember?"

"Oh, the pictures from the Halloween Spooktacular that you helped me to download and print out," she said. "I thought my friends might like to see them, even Travis might enjoy them, since he made a really good pirate."

"Oh, that's nice," Brian said. "Travis, huh?"

Again, the eyes rolled. "Dad, he's a boy."

That seemed to sum it all up, Janey Sullivan back to being the all-knowing nine-year-old.

So he let her go, hearing the beep of the bus moments later. It was the bus driver's signal that she had picked up Janey safely, they were school-bound.

Alone in the quiet farmhouse, Brian put away the last of the dishes, turned to look at the time again. Seven forty-five, according to Annie's windmill clock that hung on the wall, the two sails ticking and clicking away the seconds, as constant and reliable as the actual windmill outside. He gave the clock a quick touch, Annie's presence surrounding him, enveloping this place she'd called home. He felt her not just here in the kitchen but everywhere, upstairs in their bedroom and near the fireplace where photographs of her and Janey adorned the mantel, outside by the ever-turning sails of the windmill, and of course, always in his heart.

Annie had been gone for more than a year now, and as such, there were no more firsts to think about. No more first time they celebrated Janey's birthday, no more first time he and Janey shared Thanksgiving, Christmas, all the special days of the calendar that marked the passage of time. Why he was suddenly drudging up all these memories, he wasn't sure. Perhaps it was the memories of last Christmas sneaking up on him, when it had seemed that their fragile existence was threatening to break. A year later already and they were better, stronger, the loving duo he had always envisioned they could be. But if truths were told, and it was only something he could admit to himself when alone, he missed the time they used to spend together, just the two of them. Lately Janey was consumed with helping Cynthia take care of that cute tyke, Jake, leaving Brian more time down at the tavern, as well as more downtime. The last few months, he'd been feeling the job wasn't enough for him, that he needed something more in his life. Since his arrival in Linden Corners he had been driven first to keep alive George Connors's traditions down at the tavern, then Annie Sullivan's, and he believed he had more than lived up to the high ideals set by those two amazing folks, both taken too early from the world.

Not for the first time, did Brian Duncan wonder if there was more he could be doing.

That brought his thoughts around to Nora Rainer.

She was doing now exactly what he'd done two years ago, restarting her life. But whereas he had stumbled upon this town along his travels, she had deliberately returned to her childhood home, and the difference seemed to be that back then Brian had every choice in the world to make his stay in this village transitional, while Nora appeared trapped in some confluence of events that glued her here. So far she wasn't talking about what those events were, another thing they had in common. Not that her affairs were any of his business, just because he and Gerta were as thick as thieves didn't mean Nora was open to trusting him with her own secrets. Oddly, her being back in Linden Corners and making a go of a new business, maybe she could inspire him. Her new antique store—an oxymoron indeed—seemed to be an extension of her new self, and he wondered if she could help him figure out what the heck he was supposed to be doing with his life. Learn by example.

Janey's happiness was everything to him.

But her happiness was directly tied to his, and at this moment in time he doubted *happy* was a word he could use to describe his life.

The phone ringing broke him from his thoughts of self-doubt.

"Hello?"

"Brian, dear, it's your mother."

"Hi, Mom," he said.

"You know what time of year it is."

"Of course, Thanksgiving is coming up."

"Yes, about that . . ." she said, her voice trailing off momentarily.

Like this phone call itself, Thanksgiving dinner was a Duncan family tradition, with all the disparate members of his family gathering at their parents' house, a lovely town house in the Federal Hill district of Philadelphia that had been an upgrade over the house where Brian had grown up in the northern suburbs. Last year was the first Brian had brought Janey with him, an experience both heartfelt and nerve-racking, one destined for the books. Didi Duncan's tone today indicated that tradition was about to be thrown to the wind.

"We won't be home this year," she said.

"Okay," Brian said, tonelessly. Was he pleased, or not, or just indifferent?

"I didn't think you would mind, you're so busy with

Janey, maybe it's not the right time to take a trip all the way here."

"Sure, Mom."

"Remember that cruise we took last Christmas with the Hendersons?"

"Sure."

"We're doing it again, except this time it's a Mediterranean cruise, three weeks."

"Three weeks?"

"And while we're in Europe . . ."

"Mom, the point?"

"We'll be away from Thanksgiving until the end of the year."

"So, what you're saying is, no Thanksgiving at your house, no Christmas at mine."

"I'm sorry, dear, it's just . . ."

"Mom, it's fine, you and Dad enjoy. Look, I gotta go get Janey ready for school, she's running late." A white lie, but it would spare both of them the need for explanations and excuses, hints of guilt, feelings of remorse. In other words, all the emotions of the holiday.

"Certainly," she said, "give her our love. And we'll be sure to send a postcard or two."

"Bye, Mom, bon voyage."

Brian hung up the phone, not sure of his feelings. He tried not to think about it, not as he showered and dressed, not as he went into the barn out behind the farmhouse to gather what he needed for the day's work, not as he hopped into the truck and drove down the driveway, and certainly not when he arrived in downtown Linden Corners, its familiar businesses and grassy parks lacking any hint of surprise, unlike the phone call. Was he jealous of his parents' wanderlust? A case of same old, same old was plaguing him, in Linden Corners and beyond, to his erstwhile family. While the reserved, buttoned-up power couple of Kevin and Didi Dun-

can were spending the holidays traveling the globe, their son
Brian's level of glamour had to do with deciding between the
tuna fish sandwich or BLT for lunch at the Five O'. Not that
he wanted his parents' materialistic life, but Brian Duncan
realized just what was eating at his gut: he was in a rut, that
electric spark of life that kept people going, almost on autopilot. His had been doused. Almost like the wind had quieted
and the sails of the windmill had gone silent.

Brian Duncan needed a challenge.

"Afternoon, Martha," Brian said as he stepped inside the
warm confines of the Five O' Diner, the cloying smell of
greasy bacon strong; at least his lunch decision had been
made, hard to deny his taste buds. The lunch crowd had already dispersed, just a few lingering coffee drinkers sat at
the counter, the booths empty. It was just how he liked it, the
rush hour here was like a meeting of the movers and shakers
of Linden Corners, those who stirred the pot as much as ate
from it. Gossip was always served as a side dish.

"Ah, Brian Duncan Just Passing Through," she said. "What
can I do for you?"

"For starters, you could drop that silly nickname at last,"
he asked. "Kind of worn out its welcome, don't you think?"

"Just like you," she said, smacking her hand on the counter
for effect.

Martha Martinson, owner of the Five O' Diner, was
known for her bad sense of humor, and Brian usually took
each sharp barb with grace, but today he just felt the sting.
Brian sensed that it had more to do with his sour mood than
Martha's taste in jokes . . . barely. She must have seen him
blanch, because she reached out to him.

"You okay, sport?"

"Yeah, think I got up on the wrong side of the bed today."

"You know how to fix that? Push the bed up against the

wall, that way you always have to get up on the same side," she said.

Brian couldn't tell if she was being serious or not, so he said, "I'll try that."

"Whoa, kid, you are in some mood. Okay, what can I get you that will at least make your stomach happy?"

"Not eating here," he replied.

She laughed so loudly the coffee drinkers set their cups down and gave her a look. "Now that's the Brian Duncan I've come to know and love," she said with a smile. "Tell you what, I got a chunky chicken salad on rye, pickle, fries, that sound like something for you?"

Actually, it did. "Yes," he said, "but make it for two. And add some bacon."

"For two?" she asked, an eyebrow raised. "You finally giving Janey a little sibling?"

"Very funny, Martha. But to do that I'd first need a date, second would be a medical procedure," he said. "And both would be miracles."

"You're looking for a date, I'm right here."

"Oh Martha, I think you're too much woman for me."

She laughed again, smacking her hand down on the counter one more time, making the ceramic cups dance in their saucers. "You got that right, kid. Okay, two chicken salad specials with extra strips of bacon coming up. I assume those are to go since I don't see any companion at your side. You want to tell me who's the beneficiary of my fine cooking?"

"No," Brian said flatly.

"Fine, be that way."

Brian waited for his order, then ventured out of the diner into the mild autumn day. The trees that lined Main Street were a mix of colors, brown and orange and yellow, the streets dotted with fallen leaves and lying dormant in the windless day. Instead of crossing the street back toward George's Tavern, he strolled down a couple of blocks, ending up in front of what was once Elsie's Antiques, now a name-less, faceless business that nonetheless had a sign on the door that said OPEN.

So he climbed the steps and opened the door. The jangle of bells sounded above him.

"Hello?" a voice called from the back.

"Delivery," Brian called out.

"Delivery? I didn't order anything . . . oh Brian, hi."

Hope she didn't greet all of her customers with such a lack of enthusiasm; must be she reserved it for him. Nora Rainer appeared from the back room, dressed casually in blue jeans and a gingham blouse, both of them messy, dusty. Her shoulder-length dark hair was pushed back with the aid of a beret, though some strands had come loose and she had to push them away from her eyes to see her visitor.

"Sorry, did I come at a bad time?"

"The farmers in town would call it mucking out the barn," she said. "I don't think Elsie had touched that back room in years, and now I think I've gotten all that grime on me. Sorry, I guess I wasn't expecting any customers today, not on a Monday at least. Slowest business day of the week, that's according to Elsie. For the moment I'm content to find out myself, though I'll probably end up closing down those days. There's something appealing about not having to wake up and go to work on a day when everyone else is dreading the start of the workweek."

"As someone who doesn't start work until four in the after-noon, I couldn't agree more," he said.

"So, Brian, what brings you here?"

He forgave her her abruptness. Someone accustomed to billing by the hour probably had issue with idle, small-town chitchat. So he held up the bag of food from the Five O'.

"What's that?"

"Lunch."

"Oh, I . . ."

He cut her off, two could play the abrupt game. "What you're about to say is you've been so busy fixing things in that dirty back room that you lost track of time and wow, thanks, Brian, for thinking of me and bringing me food, I'm actually starving. Chicken salad sandwiches with bacon, thick-cut fries, all courtesy of the Five O'. I hope you don't mind, but I brought one for myself, too."

She opened her mouth, about to say something, then shut it.

"Do I take that silence as acceptance?"

"I can't even remember eating breakfast," she said.

"Oh, I'm sure you did. Gerta would never let you out of the house without."

"You know my mother well," she said.

"Frankly, Nora, I don't think I could have survived the past two years without her."

"And her, you."

"So, does that mean her daughter and her friend can be friends, too?"

"Chicken salad from the Five O', it's a good start, and I think I can smell the bacon from here," she said. "Come on, pull up one of those bar stools I've got for sale, bring it over by the register. I think it's the only clean place in the store. I'll be right back, let me wash up a bit."

Brian grabbed a stool from a mismatched set, realized they were leftovers from the tavern that he'd sold to Elsie; six months ago he'd replaced all the creaky old wooden stools. Guess no one was in the market for them, as here they remained. Which got Brian thinking. He looked around the store at all the items on display; he never understood the appeal of buying stuff that others had deemed junk, we all had clutter, who wanted more? Brian wasn't a fan of garage sales, tag sales, or whatever they were called in these parts, remnants of a life already lived, pieces of the past. Brian Duncan was currently focused on the future.

Nora returned looking more relaxed, her hair undone and dropping lazily against her shoulders, and, though he couldn't be certain, she'd added a bit of blush to her cheeks. He had set their lunch out on paper plates Martha had provided, and so the two of them sat down to their impromptu meal, Nora smiling for the first time when she took a bite of her sandwich.

"Oh, that's perfect. Brian, how did you know?"

"I almost went with the tuna fish," he said.

"Oh, ick, no. Good choice here," she said, taking another bite.

As they ate, a comfortable silence descended upon them. It was fine to start with, both of them content to make brief eye contact while they chewed, taking occasional sips from the Cokes Brian had brought. But as the sandwiches were reduced to their final bites, Brian realized they would have to start talking soon and his mind spun with various topics. He didn't want to offend her with anything probing but still, he wanted to know more about her.

"So . . ." he said.

"So . . ." she replied.

They smiled, they laughed.

"You go first," she said, biting into a tart pickle, her expression newly sour. "You've got me curious, Brian. Bringing over lunch was nice, but there must be more to this visit than being neighborly. Where I've lived the past fifteen years, the business I was in, people always come with an agenda."

He could relate. He'd once lived the Manhattan rat race. Work hard, trust no one.

For the moment, he was enjoying the quaint Linden Corners approach.

"Can't a fellow entrepreneur stop by and see how things are going with a new business?"

"No," she said, "not when he's going to get a bill for the car he damaged."

"Can we forget about that for a moment?" he asked, his voice suddenly serious enough to catch Nora's undivided attention.

"Okay, Brian, what's on your mind?"

"Actually, your store is what's on my mind," he said, learning forward with the first bit of eagerness he'd felt all day. "Tell me about it. What's your plan? Surely you're not just taking over Elsie's and doing what she's done all these years. You must have a fresh approach."

"In fact, I do," she said. "Of course, I realize that Elsie's Antiques is well known in this region, and I aim to continue to deal in her stock and trade. Lots of rich city folk come up to the Hudson River Valley in search of lovely items for their summer homes, it doesn't hurt to cater to them. But I also had to think there was something else I could do, something that was unique to me . . . for me. Something that was going to challenge me."

Brian could relate. It's like the old joke, "Why do adults ask kids what they want to be when they grow up? It's because they're looking for ideas." Aside from working as a corporate drone and now as tavern owner, Brian Duncan had never really known what he wanted from life.

"I got to thinking, the generations are changing, even what we think of as recent history is fading deeper into the past. Traditions are being forgotten, families have lost sight of what made them strong. Think about those older antiques from the eighteen hundreds and before, they're not so easy to find anymore and I suppose that's just the natural progression of time, one generation's likes giving way to another's desires. People want not so much stuff as they want to recall the memories evoked by that stuff. So out of the ashes of Elsie's Antiques has risen A Doll's Attic, a place where your past is brought back to life."

"I like the name," Brian said.

"Thanks, I thought long and hard about it and for a variety of reasons that's what I came up with," she said, "though it was my first customer who already saw through my façade, he picked right up on my literary pretension."

"A certain play by Ibsen?"

"My goodness, so many literate people in Linden Corners," she said. "You and Mr. Van Diver should meet."

Brian had been listening to every word, but it was that last comment from Nora that made him truly look up with sudden surprise. What was it about that name, why was it familiar to him? His jumbled thought made him sound all-too-much like Janey and her search for the photographs this morning. He stretched his brain to try and understand why the name Thomas Van Diver nagged at him.

"I'm sorry, who?"

"Oh, he's this kind old gentleman who lives over at The Edge, he stopped in on my first day of business last week," she said. "He had the most unusual request, one I wasn't sure I could honor. But then it occurred to me, what he was seeking and what I was peddling were one and the same, a chance to dig into the past and find something of value—and I don't mean financial, something personal. Something for his heart."

"What was he looking for?"

"I think that falls under client/attorney privilege."

"Ever the lawyer," Brian said, understanding though unsatisfied. "Sorry to pry, but the reason I ask . . . it's that name. Van Diver. It's sounds so familiar, like I'm supposed to know it . . ."

"What I can tell you is that he used to live in Linden Corners, many years ago."

"Oh my God, of course," Brian said, feeling his eyes widen with wonder. "Of course, how could I forget? The Van Diver family, they lived here years ago. Nora, do you realize who he is . . . I mean, who I think he must be? A descendant of the family that originally owned the farmhouse that Janey and I live in . . . it was the Van Divers who built the windmill. Can you tell me anything about him, about what he's looking for?"

Nora seemed to be struggling with her conscience.

"Please, Nora, this could be important," he said. "Not for me, but for Janey. The past is a place of healing, knowing more about her home and the people who lived there, it may help Janey understand more about her own parents."

"That sounds like you're guilting me, Brian Duncan."

"Is it working?"

"Fine. I can tell you one thing," she said. "He's searching for the meaning of Christmas."

CHAPTER 6

THOMAS

It wasn't every day you were invited for dinner at the house in which you were born.

Which might explain why he was so jumpy. He hadn't felt this nervous since he'd asked his Missy to marry him, though he had to take some comfort in the fact that she said yes right away. And hadn't that worked out well, sixty-two good years. So he told himself to just swallow his growing apprehension, wasn't this what he'd come back for after all these years, an old man determined to rediscover one last time the little boy who lived inside of him? Rather than try to rationalize his concerns, he instead turned his attention to which of his bow ties would complete his outfit tonight. Not the navy blue solid—he'd worn that one to meet Nora; perhaps something more upbeat was appropriate, like a polka dot or the goofy one with the little green frogs.

"Oh, of course," he said as though he should have known, and from his drawer full of bow ties (both clip-ons and traditional), he withdrew a bright scarlet tie with a snowflake pattern. It was wintery without being overtly Christmas-like, though some might say it was too early in the season for such a festive accoutrement. Putting it around his neck felt so right, soothing both any naysayers he might encounter as well as his frayed nerves. He knew instantly he'd made the right choice, one he was sure tonight's host would appreciate.

The invitation had surprised him when it arrived, he didn't even know Brian Duncan was aware of his presence in town, much less of his connection to the weathered old farmhouse. But give credit to the small network of gossipers in Linden Corners, they meant well when spreading their stories of scandals and new arrivals and old men with secret pasts, and the result had one of them (he suspected Elsie) speaking about the new-to-town Thomas Van Diver.

He'd been comfortably ensconced in his apartment at Edgestone when Susie at the front desk had buzzed him, announcing that he had a visitor.

"I'm not expecting anyone," he said, suspecting it was Nora with some news about the book, but his natural curiosity was piqued even more when the name announced was one Brian Duncan. Thomas of course knew who he was, he'd done his homework about the current owner of the old farmhouse, and subsequently the windmill. But how the young man had learned about Thomas, well, he supposed he was about to find out. He asked that Mr. Duncan be allowed in and moments later came a knock at the door.

"Mr. Van Diver," said the gentleman, tall, slim, handsome. "I'm . . ."

"Yes, yes, Brian Duncan, please come in."

He escorted his guest to a chair in the living room, asked if he could get him a beverage. The time was just after five o'clock and Thomas had already mixed his daily Manhattan, very dry. Brian declined his offer by saying he didn't touch the stuff, following up by saying, "But I have an offer for you, which I hope you'll accept. Sorry if I'm just jumping into my reason for being here, but I'm already late to the tavern, got Sara from the Five O' pouring beers for me till I can get there."

"You don't drink but you own a bar?"

"It's a long story."

Thomas raised his glass, took a grateful sip. "We all have stories, Brian."

"And I'm curious about yours," he said.

"Color me intrigued," Thomas said.

"Correct me if I'm wrong, but you're related to the Van Diver family that used to live in Linden Corners."

"As stated, no correction needed."

"So my home, it was once your home, yes?"

"Yes, many years ago."

"Well, I've come to you with an offer to join us for dinner, say this Friday night," he said. "Janey and I would love to host you and show you around the property. If that's not too much trouble . . . or short notice. Nora Rainer tells me you've asked her for a favor, something about your past—that's all she said, no violation of your privacy. But that it had to do with Christmas."

"Ah, so it was Nora, I'll have to apologize to Elsie," he said, taking another sip of his drink.

"So you'll join us?"

"I'd be very honored," he said. "What may I bring?"

"Oh, I think yourself will be plenty enough. Janey will be thrilled."

"Janey, she's the young girl you have taken over guardianship for, yes?"

"You have me at a certain disadvantage, Mr. Van Diver," Brian stated. "You appear to know so much about me, and yet I didn't even know you were in town. We'll see about changing that status come Friday night. I would love to hear about your life and about your family, and also about what brings you back to Linden Corners, that is, if you don't mind."

"Prying," Thomas said. "It's a Linden Corners tradition . . . in the best sense of the word."

"We do like to look out for one another."

"I'd be delighted to accept your offer, and I will see you both Friday night," Thomas said with a polite nod and perhaps the barest hint of a smile. And now the time had come and he still had that glint in his eye. His bow tie affixed and a red cap placed atop his head to protect against the cold, he was ready to make that long-awaited journey back in time, to a place he recalled more in the creations of his mind than he did in true memory.

Ambling slowly, Thomas made his way to the front entrance of Edgestone, bypassing all of the other residents who were either making their way to the dining room or away from it. Most liked to eat early, others like Thomas were night owls. As the seven o'clock hour approached, so, too, did his ride, pulling up alongside the curb just as he stepped out into the brisk night air. It was Brian himself, who had volunteered to fetch him and bring him back, no matter the hour.

Thomas attempted to step up into the front cab of the truck, Brian coming around to the passenger side to aid him. It was a big step up. Once settled inside the truck, seat belt fastened, Brian returned to the driver's side and they set off.

"You look quite dapper," Brian said. "Love the bow tie, the look suits you."

"I know they are a bit old-fashioned. Then again, young Brian, so am I."

Thomas rode in easy silence, just taking in the shadow on the roads as they made their way past the downtown area and toward the western edge of the village, turning up Crestview Road, melting piles of snow pushed over to the shoulders, as

though the plows had been by recently to clear for them a
fresh path. As though they knew to make way for its returning hero, a Linden Corners version of rolling out the red carpet. Feeling his heart beat with newfound apprehension, he
looked over at his concentrated driver. Brian stole a look his
way.

"You okay?"

"Just hard to believe, after all these years."

"We have a bit of a homecoming waiting for you," Brian
said, words meant to make him feel better, but all they
served to do was make Thomas feel even more nervous.
What kind of surprise had this young lad planned, and just
who else had he dragged into his little plot? He'd seen that
irrepressible Janey Sullivan at the Halloween Spooktacular,
practically reigning over the junior set, so it would come as
no shock that Brian had enlisted her help. Were there others?
He was about to find out. They'd turned up the drive, tires
crunching against snow-coated gravel. For a moment all
color slipped away, and under the cover of darkness, Thomas
was five years old again, in the backseat of a truck not too
dissimilar from the one he rode in, his parents in the front,
their mouths moving in conversation, but no sounds were
coming forth, like a silent movie reel was unspooling in the
mind. That's how he felt, distanced from them while still,
somehow, feeling their presence in this black-and-white
world.

"Here we are," Brian announced.

They went in through the front entrance, Thomas taking
in every detail: the wainscoting above the doorway, the lay-
out of the foyer, the long hallway that led into the main living area of the house; he knew instantly that the kitchen was
to the back of the house, the living room to his right, the
staircase that led upstairs to his room and even farther up, to
the attic in which he loved to hide, he remembered it all in
seconds. He looked above, down, and all around, his eyes

widening at how familiar it all looked, finally saying, "My goodness, so little of it has changed, I can almost smell the wood burning from the hearth."

"Well, that part is real," Brian said with a chuckle. "It grew cold again today, so I thought the fire would both warm the house and give off a sweet scent, perhaps evoke some memories for you. Come in, our other guests await us."

And so they were, all of them gathered in the living room, standing up no doubt when they heard the truck pull up outside. Thomas took in the guests, realizing he knew them all, at least by sight, some by name. Nora Rainer was there, and beside her was her son, whose name he didn't yet know, and beside him was the young girl who, while no longer dressed like a glowing windmill, nonetheless produced a bright smile on her face when he appeared. She must be Janey Sullivan. The only other person assembled was a lady who fell more into his age group, one with a kind expression and soft, welcoming eyes.

"Mr. Van Diver, we are so glad you could join us," the elderly woman said. "We've not been properly introduced, but I'm Gerta Connors, Nora's mother. And this handsome young lad is my grandson, Travis, and of course you already know Nora."

"Good evening, Mr. Van Diver," Nora said, "glad you could join us."

"I'm quite surprised, actually, to see you all here. I thought it was just a simple dinner."

"Dad likes to make an impression," Janey said, stepping forward and extending her hand.

"As do you, young lady," he said, accepting her handshake.

Janey giggled.

Introductions complete, Thomas settled into the proffered recliner positioned near the fireplace, accepted a glass of red wine that Nora poured for him, making sure to refill hers as well. The kids were drinking sparkling apple cider and acting like the floating bubbles were champagne; Gerta and Brian both appeared to be drinking seltzer water. Thomas was thankful for Nora, he found a drink at such a gathering to be not only civilized but a necessity. It helped relax both the body and the mind, and at the moment that's what he needed. Reality had turned surreal, his past somehow alive within him, even eighty years later. He felt a slight chill come over him. A sip of the wine warmed his insides, the nearby fire his hands.

"Well, I must thank you all for making such an effort on behalf of an old man," he said.

"When I heard the name Van Diver," Brian said, "I knew I just had to meet you."

"Me, too," Janey said. "You used to live in this house? Really?"

"When I was even younger than you are now," Thomas said.

"Wow, that's a long time ago."

"Janey!"

"Oh no, Brian," Thomas said with a hearty, good-natured laugh. "Never deny a child's honesty, they keep us all on our toes, ha ha. Yes, it was quite a long time ago, Janey, but even after all that time my mind can still see the little boy racing up and down the stairs and hiding in the attic, waiting for my mother to find me. The attic was always my favorite place, where I felt on top of the world. My mother always knew where I was hiding. Mothers are like that."

There was a moment of silence in the room, a sudden awkward scent enveloping them. Thomas looked at the crowd, saw the worried look cross Brian's face as his eyes quickly hit Gerta's. Both of their gazes then fell to Janey, who looked like she was searching for the right words, and it was then Thomas remembered that Annie Sullivan, who was Janey's

mother, was no longer among them. A gaff of major propor-
tion, and Thomas felt fresh pain strike him. He could relate
and for a moment cursed his insensitivity.

But then Janey saved the day, miraculously, with a simple
sweetness that belied her years. "Me, too. I have a favorite
place, too," Janey said. "My mom always knew to find me
inside the windmill. I think you're right, Mr. Van Diver,
mothers do have special minds."

"And hearts," he said, with a gentle tap to Janey's pert
nose.

She giggled.

"Do you want to go see the attic?"

"I don't think these old legs of mine would make those
stairs," Thomas said. "So, I'll have to be content visiting
your favorite place. What do you say, perhaps you would like
to show me the windmill?"

Janey's eyes lit up just as Brian, shaking his head, said,
"Let her do that, Mr. Van Diver, and you'll have a friend for
life. I know from experience. But what do you say we wait to
do that until after dinner? I think the food is ready, and besides, we'd all like to get to know you better and I'm sure
you've got questions for us. Everyone, shall we sit down to
the table?"

"I'll help you serve," Gerta said.

"Mom, I'll do that, you get settled," Nora said.

"Well, if you insist. Travis, will you escort your grandmother inside?"

"Sure, Grandma."

While the otherwise silent Travis attended to his grandmother's request and took her arm, and as Brian and Nora
retreated to the kitchen to start serving, Thomas was left
alone with Janey. She was looking at him curiously.

"Yes, young lady?"

"Do you like that everyone calls you mister?"

"What else would they call me?"

"Thomas. It is your name, right? That's what I'd like to call you."

"Well, little lady, to be on such familiar terms with someone, anyone, especially one so many years apart in age from you, there must exist a very special bond," he said, a twinkle to his eyes, "and I have a sense we already have that, don't we, Janey Sullivan?"

"You were born here and so was I, and I think we both love the windmill."

"You know what else we share," he said.

"What's that?"

"We both lost people important to us, and at a young age," he said quietly.

Janey's lips quivered ever so slightly, leaving Thomas wondering if he'd gone too far in his effort to win over the affections of this young girl. For a moment he felt bad, he knew her story, but she was unaware of his. Just when he thought coming here had been a bad idea, she rushed into his arms, a big, inviting smile gracing her freckled face. "I think I'm going to like having you living in Linden Corners, Mr. Van Diver," she said. "You're just what we all needed, and just in time, too."

"In time for what?"

"Why, for Christmas, silly."

"Christmas," he said with a faraway sigh. "I thought you were going to call me Thomas."

She giggled, almost to herself. "I used to call Brian silly, too, except once I tried Briany, but his name doesn't sound good with a *y* on the end. Do you like Tommy?"

Flames lit his eyes, reflecting from the fireplace. "No, no one calls me that," he stated.

"Okay, Thomas it is. All this talk of names, you know what? It's . . ."

"Silly?"

"Brian once made snow angels with me, trying to be silly. But he just looked like he was having a seizure."

Now it was Thomas's turn to look away, pain flaring up in his watery eyes. Questions were hard, answers even more so, and Thomas wondered just how he would get through this night. That's when Brian rescued them both, showing his face around the corner of the hallway. "And I'm going to call you both late for dinner. Silly."

Dinner plates were cleared and dessert was set out, two pies, one peach, the other strawberry.

"A strawberry pie?" Thomas asked. "I've never heard of such a thing."

"Have a slice and you'll never stop talking about it," Brian said.

"There's truth to what my dad says," Janey said, much to the amusement of all, not only for the half-formal way she spoke, but also because she knew Brian so well.

Seated around the dining room table as they were, they very nearly resembled a complete family, three generations gathered to break bread, share stories of yesteryear amidst lots of laughter. Thomas and Gerta, Brian and Nora, Travis and Janey, the six of them representing three separate families that had been brought together over a mutual sense of community, conscious of all they had lost in the past, embracing whatever the future held.

"As much as I would love to dig into that pie," Thomas said, setting down his napkin after a gentle wipe at the corners of his mouth, "after such a filling, delicious meal, I confess I could use a breath of fresh air first, assist my digestion. A man of my age knows of such things. And I would like to appreciate that luscious-looking pie as best I can. So perhaps now, before it gets too late, Janey could show me her windmill."

"Yay!"

"It's kind of late," Brian said, "not much to see."

"It's a clear night, stars all over, I think you'll see just fine," Nora said.

"Dad, please, can I?" Janey asked.

"You showing off your windmill, I think I'd be crazy to say no," he said. "But I think I should accompany you both."

"Maybe I could go with them," Travis said.

Looks were exchanged, between Nora and Brian, between the kids, between Thomas and Gerta, all eyes finally resting on Brian.

He looked resigned to letting the kids take charge. So he said, "Sounds like a good idea, thanks, Travis. Let the adults clean up and get some coffee brewing," he said, "while the kids of all ages go play in the backyard."

Thomas stood up with as much enthusiasm his tired body could muster, announcing that there was no time like the present to get going, so he began to shuffle off, Janey taking up on one side of him, Travis on his other. Brian cautioned them to look after Mr. Van Diver, "it's dark and the ground can be uneven. Janey, remember to flick on the outside lights to help guide you."

"He's such a parent," Janey announced to Thomas, who found that greatly amusing.

So the three of them ventured outdoors, bundled up against the cold night. The wind had picked up considerably on this cold night, Janey stating that was just the way she liked it, it gave the sails of the windmill a chance to spin, "to stretch their arms high into the sky." As much as he had bonded early with Janey, it was Travis who captured Thomas's attention now. The young lad had been mostly quiet during dinner, leaving him wondering just what he was thinking. This dinner was probably the last thing a twelve-year-old wanted to do on a Friday night. Maybe hang with his friends, wasn't that the lingo the kids used today? Thomas reminded himself, Travis was new to town, perhaps he hadn't secured the kind of friends you could depend upon. Maybe that's why he had asked to join them, just a way to get away from the adults. As they trekked slowly across the snowy back lawn, Thomas said, "You know, Travis, you and I, we, too, have something in common."

"What's that?"

"Moving."

"Yeah, but I moved here, you moved away from it."

"But it's the same thing, we did what our parents were doing, we had no choice," he said. "Youth have minds, but little authority to exercise what they are thinking. It's why kids struggle so much, they have an independent spirit that can't quite take to the wind yet. There's always someone else directing the breeze."

Travis appeared to be considering these words, ultimately deciding not to say anything, letting them float into the night sky, toward the twinkling stars for further exploration. Perhaps wishing they would not sink in, the reality being too harsh. But Thomas could see the wheels in motion inside the boy's brain anyway, contemplating their deeper meaning, and understanding. Thomas happily grinned, knowing he'd made an impact on the boy. Gave him something to think about.

A moment later, they reached the edge of a hill, the drop-off considerable during the day, precipitous in the hard-to-see dark night. Thomas looked around the open countryside, the silver glow from the outdoor light of the farmhouse reaching out only so far, the sparkling stars above like thousands of night-lights, none able to fully power the sudden blackness that encased them. He thought he'd gone far enough, his old eyes not as good adjusting to the darkness as they once were. He'd have to wait till daylight to be reunited with the windmill.

But then he saw them, dancing shadows, flickering as

they hit the ground, disappeared, only to reappear, again, again, like gentle revolutions of sparkling light. He focused his eyes and that's when he saw it, the large tower jutting into the sky, four giant sails spinning, spinning, the wind powering them. He'd heard stories for years about the old mill, how his ancestors had built it in the middle of their farm, the energy from its sails aiding in clearing excess water from the low-lying land where they grew their needed crops. By the time Thomas had been born, the farming of the once-arid land was mostly over and the previous generations had died off, leaving the windmill alone to the elements, and at age five, when finally they had left Linden Corners, the old mill was as silent as death, impervious to even the strongest wind.

"Oh my, look at how beautifully, how naturally, those sails spin," Thomas said with a breathless wonder. He put a hand to his heart, felt it beat beneath the fabric of his coat. For a moment he channeled his long-departed mother and thought, too, of his father, the final image he had of him. The windmill's large sails spun, again, again, as though turning back time to the point where Thomas was a boy again, again, an equal peer to the two charges beside him. "It's so marvelous, perhaps one of the loveliest sights to ever lay my eyes upon . . . thank you, Janey, and thank you, Travis, for taking me here and showing me the windmill."

"It's pretty cool," Travis said, his way of agreeing with the more poetic Thomas.

Janey turned to look up at Thomas. "It's where Brian and I met, he was passing through town one day and he stopped to look at it, and there I was, tumbling down the hill. . . . Momma wasn't happy that I was talking to a total stranger, but look at how that turned out, he's hardly a stranger anymore, he's the best, and you know what else?"

"What's that, Janey?"

"For Christmas last year, he decorated the windmill with

all sorts of bright white lights," she said. "I can't wait for him to do it again, Thomas, you have to see it. Promise me you'll come back and I can show you again."

Thomas nodded, not sure young Janey could see his subtle move in this darkness. But he was in complete agreement, he did wish to see such a sight, and perhaps, perhaps by doing so he might be able to complete his own journey back to this world of Linden Corners, back to the windmill and one last chance to relive that special holiday, the final one he ever spent with both his ever-patient mother and warbound father. He stole one last look at the redoubtable Janey Sullivan, realizing all that she had lost, amazed at her remarkable spirit, as though the wind fed it, her heartbeat in line with the revolutions of the sails.

As much as he had struggled with his decision this past year, Thomas Van Diver knew, finally and ultimately, at last that he'd made the right choice in coming back to Linden Corners. Back home, to the land of the farmhouse and to the windmill, where sails turned in the dark night and spun dreams into reality.

CHAPTER 7
NORA

Thousands of editions from dozens of publishers both big and small, and all of them contained the same poetic, rhythmic text, albeit with different illustrations and color palettes, that's what she found during her initial research junket online. What she found were so many variations on a theme her mind spun to the point where all the books blurred together into one holiday jumble of legend and lore. And what did all these volumes have in common? Certainly the author was one, an elusively popular scholar named Clement Clarke Moore. Also the ubiquitous red suit always worn by the lead character. Yes, there was Saint Nicholas himself, his traditional suit of red, fringed with white ruff and a thick black belt. She repeated it again, to let it sink in. A red suit—never green. Santa was jolly, red-cheeked, a sack full of toys slung over his shoulder. The images on the pages she could access never varied, the famed Christmas tale was as unchanged now as it was when the books were published, some as far back as four decades, others just this past year. The endless publishing loop of *Twas the Night before Christmas* was something for Guinness. So there the truth lay right there on the screen, practically glowing at her, Santa had never worn a green-colored outfit.

Feeling a pulsing headache coming on, Nora set her laptop down on the floor in the living room and closed her eyes, allowing them to adjust to something other than the harsh glare of the computer screen. She'd been at it all afternoon, clicking, typing, searching, and looking . . . seeking out an answer that didn't seem to exist, surfing web page after web page, and the end result was as fruitless as a juicy case where the defendant admitted his guilt. Why proceed, not when there was nothing to fight for.

Because of the challenge, that's what she told herself.

Nora Rainer was not a woman to easily admit defeat, not in the courtroom and not in life, and the more she sought out Thomas's increasingly rarer edition of *Twas the Night before Christmas,* the more determined she grew to solve the mystery. She considered the notion that his memory was faulty after all these years, or perhaps the book had been so old even back in the 1940s that the color had faded to the point where Santa's suit was indistinguishable, drenched in sepia that a five-year-old mind mistook for green. Yet his adamancy that the suit was green was so strong that she had to believe him. That, and the quiet desperation in his eyes when he spoke of the book. There was something behind his eyes that he hadn't yet revealed, which only added further intrigue to The Case of the Lost Christmas Book.

"Cup of tea, dear?"

Nora's green-flecked eyes flicked open to find her mother hovering over her. Not in any intrusive way, just . . . she was being a mother.

"Oh, uh, hi, Mom . . . what time is it? I think I've lost track of the afternoon."

"Five thirty, I was just about to start on dinner," she said. "But you looked like you could use a pick-me-up. The way you've been so concentrated on your work all day, well, I haven't seen you like this since you were in high school, determined to be the first one to get your term papers done. So different from your sisters—the three of them your father and I practically had to bribe to do their homework."

"And I always got my work done, way ahead of schedule," Nora said.

"You were always very conscientious about your schoolwork," she said. "Not like when you were younger, hiding away with your dolls and imagining whatever world you had created."

"A girl has to grow up. And being concerned with getting your work done is a good trait to have if you're going to pursue a career in law," Nora said, and then with a rueful smile added: "Or, if you're suddenly not."

Gerta opened her mouth to say something and then, apparently, thought better of it. The attempt at words didn't go unnoticed by Nora.

"Mom, something on your mind?"

She looked down at her tightly knotted hands. "How about that tea?"

"A glass of wine would go down better. 'Bout that time of day."

"Okay, dear, let me see what we have," Gerta said, starting off toward the kitchen.

She got no more than two feet when she was interrupted by the opening of the front door and, along with a cool, swirling wind intruding onto the calm inside the house was the force of nature named Travis Rainer, his almost-teenage self breathless.

"I know, I'm late, I'm sorry," he said, closing the door behind him.

"Goodness, Travis," Gerta said. "Like the wind had hold of you."

"Sorry if I scared you, Grandma. Looks like a storm is

coming in, lots of gray clouds moving fast in the sky . . . and that wind, it's really fierce. When I saw the clouds rumbling in, I just started to run, but I think the wind took hold of my feet and lifted me here."

"Well, looks like we're all in for the night," Gerta said. "You have to listen to nature."

"Seems we all lost track of time today, buddy. But next time if you're running late, storm or not, just call," Nora said, ever mindful to call her son by his name and not some affectation like honey or sweetie. She realized she had slipped, though Travis didn't seem to notice. She was trying not to baby him, not in the presence of his grandmother and not in the face of all this upheaval. And besides, if he had been hanging out with some new friends, the last thing she wanted was for them to think he was some kind of mama's boy. "Dinner's not even started, your grandma and I are gonna sit and have a quiet drink. Why don't you go upstairs, give your father a call."

A sour expression hit his face. "I'd rather not."

"Too bad," Nora said. "Call him before it gets too late. No argument."

Travis had heard that phrase often enough in his twelve years to know there was no room for debate. Tossing off his winter coat and hanging it on the rack, he trudged upstairs like it was a chore, mumbling under his breath. Nora, with a regretful ache, watched as he disappeared around the landing, listened as his footsteps hit his room. She hated that he was in this situation, hated that they'd both been put in this situation. But she and Travis would weather this storm, come out stronger. When she looked back, her mother was gone, too, presumably gone to the kitchen to fetch drinks. Nora could use that glass of wine about now.

It was Sunday, as lazy as one she could remember, even with the work she'd done online. Something about sitting around in your sweats while in the comfort of your old child-

hood home, the fireplace crackling to keep you warm, even
as your insides felt frozen, that made her realize how much
her life had changed. For the past month she'd been on autopilot, packing, driving, moving, then at the store dusting, or-
ganizing, planning, and today was the first day when she felt
she could breathe a bit easier. Not that the adjustment to life
in Linden Corners was complete, far from it, but a sense of
normalcy had set in with each passing day, to the point
where she accepted that this was no short-term visit—per-
manence was settling in. The jury was still out as to how she
felt about it all.

"Here you are, dear," Gerta said, returning from the
kitchen with a glass of red wine for Nora, a mug of steaming
herbal tea for her. Taking hold of the glass, she took a grateful sip of wine, then let it linger in her grasp. Warmth hit her
insides.

Gerta, meanwhile, sat in the chair next to hers, her usual,
only an end table with a brass lamp and a book of crossword
puzzles separating them. Nora was seated, legs crossed, in
her father's chair, still in the same place it had been for
years, even if he was no longer around to luxuriate in its soft
comfort. She gazed over at her mother, who was looking at
her even as she drank from her mug. The words she wanted
to say kept getting swallowed along with the fragrant tea.
Gerta fixated on the laptop while bubbles danced as a screen
saver.

"Have you had any luck with Mr. Van Diver's request?"

"Very little, Mom. There are so many editions of *Twas
the Night before Christmas,* not a single one of them has
jolly old Saint Nick in a green suit. Though I've been looking at the screen for so long maybe I can't trust my eyes anymore."

"It does seem odd, perhaps he just misremembers? A
child so young . . ."

"If he's still thinking about it eighty years later, I believe him," Nora said.

"What in heaven does he plan to do with the book?"

"That he didn't say."

"How very mysterious."

"Just as mysterious as his appearance in Linden Corners, after all these years," she said. "But heck, you could say the same about me."

An enigmatic comment, it brought an end to the gentle flow of communication between mother and daughter, with Nora realizing she'd opened up a can of worms she'd sooner see sealed tight. As it was, Gerta had her opening, but still she didn't take it. She just sipped her tea in silence, leaving Nora squirming uncomfortably in her chair.

"Okay, Mom, what's on your mind?"

"Oh dear . . . you know how I don't like to pry . . ."

"Mom, I'm your daughter, it's not prying, it's mothering," Nora said.

She seemed satisfied with her daughter's overture. "Well, as long as you want to talk, that's fine with me."

"Ask away, I'll tell you what I know."

"What did you mean when you told Travis to call his father . . . 'before it gets too late'?"

Talk about jumping into the deep end. "Dave is overseas."

"Overseas?"

"Germany, to be specific, Frankfurt."

"What's he doing there?"

"Working there. Living there." Nora paused. "Without us, obviously."

"I see," she said, even though it was clear she didn't.

"It's complicated," Nora said.

"Seems to me it's not. Either you're a family or you're not."

"Mom, you of all people should know that families come in all shapes and sizes and odd configurations," she said, suddenly defensive. "Look at you and Brian and Janey, talk about makeshift. Not one of you shares a surname, and look how great the three of you are together. Dave, Travis, and I, we are a family also, but we're going through a shift in its definition, and while we figure it all out, I thought it was best to give Travis some stability."

"By moving him away from all he knows?"

"No, into the loving arms of his grandmother, who I knew would spoil him."

"He does like my spaghetti sauce," she said.

"And how many times have we had pasta since we arrived?"

Gerta paused, drank her tea. "I see your point," she said. "But, Dave . . ."

"But Dave nothing. He made his choice, a big promotion with his bank came his way, with a chance to live overseas. How could he pass on that? He's almost fifty, and it was a big deal to him."

"So why aren't you there with him?"

Nora felt a quick, piercing stab to her heart. She took a big drink of wine, then two more before continuing. "He didn't ask us to join him."

"Oh Nora, I'm sorry . . . for that, and for pushing you. If you're not ready . . ."

"If I wasn't ready to talk about it, I wouldn't," she said. "You've been so patient, Mom, you've given me my space, the least I owe you is the truth. Though what that is, I'm not sure. I couldn't begin to tell you what the future holds, I think that's what appealed to me about Elsie's store, it's all about living in the past. For now, that's my comfort zone. As for me and Dave, we've agreed to a year's trial separation, he's going to live his life abroad and Travis and I will live ours, and then we'll see where we are in twelve months. Even though I already know."

"That's why you're here? Too many reminders of the life you shared?"

Nora raised her glass, a sarcastic lilt in her voice. "Here's to Linden Corners."

"There are worse places to be in this world," Gerta said.

"Yeah, Frankfurt for one," Nora said.

It wasn't a funny comment and neither woman laughed, both of them masking emotions with their chosen drinks. At last, Gerta stood up, her aging knees crackling like the burning embers in the nearby fireplace, saying she'd better get dinner started. A boy of Travis's age needed constant nourishment. Nora asked if she could help.

"I cook, you clean."

"And Travis eats."

"It's what twelve-year-old boys do," Gerta said.

"How do you know, you only had girls," Nora said.

Gerta smiled, her wisdom shining through. As she came up beside her daughter, she took hold of her hand and with a gentle squeeze, she simply said, "All mothers know their way around children, whether boys or girls. Look at yourself, Nora, at all you've sacrificed for Travis."

"See, that's what I wonder about, whether moving back here was for him . . . or for me."

"Let me tell you how I see it. If you were living your lives as you knew them, well, Dave would still be in Europe and you'd be trying to take on more and more cases to keep the money coming in, working long into the night, whether at the office or at home. Regardless, you'd hardly get to see your son, probably have to hire someone to come in and look after him after school, or get him off in the mornings if you had an early court appearance. So now, instead of a stranger he gets you full-time, and presumably, happy. And, as an added bonus, he also gets me." She paused, that knowing smile still on her face. "And lucky me, I get you both."

Nora felt like she wanted to cry. Her mother took her into her arms instead.

"Sometimes it's me who feels like the child," Nora said. "Sometimes I think it would be nice to just sit in a corner and play with my dolls again."

"Isn't that what you're doing, Nora, with your store? Recapturing your past?"

Gerta's words weren't meant to be harsh, they were spoken almost with a dose of envy. Nora couldn't find the words to agree, so she just nodded.

"Now, let me get the sauce heating," she said, "and you, how about a refill of that wine?"

"See, Mom, you always know just what your child needs, even when they're no longer a child," Nora said. "And speaking of kids outgrowing their years, let me see how Travis did with his father."

"Which one is the child?" Gerta asked, a rare, wicked sense of humor coming through.

Nora found herself laughing aloud as she went up the stairs.

Mothers, both of them, each doing for their children, no matter the age.

Nora was beginning to think Linden Corners had been the right place to come after all.

Nighttime found Nora wide awake, the wind howling at her window like a persistent dream. For the past hour she had tossed and turned, her scattered mind unable to shut down and her body uncomfortable amidst the messy pile of blankets. She was in her old room, but other than the first night when past and present had conspired against her and kept her awake, sleep had come naturally to her. With the sad status of her marriage at last out in the open, there was no reason why she shouldn't already be deep in slumber, like a load had been lifted off her shoulders. Yet her mind was still churning, thinking mostly about Thomas Van Diver and that darned, elusive book. Was she crazy to take on such an assignment, one that seemed not only improbable, but near impossible to complete by the looming deadline. Christmas . . . actually, Christmas Eve, he had said.

She realized she knew very little about the man who, like her, had been born to Linden Corners and left, only to return under a cloud of mystery. Had he been married, did he and his wife have any children, and if so, where were they? And just what was the provenance of the old book? Did his father purchase it at a store, did he find it in a store similar to Elsie's, or stumble across it . . . where? A tag sale or garage sale . . . did they even have those things back in the forties? Nora's mind swirled with possibilities, just as outside the wind continued to batter the shutters. She wondered then about the old windmill and whether its latticed sails were spinning wildly, victim to nature's blowing fury. Thomas Van Diver once called the farmhouse home, he'd been given the book as a gift his last Christmas in Linden Corners, and when they moved he'd left it behind. Which made her wonder . . . could the book still be in the village somewhere? Could it even still be in the farmhouse somewhere? Had the Van Divers sold the house to the Sullivans? Or had other family stories been wedged between them, and if so, the book could have been found by one of them and now . . . could be anywhere in the world, or thrown out, fallen apart . . . someone's garbage. If Thomas didn't have those answers, she wondered what the farmhouse's current tenant knew. All of these were good questions, none of which would be answered before sunlight.

But that didn't mean she could rest easily.

Tossing back the covers, Nora slipped out of bed and

made her way to her laptop. Firing it up, she typed in her password and waited for the screen to appear. Then she began to make notes, all she had wondered about, careful not to miss out on a single question. The furious typing of her fingers across the keyboard sounded loud in the quiet of the house and she hoped she wasn't disturbing anyone. A few minutes into her note-making, a hesitant knock came at her door.

"Come in," she said.

The door opened with a slight squeak, Travis's head pushing its way through. The glare from the computer screen created a halo effect behind him.

"Hey, what are you doing up? Did I wake you?"

"No, just couldn't sleep," he said.

"Come in, slugger."

No admonition this time either for her use of a pet name, Travis just let a quiet smile hit his lips as he shuffled his way into the small bedroom. Maybe that had just been bravado, a kid stretching his growth into adulthood. Nora closed the lid on her computer, got into bed with her son, and held him tight.

"You were quiet at dinner," she said.

"I was busy thinking."

"So, that's what that noise was," she said, attempting some humor.

"I asked Dad if he was coming home for Christmas," he said.

"Oh Travis, I thought we discussed this."

"You and I did. But not me and Dad," he said.

"And what did he say?"

" 'Not this year, big guy.' "

Nora tried to deflect the words to the point that they didn't affect her, but they sank beneath her skin anyway. Her heart felt empty, but not for her, only for a twelve-year-old boy who didn't understand what a midlife crisis was. Dave couldn't have just bought a red sports car like his wife had? No, he had to fly halfway across the world and hurt his son in the process. She didn't say anything, bad-mouthing her husband solved nothing. She held her son tighter and kissed the top of his head.

"We'll celebrate Christmas here in Linden Corners, just like I told you. You, me, and Grandma, and if I know this village like I think I do, with a few very good friends, too," she said, "and it will be more special than you can imagine."

"How do you know that?"

How indeed? For many reasons. Because she remembered special Christmas mornings from her childhood, because she had heard stories over the years from her mother and father about the beauty that enveloped this tiny town at Christmastime, a white-lighted spirit that bathed the residents in its glow until their usual welcoming smiles became holiday embraces. Because a warmth spread across this open land, even as the cold winter came knocking, the two locked in a constant battle. Just like now, with the wind again knocking at her windowpane, at the shutters on the side of the house. Heavy rain began to pelt the window, a sudden November storm sweeping through Linden Corners, but Nora had a feeling that before Christmas found its way here the precipitation outside would be turned into a white blanket of snow.

She said, "Because in a town like this, wishes dance in the wind until they come true."

But Travis hadn't heard her, he was fast asleep.

CHAPTER 8

BRIAN

"I have two favors, one of which you can't say no to, and the other . . . you won't want to."

It was an intriguing opening gambit for a Monday morning. Thanksgiving was just ten days away, and a relaxed feeling wafted through the cozy farmhouse, the sound of the telephone interrupting the calm. Answering it on the second ring, Brian Duncan couldn't have been more surprised by either the task about to fall his way or the unlikely person behind the asking. He could almost see her through the phone line, her green eyes curiously keen but naturally suspicious. She also sounded out of breath.

"Good morning to you, too, Nora."

"Sorry, hi, Brian," she said, "but I don't have time for niceties. I've got a busy day."

"You seem raring to go," he said. "Thought Mondays were your day off."

"When you work for yourself, sometimes you make adjustments."

Brian didn't have such luxuries as flextime, his and Janey's schedules were pretty much set in stone, regulated by their usual activities. School for her, work down at the tavern for him, schoolwork for her, housework for them both, each day a set pattern that enabled Brian to maintain a level of stability he knew was important to his daughter's well-being. And now with the end of the year fast approaching, all of that would have to be balanced along with the holiday traditions and trimmings that tossed even chaos theory a challenge.

"What can I help you with?" he asked.

"First of all, I need to borrow your truck," she said.

"Is that the favor I'm not allowed to say no to?"

"You did rear-end my prized Mustang."

"You weren't paying attention . . ."

"Brian?"

"And besides, Gerta has a car, one she barely uses."

"Brian." Not a question this time, just a telling statement that quieted him down.

Stifling the urge to laugh, he heard Nora sigh on the other end of the phone as though she were standing right next to him; her eye rolling could not have been more evident. Her actions reminded him of Janey—all bark, no bite, and just slightly adorable. And like Janey, he had a feeling that Nora was right, he wouldn't be able to say no to her request. She wanted the truck, fine, it was hers. He wasn't going to argue. Still, he was curious about why. So he asked her.

"It's actually a potentially good business opportunity for A Doll's Attic," she said. "I got a call over the weekend, Saturday, from this elderly woman who lives down around Hudson, she wants me to appraise her daughter's belongings. . . . Look, I don't know the full story, but I do know there's a bunch of boxes and if I'm inclined to take them on—you know, on a consignment basis—then I'll need the truck to transport everything back to the storeroom. I doubt even Mom's car would fit the boxes."

"Okay, the truck is yours. When do you need it?"

"Today," she said. "This morning."

"Gee, talk about short notice."

"Sorry about that, Brian, but it's my first inquiry of this kind and I have to act fast or lose out, you know . . . the early bird and the worm? If this works out, it might help spread the word about the new girl in town," she said. "Sorry, do you have somewhere you need to be?"

Did he? Were there errands to run, or places he needed to be? Mid-November, it was too early to bring down the Christmas decorations, even though he'd contemplated going up into the attic to start pulling boxes out. Monday morning for him was generally quiet, so while Janey was off at school, he usually just toiled about cleaning up after whatever weekend fun they had indulged in. The afternoon looked like more of the same nothingness, at least until time came to open up George's Tavern; it was his night to manage, with Mark busy at his waiter job down in Hudson. And with Janey spending the afternoon where she usually did, next door at Cynthia's, helping out with little Jake, no, he had nowhere to be. An idea struck him. "Actually, Nora, my schedule is pretty clear today, so yeah, I guess you could take the truck. Can you leave me that Mustang? I'd love to give it a test run out on Route 22."

"Up that winding, twisting road? I don't think so. I was thinking how nice it would look sitting idle in your driveway," she said with an easy laugh.

"Let's table that for now, what's the other thing you need?"

"Like I said, you won't want to say no."

"Color me intrigued," Brian said, wondering where this conversation was going.

There was a long pause on the other end, and he was about to ask if she was still on the line, but then she jumped in, words tumbling out. "As you know, I've been looking into Mr. Van Diver's request, trying to find that book he lost when he was a kid, and it's led me to a series of questions about the history of Linden Corners, more specifically about the farmhouse and maybe even the origins of the windmill. So naturally I thought of you—I mean, don't they call you the Windmill Man?"

"Among other things," he said, a comforting smile coming to his lips as he thought about how welcomed he'd been to a place he'd never heard of until he'd stumbled upon it. And Nora, back in town only a few weeks, already she'd heard stories about him. Elsie, Martha, Sara, and the Five O' crew, they sure knew how to talk a good game. "I'll tell you what, Nora, why don't you ask me your questions while we head down to Hudson to assess that estate or whatever it is the woman wants you to look at. My day is pretty light until late afternoon, we should be able to make it back in time for me to open the bar."

"Oh no, Brian, I couldn't impose. . . ."

"You've already done that by asking to take my truck and leave me stuck at home. What's the fun in that? Come on, I'll pick you up at Gerta's, say ten o'clock? We'll make a day of it, maybe stop for lunch at RiverFront, the resort up on the hills of the river, I've got a connection in the kitchen, he'll get us a good table on short notice." He paused, listening to the studied silence on the other end. Like she was having a debate with herself.

"Okay," she finally relented.

He brightened at the idea of breaking up his routine; it was a new week, suddenly fresh with new opportunities. "Great, it's a date, I'll see you soon."

Brian didn't mean for those words to come out the way they did, but once out and exposed to the open air they lingered awkwardly over the line until both of them were forced to say their good-byes. Nora's last words were tinged with nervousness. "Oh, uh, Brian, sure, I'll be ready."

Putting the cordless phone down on the counter, he shook his head. Why the heck had he said that word? Date.

A four-letter word with far more impact than any coarse word he'd ever heard.

Well, he thought, this day together ought to be interesting. Whatever they called it.

The historic, rustic village of Hudson, New York, was south of Linden Corners, located only about fifteen minutes away along county roads that today lit the lush countryside with the vibrant colors of nature, their rocky shoulders strewn with downed branches as a result of recent storms; accompanying green fields had fallen into burnt palettes of autumn. With the wind having moved out all lingering clouds, the high sky was left a bright blue, with temperatures climbing into the mid-fifties making for an unseasonably mild and pleasant November day. While the Thanksgiving holiday loomed around the corner and the region had already seen its first snowfall a few weeks ago, right now there was no sign of wintery weather.

"Unseasonable might be the word meteorologists would use," Nora stated, window open and the breeze flapping at her untethered locks, her hand occasionally pushing stray strands away from her face. "But Travis would just say the weather was totally wacked. The day we arrived it was snowing and since then, I think we've seen everything Mother Nature can throw at us."

"Come on, that Halloween snowstorm was nothing for Linden Corners, you of all people should know that," Brian said with a dismissive wave. "You grew up in this region, you know how fierce the blizzards can be, how much snow they can dump. Heck, even last year we got hit with a whopper of a storm right on Christmas Eve. Practically buried the village."

"Yes, and what I remember is Mom telling me how you

and Janey sledded your way through snow-covered streets to make sure she didn't spend a lonely Christmas by herself," Nora said. "That was nice of you."

"Anything for Gerta, she's amazing," Brian said. "Not to mention her pies."

"Aha, so the truth comes out at last, that's why you like to spend time with my mother." Still, an easy smile came to Nora's lips. Brian, concentrating on the driving, managed to sneak a look over at his passenger, glad for her company and thankful she'd accepted his offer to join her, even if he'd goofed by referring to their harmless excursion as a date. Nora seemed to have forgotten all about it, filling the drive with nonsensical conversation that came with no pretenses or undercurrents of unspoken words. She hadn't even gotten around to her other set of questions, the reason for her initial call. She was natural, both in appearance and attitude, with barely a hint of makeup on her cheeks and a fresh attire of jeans and light blue sweater, her easygoing nature making Brian relax, both when he opened the truck's door for her after picking her up, and later when he hit the highway. His only misstep was when he gazed into the rearview mirror as they left town, the image of the stalwart windmill standing tall but lonely amidst the backdrop of that big empty sky. It had left him with a nagging sense of betrayal. Annie's windmill, Annie's house, her daughter and her truck . . . now populated by Nora.

With roadside signs directing them toward Hudson, they were content to talk about Travis and Janey, noting how well the two kids were getting along, and how invaluable Janey had been in introducing the new kid in town to the other preteens at school. That made Brian feel good. Janey had such a big heart, and while it had suffered its share of sorrow, it had this rejuvenating, almost magical spirit that showed just how strong she was, how big her heart could swell.

"By the way, Brian, thanks again for this. I appreciate your company today. You didn't have to volunteer yourself, I'm a big girl," Nora said.

"I've seen the way you drive, why should I risk my truck?"

"Gee, and I was beginning to believe all that good press my mother gives you."

They both grinned, just as the truck made its way into downtown Hudson, a small, rustic village of landmark buildings and small mom-and-pop businesses, comfortably ensconced along the mighty waters of its eponymous river. It was a place well known for its artists and writers, its boutiques specializing in antiques and art galleries alive with fresh talent, all of them celebrating a region's history and heritage. For Brian, this was only his second visit to Hudson since moving to Columbia County, but the business district was small and easily manageable, with a square-shaped park laid out in the center, offset by the majestic Saint Charles Hotel looming to its north on Park Place. The entire town gave off a feeling of old-world America, a piece of yesterday living today. They journeyed down the main artery, Warren Street, headed toward the river, only to turn down a side road and travel beyond the Amtrak train station that picked up and deployed passengers along the Northeast Corridor, down to New York or onward to places like Albany, Chicago, and Montreal. A few more turns and they were high up on a hill, a series of old-style Victorian homes coming into view. Nora's client lived in the last one on the dead-end block, and as Brian pulled into the driveway he was struck by the lovely, expansive view of the river down the cliffs, the waters calm today after yesterday's storm. Again, he thought of Annie, who had loved the river, watching its languid flow from atop her own bluff.

"Wow, what a beautiful house," Nora said. "I mean, it's a bit run down, but think of the possibilities."

"This woman lives alone here? That's a lot of upkeep."

"So she says. Come on, let's see what awaits us."

Brian hopped out of the cab and before he could get around to opening the passenger door for Nora, she had already bounded down and was now halfway up the winding pathway. He had to walk briskly to catch up with her. Crabgrass grew wildly between cement squares, a clear indication the lawn was among those things not being well maintained. Like the rest of the blue-painted structure.

"You don't have to keep opening doors for me, Brian, I'm pretty independent."

"So noted," he said.

They walked up a series of stairs that were in desperate need of a coat of paint to the covered porch. The front door opened with a loud squeak, and out stepped an elderly woman, balancing herself on a wooden cane. Willowy wisps of gray hair stood out in all directions, and while the wrinkles on her face indicated she might have been around Gerta's age, mid-seventies, it was quite possible she was older. She wore an inviting smile with her ratty, red cardigan.

"Mrs. Wilkinson?"

"Yes, dear, are you Ms. Rainer?"

"Nora Rainer, yes," she said, and then turned to Brian. "My associate, Brian Duncan."

"Ma'am," he said with a polite nod.

"He does the heavy lifting," Nora said by way of explanation, with a wink at him.

He didn't comment, merely accepted his role as the hired help. Not that his body was built that way, but being a laborer with a lot of land to tend in Linden Corners had hardened this one-time city boy. They were ushered inside a musty home that felt like it hadn't been aired out in months. Brian looked around for a cat or four, but so far stumbled over none. Into the living room they went, settling onto a pair of fabric-worn chairs. On the table before them was a silver tray, again in need of a polish, like much about this house. A pot of tea and two cups were set out. Thick, voluminous draperies hung over the windows, keeping sunlight at bay. There was a gloomy sense not just to this room but the whole house, matched only by a detached sadness in the old woman's eyes.

"I apologize for only setting out two cups for tea, but I wasn't expecting a third person," Mrs. Wilkinson said.

"No problem," Brian said. "Perhaps you'll allow me to serve then?"

She nodded once, looking approvingly over at Nora. "A gentleman, how very nice. He's a keeper," she said with a sudden faraway look that gave light to her otherwise gray eyes. Like her comment had sparked an old memory. "Young man, if you go down the long hallway to the kitchen, you'll find another cup in the cupboard. Oh, and maybe you could bring in that box of chocolate cookies. I couldn't carry everything and then suddenly . . . here you were. I heard your car pull up. Thankfully I've still got all my senses working."

Brian accepted his task, returning only to find Nora and Mrs. Wilkinson already engaged in conversation. Nora said something about how glad she was to have called her store, asked how she had heard about A Doll's Attic.

"Oh, I've known Elsie Masters for years, she helped my husband furnish this house," she said. "When I phoned her a few weeks ago, she informed me she had sold her business, that the new owner was changing its focus a bit. So I was curious, and waited a week or so before calling, give you a chance to settle in. But always I thought you were the right person to handle my needs."

"A Doll's Attic is all about the past, Mrs. Wilkinson, it's about keeping memories alive."

"Call me Katherine," the old lady said.

"And please, I'm Nora. So, how can we help you?"

For the first time, Nora had included Brian with her use of the word *we,* busy as he was serving tea and chocolate biscuits. He looked up, noting her inclusion.

Katherine Wilkinson, seemingly glad to have an audience, launched into her tale, sipping at her tea only when she needed to collect her thoughts. Turned out, she had lived in this once-heralded home for nearly four decades with her husband, a noted area writer named Chester Wilkinson. They had moved up here from the city—which to everyone in Upstate New York was code for Manhattan. "Our only daughter, Mary, had just left for college and Chester and I were looking for a life change, and that's when we stumbled upon this house, quite luckily I might add, and of course my husband was not one to dawdle. Before I knew it, papers were signed and we were moving in, lock, stock, and memories . . . but no Mary. She had grander ideas than living in a big house in a small town. So we lived our lives, Chester became a bit of a local celebrity in Hudson's literary circles, always hanging at the bar at the Saint Charles with his pal, Elliot, who runs the antiquarian bookstore on Warrant Street. Yes, he'd be inventing tales, all while I tended to the house. Admittedly I did a better job back then, now it's just gotten too hard. I may have my mind, but not always my body."

"Do you have help?"

"Some," she said. "But I have my memories and they keep me comfortable."

Brian felt a crush of sadness, because not only did this kindly old soul no longer have her husband, whom she said passed away quietly in his sleep six years ago, but the daughter she had mentioned was gone too, wasn't that what had brought Nora here? There was too much loss just in this overstuffed room, not just for her but for Brian, too, and Janey and Gerta, Nora, and . . . he had to stop himself, this wasn't the time or place for regrets. He was just Nora's handyman, just playing the strong, silent role. He wondered, though, could he actually take away this woman's possessions, load them into the back of the truck and transport them to the store, only to have strangers poring over them and dickering over the price, as though they were mere objects, not cherished mementos of a person's life? It wasn't his call, but how he wished it was. Like the boxes stored upstairs in the farmhouse's attic, they were a treasure trove of Sullivan family memorabilia, a history of the life Janey had been denied.

"Oh, but my Mary was a wonderful girl, not unlike her father with her sense of adventure. But while he saw the images in his mind and put them down on the page, she wanted to see the real world, and she did. Girl couldn't even sit still as a child, so it was hardly a surprise that she grew up so free-spirited. First Europe, then the Far East and Australia and other places whose names keep changing with every government coup, or so it seems. No matter where she went she sent back so many tchotchkes her room looked like a map of the world. One of her favorites was to experience Christmas in other parts of the world, to learn and partake in their traditions. Our family is part Dutch, so of course when she went to the Netherlands it was with the intent to celebrate their holiday of *sinterklass*—which happens not on Christmas Day but on the fifth of December. Sitting in my chair and reading her postcards, I think I learned more about the world from her than from any map."

"Sounds like she was unstoppable."

"Oh, that was Mary all right, small town life wasn't for her."

"May I ask what happened to her? If it's not too painful . . ."

"Oh, it always hurts, it always will, even though she's been gone for over ten years."

"Oh Katherine . . . and then to lose your husband."

"I think her loss exacerbated his—he wrote a novel about her, but wouldn't allow it be published. It sits in a drawer, still. Anyway, Mary . . . it was when she was in the Nether-lands, just a horrible turn of events. A car accident, came out of nowhere, one of those dumb accidents. December sixth it happened, the day after a celebration in the town square of the village she was visiting. She'd gotten off one last post-card before it happened."

Brian felt a chill rip through his spine. He thought of Annie, again, and he thought about accidents, which some would call the hand of fate, and in his mind he saw the turn-ing sails of the windmill. But instead of images of Linden Corners he was swept across the ocean to the tulip-rich countryside of the Netherlands, and he saw not one but a se-ries of stunning windmills, all of them suddenly quieted. Mary Wilkinson, Annie Sullivan, lives cut short, lives blur-ring right now, like his eyes.

Nora shot him a curious look. He just turned back toward Katherine, waiting for more of her story.

"Oh, her death crushed us both, surely. But before that accident . . . Oh, you should have seen the way Chester's smile would brighten whenever one of those brown parcels from overseas arrived, always with the same unmistakable handwriting: 'From Mary,' it would simply say. And she would send not just the usual gifts like coffee cups with city names and their landmarks on them, not only key chains and magnets. Mary knew how to find those special, hand-crafted gifts, silks from Asia, painstakingly created ornaments that would decorate our Christmas tree every year. We would send her pictures, which of course only encouraged her to seek out more and more. The last one we received, sent from Hol-land, was a glass ornament with a lit windmill inside it, and, oh my . . . it was just beautiful."

Brian was shaken all over again, her heartfelt story filled with too many coincidences to sit comfortably within him. Yet he was alone in his thoughts, Katherine's story was reaching its zenith.

"We collected so many of those ornaments over the years, we would need a twelve-foot tree to fit them all, and even then there would be leftovers. Oh, and rare artifacts from expeditions she would find herself on, how she got hold of them I still don't know. I've got boxes and boxes upstairs in the attic, all marked 'Mary.' Except those we marked 'Christmas.' It's been years since I've opened those." She paused, then said, "So, Nora, are Mary's treasures anything of interest to you?"

"They sound fascinating, Katherine. I would love the chance to look them over. But, are you sure—"

"Oh, thank you, that pleases me very much," she said, without addressing the word she had interrupted. "Would you like to see them now, dear, or perhaps schedule another time?"

Brian noticed how the woman's formal address had lessened as the morning had worn on. From Ms. Rainer to Nora, now to the sweetly enveloping "dear." Here was a woman who desired company, companionship, a chance to talk about the past and her daughter in the reverential tones she deserved. And Nora was picking up on that vibe, that much Brian could tell.

"You know, I think another time would benefit us both, Katherine. It would give me a chance to really assess what you've got, especially those Christmas ornaments you spoke of—maybe they intrigue me because the holiday is right around the corner," she said. "Perhaps I could bring lunch with me next time, we could sit and get to know one another better before I get started. So you make sure your daughter's gifts are placed in the right hands."

"Oh Nora, that sounds lovely," she said with an easy clasp of her hand.

"Perhaps next Monday? My store is closed that day, so that leaves me free."

"That's perfect. Mr. Duncan, will you be joining us?"

"I think that's one date tailor-made for the two of you," he said.

As they said their good-byes, Katherine embraced them both, thanked them for their time.

Soon they were back in the truck, making their way back toward downtown Hudson.

Brian was quiet, but found Nora gazing over at him.

"Something on your mind?" he asked.

"You like that word, don't you?"

"What word?"

"Date," she said.

Brian felt his face burn with sudden embarrassment, and it wasn't because of the rays of warm sunshine beaming through the windshield. Still, that didn't stop him from shifting the visor above the dashboard, partially blocking her view . . . of him.

CHAPTER 9
NORA

Nora wasn't going to be the first to admit it, but she was having fun today, perhaps for the first time since she'd arrived back home in Linden Corners. Even if at the moment she was outside its borders, still down in Hudson and still in the company of the erstwhile Brian Duncan. In the back of her mind she still heard that dangerous thing called a date, and as they were escorted to their table at the Harbor View Restaurant, she had the sense that the other diners in the restaurant agreed with her assessment: It looked like a date. She then stole a furtive glance at Brian, who appeared nonplussed by the envious looks they were receiving.

Soon they were seated by the hostess at a corner table with a beautiful view of the Hudson River, and, as befit the restaurant's obvious name, one of the harbor, where boats were currently in dry dock; in the summer season, she imagined tables outside and the squawking of gulls as boaters enjoyed the pleasures of the water. For the cooler months, only the inside was available. Still, they had a prime table, and Nora knew it was because Brian had a connection here.

Glasses of ice water filled, Nora busied herself by studying the menu. Brian was doing the same, the silence between them more evident than the clang of dishes as they were tossed into a plastic bin by the busboy. Not able to concentrate on the lunch specials, Nora finally put her menu down and said, "Uh, Brian, you do realize . . ."

He looked up. "I know, it's not a date."

"It can't be. . . . I'm a married woman."

"So what you're saying is that if you weren't married, this would be a date?"

"Huh? No, not at all. Look, Brian . . ."

"Relax, Nora, please, it was just a slip of the tongue on my part this morning. I certainly didn't expect that this was anything more than a business arrangement, with me the driver," he said, then, attempting a bit of levity, added, "It's been so long since I've been on an actual date—much less asked for one—that my brain didn't even know what it was telling my mouth to say. So, let's forget the word and just enjoy ourselves."

"Thanks, you make it easy," she said. "Besides, aren't I older than you?"

"Now who's trying to entice me?"

She had no choice, she laughed, and the gentle sound brought her shoulders down. This day, it was so different from what she was used to back in her old life. On the rare occasions she did take a lunch, with a client or a partner or even a rival attorney, it was all business: note-taking as an appetizer, one-upmanship as an entree, and of course billable hours for dessert. Sitting at a table opposite someone she barely knew, in the middle of the day and on a Monday to boot, she couldn't ever remember an indulgence so decadent. Nora Rainer, who could be spontaneous so long as it was written ahead of time on the calendar, was actually smiling.

"That looks good on you," Brian said.

A slight frown hit her, the compliment unnecessary.

"That's not an improvement."

"You want to comment on beauty, look out the window."

Fortunately they were spared any additional volleying, as their affable waiter approached the round table, calling Brian by name. Nora gazed up to see a handsome, though scruffy dark-haired young man who couldn't have been more than twenty-four or -five. He looked familiar, but she couldn't exactly remember where she might have seen him. It wasn't until he asked to take their drink order that she recalled.

"Oh wait, you're the bartender from the tavern . . . Halloween night," she said.

"That's me, Mark Ravens."

"I'm sorry, I didn't recognize you with your shirt on," she said.

"That was Sara's doing," he said, with a slight blush.

"Remind me to thank Sara."

"She's my fiancée," he said.

"Ah, well then, I'll take whatever's available. A glass of wine?"

"Red or white?"

"Red. Merlot?"

"We've got a fab Cab."

"Fab. I'll have the Cab."

"Brian?"

He exchanged confused looks with them both, pausing before saying, "Oh, is it my turn? Didn't want to interrupt the oenophiles," he said. "You know my order, Mark, seltzer, lime."

"Right, gotcha," he said. "I'll be right back with drinks, and uh, hey, Bri? Do you think you've got a second to talk? I mean, since we're away from Linden Corners I can kind of speak freely."

"Sure. You don't mind, do you, Nora?"

"I could always go powder my nose."

"No, no, I'm not chasing you away. In fact, I wouldn't mind a woman's take."

"On what?"

"Let me get those drinks and I'll be back."

So Mark went off to the bar with a fresh spring to his step, Nora watching happily as he did. When she gazed back, she found Brian staring at her, an amused expression on his face. She nervously pushed her hair over her ear.

"What was that?" he asked.

"What?"

"For a married woman, you sure didn't mind flirting."

"Oh please, it was harmless, and besides, he's just a boy," she said, with a lingering gaze toward the bar, where he was chatting with a woman bartender likely around his own age. She appeared to not mind his company either. "Though a very attractive one."

Brian just shook his head, leaving Nora without conversation until their drinks arrived.

"So is it?" Mark asked expectantly.

Sipping at her wine, Nora feigned ignorance. "Is it what?"

"Fab?"

She just smiled his way. "Perfect."

A few minutes later, with their lunch order placed, Mark Ravens joined them by grabbing an extra chair from a nearby empty table, turning it backward and resting his arms against the back. He had asked his boss for a break, stating he just needed a few minutes to confer with his friends. Nora could see that Mark was nervous, though why was beyond her. He needed a woman's help, that's what he'd claimed, so she had to figure it had something to do with Sara. Hadn't he'd already done the hard part, though, asked the girl of his dreams to marry him and received back a yes? What could be the problem?

"You know, it's been nearly a year since I asked Sara to

marry me," he said, "and while everything is great between us, really great, I mean, never better in fact, she's been dropping less than subtle hints about finalizing a date."

Seemed to be the word of the day. The use of it here made Nora sit up straighter, eyeing Brian carefully. He just painted on a wider grin that was clearly just directed at her. She had the urge to stick her tongue out at him, decided that would be childish . . . like she was Janey's age or something. Instead, she chose to concentrate on Mark's dilemma.

"See, I wanted to have everything perfect—a better-paying job, out of debt, so she and I could start fresh, right? Except nothing has changed, we're still both in the same jobs we were a year ago, me splitting time between the resort and the tavern up in Linden Corners—don't get me wrong, Bri, I appreciate all the extra nights you can give me—and with Sara working double shifts at the Five O', it seems like we hardly have time for each other."

"So why do you think getting married will help matters?"

"No, see, that's the thing I've come to realize," he said. "Our lives are never gonna be perfect, but they'll be as perfect as they can be if we just pick a date and get it over with."

Brian was about to speak when Nora felt she had to jump in—he'd asked for a woman's perspective and he was going to get it . . . he needed it. Inwardly she was lambasting herself, here she was, a separated woman with divorce looming on the horizon, now suddenly offering up marriage advice. Like throwing a rock at your own glass house. She reached out and placed her hand on Mark's, said with knowing comfort, "Mark, you almost had it right when you said it would be as perfect as it could be, words like that would melt a girl's heart."

"Thanks, I think."

"I sense a 'but' coming," Brian said.

Nora ignored him, her focus still on Mark. "But . . .

never tell a girl you're getting married just to get it over with. Makes it sound like a visit to the dentist."

Mark nodded, understanding. "Okay, sure, I see your point, Nora. But here's what I'm thinking. I do want to pick a date, but I don't want to wait around until June or something, and I don't think Sara wants to wait that long either. So, Brian, I was wondering, are you planning to host the annual Christmas party again at the tavern, you know, like you did last year?" He turned to Nora to give her the back story. "See, that's where I proposed to Sara, and Brian here was a big help, even going so far as to quote me a good rent on the upstairs apartment. That's where Sara and I have been living for the past year. Wouldn't that be great, if she and I got married on the same day as my asking her, exactly a year later?"

"Not a bad idea," Brian said. "And, yeah, I'm sure we'll have the party, it was George's tradition . . . and with his daughter Nora here back in town, how could we not continue to honor him? What do you say, Nora, are you game for the annual Christmas party at the tavern? Bet your mom has already started planning the menu, picking out fresh ingredients for her pies from Cynthia's fruit stand. You should have been there last year, there were so many friends of mine who unexpectedly showed up, no reason why we can't ratchet things up and toss in a wedding."

"Oh my God, really?" Mark said.

"Why not, it'll give our big holiday party a nice kick in the pants," Brian said. "Though I don't suggest you make the wedding itself a surprise like you did the engagement. Girl like Sara will probably want a hand in helping with the arrangements."

"A hand? Try hands, legs, heart, and soul," Nora said with a laugh. "When I got married, I told Dave his only responsibility was to show up. And thankfully he did . . . until he decided not to."

The moment she said it she wanted to take it back. There

was no place for bitter remarks about her own troubled marriage when this idealistic young man was through the moon in love with his girl, wanting to plan an extra-special wedding day for her like a true romantic. In a way, Nora felt the string of jealousy, not because Mark seemed so earnest and she so jaded, it was that they were just starting out and the eventual baggage had not yet begun to accumulate, much less be unpacked. She was about to apologize when a bell rang from the kitchen, Mark's signal that his break was over, their food ready. He thanked them both as he retreated to the kitchen, came back not only with turkey clubs with generous helpings of fries, he set a fresh glass of Cabernet before Nora.

"Hopefully we can raise a glass together at my wedding," he said.

"I'd be honored, thanks, Mark."

"Thank you, Nora. You, too, Brian buddy. I don't know what I'd do without you. Nora, it's all 'cause of this guy that I met Sara, when I got that gig down at the tavern. Hey, who knows what next year will bring, you two look great together."

Mark departed, again with that eager spring in his step, not even noticing that both Brian and Nora had gone the shade of her fab Cab.

Turned out, all the drinks were on the house and the food came with a discount, so Nora insisted on leaving the tip, a larger percentage than the going rate. The two of them headed out of The RiverFront Resort & Spa's restaurant and into the bright sunshine of the mild afternoon. As they drove back up Warren Street, Nora reminded Brian of the bookstore Katherine Wilkinson had mentioned, asking him if he wouldn't mind one last stop. It was too good to pass up, perhaps she could kill two birds with one trip, that's what she said as they approached the store, located just across the street from the historical Saint Charles Hotel; the sign in the window stated NEW AND USED BOOKS, RARE EDITIONS.

"Are you sure you have time?"

Brian double-checked his watch. "It's only two thirty or so, I've still got two hours before I need to open the tavern," he said, nodding his approval. "Sure, let's see what we can find out. Think you'll just magically find Thomas's book on the shelves?"

"This is Hudson, it's reality."

"Meaning Linden Corners is fantasy?"

"Some days, I think so. Come on, let's go see about Saint Nick."

Brian pulled against the curb in an empty spot, the two of them then making their way toward the Antiquarian Book Shop, Christmas on her mind once again. It was a recurring theme, she thought, having first discussed Christmas with Mrs. Wilkinson and just a short while ago with Mark Ravens's wedding plans, and now here she was engaging in the next, unexpected chapter in the hunt for Mr. Van Diver's elusive holiday book. Not that she figured to find his exact edition, despite Brian's sarcasm, but it was as good a place as any to inquire. Perhaps the proprietor would offer up some leads for her.

Nora crossed Warren Street against the light traffic of midday, Brian following after her. They made their way inside, jangly bells just like those that hung over the door of A Doll's Attic alerting the lone clerk to a bit of business; he stared up from a stack of unjacketed hardcover books that threatened to entomb him behind the crowded counter. He was an older gentleman with a shock of white hair and a thick pair of spectacles, a chain hanging around his neck to keep from losing them. With his vest and neatly pressed slacks, Nora believed the very professorial-looking man may just have some answers for her; living among these stacks of books, he probably knew more about the past than he did about what was printed in yesterday's newspapers. Shelves after shelves stretched along both walls of the small store and in between, and despite its musty contents, a fresh smell like cedar pervaded the room.

"Help you?" he asked, his voice with a New England tinge.

"Yes, I hope so. Katherine Wilkinson mentioned your store, said you used to spend time with her husband. . . ."

"Ah-yuh, good ol' Chester, a fine writer, a prose stylist with the heart of a poet. A fine raconteur, shared many a story with him over at the Saint Charles. You folks looking for some of his novels?" he asked.

"No," she said, approaching the counter. "My name is Nora Rainer, I'm the new owner of Elsie's Antiques up in Linden Corners—though I've renamed it . . ."

"Uh-yuh, A Doll's Attic, or so I've heard. A clever name, I don't mind saying," he said, a friendly nod accompanying his words. "Welcome to the neighborhood, Ms. Rainer. We folks in the business have to stay current, even if our merchandise does not." He allowed himself a small chuckle at his insider's joke. "How can I help you then today, Ms. Rainer, not thinking about expanding into the book trade, are you?"

"Not exactly, Mr. . . ."

"Elliot," he said, "Everyone just calls me Elliot."

"And this is my associate, Brian Duncan."

"Pleasure," Elliot said. "So, it's a book you're looking for?"

"A particularly rare volume, one I'm not sure even exists."

"Well, if that's the case, finding it will be near impossible," he said, straight-faced.

Brian stepped forward at that point to move things along, seemed Elliot could talk around the subject all day long and not get to the point of it all. "It's a vintage edition of *Twas the Night before Christmas* by . . ."

"Uh-yuh, sure, by Clement Clarke Moore," he said, "or so the so-called experts would have us believe. Complicated history there with that tale. Legend behind who actually wrote that poem is not nearly as famous as the writing itself, but it sure makes for some interesting debate among us bibliophiles. History has it that Moore originally wrote the story for his young children, back, oh, eighteen twenty something or other, but academic scholar that he was, he was worried about his reputation after writing what many considered a frivolous piece of pop, and so he had it published anonymously. Which, of course, opens up a whole can of worms about its true authorship; some claim, you know, a man named Henry Livingston, Jr., was the original author—he was a distant relative of Moore's wife. But whoever wrote it, it's fair to say that little volume is one of the most published books in the world, even if it's only read once a year."

Nora nodded; interested as she was in the lore behind the tale, she knew they had a limited amount of time today, and thus she had to press forward. "Yes, Elliot, I've certainly discovered how many editions there are of that book, hundreds at least," she said. "But the one I'm looking for is quite unique . . . and old, dating back at least eighty years, probably longer."

"Let me guess, Saint Nick in a green suit," the man said.

Nora visibly blanched, surprised at how quickly Elliot had known what she wanted.

"How did you know?" Brian asked. "Was Mr. Van Diver here, or maybe called you?"

"Don't know any Mr. Van Diver, but I do know my books," he said. "I remember a book published, oh, maybe twenty years ago, a beautiful reproduction of a Victorian-era edition of *The Night before Christmas,* actually called *A Visit from*

Saint Nicholas; no *Twas* about it. What was special about it was the fact that the illustrations were based on an original edition, long out of print and nowhere to be found, published by the once-heralded publishing firm of McLoughlin Brothers . . . and yes, Santa Claus . . . Saint Nick himself, was dressed in a green suit."

"So it does exist," Nora said with a bit of wonder and excitement enveloping her. "But why didn't my search online come up with the new edition? I found all sort of books and saw many images, but that specific volume . . . I couldn't find it."

"Perhaps now that you know more about it, you can track it down. Like you said, you weren't even sure it existed, perhaps that colored—if you can pardon the pun—your judgment," he said. "But like I said, the book in question was a reproduction edition, as faithful to the original as possible, but certainly not the actual one you're looking for. I assume that's why your customer hired you, to find the original?"

"You certainly know a lot, Elliot, and I appreciate the lead you've given me," Nora said.

"Hang on a sec, I've got a question," Brian stated, getting their attention. "Not that I'm doubting you at all, Elliot, but you seem particularly well-versed—if you'll pardon the pun—about the book and it seems rather random that we would come in here on a whim, and learn so much. Are you sure Mr. Van Diver didn't contact you? His name is Thomas, he's eighty-four, living now at Edgestone Retirement Home up in Linden Corners, says he once lived there, in the farmhouse near the old windmill."

Elliot nodded as though he knew all of this. "Now, so you know, that's a fine little town you've got there, Mr. Duncan, and yes, I know all about the windmill and such. But alas, it was not an elderly gentleman who asked me about the book. Rather, I'm guessing she was elderly, oh, I should say late seventies, even though I only ever heard her voice, never saw her in person. But I'm good with old things, eh, that's my business? She called my store about six months ago, maybe more, asking for the exact same thing."

"A woman?" Brian asked.

"Who was she?"

"Never did say her name, all I remember is her telling me I was one of many antiquarian bookshops she had called," he said. "Left me intrigued, so I did some research all on my own, that's kind of why I'm in this business. Curiosity and a fair amount of downtime tend to lead to some surprising discoveries. That's how I learned about the book I just told you about—not that it got me any business—she had said she might call back but then I never heard from her. Didn't hear another thing until just today, when the two of you walked into my store."

"Well, Elliot, this case has certainly taken an interesting turn," Nora said. "And I thank you for imparting what you found out. Would it be too much trouble to call on you again, that is, if I can pick your brain further? Depending upon what else I can learn."

"Be happy to," he said, and then wished them both a good day.

Back outside, Nora felt invigorated, not just by the fresh air, but by having this first real clue in her pursuit of the old book. But time was fast slipping away from them, so with Brian urging her, the two of them returned to the truck and began the journey back to Linden Corners. Nora was mostly silent, thinking about what she had learned, plotting her next step. Perhaps Mr. Van Diver's request wasn't so impossible after all, and if she'd made this much progress in just a few weeks, maybe . . . just maybe she could find it by Christmas. First things first, she had to find a copy of the reproduction edition and see that she was on the right trail.

Twenty minutes later, the truck zoomed over the cresting highway, emerging back onto Linden Corners soil. The towering windmill rose up seemingly from nowhere, its sails silent, the tower riding alongside them as Brian drove along the route before turning onto Crestview Road and into the driveway of the farmhouse. He parked beside her red Mustang, but that wasn't what captured her attention now. Nora could still see the mighty sails jutting up over the land, like it was taunting her, this ever-present symbol of Linden Corners like a beacon, drawing them into its power.

As they stepped out of the truck, Nora went around to Brian and thanked him.

"For what?"

"For driving, for indulging me . . ."

"I had fun," he said.

"So did I. I think we accomplished more than we ever set out to do."

"You got a lead on Mr. Van Diver's antique book, and I was handed a dose of inspiration for the tavern Christmas party. I've been looking for some kind of distraction, and I think I found it. Who knows, Nora, maybe our paths have crossed for a reason bigger than the both of us could envision. I get to help Mark and Sara, and you Thomas. Look at the two of us, planning a Linden Corners Christmas the town won't soon forget."

"A team," she said. "So far, it's worked well."

He nodded. "Uh-yuh, so far."

She smiled at the memory of Elliot's thick accent. But then words ceased between them, both of them suddenly as quiet as the gentle wind. A nervous feeling hitting her, Nora looked away, then back to find Brian staring directly into her eyes. Inside them she felt a warmth she hadn't seen in too long, not from Dave, and it unleashed uncertainty inside her. How had things gotten so complicated so quickly, today had been just one day, a non-date, but suddenly she felt like a teenage girl coming home from the senior prom. She blinked and when she opened up her eyes again, Brian was still staring at her. She took an impulsive step toward him, then quickly pressed her lips against his. He reacted with surprise, but didn't back away either. The taste of him was sweet. The smell of cedar surrounded them, almost like they were back in the old bookstore, lost behind the shelves, horny teenagers experiencing their first kiss. When they parted, she saw a confused expression on Brian's face; she could only guess what hers was.

"Uh, wow," he said. "Not that I mind, but why did you kiss me?"

"To quote Mark, 'to get it over with.' "

"I'm not sure I understand," he said. "You told me earlier . . ."

"I know what I said, and I meant what I said," she said. "Brian, I'm married, my life is a mess, and starting over isn't easy."

"I can relate," he offered, supportive words that actually had an impact on her.

"I know, I think that's why I'm so comfortable around you, Brian. But the last thing I need is a boyfriend or a relationship or . . . whatever the experts call it these days. What I need is a friend, plain and simple. So I kissed you now just so we could end any speculation between us, stop any expectation from others. You don't have to wonder if you can kiss me, I don't have to wonder if I should let you. The moment is over, so let's move forward."

Brian nodded, but words were not forthcoming.

"Do we have a deal?" she asked, extending her hand.

Brian had no choice, he shook her hand. Her touch was warm. "Friends," he said.

"Friends," she agreed.

Making her way toward the red Mustang, she hopped in behind the wheel and then looked back to find him still standing in the same place. She waved at him, once more smiling her thanks before driving off. Again, in the rearview mirror she saw not Brian but the windmill, even as it grew ever more distant in her eyes it remained with her. Its four sails continued to stay silent in the falling darkness of the day, as though there was nothing left to say.

CHAPTER 10

THOMAS

One week until Thanksgiving, a little more than a month be-fore his eighty-fifth birthday and what he hoped would be a Christmas to remember, Thomas Van Diver found himself walking along the sidewalks of downtown Linden Corners, content to wander aimlessly as he enjoyed the mild weather. His gait was slow, but that was okay, as the fresh air filling his lungs was almost like fuel to his system, keeping him moving. He was in no hurry to be anywhere, at least that's what he told himself; his subconscious might have other ideas, might even be directing his steps. The countdown to-ward the holiday was, of course, always on his mind, but he had realized there was little he could do to control time. All he'd set in motion with Nora Rainer, it was in her hands now.

Lights were beginning to be turned on outside store-fronts, across the street at the Five O' Diner and down the street at Marla and Darla's Trading Post, where he could see one of the twins—which of them he couldn't be sure—flick-ing a switch to the point where bright lights illuminated her, and at her side two dogs happily swirled between her legs. Ackroyd's Hardware Emporium appeared to be doing good business for midweek, folks getting ready for what forecasters were predicting to be a brutal winter season. Not that the weather today held any hint of such doom, winter seemed months away still, as the day was alive with a gentle breeze and the same, mild temperatures that had been hanging over the land since that rainstorm from earlier in the week. He saw a couple emerging from the hardware store with shiny shovels and bags of melting ice; Thomas could appreciate their preparedness for the unknown future, he would have done the same.

He walked past a quiet George's Tavern, knowing Brian Duncan didn't open his business until four, and so the building was dark, uninhabited. Even upstairs, the windows were devoid of light, whoever lived there no doubt still at work. But that was life in Linden Corners, the early risers breathed fresh energy in the waking hours, while the night owls happily kept the midnight oil lit; such were the daily revolutions of a town built on the sense of community. For Thomas, such a dichotomy was what truly separated his two experiences of having lived here, then and now. Back when he was five years old, he stayed close to the farmhouse and by his mother's side, only occasionally journeying into town; now it was quite the opposite, Thomas suddenly an integral part of the downtown scene, whether with his cohabiters down at The Edge, or while meeting with his new friends back at the farmhouse.

Speaking of, Thomas watched now as Brian Duncan's truck drove down Main Street. He wasn't alone, as he could see a small head bobbing up from the passenger seat, no doubt the pigtailed, irrepressible Janey Sullivan, her mouth yammering on while Brian's head nodded either in genial agreement or resigned acquiescence. With a spirited girl of her age, sometimes it was easier to let her ramble, all that energy needed to be released somehow. He recalled the night she had brought him near the base of the windmill, her connection to it so strong, more so than he'd ever felt. Remembered, too, the way she had gone on and on about it, the way it made her feel connected to her mother. To Thomas, the windmill represented all he had lost, but for this little girl who had seen her own share of loss, she somehow managed to find inspiration there. Like the windmill spoke to her, reaching deep down to her soul.

Thomas turned the corner and made his way into Linden Corners' Memorial Park, going up the shoveled path toward the large gazebo that stood as its centerpiece. Painted a bright coat of white, with a black, gabled roof, it called to him, not just as a place he could rest but a place maybe he could find his own bit of inspiration. For just beyond the gazebo were a series of gray stones jutting up from the ground, engraved marble statues arranged in a concentric pattern; flowers adorned their sides, fresh even in the chill of November— remnants from a just passed Veterans Day. And it was to this memorial he had come, that much he realized. He stepped up inside the gazebo, settling on a hardwood bench under the protective roof, and that's when his tired old body let out a deep sigh of content. The walk had done him good, but it had also taken a lot of strength from him. A check of his watch told him it was nearly four, the light in the sky begin- ning its nightly fade. He had asked Elsie to pick him up at five outside Marla's shop, where she had needed to pick up some basic supplies and groceries. So for the next half hour he could sit and think how differently his life had become in the last six months; heck, the last eighty years. Linden Cor- ners, could this really be you? Can a person's long-ago past still exist somewhere beyond his mind, did time exist on dif- ferent planes? Looking around, his being here still all seemed like a dream.

From across the street, he could still see the two dogs playing, one of them stopping to smell the air. Both were golden retrievers with lush coats, one of them older, an adult, the other an energetic pup. Just then the younger of the two darted across the road, smartly checking for cars before doing so, and before too long it had bounded into the park, its paws sinking into the mounds of snow. Its companion, as though just noticing it was alone in front of the Trading Post, chased after it, and soon both dogs were playing, barking happily, their sound like the tune of life. Thomas watched with growing amusement as the dogs came running up the steps and into the gazebo, coming before Thomas with tongues out, tails wagging. He reached down and pet one, the second worming his way for attention as well. The dogs' antics were entertaining, and he felt a momentary rush of wonder. He could not remember a time when he had let go with such abandon, or when his body had not been filled with the ache of age. He envied them their own, playful world.

"Buster . . . Baxter, what are you doing over there?" came a voice from the porch.

Thomas stood, saw one of the twins making her way up the path of the park.

The dogs, seeing her, sensing they had done something wrong, jumped down from the gazebo and went running back into the drifts of snow. They danced around her, and she did her best to quiet them down.

"Sorry, sir, hope they didn't disturb you . . . they don't know their own power."

"Oh, they are just fine. . . . I'm sorry, are you Marla or Darla?"

"Darla," the woman said after a moment's thought, as though even she wasn't sure. Or it could just be a twin thing, keeping friends and neighbors off guard as to who was who. Served them well in town from what Thomas had heard.

"A pleasure. It's nice to see them play so happily together."

"Buster is the older one," she said, ruffling the dog's fur as it lapped around her legs in a back-and-forth routine. "I got him a couple of years ago, and like my entire life, my sister just had to copy me. So she got Baxter. Part of the litter, so Baxter is Buster's son."

The word *son* reverberated in Thomas's mind and he felt a sudden lump in his throat.

"Father and son, playing," he said, his voice almost a whisper. "As it should be."

"Some days, I'm not sure they even know which is which," she said, a dry laugh escaping her mouth. "Just like me and my sister."

Not referring to her as Marla but "my sister." Keeping their enduring mystery alive, not unlike relationships themselves, whether it was between sisters, fathers and sons, or our canine counterparts. What kept a bond strong, what events forced them to fade into memory? Such worldly thoughts occupied Thomas's mind as the twin who claimed to be Darla gathered a squirming Baxter in her big arms to carry him safely across the street, Buster following with an eagerness he could only envy. Soon the dogs were inside the store, and all that remained of their presence were their paw prints, indelibly imprinted in the deep snow. Existing only for the moment, gone at first melt.

Yes, life was fleeting, your impact on the world lasting as long as someone remembered you, and at last, Thomas knew why he had come to the park on this day. He was ready to face what he'd come here for, but another interruption kept him from advancing. Like his mind was prepared, his body still steeling itself for the next steps.

A gleeful yelp caught his attention, and he looked up to see young Janey Sullivan running toward the gazebo . . . toward him.

"Thomas! Thomas!" she called out. "I told Brian that was you!"

Rising from his seat, Thomas noticed that Janey wasn't alone on the sidewalk. There was Brian standing at the edge of the park, watching as things unfolded. Thomas indicated all was good, he was happy to welcome the young girl's company. Brian acknowledged him with a friendly wave.

"She's in good hands, I'll take good care of her," Thomas said from across the park, his voice strong, newly empowered. He hadn't set a young woman's heart such aflutter for a long, long time, making him feel more like the wide-eyed curious boy of yesteryear. Like when he met his dear Missy, that same feeling of experiencing a special connection with another person washing over him. The fact he was nearly eighty-five and she just nine, well, it meant the world to him. Generations were not gaps, they were bonds, and what sealed theirs was loss.

Janey approached quickly, out of breath as she clambered up the steps to the safety of the gazebo. She gave Thomas a big hug around his waist, looking up at him as she did so. Her smile was infectious, and he couldn't help but return it before inviting her to sit down beside him.

"So, Miss Janey, what brings you here?"

"Mark can't work his shift tonight at the tavern, so my dad had to come in, and he can't leave me by myself and Cynthia and Bradley had to take little Jake to the doctor for a checkup, so I rode with him to town. I was going to hang out till six, when Cynthia could pick me up. I don't really like staying at the bar, it smells in there; oh, and I'm not supposed to call it a bar, it's a tavern, Dad says that sounds nicer. I think he just doesn't want to hear a little girl use the word bar."

Thomas found laughter bubbling up inside him at the generous outpouring of words from her tiny body, and even though he knew she'd been blessed with a unique, earnest streak, there was something entirely refreshing about the way she spoke. Was it her zest, her wide-eyed innocence? Whatever drove this child, Thomas was happy to have it rub off on him, laughter filling his heart.

"Janey Sullivan, my goodness, the marvelous things your mind comes up with. A bar, indeed! But whatever the circumstances that bring to me your company, I am very happy for them," he said. "Now tell me, how is your schoolwork?"

She scrunched up her nose. "Why do adults always ask kids about school?"

"I guess because we don't know what else to ask," he said. "Let me try that again. How is your very nice windmill?"

"Quiet," she said.

"Quiet?"

"There's been very little wind this week, so the windmill is just standing there with very little to say. I guess it needs its rest, winter is coming and we tend to get big storms."

"Is that okay, then, that the windmill is quiet?"

She looked like she was processing the question, seriously considering her answer. "The windmill holds my mom's spirit, and when it's quiet I just think that she's sleeping. She can't talk to me all the time. Like the other night, on Sunday? Remember all that rain and wind we got, lots of kids are scared of storms but not me, because I watched from my bedroom window as the sails turned and turned while the wind battered the house; Brian even left the back porch light on, so I could see the windmill in its bright glow. I talked long into the night to my mom, told her that Christmas was coming again, but first we had to get through Thanksgiving."

"Get through?"

"Well, last year we went to Brian's parents, but this year we're not. We'll be home."

"So it's different?"

"Different, yeah, but also the same. I mean, I used to have Thanksgiving with my mom. Now I celebrate it with Brian . . . I mean, with my dad. That's what I call him, even though he's really not, but that's another story. My real father died when I was very young, even younger than you were when you moved away from Linden Corners. Why did you leave, anyway?"

Thomas felt the pull at his heart. A common bond indeed, he and this young girl.

"May I show you something?" he asked.

"You mean, like when I showed you the windmill?"

"Yes, it's my turn to share something special with you."

"Is it far? I'd have to ask Dad."

"No, it's very close, right over there in fact," he said, pointing toward the marble stones.

Taking her hand in his, Thomas led Janey down the stairs and to the series of stones, six of them in total. He watched as Janey's small fingers touched the golden leaf letters that were engraved into the marble, tracing out a random name.

"John Masters," she read.

"I think he was Elsie's uncle," Thomas said. "Do you know why his name is there?"

"Because he died?"

Thomas nodded. "Do you know what this park represents?"

"Sure, our school class came here, oh, a couple of years ago," she said. "Our teacher said it was to remember the people who gave their lives for the wars. Then we had to write a report on our thoughts about war, and why these people had to die and what it meant to us. I got an A."

"Wonderful. That must mean you really understood the lesson," he said.

She nodded once, yet her eyes were tinged with newfound sadness. "Do you know someone here, Thomas? Is that what you want to show me?"

"Yes, and yes," he said. "Come with me."

The first of the marble stones listed names that dated back to the Civil War, the second one represented local residents who died in World War I, and the next one was for

World War II. It was to this stone that Thomas led Janey, placing her hand upon the cold stone right where the name Lars Van Diver was engraved. He covered her hand with his, feeling her pulsing warmth. This girl before him was blessed with a big heart and with deep feeling. This moment, for Thomas, was powerful, a long time coming. It was one thing for a teacher to rattle off history to her class, quite another for it to strike a personal, powerful connection in one of the students. Janey again traced the name with her fingers, her red lips moving silently, like she was getting a taste of the name before speaking it aloud.

"Lars? Is that how you say that?"

"Yes, Lars Van Diver."

"Lars Van Diver," Janey repeated. Then she looked up at Thomas. "Was he your dad?"

"Yes, he was," Thomas said.

"I'm sorry," she said. "I bet you missed him a lot."

"Yes, Janey, I did very much."

"I miss my mom very much, every day," she said. "Brian . . . Dad, he's great."

"And my mom, she was great, too. She cared for me so much."

"She didn't want to live in Linden Corners? I mean, after . . ."

"We had to make a sacrifice, just like my father did," Thomas said. "Like we all do."

"That's a big word, sacrifice."

"Do you know what it means?"

"It means you give something up for the better of someone else," she said.

"Beautifully said."

"Thank you for showing me and telling me about your dad," she said.

"It was my absolute pleasure, Janey Sullivan," he said. "You know, I've been back home in Linden Corners only three months now and this is the first time I've visited the memorial. Ever, in all my life. But today was the day I decided to come here, I just woke up and knew it. I guess I needed some courage, and your being here . . . you gave it to me. I needed a friend."

"Is that what we are? Friends?"

"I hope so."

"That's weird, we're not even the same age."

"That's what makes our friendship so special."

Janey seemed content with such knowledge, and the two of them left both the memorial and the gazebo, walking down the path back toward the tavern. It was coming on five o'clock in the afternoon, Elsie would be coming for him soon, and that was a good thing, as he was now both physically and emotionally exhausted. Yet while his body was tired, his heart was full, near to bursting from this visit. They reached George's, the lights now blazing inside and out, a few cars already parked in the big lot. Thomas helped Janey up the front stairs and inside the warm coziness of the bar.

"I'll need to see some ID," Brian said from behind the bar.

Janey rolled her eyes. "He says that to me every time I visit, he still thinks it's funny."

"Indulge me, little one," Brian said. "Why don't you head upstairs, Janey, hang out at Mark and Sara's, watch some TV or . . ."

"I know, read a book."

"Always a good idea."

Before departing for the upstairs apartment, Janey again wrapped her little self around Thomas and thanked him for sharing his special memories with her. As she bounded up the stairs with an energy possessed only by youth, Thomas sidled up to the bar, settling himself upon a tall bar stool. A quick check of his watch, he decided perhaps he could indulge his nightly Manhattan here while in the company of

Brian Duncan and the denizens of George's Tavern. Elsie would find him. He nodded politely at the two gentleman sitting at the bar, both about fifty years of age, then placed his order.

"I'd like to buy you one, too, Brian, if I may. Thank you for that little gift of a girl."

"Thanks, Thomas, but I'll stick with my seltzer."

He accepted Brian's answer without question, didn't pry. Like Janey said, everyone has their stories, they share them when they're ready. Just as he had done today, sharing the memory of his father with her. Truthfully, he had journeyed to the park today in an attempt to visit the memorial, still not convinced he would actually go through with it until Janey's presence pushed him over the edge, and happily so. He felt richer for the experience.

"I'll warn you, I don't usually make Manhattans, there's not much call for them in a bar that pays its bills with beer, so pardon me if it's not perfect," Brian said, setting the highball glass in front of his customer, pouring the whiskey and vermouth into it. Thomas took a sip; he tried to hide his grimace but it was apparent Brian's bartending skills needed more work.

"It's fine. But next time . . . less vermouth. Dry means very little—"

"I barely put any in!"

"Next time, just wave the bottle over the glass, that'll do the trick."

"Noted," Brian said with a knowing understanding. "Thomas, may I ask what your plans are for Thanksgiving? I'm sure Edgestone sets out a nice meal, but Janey and I, along with our neighbors Cynthia and Bradley Knight—and little Jake—would be honored if you could join us at the farmhouse. It's a small crowd, since Gerta, Nora, and Travis are headed to New Hampshire for a family dinner with one of her other daughters. But Gerta, she did promise to leave a couple of her pies for us, pumpkin and her special strawberry . . ."

"A strawberry pie? I'm still amazed at such a concoction. How extraordinarily sweet it was that night," Thomas said, "and Brian, I thank you very much for the invitation. But alas, I have other plans—out of town."

"Oh, I . . . well then, I hope you have a wonderful holiday."

"As do I, for me and for you and yours," Thomas said, sorry not to give Brian more of an excuse. But just as the barkeep had offered up no explanation beyond his choice of seltzer water, Thomas, too, felt that certain facts were best left to the inner soul, to be revealed only when the world forced them upon you. Sometimes you wanted to keep special things private.

"But I hope you'll keep the day before Christmas Eve open," Brian said. "It's the night of our annual tavern Christmas party, with more food—including Gerta's famous pies— than you can imagine, even gives ol' Martha at the Five O' a break from cooking. The whole village turns out to the point where you'll never see George's more crowded. It's going to be a great night, filled with the kind of surprises Linden Corners excels at."

"Consider it done, my good son. I wouldn't miss a party such as that for anything," Thomas said, taking another hesitant sip from his less-than-perfect Manhattan. "And hopefully by then the fair Miss Nora will have found the book I am seeking. The clock is ticking, Brian, time is not on anyone's side, least of all mine. The holidays will be here sooner than we think, and only when I have that book in my hands will my Christmas, at last, be complete."

It would be like he and his father had been reunited.

As he'd done in Memorial Park, tracing his name, feeling as close to him as he had in years.

For a passing, joyful second, he was reminded of those beautiful golden retrievers, Buster and Baxter, and he smiled at the memory of the dogs happily entwined, their barks and their endless bounds, their uncomplicated lives. They did their breed proud, for they had retrieved a bit of magic for Thomas, their effect indeed golden.

INTERLUDE

TODAY

Family means more than just blood, more than nature's bond, it's created out of the ether from a notion called love; a concept so real and potent, yet so indefinable. That's what I've learned, my dear, a lesson as large as life itself, something I discovered in just the quick passing of a few months. I suppose when I made the difficult decision to come to Linden Corners I was uncertain about what I would find, what ghosts awaited me. Certainly the windmill still stood, healthier today than when I befriended it as a child, my little body trying to reach to the heavens but never able to soar higher than the spinning sails of the windmill. The farmhouse, too, remains as cozy as ever. Also, there is a girl here, and some days I think it is her remarkable spirit that keeps the old windmill turning, and other days . . . it's just the opposite, that she endures only through the energy churned from those magnificent sails.

She has been a dream, this child, and she speaks to my heart. She keeps me going.

Which I hope keeps you going.

There is a lot of talk about Christmas traditions around

here, they embrace the holiday with a verve the jaded would sneer at; cynicism may rule the world, but in Linden Corners it is blown far away by the wind, and the cheery residents wouldn't have it any other way. So, my dear, I have set this plan in motion, the Christmas that should be must be, and may well be. I am striving to bring my memories of yesterday into the cherished moment of today. Today it is another holiday that envelops us; it is a day I choose to spend in quiet but not alone. My heart could have soared, embraced by this new family who now live within the walls of my youth. This man and this girl, what a special, unlikely relationship they have formed, and they are not blood; they are a family as much as any. They are together first out of need, now out of want. The world found them, fate pushed their separate souls into one. Like me, like you. How I wonder, would we ever have met if circumstances had been different. Had I not left Linden Corners as a child, where would my years have taken me? Would I still call the farmhouse home, would the sails of that old windmill continue to turn for me, or would it have been destroyed by time, by the reckless disregard of progress? And if so, what of that little girl who breathes its swirling air now? What would her life have been?

But again, I am getting ahead of myself.

Yes, it is Thanksgiving Day, my dear, and I am here with my thoughts, and of course, with you. A plate of food sits beside me, turkey and stuffing, all the trimmings, and I will eat them as I always have. That is another lesson I learned long ago, from a patient mother who had only one son to care for. No matter the sorrow that stalks your heart, there is room for celebration, and it is this notion that I embrace, that I cling to. Provided the woman named Nora can find for me the second best gift I can ask for.

You, my dear, are my first, always.

That elusive book, it's the key to it all, isn't it? I have racked my mind, wondering where it could have gone to after these eighty years. But I know it must be out there, waiting for me; if I can return to Linden Corners and be welcomed into its big heart after all this time, then anything is possible. You just have to wish it, like young Janey would say, set it upon the wind and watch it fly. Sometimes the wind takes your dreams into the future, but mine . . . mine, how I wish to send them back in time. Back to an unsuspecting boy who suffered a great loss, a boy whose appreciation for all that had been given to him was stolen, both physical objects and the intangible, all gone, he thought, never to be found again.

I remember that fateful day like one recalls a recurring nightmare, coming to you not just in the dark but whenever shadows crossed over your soul. The sun could be bright, daylight lasting long into the night, summer at its peak and all of sudden there come those images, unwanted and scary, reminding you of what you didn't have. Tossing the ball in the backyard, bouncing it against the house because no one was there to catch it. Wanting to buy a treasured gift for an upcoming birthday, knowing the recipient was no longer around to enjoy it. Reading a poem on Christmas night to yourself, knowing a special memory had been lost to time.

It was the day before Thanksgiving, nearly eleven months after my brave father, Lars Van Diver, went off to fight the war in Europe. We had heard from him periodically, letters that took too many weeks to arrive from overseas, always opening with the same salutation, "My dearest family," and ending with the hopeful, "Yours, now, forever, and always."

It almost didn't matter what the contents of the letter detailed, just that we knew he was safe and we knew that he loved us. Mama and I survived on written rations just as he dined on dry ones, but truthfully none were satisfying, and we could only hope for a quick end to the war to fulfill us.

Life in Linden Corners was quieter back then, almost an antidote to the explosions that rocked the world across the expansive ocean. Mama and I, we kept the peace and we kept the farm running as best we could, hiring day laborers in the spring for the planting and the fall for the harvest, filling their coffers and our bellies. At night the two of us passed the time listening to the radio or reading by flickering candlelight. Before I slept, I would run my fingers over the photograph of the model train from the Sears catalog, the same train that I didn't get for Christmas the year before. I would imagine my dad journeying across foreign lands hearing languages he didn't understand, packed onto a train that swirled with smoke and whistled in the dark night. To me it all seemed very glamorous, a young boy who had not yet played with toy soldiers failing to understand the harsh reality of battle. Until one day he did.

A light dusting of snow coated the ground that morning, and I was outside trying to form snowballs in my little fists, all to no avail. The powder would disintegrate the moment I tried to pack them, and at last I gave up and threw the puff of snow into the air, watching as it sprinkled down like sugar atop a cookie, sweet upon sweetness. That's when I saw the car pulling up the driveway, its tires crunching against snow and gravel; it was plain, brown in color, what they would have called a sedan. As it came to a stop, a man in uniform emerged from behind the wheel, setting a stiff cap down upon his blond crew cut. He was older than Papa, with several stripes on his shoulders and colorful medals on his chest.

"Hello, young boy, could you tell me, is this the Van Diver home?"

"Yes sir," I told him easily. It was a different time then, even during war, innocence still reigned over suspicion.

"I'd like to speak with Mrs. Van Diver . . . would that be your mother?"

By now Mama had appeared, dressed in a housecoat dotted with floral colors, her hair in rollers. I think that's what I remember most, how tight she looked, how tense, as though she had been waiting for this very moment. This dutiful call from the United States Army. When she looked at the car, and saw the solemn expression on the officer's face, when she noticed the sealed letter in his right hand, that's when she knew, and when I knew. Her giant, almost stilted sob sealed it, sadness and regret and the hollow sound of loss enveloping her to the point that she dropped to the ground, her body oblivious to the fallen snow. She must have been numb to the cold, then and for days after.

The officer did his duty, speaking with soft authority: "On behalf of a grateful nation . . ."

But the other words he spoke floated into the invisible air, neither of us hearing them or remembering them, neither of us wanting to. As though by failing to acknowledge them, refusing to even open the letter, the truth could be rendered false, the past could be changed. But it couldn't, and it wasn't, and all I knew by day's end was that life had forever shifted. The world might have been emptier by one body, but it was devoid of three souls. Him, her, me, once a family, now a fraction.

Yes, it was the day before Thanksgiving, and the next day the turkey remained frozen and fresh grown peas went uncooked, and the bread for the stuffing grew stale. I don't know what we ate, Mama just sat in Papa's chair and I at her feet, and she stroked my hair for what seemed hours, her touch both embracing and tenuous at the same time, like our connection could be broken at any point. Life came with no guarantees, family could be split in a single second, a boy's heart could be shattered like glass falling to the floor.

Papa had taken a bullet, he hadn't even needed to see a medic. He was gone that fast, in an instant. The incident had happened six days earlier, the word just getting to us now, in time to ruin the holiday and our lives. No matter what day, the latter would have been true, Mama was never the same, and as for me, what I most felt was anger.

Even when I learned years later that we won the war, my young soul still ached for what it had lost.

The next month passed in a blur, like I was living inside a blinding snowstorm.

Christmas Eve came, and rather than being surrounded by a tree that glistened with tinsel, with colored lights and with brightly wrapped presents awaiting discovery underneath its branches, Mama and I lived beside dozens of cardboard boxes, our lives packed up tightly; had they been alive they would have been screaming to be let out, desperate for air. The reality was setting in; we were leaving Linden Corners, headed to Virginia to my maternal grandparents, where we would live for the next two years.

"Thomas, where are you?"

Where was I hiding? Up in the attic of course, but instead of it being a storage room overflowing with our cherished memories, it was bare and empty, wooden beams exposed to me for what seemed the first time; I had never before noticed them. Sometimes you don't see the frame when the picture inside is what draws your attention.

Lying on the floor, not caring about the dust that swirled around me, I flipped through page after page of the book and *tried to be engaged by the tale of Saint Nicholas and his fly-ing reindeer who brought gifts to all those little boys and girls who were nice, not naughty. So where were my gifts? I asked myself, all year I had helped Mama with the house and chores. My reward was a holiday that didn't exist, with-out a father and without a tree to remind us of the joys the season brought with it. Mama had explained that she had had no choice but to sell the house, we couldn't afford to stay on; we had to be out by the end of the year. We put Christmas on hold, to celebrate once we arrived at my grandparents. Our tiny family's traditions, which I had barely gotten to know, were suddenly gone; rather than hear my father's deep baritone reading me this story, me on his lap and my mother smiling from her chair, I was lip-reading, silent, fighting back tears. As Donder and Blitzen and their furry cohorts took to the night sky, as jolly old Saint Nick in his green-colored suit slid down the chimney with a rosy-cheeked goodness, I continued to turn the pages without regard for the words, and when I finished I started over again, and again, but each time I read the story its impact lessened. I was staring at the last page, "And to all, a good night," when I heard my mother's voice penetrate my mind.*

"Thomas, dear . . . oh sweetie," she said, coming up the stairs, sitting on the landing.

I closed the book, leaving the cover facedown, not that it did any good. She knew what I was reading.

"You want me to read it to you, tonight?"

I shook my head. Definitely not.

"Thomas, talk to me."

"It's okay, Mama," I remember saying. "It's just a book."

She attempted a smile, knowing I didn't mean those words.

"Come on, it's nearly time to go. The movers are here, they're loading the boxes," she said. "We can make good progress today, and more tomorrow; we should be celebrat-

ing not just Christmas late tomorrow afternoon but also your birthday. My precious boy, six years old, my goodness but where does the time go?"

Time disappears into the air, like smoke, you think you see it and then it's just gone, the smell of the past lingering only for as long as you'll remember it. I put up no argument, not if I wanted Santa Claus to remember me for next year; he would know where to find me, didn't he know everything? Santa, who now wore a red suit; everything had changed, that's what my mind told me. Getting up from the floor, I left the book where I'd been reading it.

"Aren't you forgetting something?" she asked.

"No," I said. "This is Papa's house, and this is Papa's gift. His memory should stay."

"He wanted you to have that book," she said.

"Papa needs it more than I do, his soul will come back here and I don't want him to find an empty house. Just like we leave Santa cookies, we need to leave Papa something, and this . . . it's just what he would want." I said all this with a wavering tone, and then I made my way down the stairs of the attic at the farmhouse in Linden Corners for the final time.

We left at noon on a sunny Christmas Eve, saying nothing to each other. Mama had only lived in this house for seven years, me for five. It was Papa's home, his family's, and while we had attempted to keep the Van Diver traditions alive, fate somehow felt that change was in the air. It wasn't the only thing in the air that day, because even though there was no snow on the ground or falling from the sky, the wind was strong and so the windmill's sails spun, almost as though they were waving to us, good-bye, my friend, maybe for forever.

Not forever, it turned out, but a lifetime, eighty years.

And in all that passing of time, I never again laid eyes on that rare edition of The Night before Christmas. *Only for that one year had I heard my papa recount to me the story of the visit from Saint Nicholas. Indeed, visit, not visits.*

And so another Thanksgiving comes to an end, my dear, different in some respects, strange in others. The turkey was dry and there was not enough chestnut-flavored stuffing, and the green beans were drowned in a mushroom sauce, the fried onions soggy. I ate what I could and then they took the tray away. As unsatisfying as the meal was, the company is what has filled my belly, my heart. Sitting beside you, holding your hand and telling you stories of Linden Corners past and present, it makes me feel achieving my dream is possible.

My new friends have had their own holiday, different for them, too. Brian Duncan spent his first year not at his parents' home, and Janey spent her first Thanksgiving at home without the woman who gave birth to her. And Nora, she so fiercely independent, journeyed with her mother, Gerta—you would like her, probably engage her in a pie-baking contest—and son, Travis, they went to visit other family, another sister who lives beyond Linden Corners. It can't have been an easy holiday for any of them, and yet the strains of the upcoming season have only just begun.

I watched the annual parade this morning, not far from where we are now, and of course it ended as it always does. A jolly Santa Claus waving to the masses gathered along the busy canyons of New York. He wore his red suit, he always does except in my memories. I have told you of that, and soon, I hope to show it to you, and you will hear the words as I heard them so long ago from my father. I have entrusted much to strangers, but that's what's so special about life within the world of Linden Corners, strangers somehow become friends faster than it takes that old windmill to turn a single revolution.

Yes, my dear, something special indeed is coming, a Christmas for us all to remember.

PART 2
RETURNING HOPE

CHAPTER 11
NORA

Saying snowfall was in the day's forecast was an easy understatement. A nor'easter loomed over the darkening horizon and held the region in its anticipated grasp. Having already conquered the eastern provinces of Canada, strong winds and swirling flakes of snow were quickly sweeping all across Central New York State and making their way toward the low-lying Hudson River Valley. Panicked people were out in droves buying necessary provisions, food and water, batteries, and candles. The schools had been closed even before a single flake had fallen, officials fearing the storm could hit so fast the buses wouldn't be able to handle slick, icy roads. Such hearty storms were frequent enough here that everyone knew the drill—stay home, stay off the roads, hunker down, and respect nature's fury.

It was December first and the holiday season was getting its first real blast of winter.

For Nora Rainer, the storm couldn't be coming at a better time, as the work in the storage room was piling up daily. She decided today was the perfect day in which to attack all that she'd been putting off; she accepted the storm as a gift of time. Back when she was a child, whenever a passing

thunderstorm would assault Linden Corners, she would hole
up in her room with her coterie of dolls, indulging in fan-
tasies that took her away from the howling winds, the pelting
rain, and deadly streaks of lightning. Where her mind journeyed to, the sky was calm and the women were beautiful
and the pink house in which they lived was on a beach, white
sands warm beneath their plastic feet. In her world, nothing
melted and no one froze either, no one was in harm's way.
Now that she'd passed into adulthood, she had learned to respect the ferocity of such storms, knowing the damage they
could inflict. Just two summers ago, an angry storm had
nearly destroyed the windmill, and it had taken from the residents of Linden Corners one of their own, the beloved, gentle Annie Sullivan, only weeks after Nora's father had passed
away. With dire predictions of more than sixteen inches of
snow and wind gusts of up to fifty miles per hour, Nora
wanted to keep her loved ones as close to her as possible.

Yet she also wanted to attend to business at A Doll's Attic.
What better time than when the world shut down and nature
released some pent-up pressure, and the fact she was once
again playing in her dollhouse didn't go unnoticed by her;
sometimes it was nice to have a place in which to hide. So
that's where she found herself at ten o'clock that Wednesday
morning, Travis at her side, both of them dressed in ratty
jeans and old sweaters, perfect for getting dirty amidst all
the boxes they needed to look through. Gerta had preferred
to say home, Nora telling her they would head back at the
first sight of snowfall. She wouldn't be left alone, not then.

"You ready to get to work?" Nora asked.

Travis tossed her a telling look that offered up only one
answer: no. She volleyed her own look back that said, too
bad, you don't have a choice. "I don't get it," he said. "I get a
snow day and what do you do? Put me to work in the store.
What's fair about that?"

"Who said anything about life being fair, snow day or

not?" she said, her tone playful but serious. "As opposed to spending some quality time with your tired old mum, what would you rather be doing? Playing your video games, that Wii thing?"

"Sure, why not? It's fun."

"Life isn't always about having fun, Travis."

"Not if you're a grown-up," he said. "You're always worrying about something."

"Yes, and right now my primary worry is the fact that you're going to be a teenager next year and it's only going to get worse."

"Ha ha. Okay, I get it, you don't have to hit me over the head."

Giving her son a taste of his own medicine, Nora stuck out her tongue, rolling her eyes like one of those aforementioned teenagers. "Tell you what, hang with me for a couple of hours and we'll see what the weather is doing outside."

"Where else would the weather be?"

She ruffled his hair, laughing. "Such a wiseass. Come on, let me show you what I need. Maybe after an hour we'll take a break and get some hot chocolate over at the Five O'. Martha makes a mean cup."

"Why would I want a mean cup?"

"It's just an expression. Like when you say something is bad, you mean good."

"Mom, don't try and talk street, okay?"

"How about you stop stalling, there's a lot of work waiting for you."

Indeed, much had changed in the month since Nora had taken over the place once known as Elsie's Antiques, not least of which was the sign outside, flapping now in the growing wind. Handcrafted from thick pine, the words A DOLL'S ATTIC were painted in simple, scripted red-colored letters, not unlike a lawyer's shingle hung out to attract passersby, and she supposed her subtle choice in signage was not only appropriate but deliberate. Her one concession to her lawyerly past, now just memories and mementos stored inside a briefcase. The store, too, had begun to undergo a cosmetic overhaul, beginning with the counter space that was now clean, open, and inviting, rather than encased by an array of objects for sale, those dusty old items now relegated to the rear of the showroom, some just tossed out. Sometimes you had to cut your losses on stuff that had been hanging around nearly as long as Elsie herself. A few new items had found their way to the store, first-time customers dropping in with an array of items that might just find an interested party. The curiosity factor for once fell in her favor.

With the transformation from antique shop to consignment store nearly complete, filled not just with furniture and lamps, chinaware and crystal, she now stocked vintage candy you could still actually order from wholesalers, games she remembered playing with her older sisters, like Operation and KerPlunk and even Battleship, which they hadn't played because "it was for boys." Assorted action figures had come in, too, red flyer sleds and a plastic toboggan much like one from her youth, both of which would probably move fast after the storm passed. But that's what she wanted her store to be, not so much antiques from a time no one from her generation would remember, but rather a time capsule of the simpler life, their childhoods, hers included, when toys and innocence played together in harmony. Before you learned about things like love and death, marriage and separation. . . .

"Mom, where did all these boxes come from?" Travis said, settling onto the floor in the storeroom, the first of the dozen boxes opened.

"Oh, most of those came from a woman named Katherine Wilkinson—I told you about her, she's the nice lady who lives in a big house near the river? Her daughter liked to travel and she would always send home precious gifts. I guess Mrs. Wilkinson felt it was time to start clearing some things out of the house. She lost both her husband and daughter and maybe for her the memories are too strong."

"That's sad, to not have family at Christmas," Travis said. "I don't think I want to grow old . . . not so old that all your friends and family are gone; and besides, shouldn't you want to hold on to that stuff, you know, to remember them by?"

Crouching down, she tried to read into her son's eyes, wondering if this had anything to do with his father. He wasn't dead, but he was absent, and such separation could, in his young mind, be interpreted the same way. "Everyone's different, honey, to some people it's just stuff taking up unnecessary space. Some don't need objects to remember people by," she said. "Look at me—I don't need many of my dad's things, I've got him right where I want him."

"In your heart?"

"Yup, and in your eyes," she said.

"My eyes?"

"You look just like him, Travis," she said.

He smiled widely. "Wow, you never told me that before."

"Maybe that's because I never realized it until now . . . or maybe it's being back in Linden Corners, living at home and working down the street from where he worked. You know, my dad spent his whole life in this town, met your grandma, settled and had a family."

"You think Grandma misses him?"

"Every day," she said. "But she has such a great group of friends."

"Brian and Janey?"

"Among others, but they're the best ones," she said. "Now come on, let's get to work."

Just then the jangle of bells from over the door sounded. Was someone looking to buy an old game of dominoes or some similar distraction in which to pass the time during the storm? She wouldn't think such things took precedence over milk and bread and juice, but who was she to question the

desires of her customers—she had, they wanted, they
bought, she stayed in business. Simple philosophy of surviv-
ing the retail grind. She excused herself, only to see it wasn't
a customer, just her usual mailman, the dependable Emmett
Anders. He had a pile of mail for her today, topped off by a
flat cardboard package. Her eyes lit up at the sight of it—she
knew just what it was, she'd been expecting it.

"Afternoon, Nora," he said with a tip of his hat, his New
England accent reminding her of the bookseller down in
Hudson.

"Hello, Mr. Anders, wasn't sure I'd see you today," she
said, accepting the mail wrapped in a rubber band.

"You know how it is with us mail folk, through rain or
snow . . . that's the creed," he said. "Though what they're
saying about this one bearing down on us, I best get done
fast and be home with the missus, she'll be wringing her
hands with worrying. You have yourself a nice day, stay
warm and inside. I suggest you close up, no one in their right
mind is going to be out shopping for antiques, you know?
They'll need shovels, and new ones at that, ones that can
handle the heavy snow. Keep Ackroyd's busy, won't they?"

"I'm sure they will, good for Chuck. We'll close up soon,
just got some inventory to deal with. My son is helping out
today. Snow day, gotta take advantage."

"Ah-yup, ain't that why we have 'em?"

With that, he tipped his hat again and headed back into
the blustery wind, the bells above the door once again jangling. She kept telling herself she was going to take them
down, but with Christmas less than a month away, it seemed
not in the spirit of the season to do so. She would worry
about that another day, for now she wanted to focus on her
delivery. Dispensing with the rest of the mail, she opened up
the package from Amazon.com, holding in her hand the antique reproduction edition of *The Night before Christmas*
that Elliot the bookseller had told her about, and there star-

ing back at her on the front cover was Santa Claus himself, dressed in a green-colored suit and hat. She drew in a sharp breath, because even as she knew this wasn't the exact edition that Thomas held as a child—it had only been published twenty years ago—her sense of accomplishment at finding any book with Santa in a green suit made her think she'd made the right choice in opening this store. She had the drive for success, a natural instinct to not give up until she'd satisfied her customer, and as a result, herself. She read the cover credit: "Text by Clement Clarke Moore, Illustrations by Alexander Casey."

Once Nora had been given the information from Elliot, she'd gone back online and discovered the book, and while it was out of print, there were used copies for sale. Without even checking with Thomas, she clicked and added the book to her cart, paid with her credit card, and added shipping info. Since it was from an outside seller and not Amazon.com itself, they could only estimate the time of arrival, but here it was, and ahead of schedule. She couldn't wait to see the reaction on Thomas's face; who knew, maybe this book would strike a chord with him, perhaps this green-suited Santa would satisfy him.

On closer inspection, she marveled at how beautifully it had been printed, even in its used condition. The hardcover book was unjacketed, and instead the artwork was pressed into the paper—what printers called paper-over-boards—the spine a weave of red fabric. And inside, she flipped through thick-cut pages, familiar scenes playing out of Saint Nick flying through the air with the aid of his reindeer, landing on rooftops and slipping down chimneys, where stockings hung from hearths as he scattered gifts underneath trees. As she turned the last page, it, of course, ended with "And to all a good night," and for a moment Nora could imagine a young Thomas sitting wide-eyed upon his father's lap as the story was read to him. Indeed, visions of sugar plums would have

been dancing in his head; that is, until he'd drifted off to
sleep and his father had carried him upstairs to bed. So many
years may have passed since Thomas was an impressionable
child, and while the world may have changed in ways both
good and bad, this book showed how Christmas remained a
mainstay, its time-honored traditions as vibrant today as they
had been eighty years ago, more.

She was getting ready to pick up the phone to call
Thomas when the door opened again, and this time it was a
customer, a woman who held a baby carrier; the child was
asleep inside, snuggly and warm. The woman was bundled
up good, too, but even so Nora could see she had a friendly
face, her blond hair cut short. A woman with an infant was
not concerned about her appearance, or just didn't have the
time to worry.

"Hello, welcome to A Doll's Attic, I'm . . ."

"Nora, right?"

"Yes. Wait, we've met. . . ."

"Cynthia Knight, and this young cherub is my son, Jake."

"Oh hi," Nora said. "Please come in, come in . . . what
are you doing out in this weather?"

"Picking up some groceries, and then I was passing by
and . . . well, I decided to stop in on a whim. I've heard so
much about the store, thought I should check it out."

Nora believed the first part of her story, but not the second. The lawyer inside her was anticipating the big reveal,
her mind all ready with an objection. She cut to the chase.
"Is there something I can do for you, Cynthia?"

"I wonder, do you time for a cup of coffee, maybe over at
the Five O'?"

Though the invitation took her by surprise, actually the
idea of girl talk over a coffee was appealing. "Oh, well, sure,
there's not much going on here. But can I ask what this is
about?"

"Brian Duncan," Cynthia said.

Nora's smile turned upside down, as the saying goes. Of course, now she remembered who this woman was. Cynthia Knight was Brian's best pal in town, and no doubt he'd told her about the kiss. Objection overruled.

The Five O' was pretty quiet at the moment, the lunch rush hadn't yet begun and breakfast had been digested hours ago. Even so, with the forecast as it was, Martha Martinson, proprietor and all-around jokester, told the ladies to take their pick of booths as only two of them along the long bank against the wall were currently occupied, both of them with burly men in flannels drinking coffee.

"You can have your pick of them, the booth or the guys," Martha said and then laughed heartily.

So much for a quiet cup of coffee.

"The booth is just fine," Nora said, wishing Martha could tone it down a bit.

Cynthia just waved off Martha's attempt at humor. "Pay her no mind, Nora, it's what we all do in Linden Corners."

"Just for that, I'm putting sour milk in your coffee," Martha said.

"Ah, so it will be an improvement over the swill you usually serve," Cynthia said, who grinned up at Martha. Having been one-upped, she retreated back to the kitchen.

Nora gave her . . . what, friend . . . friend of a friend . . . frankly, she didn't know what to think of Cynthia Knight, about their relationship or what she wanted. They'd already established their topic of discussion: one Brian Duncan, but so far Cynthia hadn't been very forthcoming with details. On their short walk over, Cyn had talked casually about the store and the coming storm and other safe subjects. Before leaving, Nora had told Travis she was going to have coffee with "Mrs. Knight," promising to return soon with hot chocolate for him. He was actually fine with being left alone, turned out he was having fun pouring through the boxes and discovering the shiny Christmas trinkets and ornaments. Nora had reminded him to be careful, and he just rolled his eyes at her, the "duh" heard but unspoken. "Look what you have to look forward to with Jake," Nora had said as they headed out the door.

Now that they were settled with coffee and pastries set before them, Nora peered over the mug at Cynthia, eyes narrowed.

"So, Brian Duncan, you said. What about him?"

"Wow, you don't waste time, do you?"

"I'm used to it, I was a lawyer for too long."

"Aha, billable hours," Cynthia said. "My husband, Bradley, he's an attorney, too."

"What kind?"

"Tax. Offices up in Albany."

Nora nodded. "So he spends all his time in an office or worse, a cubicle, pouring through files and watching the ticking of the clock. I'm familiar with it, even though I practiced criminal defense, so fortunately many of my days were spent in court. Broke up the routine." When she said those words she surprised herself by having spoken of her career in the past tense, as though being confined to Linden Corners had closed her off to her previous life. Her past had lost its place in the world.

"Linden Corners must be quite a change of pace."

"From sixty to zero," Nora said.

"That's funny, never heard it said quite so . . ."

"Succinctly?"

Again, Cynthia laughed warmly, this time loud enough to catch the attention of the other people inside the diner. The burly guys ignored them, going back to their coffee, but the waitress who was refilling their cups came over to the booth. Nora noticed she was a cute young thing, blond and slim,

with lots of makeup that made her cheeks rosier than . . .
well, Santa Claus, she thought. Her name tag read SARA.

"Sorry, ladies, I don't mean to interrupt your day, but,
Cynthia, um, do you mind if I ask you a question?"

"Sure, Sara. Hey, do you know Nora Connors? She's the
new owner of Elsie's."

Sara said hello, then, "Yeah, sure, you come in for lunch
sometimes, always to go."

"Nice to meet you, officially, Sara."

It was then Nora realized who this Sara was, the lucky
woman engaged to Mark Ravens. Funny, she thought, meeting both of them in their place of employment, both of them
waiting tables in places as different as could be, a greasy
spoon and a fancy resort. She thought of Mark's comment
about wanting more out of life and trying to make things
perfect for his girl. Nora stole a look at the modest engagement ring on Sara's finger and felt a stab of jealousy hit her.
Starting out, they were full of optimism and love.

"What's up, Sara?"

She hesitated briefly, then blurted out: "I want to kill that
Mark Ravens!"

"Whoa, honey . . . relax," Cynthia said. "I thought you
two were getting married."

"Yes, we are, and if he has his way, well . . . he wants us
to get married in a bar!"

She spoke that way, with forceful exclamation points giving her words additional impact, so much so Nora felt she
could actually hear the punctuation.

"Oh, Brian told me about that," Cynthia said. "Not a good
idea, huh?"

"Where's the magic in that?" Sara asked. "Oh, we had
such a big fight over it!"

"Actually, Sara, if I can interject a moment," Nora said. "I
know it's none of my business being the new girl in town,

but I was there when Mark asked Brian about the idea, and he seemed so earnest . . . he just wanted to make you happy."

Sara rolled her eyes to the point that Nora wondered if kids ever outgrew the silent weapon known as sarcasm. "Oh please, two men planning a wedding, what, they want to raise a toast with cans of beer? That's not the day I've been dreaming about since I was five!"

"And did you tell Mark that?" Cynthia asked.

"Yeah, but he just stormed out, as though I'd done something wrong."

"So how did you leave it?"

"Oh Cynthia, I think I just hurt his feelings big-time," she said. "I mean, I guess I've been putting too much pressure on him lately, telling him I wanted to settle on a date, and I know he was trying to be sweet and romantic and . . . so Mark, by having us get married at the same place that he proposed—and on the anniversary of the engagement to boot—but really . . . a bar? Where's the honeymoon? The Five O'?"

"Hey!"

It was Martha from over by the counter saying that, and all the women just erupted into peals of laughter, Martha included. The moment broke the ice, and finally Cynthia took hold of Sara's hand and imparted a bit of wisdom. "Sara, if you don't want to get married in a bar, then don't. Talk to Mark, calmly, leave the exclamation points here, okay?"

"Thanks, Cynthia, I knew you'd be rational."

"I think that's a compliment," she said.

Sara was about to return to her station when Nora stopped her. "Can I tell you a secret?"

"Sure, I like secrets."

"When it comes to what women want, men are usually pretty dumb. They don't really understand what makes us tick," she said, "but what I saw in Mark's eyes that day, he adores you and only wants to give you the best, and not just on your wedding day but for your entire lives. For a man to admit such a thing in front of a perfect stranger—well, you're a lucky girl."

"Thanks, Nora, I'll remember that."

So Sara left them alone again, having forgotten to refill their coffee, which by now had grown a bit cold, not unlike outside, where the snow had begun to fall. Both women observed it, nervously checking their watches before looking back at each other.

"Yeah, I think we should head out, no telling how quickly this storm will hit," Cynthia said.

"We never had a chance to talk, about Brian."

Cynthia reached over, placing her hand over Nora's. "Just heed your own advice, men don't understand women, and so if a woman is going to kiss a man and then tell him she just wants to be friends, well . . . that's as mixed a message if ever I heard one. Look, Nora, we barely know each other and so maybe I'm overstepping my bounds . . ."

"No, it's okay, Cynthia, I appreciate it," Nora said, feeling a little hot beneath the collar. Of course Brian had told his best friend about what had happened that day in his driveway, how foolish was she to think he'd keep it bottled up inside. Unlike her, who hadn't told a soul. Who did she have to tell anyway?

"Brian is a helper . . . a fixer. When he came to Linden Corners, he was a bit of a mess, he didn't know who he was or what he wanted from life, he was just passing through—that's where the nickname came from, coined by our own Martha Martinson over there. He could easily have blinked twice and been driving out the other side of town, but instead something called to him here. When his weeklong stay became a month and then a whole summer, he did nothing but help out others. What he did for your mother after George passed away, what he's done for Janey, the sacrifices he's made in order to make others happy, it's a rare quality.

But in all this time, I still don't think Brian has rediscovered himself. He helps everyone but himself. I think you're his latest reclamation project."

"I didn't ask for that."

"See, that's the thing, you don't ask, he just does."

"So what you're saying is, don't mess with Brian."

"Be his friend, as you said. Just don't mess with his heart."

Nora nodded, words forming on her lips. "That's why I did it, Cynthia, kissed him. So we could remove that element from our relationship . . . gosh, that sounds so lame the way I say it. Like a man and a woman can't be friends without romance getting in the way? Not very evolved for a defense attorney."

"Don't be so hard on yourself, Nora. Remember, you're not a lawyer anymore, you're a person."

Nora allowed herself one last, wide smile. "Thanks for that. I think you're funnier than Martha. This was actually nice, girl talk, something I've missed."

"Then we'll have to do it again, soon," she said. "But for now, I think the storm is doing all the talking."

As they settled their tab and made their way into the fresh falling snow, they parted with a hug. Nora watched as Cynthia got into her car, settling little Jake into his car seat, and that's when she realized the tyke had slept through the entire conversation, about weddings and love and relationship issues and kissing men when it wasn't appropriate to do so. In a half hour's time, Jake had learned a valuable lesson: When the ladies start to chatter, just roll over and sleep. Nora found her mood improved as she made her way back to A Doll's Attic, the bells above the door jangling, announcing her presence. They didn't bother her.

When Travis came running out of the storeroom, she realized she'd completely forgotten to order his hot chocolate, a wave of regret washing over her. What kind of mother was she? But her son didn't seem to mind, as his face was lit with an enthusiasm she had rarely seen in him lately, his hand dangling a glass ornament before her.

"Mom, look what I found among Mrs. Wilkinson's boxes," he said.

She looked closely to see what had so intrigued him, and what she saw inside the round glass globe was a snow-coated windmill, its sails turning as white lights blinked on and off, on and off. A small inscription said SINTERKLASS, THE NETHERLANDS.

"Just like in Linden Corners," he said.

No matter where she went in this town, Nora Rainer couldn't escape Brian Duncan, nor the specter of that old windmill. Just then the howling wind rocked the windows of the store, and Nora gazed out to see snow being blown sideways; the lights inside the store flickered. The storm had hit fast, its fury increasing exponentially with each passing second, it seemed. As she and Travis gathered up their stuff, she thought about the real windmill alone on that open field, and how its mighty sails would be answering nature's call. She hoped it would be safe, it and the people who lived to see it spin.

CHAPTER 12

BRIAN

"Wow, Brian, it's not even Christmas and already we have so much snow."

"We sure got walloped."

"Walloped? What does that mean?"

"It means Linden Corners took a beating from Mother Nature."

"You mean, like getting so much snow."

"Like you said."

"So why did you have to use that big word to say what I said?"

Brian didn't know how to respond to that, he often didn't to Janey's unique sense of expression, so he just looked at her exasperated, freckled face and decided the debate wasn't worth it. When a nine-year-old girl got an idea in her mind, it was best to just let her alone to work it out. She'd be on to another topic in a matter of minutes, if not sooner.

"Can we go sledding?"

A related topic, sure, but different enough to know their morning was progressing. Brian just laughed at his daughter's spirit, reaching for her empty plate of pancakes as she continued to stare out the window at the drifts of fluffy white snow. "Maybe later, okay, and we can make snow angels, too. There's just a few things I need to take care of this morning. What do you say you head on over to Cynthia's, Jake probably needs to learn a lot about snow."

"He has a lot to learn about everything," she said.

"Well, baby steps."

"Well, duh, he's a baby."

Some expressions just didn't need translation, so Brian let the conversation die off, with Janey hopping off her chair and running upstairs to get her stuff ready for a visit over at the Knights' house. It was one of her favorite places to spend time of late, and while Brian could easily have been jealous of the attention she paid over there, he knew it was important—not only did Jake give her an excuse to play older "sibling," but there was no denying the strong influence Cynthia had over a girl with no mother, one who had to rely too much on a hapless legal guardian, one Brian Duncan . . . *me,* he thought with a gulp. Some days he wondered how all of this had happened, feeling like he'd been on autopilot since the moment Janey had come under his supervision, and as much as he loved her, and he did . . . tremendously, feeling that his heart was bigger than his entire body when it came to providing for her, he would have traded it all to have Annie back. Annie and Janey together, as it should be, he the man Just Passing Through.

As though hearing him, the clock on the kitchen wall struck, the windmill's sails at nine and twelve. He stole a look at the pile of dishes waiting for him in the sink, decided they could wait. There was too much to do, and none of it could get off the ground without him, and so after dropping Janey off next door—a hike itself, through the dense drifts of snow that had Janey's cheeks glowing a bright red both from the anticipation of playing with Jake and from the cold—Brian returned to the quiet of the farmhouse and began to think about Christmas. Last year he and Janey had begun the holiday preparations too late, not chopping down the tree until mid-month, and even then it had taken a few days for them to decorate it as he and Janey were going through a rough patch. He was thankful there were no signs of any this year. It was smooth sailing for her, if not for him.

Why then did he still feel a sense of incompleteness enveloping him? It was the same lingering notion that had attacked his gut the day his mother had called to say there would be no Thanksgiving, not at the Duncan household anyway. He had not heard from her since, nor had he heard from his sister, Rebecca, less of a surprise. She popped up when she felt like it. Divorced, she used her son as a tool against her ex, and frankly, Brian was glad to be spared her drama. So that just left Brian and Janey fending for themselves this holiday season. Even Gerta was missing in action, since she had Nora and Travis living with her, and not that Brian begrudged the sweet lady time with her family, truth was . . . he missed her company, the way she would just drop by with lunch and a home-baked pie for dessert. That hadn't happened since Nora returned to town. As for Nora, he tried not to give her much thought and aside from a post-Thanksgiving dinner at Gerta's house, he hadn't even seen her.

She had her Christmas mission, helping Thomas find his antique book.

Brian had his assignment, too, helping to plan a joyous wedding celebration at the annual George's Tavern Christmas Party, not that he'd done much on it yet. He was still waiting to hear from Mark about how his proposal had gone over with Sara. He reminded himself to call Mark later, if it was going to happen then they needed to coordinate some ideas. For now, he had a job to do in the attic.

Before heading upstairs, Brian caught a glimpse of himself in the hallway mirror and stopped. He studied his face, the lines around his eyes a bit more pronounced; where had those come from? He was only thirty-six. What was he doing in this crazy town—caring for a nine-year-old girl, planning a wedding, accepting friendly kisses from a married (albeit separated) woman. Who was this Brian Duncan, the man who had once dreamed of climbing the corporate ladder alongside Maddie Chasen, a Southern beauty who by now should have been his wife. He had traded the dreams for the ones that spun magic inside an old windmill. It had been an eventful two years since he'd left New York, and now here he was, feeling like a virtual stranger in this house he called home. If he was going to be any good for Janey, he had to finally solve the question of himself: just what did he want from life? Running a tavern a few nights a week just wasn't cutting it anymore, he needed to show Janey that happiness came from fulfillment, and what that was . . . well, therein lay the problem. He didn't know what he wanted to be when he grew up. Even though he'd donned the cap of responsibility real fast the moment Annie had left them and Janey had come into his care, he still felt cold.

But all those life questions could wait until the New Year, couldn't they? Concentrate on the here and now, Christmas and the annual tavern party and Mark and Sara's imminent wedding, wasn't that enough purpose for the last month of the year? With that in mind, he started up the stairs to the second level of the farmhouse, unlatching the ladder that allowed access to the attic. He figured it was as good a time as any to start bringing down the Christmas decorations—not just for the house but for the tavern, whose exterior he would populate with colorful lights. This year he was determined to beat Martha over at the Five O', who last year had kidded him but good for his tardiness.

He climbed up the stairs, ducking his head as he made his

way into the attic. It was musty, as attics tended to be, and cold, and for a moment he was reminded of Nora's store, an entire business dedicated to the items regular folk kept hidden away in rooms hard to get to. The image of Katherine Wilkinson came next, she who was parting with her daughter's gifts from around the world, and wondered how she had been brave enough to let them go. With all that Brian and Janey had in their attic, he knew he couldn't possibly give any of it away, for sealed in several boxes was a history of the Sullivan family, Dan, who had been Janey's father, and Annie, with picture album after album recording the limited images of the three of them as a family. Which got Brian's mind thinking, an idea sparking his imagination. Quickly he made his way to the back of the attic where the Christmas decorations were stored, boxes containing the tree stand, strings of lights, an array of ornaments, among them two very special "name" ornaments.

Wiping away a year's worth of dust, tearing back the duct tape, he opened the lid and found right on top two rectangular white boxes, and he withdrew them carefully, one at a time, resting them on the floor. Opening the first one, he picked it up and watched as the red glass caught the glow of the exposed lightbulb over his head. "Janey," it read in sparkling glitter, as beautiful as the girl whose name adorned it. It had been a special gift last year, and Brian smiled at the memory of her bright face, mixed as it was with tears and joy as she dangled the ornament before her. Returning it to the safe care of its cotton bed, Brian then opened the other box and pulled out the ornament with his own name written in silver glitter, the glass a shiny green that looked as new as Janey's and that's because it was. He'd needed to replace the original; this year the new orb would make its debut on their tree, having arrived too late for last Christmas. The drama of last year was more easily replaced with the growing excitement he was feeling now. Because this year, Brian knew, his ornament wouldn't be the only new one.

As he set his ornament back inside the box, he heard the telephone ringing throughout the house. Making a quick dash down the steep stairs, wondering if it might be Janey or Cynthia, he grabbed it just before the answering machine clicked on.

"Hello?"

"Hey, Brian, it's Mark." His usual chipper tone was missing.

"Mark, hi . . . uh, something wrong?"

"Man, you're good."

"I can hear it in your voice, practically see your sour expression over the phone," he said. "Let me guess, Sara's not pleased with your idea of a bar wedding?"

"To say the least."

Secretly, Brian had been expecting this, it was why he hadn't planned anything yet. "Sorry, Mark."

He let out a frustrated huff. "She said the setting wasn't magical enough and that if we wanted a Christmas wedding than we should just get married on Christmas Day, or on the Eve," he said. "Not like other people have traditions of theirs to see about on those two days, the last thing our friends need is a wedding to distract them, too. Look, I really don't have time to get into it now, I've got to get down to RiverFront, they're short-staffed and are depending on me, the storm really socked them in down there. They lost power for a few hours. So I just wanted to call to give you the heads-up, okay, don't plan for a wedding, just have the tavern party like you would."

"Everything okay, Mark . . . I mean, between you and Sara?"

"Oh yeah, we're still nuts about each other. But now she knows hopeless romantic is not one of my qualities."

"You'll think of something," Brian said.

"What I think is I should just let her do everything and then just show up."

"You wouldn't be the first groom to adopt such a strategy," Brian said with an attempt at humor that fell flat. Mark just said his defeated thanks and hung up, leaving Brian with an empty receiver and an even emptier heart, not only because their wedding would have been a capper to the holiday party but now it gave him one less thing with which to occupy himself. He wouldn't have minded the distraction.

Returning to the attic, he put away the Christmas ornaments, feeling almost as though he were packing away a bit of magic himself. Instead, he carried down a box of colored lights, and walked outside, placing them on the passenger seat of the truck. Cold wind circulated around him, making him rethink what he had been planning to do, but then realized no snowstorm could stop a true resident of Linden Corners. And wasn't that what Brian Duncan was, no longer Just Passing Through, he was the Windmill Man, and as such he kept life spinning in this little burg, for himself and for a little girl named Janey and a sweet old lady named Gerta, both of whom were responsible for instilling within him the renewal of hope.

In fact, the entire village had been supportive of him, welcoming him into their fold, their families, and so it was time for him to return the favor. Another idea was forming in his mind, and so with fresh determination, he hopped into the truck and made his toward downtown Linden Corners.

"Should I cook up some worms for you?"

"The Early Bird Special, huh? Might be an improvement on that chicken noodle soup I had the other day," Brian said, tossing a conspiratorial smile Martha's way.

"Geez, what's with everyone attacking my food lately, first Cynthia, now you?"

"When did you see Cynthia?" he asked.

"Just yesterday, she was having coffee with our newest business lady, Nora."

That surprised Brian, he didn't even know the two women were on friendly terms. "Are you sure? Did Cynthia and Nora come in together, or did they just happen to show up at the diner at the same time?"

"Seated in a booth, swapping stories, advising poor Sara about her wedding."

A lightbulb went off over Brian's head. Mark's phone call now made complete sense, and he had his old friend and his new one to thank for it. As for Brian, parked in the lot of the tavern and in the process of unloading the box of lights, that's when Martha had come upon him and seen that he was the first among the business owners to start putting up decorations; soon the entire village would be bathed in colors, flickering blues and vibrant greens, scarlet reds and golden yellows, the holiday spirit bright and alive to residents and passersby alike. Brian knew he'd first need to shovel a path to the front entrance before he could attempt to put up the lights, might take him all afternoon just to remove the snow.

"You sure you're gonna put those up today? Mighty cold out," Martha said.

"What, I should stop, only to come in tomorrow and see that you've put up yours?"

"Nah, last year was last year," she said. "I was testing you, Windmill Man."

"So that means I passed?"

"Oh, you passed long ago, kid," she said. "So, when's the party this year?"

Just then Brian saw a car pulling into the lot of the Five O', saw Elsie Masters and a couple of the ladies from The Edge emerge. They walked hesitantly on the salted sidewalk as they made their way inside the warm, cozy diner. Brian saw that Martha had noticed him watching, said, "Hey, you're not answering me . . . what, you got a thing for the older set? Thought you said I was too much woman for you. That means Elsie would have you crying uncle in no time."

"Ha ha, Martha," he said, returning his gaze to his neighbor. "No, it's just . . . I've got this idea about Christmas, but I need to run it by a few people, Elsie's as good a one to start with."

"Tell her, the whole village will know in seconds," she said. "Well, come on over why don'tcha, the diner's full of regulars, Marla and Darla are there and so is Chuck . . ."

"Oh joy," he deadpanned.

"And Father Burton is there, too. I think he might have a few Christmas ideas himself."

"Indeed," Brian said, "and what about Sara? She working?"

"Of course, what kind of boss do you think I am, allowing my best girl a day off?"

"You may have to arrange for one soon," Brian said, and without further explanation he dashed across the street, Martha following close behind him, asking him just what he meant by that comment.

It wasn't until he'd entered the diner that Brian realized just how cold outside the air was, and all of a sudden he was grateful to Martha for having interrupted his planned lighting of the tavern. He rubbed his hands as he sat down at the counter, took a cup of hot coffee from Sara without needing to ask. That was as nice a greeting he got from her, obviously she was still annoyed with Brian's part in hatching the tavern-set wedding.

"Hey, Sara . . ."

"I got a customer," she said, briskly, but not before tapping her nails on the Formica counter for effect.

Brian turned to see her make the rounds of the tiny diner, pouring fresh cups for nearly everyone. It seemed he knew the entire gang that had gathered; regulars indeed. Elsie and her posse were just getting settled and ordering tea, and Father Burton was breaking bread with Gerta, and Chuck Ackroyd sat just a few stools away from him. Marla and Darla hid in the back, talking quietly amongst each other, like always. Brian still wasn't sure which twin was which; they had such a strong connection they may as well have been born Siamese. Of the principal business owners on Main Street, only Nora seemed to be missing, and of the usual suspects Brian seemed only to be missing two of the actors in the play he was formulating in his mind, Mark, busy at work down in Hudson, and Thomas Van Diver, who seemed to have pulled his disappearing act again.

"Hello, Brian," Gerta said, waving to him, "would you like to join us? Plenty of room."

He accepted the invitation, sliding away from Chuck Ackroyd with pleasure; he was the one guy in town who just rubbed him the wrong way, a guy who wore his problems on his flannel sleeves. Short of needing supplies for the farmhouse or the tavern, Brian did all he could to avoid the surly natured Chuck. Life was too short to live in his bitter world. Still, if Brian was to put his plan in motion, he'd need Chuck's help, or at least, his hardware store, and didn't the two come as a package deal?

Sliding in next to Gerta, he planted a kiss on her wrinkled cheek, then shook hands with Father Eldreth Burton, the priest at the local Saint Matthew's Church. "How are you, *padre*, it's been awhile."

"Tell me about it, Brian."

Oops, that was the wrong thing to say to a priest; weren't you supposed to see him at least once a week? Gerta saved the day, steering the conversation away from church to whatever was on Brian's mind.

"I know you, Brian Duncan, you have that look on your face like you're planning something. Spill it." And after a pause, added, "And also, how can we help?"

So Brian told his short tale of his conversation with Mark, first the one at lunch, then the one just this morning. "I've never heard him so deflated, here he was just trying to give Sara the perfect day she wants and she shot him down. But it was something she said that got my mind thinking, a phrase that Sara said—if she was going to have a Christmas wedding, it may as well happen on Christmas Eve." Brian, his voice a near whisper, "What do you think?"

"Isn't it up to them?" Father Burton said.

"Oh, I think they're so confused at this point, they need some prompting," Gerta said. "And I for one think it's a marvelous idea, one I think the entire village can get behind. It's what we do best in Linden Corners, plan celebrations. Just think, what better night for them to share their love than on the holiest one of the year? Oh Brian, just think how magical it could be."

"What's magical?"

They all looked up to find Sara standing over them, coffeepot in one hand, almost like a third appendage.

"A Christmas wedding," Gerta said.

"Nuh-uh," Sara said. "I told Mark I'm not getting married in a bar."

"No, my dear," Gerta said with a friendly cluck. "A church wedding for you and Mark, and on Christmas Eve, what do you say? You want magic, what better place?"

Her eyes lit up, warming to the new idea. But it was Brian's comment that really won her over, and sent her squealing to the point that everyone at the Five O' heard her, one cup even splattering to the floor with a loud crash. But no one paid it any mind, least of all Sara or even Martha, as nearly everyone was suddenly chattering about the idea that Brian had presented the bride-to-be with.

"You can get married at the base of the windmill, amidst all those glittering white lights," Brian had suggested. "You want magic to swirl around you, there's no better place than beneath those ever-turning sails."

CHAPTER 13

THOMAS

"Did you hear that sweet waitress down at the Five O' is getting married . . . finally."

"On Christmas Eve of all days, I hear."

"By the old windmill, it's what everyone is talking about."

"I can't imagine a lovelier setting. Remember that time last December when we all took the trip to see the windmill, it was the talk of the town, lit with what seemed like thousands of bright white lights. Like the blinking lights from heaven."

"Which you're not too far from visiting."

"Why, Elsie Masters, you're more of an antique than that junk you used to peddle."

That comment was followed by peals of laughter; elder humor, supposed Thomas Van Diver, sitting as far from the yammering ladies as he could and still be in the same room. He wasn't in the mood for their antics this morning, and thankfully they had respected that. Elsie, Myra, Edna, and, reluctantly, Jack, and assorted other cronies—the "Edge Mafia"—were sitting around a long, folding metal table, supposedly playing a game of mah-jongg but instead just plain gossiping about the latest news to hit Linden Corners, news they couldn't wait to spread, comment upon, and toss around their opinion on. Some of the ladies had been there at the diner when Brian Duncan had suggested to Sara Joyner a Christmas Eve wedding at the windmill, others of course claimed they were there, while a few just waved the news away with an apparent display of disinterest.

"Hogwash, who gets married on Christmas Eve?"

Thomas jolted to attention at the comment, turned to see who had said such words. Myra Cole was shaking her head, as though agreeing with herself.

"Well, at least the groom won't forget his anniversary," Edna said pointedly.

Jack had the look of a man who wanted to be anywhere but where he was.

Such was life here at Edgestone.

All this endless chatter in the otherwise spacious recreation room was starting to close in on Thomas. He was awaiting a guest who had her own news to share. For now, the breakfast dishes had been cleared and those who were hanging around were doing so for companionship, a way to pass another long day filled with nothing but the busy lives of others. Thomas Van Diver missed the old days when he relied less on reliving memories, always forward thinking in his approach to his life. Yet since he'd returned to Linden Corners, it was the past he'd been absorbed by. Even at his advanced age, he liked to think new memories were just waiting to be made, wasn't that what all this effort was about? One final, beautiful memory?

It's not that he didn't appreciate a heartwarming story about an upcoming wedding or the pleasant-natured preparation of Christmas coming from the other corner, where a few spry folks, along with the aid of The Edge's staff, were putting up their artificial Christmas tree, but because he was anxious about what his soon-to-arrive visitor had to show. Christmas, indeed, he thought. Today was the fifth of December, and for Thomas, watching the tree go up filled his mind with memories of yesteryear. Lately signs of the encroaching holiday were appearing everywhere, and why not, December had settled in for its thirty-one-day marathon, with much to look forward to in a busy month that culminated with folks taking a breather from the stresses of the regular routine of life.

Stress, he supposed that was what most affected him, and why he could barely keep his eyes open, even at eleven o'clock on a bright, sunlit morning, with the village still coated with a layer of snow that had fallen just a few days ago. It was what kept him awake at night, his tired eyes watching as three, four, five o'clock rolled around on the dial, constantly thinking about the countdown to Christmas and whether his deadline would be met. The phone call he'd received just two hours ago from Nora Rainer had filled him with apprehension. Had she found the book? he had asked her. She wouldn't say exactly say, "Not on the phone, it's something I need you to see without prejudice."

So here he sat, a newspaper at his side but unread, still watching the slow progress of the clock, still listening as the old biddies talked about a new Linden Corners Christmas tradition, a parade of lights that would wind down the hill from the farmhouse on Christmas Eve, leading up to the wedding of Sara Joyner and Mark Ravens in the presence of the windmill. Though he barely knew the happy couple, Thomas was sorry he would have to miss out on the village party. The way he'd been embraced by all of its residents had kept his heart warm for months; but Christmas Eve for him would hopefully find him elsewhere, and it was the presence of the book that would dictate just where that was.

His thoughts were interrupted by the arrival of Nora Rainer, a large bag slung over her shoulder, like a female Santa come to leave presents under the tree. But their tree here was not yet lit, old Charlie and Harry still arguing over whether you strung the lights from the top of the tree down or from the base to the pointed tip. At this rate, the baby Jesus would be a teenager before the men could agree.

"Thomas, hello," Nora said, coming up to him.

"Ms. Rainer, a pleasure to see you again," he said.

"Please, it's Nora. We discussed that."

He allowed himself a polite smile, feeling his bow tie constrict against his throat. Today he wore one of deep, rich navy, a splash of yellow coming from the waddling ducks that adorned it. "Of course, Nora. Please, have a seat. Don't mind all the activity around here, from what I can tell, my neighbors really get into the Christmas spirit here, even though the tree is artificial—too many allergies among us all, I suppose. What I miss is the evergreen scent of pine."

"You'll have to visit my mother's house sometime, she believes a real tree is the only way to go. Besides, The Edge is hardly alone in getting ready for Christmas," she said. "Already the other businesses downtown have begun to hang lights outside, and there are several snowmen populating the park at Linden Square, turning its gazebo into a village hotspot—or, I guess, a coldspot, really, keeping them from melting."

"And at your store?"

"The only thing that says holiday there are those annoying bells over the door," she said.

"I'm sure you'll do the village proud," he said.

"We'll see. I've been so busy getting the interior of the store ready, I haven't yet had the chance to worry about the outside, my little red shingle notwithstanding—which is buried in snow right now. I don't even have any decorations for the outside."

"I'm sure Elsie would be happy to tell you how she used to do it," he said. "She's just back there, talking with her gals about the latest village gossip. Or creating more."

Nora stole a look behind her, saw the gaggle of gals and

two elderly men, both of whom seemed to be nodding off. "I'll take a pass. It's a new store, so new traditions," she said. "But of course that's not why I'm here, as you know. I have something special for you, but before I hand it over, I wonder, Thomas, how you've been feeling. It's seems you've been MIA lately from Linden Corners. I called the day of the storm and left a message with the receptionist at the main desk, she said you were out of town."

"Ah, yes, a weekly trip of mine," he said with a slight pause, "a doctor's appointment, up in Albany. And I'm afraid with the storm that battered us, this untrustworthy body of mine found it easier to stay holed up in a hotel in the capital until the worst of it had passed. A simple explanation, really, just an old man playing it safe. Elsie does me the great favor of taking me to the train station down in Hudson, where I catch Amtrak—a bit of going backward to go forward, but I have little choice. Driving is not an option I myself have."

Even as he offered up his explanation, the words rang hollow inside his mind, sounding like a sentence in search of a period. Thomas wondered if he had revealed too much. Nora had not really been grilling him, yet he suddenly felt like a suspect under interrogation lights, wiping at his brow. His hand came away sweaty, and he realized it had nothing to do with any suspicion on Nora's part, instead his eyes were gazing at a thin, hardcover book jutting out from the heavy bag she'd brought. Had she indeed found the book? How had she discovered it so quickly after its having gone missing for eighty years?

"My mother is the same way, she drives but she doesn't like to," she said.

"Time is not on anyone's side, Nora," he said. "Speaking of . . . perhaps I could see what you have uncovered?"

With such a prompt, Nora had no choice but to withdraw the book from her bag, and with a hesitant smile gracing her lips, she handed it over to Thomas. For a second he closed

his eyes, even as his shaky hands took hold of the thin volume, almost as though he wanted his senses to experience
this moment on separate planes, touch giving way to smell
as he put it up to his nose to breathe in its musty odor. But
then his eyes flew open and he gazed down on the once-
familiar image of Santa Claus himself, ol' Saint Nick and his
green suit. Green, he breathed, green, he heard himself speak
inside his mind . . . green, not red, and he felt the world grow
fuzzy around him, as though his body were being trans-
ported back in time to his initial discovery of the wrapped
present up in the farmhouse's attic and the subsequent pre-
sentation of the gift from his father. Oh, how he had reveled
in such joy that night, sitting on his father's lap and hearing
the sweet rhythm of the poem bounce off his tongue, swirling in the warm air around them, the pictures embedding
themselves in his subconscious.

"Nora . . ." he spoke, his voice a whisper.

"Is it the book? I mean, I know it's not the actual one you
owned, but . . . it's good?"

He stared at the cover, and then without another word he
began to flip through the pages. It wasn't the text he concentrated on, or the colorfully antique-looking illustrations, the
physical book was what captured his attention. Similar to the
book from his youth, it was hardbound but came without a
dust jacket, the artwork printed directly on the case. An
image of a friendly Saint Nick graced the cover, and on the
back was an illustration of his sleigh and reindeer flying off
into the glow of the night's silver moon. And just then he felt
the prickle of tears at the corner of his eyes and let them roll
down his cheeks.

"Oh Nora, what you have done for an old man . . . I can
never repay you."

"So . . . it's the same edition?" Her voice was a curious
mix of hope and worry.

He said nothing again for a while, silence falling between

them, nearly enveloping the entire recreation room. Like the gossip and the decorating had ceased, leaving Nora and Thomas alone to this moment in time, so long in coming, so fraught with doubt. Yet it was actually happening, the past somehow reaching beyond yesteryear to make a revelation in the present.

"Tell me more," he said, "like a piece of art, it must have a provenance."

And so Nora launched into her tale, detailing to him her online research and random visit to Elliot's Antiquarian Book Shop down in Hudson, and finally to ordering a used edition from a bookseller. Thomas listened and nodded, asking questions and commenting when he felt it was appropriate, and as the words spilled from Nora's mouth he wanted nothing more than to embrace her and thank her for her resourceful efforts. Yet a part of him held back, because he knew, deep down, that while this edition of *The Night before Christmas, or A Visit from Saint Nicholas* did indeed include a Santa dressed in a green suit, it was just a facsimile. But how to tell her? He saw the joy on her face, the look of a woman who took pride in the completion of her job, and so he had to weigh the impact of telling her the truth and have her keep looking for the original . . . or be content with her efforts.

"Nora Rainer, you are an angel," he finally said, clutching the book close to his heart.

"No, Thomas, I'm just a businesswoman," she said. "You hired me to do a job, I did it."

"And very well indeed, I might add," he said, not looking at her, focusing on the book cover and Santa in the green suit. "And you performed your duties with such great respect for the needs of your customer, no matter how crazy they may have sounded. This is just beautiful, the memories this volume evokes . . . I believe I need a moment to myself.

If you do not mind, my dear, I think I need to retire back to my apartment to peruse the volume very carefully. I'm afraid I've been left with an emotion I'm not quite ready to process, not in front of others. After so much time, to hold this dream in my hands, it's almost too much. Yes, much to absorb. And so I bid you *adieu,* Ms. Rainer . . . Nora, and wish you a very good day."

With that, Thomas stood up, his legs a bit unsteady as he grabbed the arm of the chair to balance him. He waved off any assistance from her, and began to walk out of the recreation room. That's when he found Nora suddenly at his side, looking like she had something on her mind.

"Yes, Nora?"

"It's not the book, is it? Not your book."

"It is. I assure you. Saint Nick is wearing a green suit," he said. "You did as I asked."

"Thomas . . . it's just a reproduction. It's not what you wanted."

"What I want is not achievable, Nora, too much time has passed. The world I knew has passed me by, and the only one who doesn't seem to realize that is the man I look at in the mirror every morning. It's high time I faced facts. I have lived so long . . . too long, they are reproducing things that should have already been put to rest. And speaking of rest, I think that's what I need most. Thank you, Nora, with all my heart," he said. Then, his voice grew serious, as he added, "Please do send me a bill. And merry Christmas."

And then, with the book securely tucked underneath his arm, he shuffled slowly down the corridor, knowing that his lack of speed denied him any chance at a dramatic exit, but his words more than made up for it. As though, even with three weeks remaining before the world would celebrate Christ's birthday—and indeed he would celebrate his eighty-fifth—he was saying good-bye to her.

"Thomas . . ."

Her voice lingered down the hallway, only to fall flat as it hit a closed door.

Three forty-seven A.M. according to the clock on his bedside table. Shards of moonlight slipped through closed blinds, cutting across his eyes to the point where they opened wide with weary exhaustion. Not that his usual twinkling eyes needed much prompting; sleep had already proved elusive during this long night, like so many others the past few weeks. His mind absorbed with matters more important than rest. He lay there, alone of course, in the soft comfort of his twin bed, staring at the shadows on the ceiling, trying to lull his mind into shutting down and falling into peaceful slumber. Such thoughts were only making the situation worse, to the point that he gazed over at the photograph on his bedside, edged by a silver frame, a black-and-white shot of a man dressed in a sharp-looking tuxedo, the woman at his side beautiful in pearl-encrusted ivory, a lace veil partially obscuring her features. Still, he could see her beaming face, her porcelain skin. Usually he took great comfort in the image, but tonight he knew nothing would soothe him. So he just gave up on forcing sleep's elusive muse to visit him, tossing back the covers. He stretched his legs out over the bed until they came to a rest on the floor.

Slowly padding his way to the closet, he slid open the door and pulled out his navy silk robe, wrapping it around his pajamas and cinching the belt tight against his waist. He then slid his bare feet into a pair of matching slippers that had been given to him just last Christmas; the contours of his toes already well imbedded.

Making his way to the darkened living room of his apartment, he reached for the book he'd placed earlier that day on the glass-topped coffee table. *The Night before Christmas, or A Visit from Saint Nicholas* was its officially published title—he'd forgotten this volume hadn't used "T'was." He ran his slightly bent fingers over the lettering, like braille to a blind man. The title said so much about what awaited you within its pages, like the use of the word *visit*. With such homespun images throughout the volume, who wouldn't want Saint Nick to pay a call to their home? Who didn't want gifts delivered to them, an acknowledgment of how nice they were? Why receive, when giving filled you with such joy?

Thomas sighed, a soft echo present in the hollow morning. What to do about the book, that was the decision mostly weighing on him. Did its presence really complete his mission, or was this facsimile edition simply another bitter disappointment in a life filled with them? Yes, Santa might be dressed in the green suit, but aside from that detail he just wasn't satisfied with the reproduction—it wasn't about quality, the book was wonderfully, lovingly reproduced. It was about having the original that continued to evade him, a lost treasure of his childhood, not unlike his father himself. Thomas had so much riding on possessing the book that had defined his early holiday memories, he shouldn't be surprised at the disappointment that had settled inside him. To him, the book was the bridge between life and death, a final, tenuous reminder of the bond he had shared with a father he'd barely known, a representation of what he'd lost when his father went off to fight—and die—in the war. While the situation he was in now had its differences, one fact remained a constant: the looming sense of loss.

Cradling the hardcover book in his arms, Thomas made his way toward the front door of his apartment, unlocking it to emerge into the harshly lit corridor. All of Edgestone Retirement Home was quiet, the squeak of his door echoing down the hall. In his mind he heard the phrase "not a creature was stirring, not even a mouse," and the famous line brought a tentative smile to his lips. He gingerly made his way to the quiet recreation center, bypassing the front desk, which was not occupied at this late hour; perhaps the night nurse was grabbing a needed cup of coffee in the kitchen. He found his way to the Christmas tree, situated near the fireplace, finally decorated with lights and shiny ornaments, with tinsel that had glistened. The tree seemed tired, its lights turned off, silent as the cold night. Such a thing didn't last, if he was awake, so, too, could be the tree, and so he flipped the light switch and the darkness of the room suddenly was cast in a colorful glow of illumination.

Pulling up a chair, Thomas settled down and opened up the book. He began to read, silently, his lips reading the couplets even though he knew them all by heart. What captured his attention were the illustrations, Santa in that green suit. The effect made Thomas remember his father, who had also worn a uniform of green, a faded, muted palette the army somehow found appropriate for sending innocent men off to battle. Closing his eyes, he conjured an image of his father, and then at his side, his mother, also long since gone from this world. She had lived to a ripe age of seventy-seven, having watched as her son grew, graduated from high school and college, saw him secure a teaching career at the local university, witnessed his wedding to the beautiful Missy, craved the grandchildren that never came. Never once had she wavered in her support of the boy she'd given birth to. She'd never remarried, Lars Van Diver had been all she ever desired, and now Thomas held tight to the belief they had long since been reunited.

The shuffling of feet on the hard flooring drew him out of his world and into the present. Approaching him was a figure backlit by the glow of the tree, her shadow approaching first.

"Well, Thomas Van Diver, shouldn't you be asleep?"

"I could say the same for you, Elsie Masters."

"Oh, some nights, I just can't rest. Guess my body is still getting used to this new life. It's always nighttime when doubt creeps in, when I question my recent decisions. Selling the business . . . renting the building, moving here. When you reach a certain age, you start doing things because that's what's expected of you. You listen to your brain rather than staying true to what your heart is telling you. Age brings wisdom, the experts say. The experts must not be elderly."

"Very well said, Elsie," he replied with a gentle nod, his voice quiet, almost reverential at this late hour . . . or was it considered an early hour? No one really knew whether it was the dark of last night or the dawn of a fresh day.

"I've never seen you here," Elsie said. "Not at this hour."

"That tells me that this isn't your first nocturnal visit."

"Oh, I've wandered these halls many nights since I moved in," she said, "but tonight was different. When I saw the lights of the Christmas tree I knew I wasn't alone in my insomnia. You switched on the tree lights?"

"Indeed, I did."

"May I ask why?"

"Do you know what today is . . . I mean, what yesterday was?"

"December fifth," she said. "*Sinterklass*. The annual Dutch celebration of Saint Nick."

"Linden Corners has never forgotten its Dutch heritage, has it?"

"The windmill is a constant reminder of the original settlers of this land."

"Including the Van Diver family," he said.

"They built the windmill, right where it stands today."

He felt pride strike his heart. It was an uncommon feeling for him.

Without asking, Elsie took up a seat beside him, touching her hand to his arm. "Can you tell me something, Thomas?"

"If I can."

"You obviously are a man of traditions. Does *Sinterklass* have meaning for you?"

He smiled despite his unsettled mood, reaching far into the past for the warm memory. "Family, for starters," he said with a hint of remorse lodged in his throat. "Not that my young self ever understood it, but my father insisted that every December fifth we decorate the Christmas tree, it was his way of honoring his ancestors. All those Van Divers who came to the Hudson River Valley way back in the eighteen hundreds and made this their new home—the very same men and women who built the farmhouse and established a community farm, and one summer built the windmill that still stands today."

"After you left Linden Corners, did you continue those traditions?"

"Some, not all," he said, sorrow laced in his quiet voice. "My mother was not Dutch, so when we moved to Virginia to live with her parents—my maternal grandparents, the only ones I ever knew—traditions changed. As the years progressed I guess we lost our appreciation for all my father had taught us, taking on more of the O'Neil clan's identity. The Dutch influence I'd been introduced to early in my life gave way to the Irish, and our once-solemn holiday became a raucous celebration of life. And when I married, I, too, married an Irishwoman—and even more of my childhood traditions faded away. But the one thing I insisted upon, each year—and that included my teen years and my married days—was that the Christmas tree went up on December fifth—on *Sinterklass*. That was the one thing I would not change."

"Thomas, oh, I know I talk a good game around the others and I know what they think of me. Elsie Masters, she's the life of the party because she's always getting into everyone's business," she said, "but it's not just about gossip, I do care. About people, yes, but mostly about the keeping alive of this village's past, its history. Who knows, maybe it's the late hour that's got me confessing to such things. Think about it, though, I would not have devoted my entire life to selling antiques if I was a person who dreamed of what the future held. I like to see how the past impacts our present day, it's one of the few parts of life we can control. The future? Eh. For my money, we may as well call it the unknown. So while some folks may find my style abrasive, I'm really a gentle soul."

"Oh Miss Elsie, that is clear to me," he said, "the generosity you have shown me . . ."

She waved off his comment, embarrassed by the easy compliment. She was quiet for a moment, but Thomas could tell there were words waiting to spill out from her, and he readied himself for her revelation. He knew that Elsie Masters had suffered a loss, too, it was why she was here among friends, seeking comfort in their company, not unlike himself. That said, it might be four in the morning, but Elsie was still Elsie and that brought a smile to his lips. "Thomas . . . I don't mean to pry, it's not my nature . . . no, don't laugh, it's not my fault people tell me things, I rarely ask them. But tonight I will, because I think it's important." She hesitated, Thomas saying nothing, just waiting. "Those rides I give you to the Hudson station, you're not catching the train to Albany, that much I know. I stayed behind one day to make sure the train was on time . . . and there I saw you emerge from the station and board the train that went in the opposite direction. Toward New York."

Thomas remained still for some moments, lost in his own thoughts. The entire retirement center was so quiet, peaceful, it was almost like all of the residents were listening for his answer. But in truth it was just him and Elsie and a tree that sparkled with the spirit of the season. Since Elsie herself had been so kind to him, he felt there was no holding back anymore.

"No, I do not go to Albany," he said, "New York City is my destination."

"To see someone?"

He just nodded, even though he would not allow words to confirm hers.

Expecting her to push the issue, her next action caught him by surprise. Rising from her chair, she put a warm hand to his shoulder and squeezed ever so gently. Her rare bit of subtlety washed over him like a gentle wave of gratitude. He reached up, his hand resting atop hers. The warmth spread from their hands to their faces, rueful, regretful smiles cementing their friendship.

"I'm sorry if I pushed too far, Thomas," she said.

He nodded, not sure if his action was forgiveness or just acknowledging her apology. She understood him so well, it seemed, even though she was fifteen years younger than him. She knew about growing older, people and objects both, she knew their value.

"Thank you, Elsie, for all you've done for me . . . for us."

"That book in your hands, I can see its title," she said. "Am I to assume it's part of the reason you're here in Linden Corners, right?"

"No, Elsie," he said with a shake of his head, fighting back tears. "It's the entire reason I came back to Linden Corners. As you said, it's time for the past to meet the present, and I only hope this book is enough."

CHAPTER 14

NORA

She listened to the plan and thought they had both lost their minds.

This was not a day to go trekking through the woods to chop down a tree.

"Mom, it's freezing out. Ten degrees, last I heard."

Gerta Connors, seventy-five years young and with a determined mind of her own, simply waved off her daughter's worries. "Nonsense, Nora, if you wait until the weather improves then you'll be celebrating Christmas in July. Besides, I promised Travis he could help cut down the tree. . . ."

"Mom! That could be dangerous. You should have consulted me."

"Goodness, your reaction, Nora. It's just a saw, no one's talking about using an ax. And Travis said he would be careful, and besides, we'll have plenty of help around us, Green's Tree Farm has a sterling reputation. Albert, Sr., himself has been running the place for more than thirty years. I've certainly never heard of any accidents occurring there." Then, placing a comforting hand upon her daughter's shoulder, Gerta offered up a bit of advice whether Nora wanted to hear it or not. "Dear, you have to let the boy grow up. With his father away doing whatever it is he needs to do to find himself, Travis has got to learn he's responsible for his own happiness—and I don't know a better influence on such matters than his headstrong mother. Look at what you've accomplished already in coming back to Linden Corners—for yourself and for him."

"Now you're just manipulating me," she said.

Gerta shrugged, a knowing grin making her gray eyes dance. "I'm a mother, it's what we do. Something you should know by now. Nora, you may be a grown-up, but I'm still the mother, so I'm telling you right now to go upstairs and get properly dressed for the day. We'll be outside in the cold most of it, and we don't want to disappoint Travis. That poor boy has been talking about nothing else all week, he said he'd never chopped down his own tree before, you always bought yours at the stand by the grocery store."

"Until Dave realized a few years ago he had an allergy and we went artificial," Nora said, realizing the tree metaphor could also be used to describe the state of her marriage. She would have laughed had she found the irony even remotely funny.

"Well, Dave's not here and until he is, Travis gets a real tree," Gerta said. "A visit up to the Berkshires is just what this little family of ours needs to put us in the holiday spirit."

As Nora started up the stairs, Travis came bounding down them, nearly crashing into her. He was all bundled up, his parka making him look like the Michelin Man, big and puffy, and the color on his cheeks made him seem like he'd already spent too much time outside. Nora knew it was the flush of excitement, and seeing him leap off the landing and practically fall into the arms of his grandmother she felt a wave of affection. Her mother was right, today was all about Travis, and even though it was a Saturday and she should be opening up the store, what were a couple of hours to play hooky in the snow-encrusted woods? She was back downstairs in a matter of minutes and ready for their adventure.

"Okay, Travis, ready for the checklist? Hat, scarf, mittens."

"Check, check, and sort of check. I have gloves, since Grandma says they'll give my fingers better flexibility," he said, raising his hands in the air to show his thick woolen gloves.

"Sounds like a plan. Mom? You ready?"

"Oh, I'm all set, just waiting for our ride."

"Our ride? We'll just all pile into the Mustang and . . . oh wait, that reminds me, we need some rope to tie the tree to the roof . . . or will Mr. Green take care of that?"

"Oh no, Nora dear, you don't understand. We have company today, so you won't have to worry about the tree. We'll just put it in the truck along with theirs."

Nora felt a sense of dread; wasn't this just a family day?

Just then the crunch of tires on frozen snow could be heard, along with the honk of a horn. Nora peered out the living room curtains, saw the familiar old truck come to a stop. Brian Duncan emerged from the driver's side, helping Janey down from the passenger seat like she was used to it. She was bundled up like the rest of them, with only Brian less than prepared for the cold, his jacket open to reveal a simple shirt and no sweater. Did the man not even own a scarf, she wondered, and then wondered again why she was even worrying. He wants to freeze, let him.

"Brian Duncan, you'll catch your death," Gerta said as she opened the door.

"At least he's wearing a hat, that's how you know it's cold," Janey added. "Otherwise, he does not set a very good example on how to dress for winter. Sometimes I need to be the adult."

"Well, at least I've taught you how to be that," Brian said.

"I'm an adult, too," Travis piped in. "I'm going to chop down our tree."

The two kids chatted amiably about Brian's misadventures with the ax last year, even as they eagerly hopped into the backseat of the truck. Nora found herself stuffed in the middle of the front seats, the conversation between Gerta and Brian making her feel like she was watching a tennis match, with commentary from the row behind messing with her concentration. This day wasn't shaping up in any way she'd envisioned, and truthfully, she had other things on her mind.

Four days of bitter cold temperatures had passed since she had handed Thomas the book he'd asked her to find, and his quiet reaction was something she'd given much thought to since. As much as he had tried to mask it, she knew he was disappointed that all she had found was a facsimile edition of the book, published within the last twenty years. He'd attempted to assuage her guilt by saying she had performed a near miracle in finding even this edition, but she knew it was just hollow praise. What, exactly, should she do about it? Continue her search, and even if by some spark of inspiration she did begin again, could she ever hope to find the book in time for his deadline? From the start, Thomas's request had come with a ticking clock, even if he wasn't willing to admit to her the reason why. Even now, she still didn't understand the book's significance beyond it having been a gift from his father. It wasn't like she had months to keep searching for the original, Christmas was looming, and she needed no further proof than today—lights lining houses stretching beyond the village, the five of them en route to chopping down their own trees. No doubt their trip would lead to an afternoon of decorating, perhaps dinner with Brian and Janey, and before long she would have lost yet another day.

"You're quiet today, Nora," she heard Brian say, breaking her from her thoughts.

"Sorry, I've just got a few things on my mind," she said.

"Care to share? Still got another ten miles till we reach Green's Tree Farm."

"Just drive," she said.

With a free hand, he saluted her. "Yes, ma'am."

Gerta chuckled. "Don't even try, Brian, she's been in a mood for days."

"I have not!" Nora protested.

"Mom has trouble relaxing."

"Hey, you know, I do know how to wield an ax," Nora said with mock protest.

"And just think, when the police arrest you, you already know a good defense attorney," Brian responded.

Everyone in the close confines of the truck laughed aloud, except Nora, of course, but then she couldn't help but laugh, too, when Janey said, "What does wield mean?"

The mood in the truck much lightened, they made their way up the winding roads that took them beyond Linden Corners and neighboring villages Craryville and Hillsdale, the latter the largest of the villages in this part of Columbia County. Northward they turned, gradually pushing up Route 22 toward the border between New York State and Massachusetts and the lush countryside of the often misty Berkshire Mountains. Nora gazed out the windshield, admitting to herself how beautiful it all looked, like a postcard. Sure the air outside was freezing, but from the truck the expansive sky looked like blue crystal, and the rocky terrain was so different from the verdant, low-lying Linden Corners it was amazing to her they'd only driven a short distance.

At last they turned into the large lot at Green's Tree Farm, parking amidst many other cars and SUVs, where they unloaded themselves and their supplies from the truck. The jolly, old Albert Green, Sr., greeted them warmly, giving Janey and Travis extra attention. He even remarked that he remembered Janey from last year, with her scrunching up her nose in that way that even Nora had come to recognize.

"You do?" Janey asked.

"Think this round belly of mine and white beard is pretend?"

"That does not make you Santa," she said matter-of-factly. "He lives at the North Pole."

"Cold enough today, we might as well be living there," he said with a hearty laugh of ho, ho, ho. "Okay, you all have yourselves a nice expedition up into my hills, I'll be here when you get back, give you some instructions . . ."

"I know, I know, on how to care for it so well, it'll keep alive through June," Janey said. "That's what you said last year."

"And the same holds true this year, little lady."

Again, she scrunched her nose. "I still don't know why . . ."

"Why you'd want to have a tree in your house that long," he said, leaning down to tap a cold finger upon her red nose. "See, I told you I remembered you."

"That still doesn't mean you're Santa Claus," Janey said, and that's when Brian stepped in and told her enough with the chattering, let's not waste any more time finding our trees.

"Before it's our teeth that are doing all the chattering," Gerta added.

And so the five of them began the trek up winding, snowy paths. Travis dashed ahead with his strong athleticism, Janey's little legs trying in vain to keep up with his long strides. Nora remarked to herself how much her son had grown in the six weeks since they'd arrived in Linden Corners, with his voice deeper and his body developing a sinewy grace. Just then she heard her own knee crack as she bent down to clear random sticks that hindered her mother's progress. If Travis was getting older, she had to admit, so was she.

"Grandma, come look at this one, do you think it's too tall . . . ?"

Travis took hold of Gerta's hand and led her gently up a side path to where he'd picked one out of the tallest pine trees around. It looked all the more taller with the two kids dancing around its base. Janey was pointing upward at its top and wondering how they would get the angel positioned there, with Gerta adding maybe the angel would just have to fly there, and that sparked a whole fresh debate among the three of them. As laughter and squeals of delight filled the fresh-smelling canyons, pines and firs lined up like sentries, Nora felt a chill seep beneath her zippered coat.

"You cold?"

"Aren't you, Brian?"

He shrugged indifferently. "I've grown impervious to the cold. Guess I've gotten used to the winters up here, I'm fine."

"It's so cold, I doubt even snowmen would want to venture outdoors," she said, "and yet . . . here we are. I don't know how my mother does it, must be the fact she's lived here all her life. As you said, impervious."

"Speaking of, how goes things with Thomas?"

"Not sure the transition works, Brian, but I'll play along. I found his book, sort of."

"Sort of?"

"It's a long story, I'll tell you in the summer when it's warm."

Brian grinned, his breath misty. "I eagerly await your tale," he said. "You know, you never did get around to asking me about the Van Diver family and their history at the farmhouse. That was one of your favors, right? Something about other families that lived there?"

"I did, yes, but once I got the lead on Thomas's book, well, it all seemed irrelevant."

"I could have told you that day we traveled down to Hudson, it's an easy enough answer. The Sullivans bought the house directly from the Van Divers," he said. "Dan Sullivan—Janey's biological father—he grew up in the farmhouse bought by his grandparents and lived there after his parents passed and he married Annie."

"Doesn't seem to be a house with much luck," she said.

"Oh, I have a feeling Janey will break the curse," he said. "No matter how old she gets, she'll still retain that youthful vigor, it's just inherent within her. And as much as I have Dan and Annie Sullivan to thank for her genes, I think it's the Van Diver ancestors who deserve more of the credit for what Linden Corners is today—after all, it was their decision to build the windmill. And while I know the Van Divers built it for practical purposes back then, today it just spins its daily dose of inspiration. Who Janey would be without it, I hesitate to say."

"Travis is the complete opposite," Nora said. "He's had to grow up so fast, more so than if Dave had not decided to play to the stereotype of a man fast-approaching fifty. A midlife crisis, I mean, really? I didn't know I had married such a predictable man. The way Travis has rallied during this adjustment, sometimes I believe he's the one holding me up."

"I think it's different when you lose a mother at such an impressionable age, it's like Janey wants to stay a little girl—despite her claims of having to play the adult sometimes," Brian said. "The older she gets, it just means she's that much more removed from the time she had with Annie. This time of year is particularly sensitive, she and Annie had what seems a treasure trove of traditions that I've tried to uphold. The annual visit to Green's Tree Farm is one of them."

"That's so good that you're so considerate of her feelings," she said, but in a defensive tone added, "But you know, their situations are hardly similar. Travis didn't lose his father."

"It wasn't a case of comparing the two of them," he said. "It's just . . . maybe in a kid's mind, death and desertion are not dissimilar."

"He didn't desert his son," she said, her voice rising in anger. "Bastard just . . . just . . ."

"Nora, it's okay."

"No, it's not," she said, angry with herself for letting the conversation go even this far. "I'm better than this. I've had more pressure in the courtroom, and trust me, Dave is a pussycat compared to some of the brutal judges I've been before. No matter, I've never once spoken ill of Dave, not in front of my son and I'm not going to start now. He made his choice, I made mine."

Brian put a comforting hand to her face, trying to soothe the anger lines from around her eyes. "I don't know how we got started on this, but what do you say we drop it? This is supposed to be fun. Let's just go pick a tree."

"No, no, let's finish it. You've got a question, I can tell."

"Okay, but if you don't like it you can tell me to take a flying leap," he said. "But, I will remind you that it was you who said she needed a friend."

"Fine, Brian, my good friend. Ask away."

"What's the real reason Dave left?"

She didn't respond, not right away, not even sure she could get the words out. Set amidst this seemingly endless forest of trees, the sky was smaller somehow, like the world was closing in on them, around her heart. The only way to conquer this growing sense of claustrophobia was to let out a scream, something she wasn't all that keen to do, not here, and not now. She didn't want to scare Travis or her mother . . . or any of the other people who were busy wandering the trails with axes and saws and other tools. So she just allowed herself a tiny chuckle, one tiny slip of emotion.

"His boss recommended him for the job, and he accepted it."

"And the rest of the story?"

"Oh right, Dave's boss was going overseas, too," she said, "and of course the two of them were, and continue to be having, an affair."

"And Dave's boss is . . ."

There was a protracted silence before Nora realized what he meant and she laughed so loud the sound rattled nearby trees, snow on their branches floating to the ground. "Oh, oh . . . no, thankfully we didn't have to deal with that issue, too. No, no, Brian, Dave's boss is female. That was rich, though. I don't think I've laughed that hard in weeks. Oh boy, that would have been something. Come on, enough of this nonsense, we came to get a tree, let's go grab one."

"Two," he said, "things always come better in twos."

Nora decided the better response was to just punch him in the arm, and she did, her fist landing hard. He seemed to accept the jab with ease. When they rejoined the group, she noticed Janey tossing her one of her patented, curious looks, but the young girl didn't say a word. She simply grabbed Brian's hand and pulled him helplessly toward the tree of her choice.

Travis finally picked out the perfect tree, an eight-foot Douglas fir that smelled as beautiful as it looked, with full, green branches spreading out above a thick stump that was proving difficult against the rusty teeth of the saw. With Brian's assistance, Travis sliced at the base of the tree and as Nora urged them on, the tree finally separated with a crack. One crack and then it came crashing to the ground into a powdery puff of snow. In short order, Janey's tree followed, almost as though she'd chosen it already but didn't want to be upstaged by Travis. Their bodies near frozen from the long trek deep into the farm, they dragged their bounty down the snowy hill and to the truck.

Mr. Green complimented Travis and Janey on their fine choices and helped first tie them then load them into the rear of the truck. Glad to be back inside the heat of the truck, they drove back to Linden Corners poorer in pocket though richer for the experience, Travis going on and on about what it had felt like the moment his saw sliced through the last of the stubborn bark. With Gerta promising fresh apple pie and steaming cups of hot chocolate, "yeah, with tiny marshmallows," Janey happily adding as an afterthought, they headed back to Linden Corners with the promise of heat and nourishment.

But as they arrived into the dusky downtown area of Linden Corners, Nora asked if Brian wouldn't mind letting her out in front of A Doll's Attic.

"Mom, what about the hot chocolate?"

"Save me some, okay? There's something I've got to take care of at the store and it can't wait," she said, turning her head back to assure Travis that she'd only be an hour, not more. "Besides, nothing we can do with the tree yet, it needs to relax its branches before we can start decorating it. Help Brian get it out of the truck and into the stand, I'll be home before you know it."

Brian pulled into the small parking lot near the old Victorian-style home, the truck idling as Nora quickly hopped out. Before pulling away, he remarked on how dark the building looked, even in the falling light of day. "You should put some up Christmas lights, compared to the rest of the village the outside of your shop looks like the single burned-out light on a string of bulbs. If you want, I can help. Janey gave me boxes of staples last year for Christmas, there are plenty left to attach them to the building."

"It's because he used so many when lighting up the windmill," Janey offered.

"I'll keep it all under advisement," Nora said, wishing she hadn't. She sounded too much like a lawyer right then, all businesslike. She smiled meekly in an attempt to keep her options open and then closed the passenger side door. The truck drove off with a friendly honk sounding in the air, but to her the effect was hollow, emphasizing the fact that she was alone.

It might have only been three in the afternoon, but around her she felt the sunlight was fast diminishing, darkness coming sooner for her than others. Maybe that had to do with the lack of Christmas lights around the edge of her store, lacking any kind of invitation. For half a second she reconsidered Brian's offer of help, told herself that could wait. Something else was motivating her, and so she made her way up the path toward her entrance, unlocking the door. Again she encountered that jangle of bells overhead, their sound lingering as she closed the door, making her way quickly behind the counter. Without hesitation, she fired up her laptop and, waiting for the screen to come to life, she ran to the kitchen to boil water for tea—she was still freezing from their winter excursion into the woods.

At last settled in the quiet of her store, she sipped at herbal tea while she looked through her recent online searches. Because somewhere between complaining about the cold and cutting down a Christmas tree, Nora had found herself thinking not of her family but one that had existed years ago. No, the moment was not about she and Travis and her mother celebrating the holiday on the twenty-fifth, not about Brian and Janey waking to another Christmas morning in the shadow of the windmill reminding them of Annie. Who consumed her thoughts was Thomas Van Diver, he who seemed to have no one in the world with whom to exchange gifts. Yet for some reason he still sought out the book he had lost during his childhood, and if not to give it as a gift to someone, then what purpose did it serve? He hadn't been very forthcoming with a reason why, all he'd asked of her was to find it. And she knew she had failed him, settling rather than pushing.

The sense of failure ate at her, as it had all week. Even without Dave—the man to whom she had promised a lifetime of love to, even with him gone from their lives, probably for good—she still had a lot to be thankful for this season. Her son and ever-patient mother, this store and the opportunity it had afforded her, they all played their part in giving her the chance to strip away the façade of her business life and return her to a simpler time. That was life in Linden Corners, embracing a quality of life where neighbor looked after neighbor, where help was just a phone call away. Or, in this case, in an attempt at modernization, an Internet search away.

She went online and returned to the bookmarked pages where she had found the facsimile edition, looking at the picture of the cover on the upper left-hand corner, reading through the details that helped potential buyers make their decisions. Something about the book was nagging at her, a detail that she had overlooked. She read over the specs one more time—the title, author, illustrator, publication date, as well as the many customer reviews posted below, and that's when she found it . . . wonder filling her eyes, a true *eureka* moment. Because there among the posted reviews was a five-star review from a man named Nicholas Casey, who wrote the following: "This lovingly restored edition is a faithful reproduction of my great-great-great-grandfather's personal interpretation of Moore's classic story, complete with the Victorian legend of Saint Nick dressed not in his traditional red suit but in a green suit."

Nora looked back at the credit line again and for once her eyes focused beyond the author's name, Clement Clarke Moore, and instead on the illustrator's name. Of course, how could she have been so stupid? The key to the book lay in the unique illustrations; Moore never wrote of a green suit, it was something that grew out of the painter's fabrication. With each book published, the variable in each edition came courtesy of the artwork. Alexander Casey was credited as the illustrator here, and now, over one hundred years later, his descendant was posting an online review about the publisher's restored version of the long out-of-print volume.

Closing out of the web browser she was on, Nora typed in the name *Alexander Casey* in a search engine and found a short Wikipedia article about the little-known artist. He had been born in 1842, died in 1907, and he had spent his life as a vibrant, colorful chronicler of scenes of the Northeast region of the United States, having resided in Lee, Massachusetts, a historic village located in the heart of the Berkshires. Not quite an artist of Rockwell's reputation, Alexander Casey was not without his admirers. Nora couldn't believe what she was reading, just a couple hours ago she had been in the midst of those lush mountains, no more than thirty minutes from Lee. Now she knew the secret to Thomas's lost book might just lie close over the border. With her heart beating over her surprise discovery, she began to type furiously, the *tap tap tap* of her fingers across the keyboard like a staccato burst of ideas. When she was done, she had found the descendant, Nicholas Casey, still alive, still living in Lee, and with it came a phone number. His first name was not lost on her.

But she didn't call, not right away.

She thought of calling Thomas to tell him she had a lead on the real edition. She thought then of the expression on his face when she had handed him the facsimile edition and she wasn't sure she could handle a second dose of disappointment. Despite what she'd learned, what if this Nicholas Casey couldn't help her, what if the reproduction had been published because there were no original editions left, long out of print and gone from this world? She had to tread carefully here, it was when you tried too hard to do your best that you offered up the biggest risk.

Heck, she thought, nothing ventured, nothing gained.

She was about to pick up the phone when it rang, the sound reverberating off silent walls.

"Hello?"

"Mom?"

"Hey, baby."

"Hey, you promised . . . no more nicknames. . . ."

"Sorry. Yes, Mr. Rainer, how can I help you?"

"And you don't need to be so formal," he said, "but you do need to come home."

"Soon, I said I'd only be an hour."

"Mom, it's six o'clock, Grandma's got dinner on the stove, Brian and Janey are still here."

She'd lost all track of time, the hours flying by as her search had consumed her. Right now she was torn between her son's needs and Thomas Van Diver's request and realized there was little choice. She remembered her promise to Travis on the day they'd pulled into Linden Corners. She'd messed up big-time with Halloween, and Thanksgiving had been a cloying day at her sister Victoria's house, with Travis lost among all his girl cousins. She had assured Travis that Christmas would be as special as she could make it. He was her priority.

Thomas Van Diver had waited nearly eighty years to find his book, what was one more day? Nora knew she could phone the illustrator's relative tomorrow and who knew what she might learn? She just might be journeying farther beyond Green's Tree Farm and into the misty hills of the Berkshires, where perhaps she would finally find the solution to a mystery that until today had seemed to offer up no clues.

"Tell Grandma I'll be right there, and . . ."

"I know, have a glass of wine ready when you get here," he said. "I mean, why not, we drank all the hot chocolate. And Janey finished all the marshmallows. She said it was one of her family traditions, but she seems to have a lot of them. What about us, Mom? Do we have any traditions left, or is everything about Christmas brand-new?"

CHAPTER 15

BRIAN

The morning after the adventure at Green's Tree Farm, Brian Duncan awoke with a mission to launch his and Janey's second Christmas celebration in grand fashion, and it began with an early wake-up call that found him making his way to the kitchen. He put on coffee knowing that with all he needed to accomplish today, caffeine was just the opening gambit. He would crave all the energy he could muster, and what better way to get started than with a hearty breakfast. It was the irresistible sizzling smell of bacon that awakened Janey, she appearing in short order dressed in her purple pajamas and rubbing her eyes with the lingering effects of sleep.

"Morning, sleepyhead."

"Hi, Dad, wow, you're up early."

"It's going to be a busy day."

"But it's Sunday, usually it's nice and quiet, we just play."

"But with Christmas getting closer, we have to get ready."

"There sure are a lot of things to do to get ready for just one day," she said.

"Yes, but isn't it all worth it? Remember last year, all those great gifts?"

"That weren't under the tree," she said.

She would never let him forget that Christmas morning, when he'd fallen asleep on the sofa while all of her wrapped gifts remained securely hidden inside a locked closet inside the windmill, once Annie's hiding place. Their first Christmas morning together had been a near bust, but in the end he and the red toboggan won out over thick banks of snow and had saved the day. Sometimes he thought it was Annie's magic that had done it, fueling their day with the revolutions of the windmill, a day after a blizzard had blanketed the countryside.

"Hey, our Christmas worked out pretty great, I seem to remember."

"Yes, it did. And don't say 'hey.' "

Brian had become a stickler for proper grammar and full sentences, picking up where Annie had left off. Even on a cold, early Sunday morning, it was proper to speak properly.

"Okay, little lady, will it be French toast or pancakes?"

"Dad, it's Sunday!"

Janey was a stickler for routines. "Right, pancakes it is."

He busied himself with batter made from scratch, the sizzle of butter on the griddle filling the kitchen with wonderful scents. Janey set out plates and silverware and real maple syrup, and before long they were sitting down to their usual Sunday feast, Janey pouring more syrup on her plate than was needed.

"You're plenty sweet already," he said.

But her reaction surprised him, because she didn't respond at all. She just cut a fork into the stack of golden pancakes, taking a big bite, repeating the process again, again. Oh, uh, Brian thought, he knew this version of Janey. Something was on her mind and from her silence he took that to mean she hadn't yet formulated her thoughts. This ought to be interesting. What had changed since yesterday? Just a harmless day in the woods with Gerta and her family.

"Did you have fun yesterday?"

"Yes," she said. "I always like getting the tree."

"And tonight we're going to decorate it."

"I'm glad, I can't wait to hang my name ornament on one of the highest branches."

"I'll help you," Brian said.

"I'm sure I can do it myself."

Yup, there it was, that streak of independence that only showed up when she was upset or concerned about something; he'd seen it all during the holiday season last year, less times during the past year. He thought they had worked out their issues, learned to communicate. But with an impressionable girl like Janey who rarely missed observing human nature, you had to stay on your toes. She could blindside you with a comment faster than Nora Rainer could pull out from a parking spot. And if his metaphor seemed out of the blue, turned out . . . it wasn't.

"Do you like Nora?" Janey asked, her voice serious.

Brian's fork was midway to his mouth and it never got any further. He set it down on his plate, gathering up his thoughts as he chewed the last bites of bacon. "Sure, she's a nice woman," he said, being deliberately obtuse.

"No, I mean, do you like her, like her?"

"Oh, you mean like in school, when boys have secret crushes on girls?"

Janey rolled her eyes. "Dad, now you're being silly. And I'm being serious."

Guess "like her, like her" was a serious topic for a nine-year-old. He would have to be very careful with this issue, last year Janey had become fascinated with couples—with his friend John and his new girlfriend, Anna; with his sister, Rebecca, and her boy-toy friend whose name escaped Brian at the moment; and of course with Mark and Sara, accurately predicting their engagement before they had made an announcement. She'd also been interested in Brian's past love life when she heard about his high school sweetheart,

Lucy, his big city girlfriend, Maddie, not to mention his love for her mother, Annie Sullivan. Fear had kept her awake many nights, her trembling body scared that Brian would fall in love with some new woman and want to leave her behind. He'd managed to avoid that subject most of the year, mostly because there hadn't been a woman in the picture . . . until now. Until Nora.

"No, Janey, I'm not interested in Nora, at least, not in the way you're thinking," he said. "Remember when I showed up in Linden Corners? I had problems to work out and everyone in town helped me out, which I'm still so thankful for. Well, now it's Nora's turn, and she needs friends."

"So you're her friend?"

"Just her friend."

"Because she's married? Travis says his mom and dad are still together."

Wow, she was really throwing the book at him this morning, it wasn't even nine o'clock. "No, Janey, Nora being married has nothing to do with it. Even if she was single and I was available, she and I would still just be friends. Like me and Cynthia."

That comment seemed to appease her, as she went back to eating her pancakes.

"I don't think I would want Travis as a brother," she said.

"Why is that, Janey? Do you like him, like him?"

She stopped chewing as she dropped her fork; her face grew three shades of red. Even so, her words defied her flushed look as she said, "Oh, ick! Brian Duncan, you have to be the silliest man ever. Me, like Travis. I don't like boys."

He had to stifle the laugh, hoping not to choke on his pancakes.

"Eat up, young lady, you've got a big day ahead of you," he said. "You promised Cynthia you would go Christmas shopping with her and Jake."

"Jake I like, he's not like other boys."

No wonder. Janey liked to do all the talking; it was no surprise she preferred the company of an infant.

The shopping spree up to the mall in Albany was really just an excuse to get Janey out from underfoot. Not that Brian necessarily wanted to get rid of her, but with what he had to accomplish this afternoon it would be easier without her darting around the windmill all day, asking questions, wanting him to stop and make snow angels or go sledding down the snowy hill. Plus, he wanted to surprise her upon her return; the mere thought of her reaction was fuel enough for him to get started.

And start he did, the moment Cynthia had driven off with Janey in the backseat keeping little Jake company. Brian made his way to the barn, a rickety old building that had seen better days. There he climbed up the ladder attached to the inside, emerging onto the second level. From a big box he withdrew what seemed an endless string of lights, unraveling them to create one long thin line; he plugged one string into another until they were all connected, and then inserted one of the ends into the outlet. The barn lit up with a bright white glow, so powerful it was like the sun itself burned against the walls and ceilings. Checking them one by one, he made some replacements for those that had burned out, though for the most part the lights were as good as they were last year. Even so, he'd bought a few extras down at Ackroyd's just in case.

Gathering them back into the box, he then opened the swing door on the second level, figuring that was a far easier way to get them down than risking the box on the ladder. He pushed the box off the ledge, watched as it fell down ten feet to the snow-covered ground, a thick white drift helping to break its fall. Then he scrambled back down the ladder, pulling out a sled from the side of the barn. Outside, he placed the box on the sled, gathered up his staple gun and supplies, the ladder, then made his way down the hill and toward the windmill.

Compared to the past week's chill, today the air was a balmy thirty-four, with the wind all but quiet, which meant the windmill was silent as well, its sails thankfully sleeping. This would make his task that much easier, and so before the fickle forces of Mother Nature decided to play with him, he set about working. For the next hour he concentrated on the lights, trying to remember the pattern he'd used last year. From the base of the tower, all the way up to the cap that contained the spinning mechanism, Brian stapled string after string, until the lights coated the old mill. When he'd come up with the idea last year, he had pondered how to put the lights on the sails, knowing that in a strong wind the cords would get tangled and snap, and so in the end he'd foregone the sails. He did the same today, hoping for the same shadowy effect upon the reflective snow he'd produced just a year ago.

As he was nearly done with the first side of the windmill, he saw a figure emerge over the hillside. He checked his watch to make sure he hadn't lost track of time; he wanted to be done before Cynthia and Janey returned. But it was neither of them, instead he saw the familiar face of Bradley Knight coming toward him. Brian waved, receiving a hearty one back.

"Need some help?" Bradley asked.

"You? I wouldn't want you to soil your clothes."

"This old shirt?" asked Bradley with an affable laugh. He was dressed in a crisp white dress shirt, visible beneath his yellow Lands' End jacket and scarf; he looked cool and refreshed, with his blond hair perfectly combed, the preppy tax attorney very much in weekend mode. Bradley's philosophy in life was a simple one: If he wanted something done, he was perfectly willing to pay someone to do it. Such was life when your world revolved around billable hours, he understood the concept of work-for-hire. As opposed to Brian, a sweaty mess in his jeans and sweatshirt, his once corporate self turned hard laborer, and he wasn't seeing a dime from this venture.

"Cynthia told me what you were planning, thought you could use some company at least."

"Thanks. Feels like I've been at this for days, might as well take a break."

From a knapsack slung over his shoulder, Bradley produced a thermos and two cups.

"Coffee?"

"Oh, you are a lifesaver," Brian said. "I think my hands are numb."

"At least it's not that cold out today, we finally got a break after the week of bitter temperatures."

"Nah, it's not the temperature, it's that staple gun."

Bradley surveyed Brian's handiwork, pronounced it a disorganized mess.

"Yeah, well, wait till the night, that's when it matters," Brian said.

"Where did you ever get this idea? And why all white lights?"

"You know, I was thinking about that," Brian said, "and I realized what I had done last year was an extension of a tradition back we used to do in the neighborhood I grew up in outside of Philadelphia. All of our neighbors would line the curbside with luminaries—votive candles that would flicker in white paper bags; the entire development would glow all Christmas Eve, supposedly it was used as a guiding light for Santa and his team of reindeer. Except in our neighborhood, Santa would arrive on the back of a fire truck, the siren's wail a signal to all the neighborhood kids that he was coming. Santa would have a gift for each kid."

"That sounds nice."

"I later learned it was actually our parents, dropping one of our Christmas presents at the firehouse," he said. "Still, the neighborhood looked so beautiful. So I guess that's what I see in my mind when I'm lighting the windmill, my past mixing with Annie's world . . . with Janey's."

"I remember how nice it looked last year," Bradley said. "Still, I thought you were nuts then and I remain convinced of that today."

"Now you sound like Chuck Ackroyd."

"Ouch. That's really not nice, Brian," Bradley said, but the two of them exchanged knowing smiles, a Linden Corners in-joke. "Cynthia tells me that you're decorating the windmill not just for Christmas, but for some wedding? What's up with that? When did you go from farmer to becoming a wedding planner?"

"I'm just in charge of putting the lights on the windmill, maybe help calm Mark's nerves, too," he said. "Martha is handling most of the details. Sara is like a daughter to her. But this being Linden Corners, she's enlisted the help of many others—including Chuck, who has agreed to come by with his sidewalk plow and cut a path through the snow so Sara has something to walk down; oh, and Father Burton has agreed to perform the ceremony outdoors, switching the Christmas Eve vigil mass later, to nine o'clock. We're also redirecting the children's parade to help light the way, and even Santa Claus may show up."

"On a fire truck?"

"Maybe. Just maybe."

"Please don't tell me you're playing Santa."

"That's a promise I can keep."

"The whole day sounds very ecumenical," Bradley said. "What, no manger scene?"

"Not a bad idea, Bradley," Brian said.

"I was kidding, please don't credit me with that one," he said.

Brian assured him that one was just between them. "I'm sure there's a lot more going on behind the scenes, but with less than two weeks to go before the big day, it's going to sneak up on us fast, just like the holidays do every year. But that's for then, this is now and I've got to finish lighting the windmill. So, you want to get a little dirty and help me finish getting these lights up? Might even score you an invitation to the wedding."

"Gee, can't wait," Bradley said, but that didn't stop him from stepping up and assisting.

It was about fifteen minutes into the next stage of stringing the lights around the windmill that Brian noticed they were getting additional company. It was Mark Ravens, the groom, who had parked his car along Route 20's shoulder and made his way through the big open field, coming upon Brian and Bradley.

"Hey, Mark," Brian said from atop the ladder, wrapping lights around the rail of the upper level's catwalk.

"Saw you guys from the highway, thought I'd stop by."

"To help?" Bradley asked, hope in his voice.

"Sorry, I'm on my way to RiverFront, but when I saw you . . . hey, Brian, got a sec?"

"Sure, what's up?" he asked, hopping off the ladder.

Mark looked at Brian, then passed a quick look at Bradley.

"You want, I can take a breather up at the house," Bradley said.

"Oh no, I didn't mean . . ."

"He's cool, Mark. What's going on?"

"Well, I mean, I really appreciate what you're doing for me and Sara, and I . . ."

He was fidgeting where he stood, feet crunching the snow beneath his feet into slush.

"Mark, you're gonna be late and I've got to get this finished before Janey comes back."

"Right, sorry, it's just . . . I need a best man. I thought of you."

"Me?" Brian asked. "What about your uncle, Richie . . ."

"You know Uncle Richie, he lives in his own world down at the Solemn Nights, and yeah, he was there for me a lot when I was a kid, but no one has done more for me lately. But if you don't want to . . ."

"No, no, Mark, that's not what I meant. I'd be honored, thank you," he said. "And am I to assume that Martha is Sara's maid of honor?"

"Yeah, old maid," Mark said, a grin striking his scruffy face.

"Have Martha hear that, your marriage will be short-lived," Bradley said.

"Nah, I'm in it for the long haul, for better, for worse," Mark said. "The way it's supposed to be."

And with that, he started off, soon zooming down the highway, his car cresting over the hill and disappearing from view. As for Brian, his heart warm after his exchange with Mark, again amazed at the generosity of spirit that existed in this tiny village, he climbed back up the ladder with new-found determination and resumed his post on the catwalk. With Bradley giving an able assist, they managed to finish off the remainder of the lighting of the windmill in just under two hours, and so, as daylight began to fall and the shadows emerged onto the land, Brian stole a look at his handiwork, and then in a test run flipped the switch inside the windmill. At four o'clock in the afternoon, already the glow was so bright it could probably be seen from high above, and that's when Brian sent up a quiet message of hope. *Here it is, Annie, here's your windmill and soon your little girl will see it and her face will light up so brightly, she just might give it a run for its money.*

"You know, Bri, you've got a lot of lights on that thing," Bradley said. "Ever worry about a power outage?"

"You know, Bradley, what is with you lawyers?"

"What's that supposed to mean?"

"I think sometimes you forget to find the joy in life," he said.

"You talking about me, or some other lawyer you know?"

And so at eight o'clock that same night, the farmhouse was aglow, the refreshing scent of pine swirling through nearly every room. Inside the living room, the fireplace crackled with heat, stockings hung just above it. The tree stood proud in the corner, alive with colorful lights and from the angel glowing from atop. Only two ornaments remained to be hung on the tree, they'd saved the best for last.

"You ready?" Brian asked.

Janey simply nodded, her face filled with eager anticipation.

From its box, Brian withdrew the glittering red ornament, the name "Janey" written on it. He handed it to her, watched as she hunted for the perfect branch from which to hang it, and at last she did. The hook caught, and the ornament dangled in the glow of a tiny red light beside it, the effect like the rosy glow of Santa's cheeks.

"Your turn," she said.

Indeed it was, so Brian removed his own ornament, this one green. He placed it near hers but not so close they lost the effect of them both. As she had done, he placed it near a bulb of the same color, and again the reflection that came off the tree was an emerald glow. That's when it struck him, her ornament was red, like Santa's suit, his was green, like the Santa suit in Thomas Van Diver's antique book. Years ago in this very room, with the fire crackling and spreading warmth, a young boy had sat on his father's lap and listened as the story of Saint Nick unfolded with holiday joy. Many other Christmases had been celebrated here since then, with Dan Sullivan and his parents, later with Dan and Annie and one day with little Janey. The photos of those times were all upstairs in the attic, tucked away in the boxes marked "Dan." Brian reminded himself that one night this week he would take that box down and he and Janey would share the memories; it was important to her heritage, her well-being, that she remember both Dan and Annie.

But speaking of Annie, he took hold of Janey's hand and led her to the back door. They put on their boots and wrapped their coats around their bodies, and together they trekked over the wide, snow-coated lawn, reaching the crest of the hill with heavy steps. And it was there, on this night when Christmas inched ever closer, a night that he and Janey had joyously celebrated both Sullivan and Duncan family traditions, the two of them held hands as they gazed down at the sparkling windmill, its glow like a halo from a faraway world.

"Hi, Mama," Janey said.

Brian Duncan squeezed Janey's hand in support, felt his heart about to burst.

So many of the residents in this little town had felt the sting of loss. Yet promises still existed out there, whether through planning a long-awaited wedding or the eager anticipation of gifts to be given, to be received, some still to be bought, or through some unknown surprise that still awaited discovery. Christmas in Linden Corners was fast approaching, no more evident than those newly spinning sails of the windmill, today awash with light, with life, with hope.

CHAPTER 16

THOMAS

"I'm sorry, I didn't know who else to call."

"That's okay, Thomas, I'm glad you felt you could reach out to me."

So said Brian Duncan as he helped the old man into the passenger seat of the old truck, getting him settled as comfortable as possible, securing the seat belt with a noticeable click. When he pronounced himself ready to go, Brian hopped back behind the steering wheel and drove away from Edgestone's circular driveway. Thomas breathed a sigh of relief as he realized there was still time to make his scheduled train, something he hadn't thought possible even a half hour ago when Elsie called to inform him she wasn't feeling well and wouldn't be able to drive him today.

Since his arrival in Linden Corners nearly three months ago, Thomas Van Diver had not missed a single one of these trips, had not even considered the idea. Every Thursday his pattern never deviated, he awoke early and ate sensibly and then got dressed, always careful to pick out a colorful bow tie he knew would go over well. The staff there always commented on his sartorial appearance, and today promised to be no exception, as he had chosen a classic blue and yellow-striped rep. It was when he was still securing the tie around his neck that the phone had rung and the tone of his day had shifted.

With the tails of his tie dangling, unfinished, he had sunk to his chair, his old body weary all of a sudden. Maybe he should just stay home, see if for once Elsie needed his assistance; he could return her favors, take it easy, relax. With his restless sleep keeping him from getting a full night's sleep, he had to face facts: He'd been pushing himself too much, and so perhaps Elsie's call was a message to be heeded. The idea of not going left him more bereft, however, so he thought about whom else he could call to take him. A cab service came first to mind, something he'd done for a few weeks until Elsie had volunteered to drive him. But even so, time was ticking away loudly on the clock, the cab could be late and he might miss his train. Then inspiration had struck and next thing he knew, he was calling over to the farmhouse.

Brian had happily accepted, wasting no time in arriving at Edgestone within twenty minutes, and now here they were hurtling toward Hudson on a brightly lit mid-December morning.

"This is really very kind of you, Brian, such a very big favor."

"Mornings are my slow time, once I get Janey off to school, that is."

"Kids do not like to get up for school, especially when it's cold out."

"You're telling me," he said, with an appreciative laugh. "Last week's bitter temperatures, Janey acted even worse. She practically hid under her blankets."

"I remember the farmhouse being toasty warm in the winter."

"No complaints so far, but when there's an occasional draft running through the house—you know, when the wind really picks up over that big open field behind the house—

that's when I strike a match in the fireplace," Brian said. "Actually, speaking of the farmhouse, Thomas, you should come over for dinner again, and soon. Or better yet, we'd be happy to host you on Christmas—that is, if you don't have previous plans. I know both Janey and I would enjoy your company. Just think how much you both have in common. Each of you having been born to the farmhouse, both of you having celebrated early childhood Christmases there. Perhaps you can even join us for Christmas Eve, after the wedding and vigil mass. I'll even let you read Janey *Twas the Night before Christmas*. I bet she'd get a kick out of that."

"Oh Brian . . . how very kind of you," Thomas said, feeling an odd mix of emotions. Joy, regret, sadness, and for a moment he wished his answer could be different. How to explain to this kind, giving man the reason why without offending him, or hurting his feelings? "I, I do have plans already. Otherwise . . . it's a very nice invitation."

"No worries at all," Brian said, his tone, however, indicating a hint of disappointment. "I suppose it was presumptuous of me to think you wouldn't have plans. Look at today, here I was available on short notice to drive you to the train station. Seems you're the one with the busy social calendar."

"Not so much busy plans as a necessary appointment," Thomas said. It was a comment that inadvertently invited further discussion, he realized, one he was neither ready nor eager for. He quickly changed the subject. "You do know where the train station is located, correct? I have perhaps ten minutes to spare."

"Not a problem, Thomas, we're almost there," he said. "I was down here in Hudson just a few weeks ago with Nora, we passed right by it on our way to see a customer of hers. It's funny, actually, both of Nora's first two customers—you and Mrs. Wilkinson—hired her for Christmas-related jobs. You, the search for the book from your childhood, and she was giving away a few boxes of old ornaments. It's like the two of you were diametric in your Christmas wishes—you wanted to find the past, just as she wanted to cleanse herself of it. Guess the holidays tend to bring out a strange array of emotions in people. No wonder we're all exhausted come Christmas Day, we've put our bodies through the wringer."

"Not just our bodies, our hearts and our minds," Thomas said.

Brian shot his passenger a curious look, careful, too, to watch the road as they made their way into Hudson. Coming to a quick stop at a red light, Brian, hesitating ever so slightly, said, "Thomas, is there something I can help you with? You know, all you have to do is ask. If I've learned one thing about Linden Corners, it's that we take care of our own."

"Brian Duncan, there's nothing anyone can do, not anymore," he said.

Thomas found his new friend staring at him, lingering to the point that he missed the light changing over their heads. The impatient driver behind them honked him into moving, and soon they were riding west down Warren Street, the train station just a few blocks away. Thomas was glad the ride was nearly over, he'd come dangerously close to revealing to Brian everything—why he'd come back to Linden Corners and the importance of the book, where the train took him and why. When the tracks came into view, Thomas knew he could escape unscathed, the secrets of his heart still his and his alone.

Or so he thought. He should have seen it coming, as Brian parked and insisted he stick around with Thomas until the train came. Despite his subtle protests, Brian accompanied him to the small, historic station, waiting on a bench while a dozen or so other passengers milled about, some with several pieces of luggage, Thomas with his lone overnight bag. To him, the bag was a red flag: He wasn't going far, and he wasn't going for long.

"Really, Brian, I'm sure you have more important things to do today than waiting for a train you're not even taking, especially since the board says it's running ten minutes late. I'm perfectly fine, just as I am every week."

"Ten minutes late? The train to Albany is not for another thirty minutes and is right on schedule. All this waiting around, I could have just driven you straight up to Albany, it's not that much farther and avoids the extra time you spend traveling. The train you're looking at is the one to New York . . . unless that's the one you have a ticket for." That's when Brian paused and studied Thomas, who looked away in guilt, like a child caught in a lie. And wasn't that just what it was? Silence echoed between them, as mournful as the whistle of a train.

"I'm afraid you've caught me in a bit of a fib," Thomas finally said. "I apologize."

"Thomas, you're under no obligation to tell me anything, you asked for a ride and I was happy that I could provide it. Your business is just that, yours, and whatever you wish to share is just as fine as whatever you don't wish to. Obviously it's a very personal mission you're on, and I don't mean in Linden Corners but wherever your weekly trip takes you—I respect your privacy and will say no more." He paused, resting a palm on the old man's wrinkled hand; Thomas could feel the heat emanating from his friend, how comforting it felt in the cool air of winter.

Thomas opened his mouth to speak, just as the train came 'round the bend, its whistle blowing in the quiet of morning. The effect was almost as if Thomas himself had let out the wail, his voice reacting to being found out, his heart unable to process anything. Thomas rose from the bench, turned to Brian, and said, "I thank you, for your concern and your respect. Perhaps one day I will tell you all, Brian, because if I feel anyone in Linden Corners could understand my situation, it is you. For now, I bid you a good day."

"Wait, Thomas," Brian said. "I have one more request, please . . . just listen?"

The train was still several hundred feet away; while the other passengers made their way down to the platform, Thomas remained behind, waiting with a mix of anticipation and fear. He had opened himself too much to the kind people of Linden Corners, more so than he had ever intended, and here was one of its finest folks with a request on the tip of his tongue. Thomas hoped he could easily refuse.

"About Christmas Eve," Brian said, "I know you say you have plans, but we need you as part our village celebration. I know how much it would mean to Janey and myself, what it would mean also to the residents of the Corner and . . . heck, ask anyone in town. You came to Linden Corners to find your Christmas of the past and now you have an opportunity to bring it into the present. With our parade of children, the wedding, Christmas itself, it's a chance to make new memories that will last far into the future. All three worlds colliding in a beautiful medley of traditions."

"Brian, the train is approaching . . . what is it you want of me?"

"I . . . we, we want you to play Santa Claus."

The whistle blared again, loud, as the train rumbled into the station. Its doors quickly opened.

Thomas said nothing to Brian, he couldn't find the words. He just stepped onto the train and inched his way down the crowded aisle. He found a seat on the side that faced the river, which provided a spectacular view of the mighty Hudson, its ebbs and flows, the train hugging the banks so closely the many sides of nature—land, water, sky—may well have been melded into one stroke of crystalline, sunlight blue. But connections were a funny thing, how easily they could be broken, like when the tracks curved away from the river and nature returned to its individuality. You could be lost in the woods, the sky closed off, the river's path leading you astray. As the train pulled out, Thomas stole a glance back at the platform, but it was empty, Brian Duncan was gone. Another connection, gone.

Like the one he'd shared with his father, like the one he'd discovered with the antique edition of *Twas the Night before Christmas,* both of them strong once upon a childhood, only to be taken away from him through the cruel twists of an angry fate. Was the bond he'd established with Linden Corners slowly beginning to slip away, too, not unlike a certain someone who meant the world to him?

It was like his past had just swallowed him up. No longer was the train from the Sears catalog up on his wall, instead it took to the tracks and inside it was a five-year-old boy who didn't understand why life took the turns it did. There were no tracks, just mysteries and unseen curves along for the ride.

"How is she?"

"Resting comfortably, Mr. Van Diver," the woman said with a reassuring smile. She was fifty-ish, plump around the middle, and with wise eyes that said she had seen much in this world, both the good of the human spirit and sorrowful regrets, much of it witnessed in these stark white corridors. "Why don't you go on in? I'm sure she could benefit from your comforting touch."

"Thank you, as always," Thomas said, removing his coat and draping it over his arm.

"Oh my, that's another lovely tie, very old-school," she said.

Thomas smiled, nodded politely. "Another gift."

"Weren't they all?"

"Just as she was . . . is," Thomas added, only to receive in return a supportive pat upon his shoulder.

And so she went back to her desk duties while he shuffled along the end of the corridor to the last room on the left, the final steps of a journey that had begun earlier today. All during the train ride he'd been distracted, thinking not of her but about Brian Duncan and his surprise, final request at the train station . . . and how he had let the question go unanswered. It remained that way when he pushed open the door and came to the side of the bed, the steady, artificial sound of breathing filling the silence. He sat down on the edge of the bed, his knees creaking as he let out a deep sigh. He stared at her quiet face, unmoving, her eyes closed. A shadow crossed over the pattern of wrinkles as though smoothing them out, a deceptive attempt at reversing time. Bending down, he planted a kiss upon her cheek and when no reaction was forthcoming, he knew none of this was a dream.

Placing a hand to hers, he felt for a pulse. It was steady, but hardly filled with energy.

"My dear," he said softly, "a most strange thing occurred today. I have told you of my old home in Linden Corners and the wonderful people who populate the town, but this morning I received help from the man who owns the farmhouse . . . this Brian Duncan fellow, a nice chap, so giving to others of his time. Well, he hit me with the most extraordinary offer and I'm afraid to say my response was less than honorable. Rather than tell him yes or no, I simply just walked away as though I hadn't heard him."

Still no reaction, still she just rested. The machine pumped air into her lungs. Her cheeks remained hollow.

"The village of Linden Corners is hosting a Christmas Festival, to be followed by a wedding, and all of it is happening on Christmas Eve—think of that! As part of the festivities, they have asked that I dress up as Saint Nick and read to the children of the village my story. Oh my dear, if only these good folks knew what they were asking of me, and when. Because we both know there is only one place for me to be on the eve of Christ's birth . . . on mine, too, and naturally, always, that is by your side. Because nothing will stop me from being with you, a final Christmas, one in which to seal our hearts and remember our life together. And as much as I have tried to make our celebration as authentic as possible, I fear I may just come up short on that end. Some pieces of the past, they just cannot be found."

CHAPTER 17

NORA

"Travis, honey, are you upstairs? Let's get a move on, we'll drop you off at school today. I'm going that way anyway, save you a bus ride," Nora said, calling from the downstairs landing, her voice carrying upward. She waited for a response but didn't get one. Checking her watch, she saw it was seven thirty-five; he'd have been getting a ride from her anyway, since he'd missed the normally scheduled bus departure. Which meant if he was running behind, so was she. Like always, even her day off was carefully mapped out. "Hey, Travis . . ."

"I'm here, I'm here," he said, approaching the top of the staircase. He was putting his sneakers on his feet while hopping on each foot, the laces undone, and if the one action didn't make her fear he could fall down the stairs, the second certainly did. Kids, they were so fearless, that is until that first tumble rocked their confidence. But Travis made it downstairs without incident.

"What's the rush?" he asked.

"First of all, you're going to be late for school, which is not something I'm happy to be reminding you about," she said. "And second, I've got an important meeting out of town and I need to get moving. Oh, and just in case we're not back by the time you're home from school, I told Brian to expect you over at the farmhouse, you can just get off the bus with Janey there. I'll send you a text to let you know when we'll be home."

"Who's this we? Why can't I just come home, where's Grandma going to be?"

Emerging from the kitchen, all dressed in a long red winter coat and green scarf and gloves, her wire-framed glasses perched atop her nose, she gave off the look of a Rockwell-like grandmother figure. Nora supposed that was appropriate given the part of the world where they were headed; Gerta was indulging her part. "Your mother and I are taking a little trip today. Like I said, I expect we'll be home sometime around three but you never know, time could get away from us or weather up in the mountains could delay us. So keep close to your phone," she said, with an easy laugh. "Which is like telling a fish to stay in the water."

Nora, Gerta, and Travis made their way out of the house and into a wintery mix. It was Monday and the start of a new week, Christmas just six days away and Travis already had that distanced look of a kid who believed school break was in full bloom. He forgot his books and had to go rushing back upstairs, delaying them once again. Nora waited until his return to have him assist his grandmother down the icy path and into the front seat. All day Sunday and overnight a mix of snow and rain had fallen, the temperatures falling then rising, so coating the sidewalks and road was a slushy, icy mess. Nora had considered cancelling, but she'd worked hard to get to this appointment. Today's trip wasn't about her, others were depending upon her. She was going, of course, but just this morning had tried to talk her mother out of joining her.

"Nonsense, I'm looking forward to our little adventure, if you wait for the weather to be perfect you won't be doing anything until . . ."

"I know, July," Nora said. "Okay, fine."

"High time the two of us did something fun like this, just you and me."

"Mom, it's work."

"Maybe for you it is," she said with a smile.

So now the Mustang pulled out onto the road, Nora testing the road with her brakes. The plows had been out and the salt was doing its job, so the driving was smooth sailing. First stop the Linden Corners school complex, where they dropped off Travis with just minutes to spare before homeroom. Both mother and grandmother kissed him on the cheek good-bye, and when he wiped them away with a shade of embarrassment to match Nora's car, she said, "Next time, don't miss the bus." The laughter shared by both women carried them to the village borders, and soon the sporty red car was zooming along country roads toward the New York State Thruway, following signs pointing them to the Mass Turnpike. Their eventual destination: Exit 2, and the village of Lee, a lovely village set high among the Berkshires, the home of Nicholas Casey, the ironically named descendant of Alexander Casey, an artist with an affinity for ol' Saint Nick and the green suit.

"Nora, honey, do you really think you'll find the book that Thomas wants?"

"All I can do is try," she said. "Mr. Casey was evasive over the phone, he just told me that if I had an interest in his great-great-grandfather's—or is that three greats, I can't recall right now—and I lived so close by, why not come for a visit. It would be easier to explain in person." Indeed, Nicholas Casey had been intrigued by the phone call from Nora, and not just because of her interest in the edition of *A Visit from Saint Nick* but because of where she said she hailed from, "Yes, Linden Corners, that's the home of the famous windmill," he had said. So the intrigue went both ways, Nora wondering about Nicholas's knowledge of the windmill.

As daughter drove, mother continued to look out at the passing countryside, remarking how beautiful the mountains looked with the fresh dusting of snow that had fallen. It had been so cold up here they had seen none of the rain, and so the morning's sun exposed a picturesque setting that any photographer or nature artist would want to capture. Then, as the Castleton Bridge approached, Nora actually gunned her engine a bit, and the fiery little Mustang shot across the wide expanse, both of them sneaking peeks at the spectacular valley below as the Hudson River cut through the rocky banks on its endless journey. Before long the Berkshire exits B1–3 fast approached, and eventually the border of Massachusetts.

Knowing they were closing in on their destination, thoughts of the original edition of Moore's book filled Nora with a sense of anticipation. What if she found Thomas's book after all these years? How would she feel? More importantly, how would Thomas react, especially considering the old man had no idea Nora was still on the case. She laughed at the idea, not a job but a case, like she was Nora Charles, and here she was seeking her own Nick. A black-and-white movie flashing before her eyes, the tarmac and the snow a bland match for the nostalgic backdrop. Depending upon how the day played out, she might be able to erase the memory of that night when she had handed Thomas the reproduction edition. Instead she would be putting into his hands the same one he had held as a child, doing so as mutual smiles sealed their fates. There was much to be said for the satisfaction of a job accomplished.

But she was getting ahead of herself, she warned herself, there were still a few exits until their destination, still miles to go before they could bring a resolution to their mystery, whether good or not. As she drove on the near-empty highway, the questionable weather and early part of Monday a factor, Nora was busy anticipating questions that Nicholas Casey might have for her. If his ancestor's book was so rare, he might wish to learn the provenance of the book Lars Van Diver had given his son, a detail Nora didn't have. She wondered if Thomas had said anything of his past to his neighbors at The Edge; he'd been elusive with her, did a man of eighty-five years open up to people his own age, or had he lost so many friends that all his words were kept inside his mind?

"Mom, what do you know about Thomas Van Diver?"

"Oh, I hardly know the man, met him of course at the dinner Brian had in his honor at the farmhouse," she said, "and I've seen him around Edgestone a few times when I've gone to play cards with Myra and the girls. But other than mealtime they say he keeps mostly to himself, sitting in a corner of the rec room, watching rather than partaking in the various activities, despite Elsie's attempts. Or maybe, observes is a better word; like he's studying us, wishing he could join in but something holds him back. I wonder if he envies us our connections, the fact we've all known each other for so many years. We may be old, but that doesn't mean our lives are over. Thomas, to me, seems like a man thinking too much about the end, not the now."

"But what about his family?"

"I don't know about that," she said.

Nora pursed her lips just as she saw the approaching green sign indicting their exit. She needed to concentrate now, she was in unfamiliar territory. But she felt she was on the verge of discovery, so she pushed the conversation a bit further. "Was he ever married? And if so, where is his wife? Was he widowed? That's the only thing that makes sense to me, why else would he return to his childhood home at this point in his life if not to look back on all he's lost? I don't know why I think that, he just doesn't seem to have the soul of a divorced man."

"Divorced men have souls?" Gerta asked, her tone genuine.

It was Nora who responded with a derisive snort. "I'll be sure to let you know," she said.

"Oh Nora . . ."

"Mom, we're talking about Thomas, not me."

"Why are you so curious about this man's personal life?"

"Because, Mom, when you understand the customer, you better understand his needs."

"You know what I think?"

"No, but I think you're going to tell me."

"You're trying too hard, dear."

"Trying too hard? To do what?"

"To find Thomas's book," she said.

"Of course I am, a job well done means a job accomplished," Nora said. "To not get him what he's looking for, it'd be like a hung jury coming back on one of your big cases. Neither side goes home happy. And much to the displeasure of the judge, in the end the prosecution and defense commiserate over drinks while the defendant's life lies in limbo."

"Hmm, an interesting metaphor, Nora."

"Mom, can we stop dancing around the issue? Just tell me what's on your mind?"

"Thomas was your first customer and I think it's important to you to finish out the job."

"Yes, for him."

"No, dear, that's where you're wrong. It's for you . . . to justify your new life."

Such strong words coming from her usually tight-tongued

mother shocked her, so much so she nearly missed their exit.
But she corrected at the last minute, a honk from the driver
behind her snapping her to attention; my God, she thought,
it's nearly like my first day back in Linden Corners when I
had the fender bender with Brian. She had been lost in doubt
then about her store, and now here she was faced with those
same demons now, and at the unlikely hand of her mother. It
wasn't true, she wasn't looking for personal satisfaction.
Like any businessperson she wanted her customer to feel
satisfied . . . right?

"Mom, I don't know what you're trying to do to me. Let's
just go see if you can locate the book and on the ride home
you can play psychiatrist all you want," she said, feeling the
heat rise up in her throat, words bubbling to the surface that
she couldn't control. Like the lid had been taken off a boiling pot and now its contents were spilling out. "You can tell
me that what I've done is all wrong and that I've messed up
Travis for life, and in the end all I'll be is a divorced woman
of fortysomething with a smart-mouthed teenage kid and a
store that I use to escape from my real problems by immers-
ing myself in junk from the past. Oh, and the past is supposed
to evoke fond memories, everything tinged with fondness,
nostalgia. Nothing bad ever happens in your past. It can't,
because you can rewrite it to your satisfaction."

"Looks to me like someone has already done the analyz-
ing," Gerta said.

"Mom!"

Nora was beginning to wish she'd never invited her
mother along.

But that was just one in a long line of regrets that threatened to overwhelm her. Buying Elsie's Antiques, moving
home to Linden Corners with her son in tow, uprooting their
lives, allowing Dave to go running off to Europe with a boss
who dominated him in more than just the boardroom, impul-

sively kissing Brian Duncan in the shadow of the windmill, and most of all, agreeing to this fool's errand of finding an antique book in a world where the printed word meant about as much as yesterday's fish, much less news.

She thought they might as well turn around.

Until her GPS told her they had arrived at their destination, downtown Lee. More specifically, the Casey Gallery. So the sign stated, in a thin black script. KEEPING THE PAST ALIVE was the motto printed beneath its name. Nora just exchanged a wide-eyed look with her mother, who finally nodded with a hint of approval.

"You may just be on to something here, Nora."

"Shall we?"

"We shall," Gerta said.

When they opened the front door to the gallery, Nora was comforted not just by the blast of heat that welcomed them inside, but by the fact there were no annoying bells ringing over her head doing the same. Plus, the walls, painted in a fresh coat of white paint, were adorned with an array of paintings—bright watercolors and oils, penciled black-and-white sketches, canvases both large and small. The friendly face that looked up from behind a newspaper was as warm and inviting as the atmosphere. A cup of fragrant cranberry-scented tea enveloped the room, and both Nora and Gerta found themselves closing the door behind them, like they were here to stay. She immediately sent Travis a text. They wouldn't be home for a while.

She was smiling for several reasons. Nicholas Casey surprised her, and in a good way.

First of all, she supposed she'd been picturing an elderly man in his late seventies or early eighties, not unlike her own client, white-haired, genial, and slightly hunched over, holding on to his family's rich legacy like so many of the older generation do. From the two conversations she had had with him over the phone, she hadn't ascertained anything from his voice, but now as he greeted them she heard a mellow, relaxed tone that went well with his slightly bohemian look, shoulder-length brown hair and round wire glasses, his casual attire. He looked all of thirty-five, maybe thirty-seven. A scruff of a beard on his face seemed to grow as his smile widened; her first thought: what an attractive man, and then she had to shut down those thoughts, this was business and she was a married woman.

Both excuses rang false; why couldn't she appreciate a handsome man?

"Mr. Casey?" Nora asked.

"Yes, you must be Nora Rainer," he said, "and please, call me Nicholas."

"Thank you . . . uh, Nicholas. And this is my mother, Gerta Connors."

"A pleasure to meet you both," he said, coming over and warmly shaking their hands.

"Likewise, thank you agreeing to see us," Nora said.

"You mentioned my triple-great-grandfather's Saint Nicholas book," he said. "While it was one of his most acclaimed books, I don't get many calls about it anymore. So I was interested to learn more. Come in, let me make us all cups of tea and we can start from the beginning. Lemon, cranberry, mixed berry? Anyway, you tell me your story, I'll tell you mine. How does that sound?"

Nicholas Casey had an easy style to him, and Nora found herself agreeing to his offer of tea. He left them for a few minutes, returning with a tray of teacups and the same herbal scent they'd walked in on wafting from the kettle. Nora was busy looking at the paintings on the walls, which Nicholas explained were part of a new series the gallery was getting set to show, ten young local artists who were being given their chance to show their work. "It's an initiative we support each year," Nicholas said, setting out the tea. "The Casey Gallery can't be all about the past, with each passing year my triple-great-grandfather becomes even less known. We do what we can for new artists, they do what they can to keep us in business. And also, Alex Casey was talented, but he was no Norman Rockwell, and when you come from these parts, he's stiff competition to overcome. So I welcome the chance to talk to you two ladies about Alex."

"I can imagine," Gerta said. "Rockwell defines small-town charm, even today. Which is a nice thing, big cities and technology are very much overrated. Keeping alive the past, it's a noble profession. And like you, Nora's store is doing the same . . . she calls it A Doll's Attic."

"Yes, so she said. It's an interesting name. Are you an Ibsen fan?"

Nora shook her head. "No, not really."

"But I was, I just loved his love of language," Gerta said with a nod of her head. "And when this firebrand of a girl was born, well, I just knew who to name her after. She can be an impulsive girl—but only when she plans ahead."

Nicholas laughed, even as Nora looked away with embarrassment. What was going on here? Was her mother actually flirting with Nicholas on her behalf? "That sounds like quite the juxtaposition," he said. "Nora, is your mother telling tales out of school?"

"I think my mother should just drink her tea before it gets cold," Nora said with a pointed arch to her eyebrow.

That seemed to only solidify the growing bond between Nicholas and Gerta.

"So, Nicholas, I don't see any of your . . . what do you call him?"

"My triple-great-grandfather," he said, "but to expedite matters, let's just call him Alex."

"You said on the phone that part of the reason you keep

the gallery going is so Alex gets the recognition he deserves, yes? I don't see anything on the walls here that looks like it was painted by a nineteenth-century artist."

"That's right, Alex's work is kept elsewhere," he said. "But why don't you tell me about your client and what he's told you about the book and we'll take it from there."

So Nora began her tale from the moment Thomas had entered her store that day, asking her to find a rare edition of *Twas the Night before Christmas* that had Santa himself dressed in a green suit. Her story continued with the chance visit to the antiquarian bookseller in Hudson, the lead he gave her about the reproduction edition, and her purchase of it online. "I'd show you the book, but I already handed it over to the client," Nora concluded. "It was his reaction that has me at your gallery."

"Let me guess, he wasn't pleased with it," Nicholas said, matter-of-factly. "There's a lot of confusion about that edition. Sure, it was an authorized book by the Estate, but the plates the publisher was working from were not complete; some of the original illustrations had been damaged over time. So we hired another artist to redraw them as faithfully as possible, and while she did a beautiful job and the publisher's edition was lovingly printed . . . to anyone who had seen the original edition, it pales in comparison."

"So why was it published? The reproduction, I mean," Nora asked.

"It was done as part of a retrospective my family sponsored. We were gearing up for the one-hundredth anniversary of the original edition, so we wanted to do something special. A friend knew a friend who worked for a children's book publisher. The editor simply fell in love with Alex's illustrations, said they evoked a Victorian charm rarely displayed by an American. So, tell me what you can about this client."

"He was born in Linden Corners, but left when he was just five," Nora said, launching into Thomas's story without giving away his identity; a lawyer, even non-practicing, knew all about client confidentiality. The details, though, she was happy to relate, and when she finished telling him about Thomas and his father who had gone off to war, of the last Christmas gift he'd ever received, Nicholas Casey was on the edge of his seat.

"I'm with your client, I wish I could get my hands on that book," he said.

"Well, surely you have one," Gerta said.

"Not anymore, sadly. The last of the family's private collections were destroyed, waterlogged one spring after a particularly snowy winter," he said, "which is also when the original artwork was damaged. All of this happened before I was born, back in the fifties sometime. So the book your client's father gave to his son that one Christmas Eve, it might have been one of the only copies left in existence."

"If only we knew where it had gone," she said.

"You say the boy left it in the house when they moved? Can he be sure? I mean, it's eighty years ago, perhaps his memory is faulty?"

Nora shook her head. "Not likely. When he told me of his last day in the farmhouse, the details were so vivid, it was almost like he had abandoned the book all over again. I could even see the windmill's sails as the boy and his mother drove off, never to return to Linden Corners."

Nicholas's eyes lit up. "The windmill?"

"Yes, surely you know of our town's landmark, an old Dutch style . . ."

"Yes, yes, certainly I know of it. I had forgotten it was in Linden Corners, where you hail from," Nicholas Casey said with obvious excitement. "Ladies, I think we've told enough, now it's time for show. Please, if you'll join me, I think we each have some surprises ahead of us."

Nora and Gerta, intrigued, exchanging quick glances, quickly gathered their belongings and followed Nicholas out the back door of the village gallery. He helped them into his car, assuring them where they were going was just a short ride. "A couple of miles, but well worth it," and so they quietly drove out of downtown Lee, back into the countryside where they followed along the trickling waters of a rock-crusted steam, over a covered bridge whose roof was coated with snow. It was as beautiful a scene as Nora had witnessed, a wintry wonderland that had her thinking of Rockwell and seeing what so inspired his devotion to Americana.

At last they pulled into a driveway partly hidden by the curve in the road, made their way up to an old Colonial-style house; Nicholas explained this was his home, "been in the family for generations."

"You live here with your family?" Nora asked.

"Mom, Dad, brother and his wife, their three kids. And me, sort of the caretaker, not just of them but of Alex's legacy."

"How interesting," Gerta said with an eye toward Nora.

Thankfully that part of the conversation ended. It wasn't the house that he had brought them to see but a large, re-stored barn in the wooded backyard. As he brought the car to stop, he helped Gerta out, steadying her feet as they tromped through the snowy drift and into the warm confines of the barn.

"This is the family jewel," he said.

As Nora stepped in, her green eyes expanded with sudden wonder; all over the walls were paintings, lush illustrations and faded ones, too, an array of artistry that drew her attention from one to another, another, another. There must have been hundreds of them, some behind protective glass, others simply mounted on a canvas, frames made of wood or edged in shiny gilt.

"What is this place?" Gerta asked.

"By proper standards, it's the Alexander Casey Museum, open only to private collectors and museums, by appointment only. Of course, I like to show it off to close friends, as well, and I think after what I have to show you, friends are just what we'll be. Come, there are two places I wish to show you, if you'll follow me."

Nora thought she would have followed this interesting man anywhere, as his passion for art was infectious, his joy at his ancestor's talent admirable. Gerta took hold of Nora's arm, for support, but also giving it a squeeze of excitement. They walked the length of the barn, its exposed beams and high ceiling making it seem almost like a cathedral, and with the only sounds coming from their footsteps, there was also a reverence instilled within these walls. As they passed paintings of churches and landscapes of the Berkshire Mountains, they at last came to the back wall, where a series of illustrations hung, all of them behind glass to preserve them.

"Oh my," Gerta said.

"How beautiful," Nora added.

"It's not all of them," Nicholas stated. "Like I said, some were damaged. But there he is, your Saint Nicholas in the green suit."

From the cover art to the final back cover circle of Santa Claus and the reindeer flying toward the shining moon and many of the interior drawings in between those covers, here were the original illustrations of Alexander Casey's version of *The Night before Christmas, or A Visit from Saint Nicholas*. And at last Nora could see why Thomas had been so disappointed in the reproduction edition, because, as beautiful as it had been printed, it was no match for these original drawings. Even behind the glass she could see the expert brushwork, oil on canvas and still bright with color; Santa's suit was a more vibrant green here than on the book she'd held. His twinkling eyes were that much brighter.

So were those of the Nicholas standing before them.

"That was for your client," he said, "and while it's not the book itself that he could hold and keep, he's welcome to come up and see them for himself. Perhaps that will be enough for him. You'll have to let me know. But this next series I'm about to show you, it's for you both."

They turned around, faced a fresh panel of illustrations, none of these behind glass. They were exposed, vulnerable to the elements but still beautiful. A series of three paintings titled *The Windmill's Creation* had Nora and Gerta both easily drawing in their breaths.

The first of the illustrations showed a barren land, the unfinished sails of the windmill lying flat and on the verdant lawn, two men standing beside them, dressed in period clothes from the 1800s; the second illustration was of the windmill's tower, the men on ladders, hammering nails into the wood; and at last the third illustration displayed the sails at last mounted on the windmill, the two men shaking hands at its base.

"One of my triple-great-grandfather's favorite pieces, done during his most productive period. He embraced this countryside with such verve, he felt there was no more perfect place on earth, since with each season came its own glories—the heat of summer and the crisp burnt colors of autumn, the snowy landscape of winter, the burgeoning return of nature in a verdant spring. It helped inspire his art year-round. He was present for many of the days the Van Diver family spent building the windmill, he sketched these and other pictures, but committed only these three paintings." He paused. "So, what do you think?"

"I wish I could buy them," Gerta said.

Nicholas smiled as though he'd been expecting the question and had his answer all ready. "Well, in a way, Gerta, you can," he said, his eyes dancing behind his glasses. "Are you looking for that perfect Christmas gift?"

CHAPTER 18

BRIAN

The moonlight shined down on the land, creating a shadowy sheen across the snowy field. Stars dotted the sky, the North Star bright and sparkling. No rain or snow was falling, and just a slight wind blew in the otherwise quiet of the night. For Brian Duncan, this was as peaceful as life got, especially as he sat upon the roof of his car watching the sails of the windmill turn, the white lights that adorned the tower glistening against a black canvas. Compared to where he'd been just an hour ago, the difference was as stark as Linden Corners was to the big city.

The annual George's Tavern Christmas Party had been a smashing success, with more food and drink than necessary, all of it capped by dozens of Gerta's homemade pies, a rich selection of apple and peach, pumpkin and mincemeat, and of course, for Brian her sticky sweet strawberry. He'd managed to gobble up two slices, taking quick bites as he served drinks from behind the bar. He and Mark barely had time for a break, that's how crowded and busy the bar was. The regulars had come early, found their seats, and barely moved. The twins, Marla and Darla, sat at the corner edge of the bar, knocking back tequila shots, just as they had done last year.

Chuck drank cheap beer and kept looking at the door, as though waiting for some vision of Christmas to come entertain him. The senior set was out in full force, Elsie leading the charge save one person; there was no Thomas Van Diver to be seen, which disappointed Brian. He'd been working on his Manhattan-making skills in anticipation of the old man's presence, but Brian had not had seen or heard from him since dropping him off the other day at the train station. Martha Martinson enjoyed herself, too, glad to have one day off from the Five O', and Sara was the belle of the ball, with everyone saying how they couldn't wait to see her in her wedding dress tomorrow. The tavern barely needed any light, that's how much Sara glowed. The kids had a blast, too, Janey and Travis and Janey's best friend, Ashley, all hanging together, playing darts like the grown-ups, drinking down their sparkling cider like it was champagne. Even Cynthia and Bradley managed to stop by with little Jake; despite the noise he'd fallen fast asleep and Bradley had opted to return back to their home, leaving Cynthia to hang with Nora, the two of them chatting nonstop. A sight that left Brian filled with more than a bit of paranoia.

But while the village of Linden Corners started off the holiday season in full tradition, it was Brian who was left with a touch of sadness. Last year at this time he'd had his own guests attending—his pal, John Oliver, along with his girlfriend, Anna; and Rebecca, his sister, who had brought Junior along. This year none could make it, John and Anna were now engaged and spending the holiday with her Italian family in Brooklyn. Rebecca he hadn't even heard from. So if those traditions could not continue, there was one Brian wished to retain, and thankfully he could control that. Atop the roof of the truck with legs crossed, he stared wonderingly at the windmill, thinking about Annie and a thing called destiny.

"Hi, Annie," Brian spoke into the wind, letting his words

flow on its current. "Janey's good . . . no, she's great. Thriving and growing like a weed. But she's still your sweet girl and misses you every day. I'm sure you know that, she talks to you, too. Cynthia is doing well, too, with Jake. Janey is over at the Knights' house so often I think they are thinking of charging her rent. She's there tonight because it was the annual Christmas party, so I had to work late. And then tomorrow is Christmas Eve. There's going to be a big party here in front of the windmill, a Christmas Festival topped by a wedding, actually, which I know would fill your heart with joy. You might have been called the Woman Who Loved the Windmill, but so many in Linden Corners seem to be vying for that title now. You should have heard all the chatter tonight about how lucky Sara was to be getting married under all these lights, in such a picturesque scene. But don't worry, the title remains yours in spirit, Janey's in reality."

He paused, crossing his arms over his body as the cold seeped beneath his coat. Watching the windmill spin, he felt the wind pick up and turn those sails that much quicker; like Annie was letting him know she was listening to every word. The lights on the windmill flickered, like the blink of crystal eyes. Wait, he thought, what was that? They flickered again, then returned as bright as ever. His heart beating, he feared the worst and then took a moment to settle them.

"Power is an amazing force, Annie. These lights power the windmill just as the stars do the sky. And Janey, she's a power all her own, and thankfully she's got enough to fuel me. She's my first thought in the morning, my last one at night, the light inside the farmhouse, like the twinkling bulbs on our Christmas tree. Annie, I can't wait for Christmas morning to see the look on Janey's face when she opens my special gifts. We'll open them in your presence, we'll be here again that morning, just like last year, just like always."

He sat for as long as he could, but after thirty minutes the wind blowing across the open field grew too much; it was two thirty in the morning, he should get home and try for sleep. There was much to do in the next two days, a wedding, the Christmas Eve festival, and of course Christmas Day itself. For a moment he thought again about Thomas; where was the kindly, but enigmatic man? Brian had hoped to convince him to read Saint Nick's story to the children as part of the festival, and though he wasn't yet giving up—even going so far as to rent a Santa suit—time was fast running out. He would go tomorrow morning to visit the man at The Edge, hoping to catch him before he left for his mysterious Christmas Eve trip.

Hopping off the truck's roof, he set himself behind the wheel and with a wave at the windmill, drove off onto the highway. A minute later he had turned up Crestview Road and into the driveway, his headlights guiding him, one more beam of light against the dark night. Heading inside the farmhouse, he listened for the sounds of the slumbering girl who called this place home, even as he knew that wasn't possible, she wasn't here now. He was all alone, not unlike last year, a stranger inside the Sullivan home. He thought again of Thomas, he who had called this home even before Dan Sullivan's parents had bought it. Brian wondered, was there something more he could do, both for Janey and for Thomas, too, that would make Christmas as perfect as it could be? A way to bridge past and present, creating a brand-new future for them both.

Foregoing sleep once again, Brian went upstairs, where he brought down the ladder to the attic, its squeaky hinges exponentially louder in the quiet of the early morning. Making his way up the stairs, he walked past the boxes that had usually contained their Christmas decorations, empty now, settling himself on the wood floor before the boxes filled with the Sullivan family memories. The tape was old, browned and loose against the cardboard; Brian hoped the contents of the boxes were secure and undamaged. Janey had lost enough already at such a young age, to be denied her father's family legacy would be too much. So Brian tore open the first of the boxes, which were filled with trophies and photographs; a handsome collegiate man with blond hair and an easy smile. The name DANIEL SULLIVAN sketched on all the plaques and trophies—he was a star runner, a winner of his college's triathlon. Brian quickly flipped through various items, photographs of Dan at a younger age and in the company of what were undoubtedly his parents. People who had populated this world and left it early, only their memories alive inside the place they had called home. He found nothing that connected Dan to either Annie or Janey, so no doubt there was more information to be gleaned from inside the other boxes.

He paused, unsure if he should be doing this. He felt like an intruder, delving into a life he had stolen despite the fact he had never met Dan. In his company Annie had rarely mentioned her husband, who had died in a car accident when Janey was not even five years old. But one day Janey would want to look inside these boxes and learn all she could about her birth father, and Brian thought he best be prepared. What was the rush, why tonight? Because of the gift he had for Janey, he knew it would spark emotions within the little girl. And so he opened up the second box.

There he found Dan and Annie's wedding portrait, he in a tux and she in a simple white gown, nothing fluffy or extravagant, and he wasn't surprised by this. Annie had been a simple woman in her tastes, elegant in an understated way, and so for her to shun decadence for love was in keeping with her spirit. Brian realized he was holding on to the frame for too long, his eyes focused on a happy couple, who should have had their whole lives ahead of them, neither knowing at the time how short their time together would be. Neither knew of the blessed young girl who would carry their traditions forward to a new generation, a new world. Neither knew how a stranger named Brian Duncan would figure into this family equation, as unlikely an event as Brian's first sighting of the windmill along the Linden Corners landscape.

Near the bottom of the box, an object caught Brian's attention, not because of what he saw but what he couldn't. It was wrapped in paper, and as he carefully pulled it from its long hidden home, he recognized Christmas paper—faded red backdrop, a Christmas tree pattern designed all over; a simple tag was attached.

"To Janey, a gift to you from beyond the wind. Love, Dad."

His heart heavy, Brian stifled a tear as he realized this was a gift nearly lost to history, a Christmas memory that had been trapped inside a piece of the past. Had Annie known of its existence, and if so, was she holding it back from Janey because the emotion would have been too much for her, for them? Which left Brian with a tortured dilemma. He was Janey's legal guardian, and even if he wasn't he still had her best interests at heart. And so he asked himself: Should he remove the old wrapping and see what Dan had intended to give his daughter, or should he just leave well enough alone and wait until Janey was older, more mature?

But that would mean Brian would be left with a sense of mystery about the gift, not able to get it out of his mind. Not just during the holiday, but every time he ventured into the attic or even just past the door, always he would be thinking, what is this gift . . . how would it impact her life? He had little choice, he had to find out what it was, and so he stripped the paper away to reveal a cardboard shirt box. Sliding a nail beneath the tape that held the box together, Brian finally had it open, drawing back the tissue paper to reveal . . .

His eyes flew open, his heart skipped a beat, a nervous tingle rippled across his back. He dropped the box to the floor, its precious content sliding out of the box. Brian stared

down at the faded image of the one and only Santa Claus . . .
his face filled with a jolly mirth, as though he were smiling
directly at Brian and thanking him for finding him, releasing
him.

"Oh my God," he said.

Even without picking the book up, he could read its
musty-looking cover: it stated *The Night before Christmas,
or A Visit from Saint Nicholas,* and what was most unusual
about the volume was Santa himself, dressed as he was in a
green suit. Brian still couldn't touch the book, his heart was
pounding so furiously, because not only had he discovered a
gift for Janey left to her by her deceased father, he had
solved the mystery of Thomas Van Diver's lost book. It had
been in the farmhouse all this time, never having seen the
light of day . . . never having been read for who knew how
long.

Finally, with kid gloves, Brian took hold of the precious
book. It was in good condition for such an old volume, and
he supposed the paper wrapping and secure location inside
the cardboard box had kept dust and air from further drying
its pages. He opened the front cover, heard the spine creak as
he did so, the binding challenged after so many years of
being sealed. A piece of paper slid to the floor, but Brian
paid it no mind, not now. Because, there on the first page was
an inscription that captured his attention, a strong, handwrit-
ten script that was thankfully distinguishable after all these
years. *"For my son, Thomas, on his birthday, this book is for
Christmases Yesterday, Today, Tomorrow. With love, Papa."*

Brian set the volume down inside the box, keeping it safe.
Then he retrieved the piece of paper that had fallen to the
floor and read its contents. *"My dearest Janey. For much of
my childhood my father read this book to me every Christmas. It was discovered here in the farmhouse's attic when we
moved in, and has remained in the Sullivan family since.
Now I give it to you to pass on to a new generation, a gift*

from another family who could no longer celebrate its future. For us, you and me and your treasured mother, that is all we will embrace, the notion that with tomorrow comes a special thing called hope. All my love, Dad."

Brian couldn't believe this unexpected discovery, not after all he'd heard about the book, from Thomas and from Nora, and all this time . . . it was here, inside the attic. He blinked away a tear as he realized this gift that Dan Sullivan had intended for Janey was not going to end up in her hands after all, because it belonged to Thomas, and it had been discovered just in time for Christmas Eve . . . no, correct that, it had been found on Christmas Eve, like a gift from Saint Nick himself.

A sudden sense of darkness fell over the attic, and Brian looked up to see if the bulb above him had blown. But no, he was still bathed in that yellow light, realizing the fresh coat of darkness was coming from outside. He moved over to the window, which faced west, and he looked out over a land that was encased in blackness. Not even the moon was visible from here, just a blank, black landscape. He couldn't even see the windmill . . .

"Oh no . . ." he said.

He went running down the stairs and out through the back door, not even stopping to grab his coat. Into the cold of the early morning, his legs swept him across the land almost without touching, and when he reached the crest of the hill what he saw was that the windmill had been silenced, its white glow vanished. The wind had picked up, a strong force gale nearly blowing him over in his vulnerable state. Flakes of snow had begun to fall.

Christmas Eve had arrived, and with it had come a winter storm.

As though the wind had swept in one miracle, and taken with it another.

* * *

"You completely blew out the circuits."

"Yeah, I could figure that part out myself."

"So why'd you call me?"

"Because I need you to fix it, and fast."

"Hmm, not sure I can."

There was a reason Brian had never taken a liking to this guy, and he was trying his hardest right now not to strangle him, seeing as how it was Christmas Eve, time for goodwill toward men and all that other holiday gibberish. Brian was frustrated, to be sure, but Chuck . . . all of his comments were negative and carried a notion of cannot rather than can. While that was Chuck Ackroyd's usual nature, it wasn't what Brian wanted to hear on such an important day.

"Too many lights on the windmill, I told you that last year," Chuck said. "Looks like you added a few more strings this year, so it's no wonder the circuits failed. Even these little lights require power, despite their low wattage."

"I get that," Brian said. "But we've got a wedding here at four o'clock, sundown."

"Gonna be hard to see everything," Chuck said.

"No, it's not. Because you're going to repair it and get the windmill glowing again."

"Doubt I have the parts. I can order them, but given the time of year probably won't see them till after the New Year. So, Duncan, what's your Plan B? Got any other ideas on how to light up your precious windmill?"

Plan B? Brian hadn't even considered the possibility. He just stared at the darkened structure, denied even the bright glare of morning sunlight. Not with all the gray clouds hovering overheard, not with the snow falling. Brian's mind was spinning, wondering what he was going to do. What was he thinking, helping to plan a wedding? He didn't even know how to plan his own life, hadn't that been his problem all these past months, wondering just what he was going to do after the new year? Helping to plan today's holiday festival, capped by the wedding of Mark Ravens and Sara Joyner, had worked its wonder, kept him from digging too much into his own mind. But now, even this had failed. At this point, Mark and Sara would be saying their "I do's" with candlelight.

With a determined clap on the man's shoulders, Brian said, "Just do your best, Chuck. Get those lights burning so bright they cast Linden Corners in its own glow."

Leaving him openmouthed around the silent windmill, Brian started off toward the farmhouse, his feet crunching through the snow.

Chuck called out, "Hey, wait, where are you going?"

"Like you said, I need to implement Plan B."

What that plan was, he still had no idea. As he crested the hill, he could suddenly hear the telephone ringing from inside the house. He picked up his pace, tracking melting snow into the warm comfort, picking up the cordless hoping to still catch his caller.

"Hello?" he asked.

"Brian, hello, it's your mother."

"And your father."

The latter voice hollered from the distance, though considering they were overseas Brian could say the same about his mother. He shouldn't have been surprised to hear from them, for the Duncan family Christmas had always held its own special meaning, wrapped up as it was in the story of the ornaments adorned with their names. Still, to hear her voice, and on Christmas Eve, meant the world.

"We just wanted to call and wish you a merry Christmas," Didi Duncan said.

"Thanks, to you, too," he said. "Where are you?"

"Rome, some beautiful apartment right near the Colosseum, it's really quite lovely."

"I'm glad."

"We're going to try and make our way toward Vatican

City, though I think half the world has that idea, too," he heard his father announce. "You know, when in Rome and all that, as they say. The entire city is awash with white lights, gives Paris a run for its money, though I suppose it's only this way for the holidays."

"It reminds me of our old house back in Philly, doesn't it, Kevin?" Didi asked. "The way the neighborhood was left so bright from the luminaries we would set out on Christmas Eve."

"It's one thing I miss," he said. "Traditions are important."

Great, now they were having a conversation with themselves, with him as a long-distance listener. Still, his silence gave his mind a chance to think, and what it saw were the flash memories of Christmas past his parents were talking about. An idea began to flow.

"Brian, dear, are you there?"

"Yes, sorry, just daydreaming," he said.

"Well, daydream on someone else's dime," his father said, though with a laugh.

"Good-bye, Brian, and again, merry Christmas," she said.

"Think of Phillip," he said, and received back a studied silence before he heard the word, "Always."

When he set down the phone, he found he needed to wipe a tear from his eye. Of course on this wondrous day he was thinking about his long-gone brother, Phillip, who instilled within the Duncans a holiday tradition that embraced family. Making his way to the living room, he turned on the bright bulbs of the Christmas tree he and Janey had decorated, sought out his name ornament, the green glass glistening against the tinsel. He wasn't sure how long he stood there, but when he turned around he found himself faced by a small group of people. Janey, Bradley, and Cynthia with little Jake wrapped in her arms.

"Oh good, glad you're all here," Brian said.

"Why, what's going on?" Cynthia asked.

"Why is the windmill turned off?" Janey asked.

"And why is Chuck down there?"

"We've had a slight setback," Brian said. "So I need everyone's help."

"With what?"

"With pulling off a Christmas miracle."

CHAPTER 19

NORA

Add a weekend day, plus a holiday, toss in a winter storm, it all equaled time off from work, and so Nora Connors was quite content on that Saturday Christmas Eve to relax under the toasty cover of her blankets, the minutes of morning ticking away without a tad of worry to spoil the peace. She was all set for Christmas morning—gifts were bought and wrapped, the decorations were up inside her mother's house, the tree beautiful, the lights around the perimeter of the house glowing, the smell of pies and cookies already wafting up the stairs. There was nothing left to do but lounge around and enjoy this one-two punch of rest and relaxation, where she could sit quietly with a cup of tea and watch as the snow piled up.

The ringing of the doorbell downstairs announced that the world had other plans for her.

"Who could that be?" she asked, sitting up in bed, looking at the clock on the bureau. It was eight forty-four . . . five. As though that just-passed minute was a signal to her that a shift had occurred, peace had become chaos, a second, persistent ringing of the bell confirmation. She tossed back the covers, listened from atop the stairs as she heard a commotion in the foyer, a happy chorus of voices that told Nora it was more than a visitor . . . it was visitors. Certainly not carolers at such an early hour.

"Nora, Travis, are you awake? Come down, please," she heard her mother call out. "Put on your robes, we have company."

Just then Travis emerged from his room, wiping sleep from his eyes.

"What's going on?"

"I suppose there's only one way to find out," Nora said.

Two minutes later, with robes wrapped around their bodies, she and Travis entered the living room to find Brian, Janey, and the Knights all sipping hot beverages, Gerta arriving from the kitchen with fresh toast and jam. Was this an impromptu breakfast, or had Nora not gotten the memo about another crazy Linden Corners holiday tradition? The Forty-Eighth Christmas Eve Toastacular, or something charmingly inane like that. She was about to ask what was going on when the doorbell rang again, and without waiting for it to be answered the door opened and in walked Martha Martinson and Elsie Masters. Now Nora knew this wasn't any ordinary social call, from the looks on everyone's faces it appeared to be a call to action.

"Good, you're all here," Brian announced, taking center stage in the room. "First, let me thank Gerta for making her house available as the staging area, we couldn't meet at either the diner or the tavern, not with Mark and Sara potentially at either location. Seeing us all together like this, might sound some alarm that something's wrong, that's the last thing a bride and groom need on their wedding day."

"Brian, what's going on?" Nora asked.

"One second, Nora," he said, turning his attention to Elsie. "Has Thomas left yet for the train station? He's expecting you to drive him today, yes?"

"No and yes, so I can't stay long, I need to get back. Fool weather be damned, I cannot let him down."

"Don't worry about it, you'll stay here. I'm going to drive Thomas."

"Oh well, this sounds intriguing. What can I do?"

"It's what you can all do," Brian said, explaining to the group how the lights on the windmill had blown last night and how doubtful Chuck was that he could repair it in time for the Christmas Festival, "and so, we need to come up with an alternate plan, and it's going to take all of Linden Corners to come together and get it ready in time. Nora, in lawyer-speak, we need a change of venue, as romantic as the windmill would have been."

"Got any bright ideas?"

"Yes," Brian said. "See, that's the key—bright. That's what Sara wanted, a day of lights to brighten her wedding day. We're going to host the festival at Memorial Park, and Father Burton will perform the ceremony there—inside the gazebo."

"That's a perfect choice," Martha said, "if all this falling snow doesn't bury it first."

"So, Brian, tell us what we can do to help," Gerta said.

"We need to turn our village square into a Christmas wonderland," he said, and then, with a check of his watch, added, "and we've got less than seven hours in which to do it. So, Bradley, I need you to take charge of the decorations—Travis, how would you like to help him?"

"And me, too!" Janey piped up.

"Fine by me," he said. "Be good to have such sturdy troops."

"And hey, I've got a great idea," Travis said.

"What's that, honey?"

"All of Mrs. Wilkinson's ornaments . . . wouldn't they look good on the trees in the park?"

The idea sparked a fresh discussion, and soon all of the assembled parties were talking and planning, Bradley jotting down notes and Martha interjecting with some comments of her own. As they made plans, Nora followed Brian into the kitchen.

"You got a job for me, too, Windmill Man?"

His grimace displayed his disappointment. "I'm hardly that, not today," he said. "Of all the luck."

"The universe is telling you something, Brian, sometimes you can't pull off perfect," she said. "Even in Linden Corners."

"Now what kind of talk is that? Especially when I show you what I've found."

It was the way his brown eyes danced in the glare of the overhead light that grabbed Nora's attention. Setting down her coffee cup, she steeled herself for what further surprise awaited her on this unexpected morning. But when she saw it, when Brian opened up the box he'd put on the counter and placed the objects into her hands, she felt an electric spark pass through her. Like a piece of the past had shot forward into the present, leaving a heated trail between that world and this. She stared down at the book, and even as she read the title and realized what it was, her mind still refused to process it.

"But . . . where . . . how?"

"Believe it or not, it was in the farmhouse, packed away nicely in Dan Sullivan's things," he said. "I'll tell you everything, but right now you need to get dressed because we need to get over to The Edge and give Thomas his Christmas present—and we need to do it before he catches his train. In fact, I need to convince him not to leave, and I can only do it with your help. We need him for the Christmas Festival—and now that we have the book, I think we'll be able to convince him."

"Brian, this is just remarkable, I can't believe this."

"See, Linden Corners is not without hope after all, and the day is just beginning."

* * *

In just thirty minutes' time the snowfall had intensified, with the streets and sidewalks coated in a few inches of soft, powdery fluff. That's how long it had taken Nora to get ready and for her and Brian to make their way toward Edgestone Retirement Home. The roads were wet, slippery, which might just work in their favor, Mother Nature's plot to keep Thomas from his trip.

"Though you know Thomas. He's very determined," she said.

"So are we," Brian said.

"What's your plan?"

"Just follow my lead," he said as they made their way inside The Edge's main lobby. A joyful sound of Christmas music and the chatter of many people filled the air; an early breakfast gathering was taking place in the recreation room, Nora recognizing the familiar gang of her mother's friends, Myra and Jack and other of their cronies. Approaching the lobby desk, Brian asked the attendant if she could ring Mr. Van Diver's apartment.

"Oh, I'm sorry, Brian, he's already left."

"Left, where?"

"I saw him get into the back of a cab, said something about wanting to leave extra time because of the weather," the woman named Julie said. "My guess is the train station, just as he does every week . . ."

"But I thought Elsie was driving him to the station?"

"In this weather? I doubt a man as honorable as Mr. Van Diver would have asked Elsie to drive him in this weather. It's awful out there, coming down harder now than it was when the party started."

Brian and Nora exchanged looks that said the same thing: *Now what?*

"We drive to Hudson, see if we can stop him," Brian said.

"Brian, maybe we should just leave it alone . . . he's got his own destiny."

Holding up the box with Thomas's original edition of *The Night before Christmas,* Brian begged to differ. "Not without this book—it's why he came back to Linden Corners, and he's not leaving without it. Didn't he tell you he wanted it for Christmas Eve? Well, that's today and we found it."

"You found it. Fine, Hudson it is," she said, knowing Brian was right, this was the only way, even if they couldn't stop Thomas from hopping on that train, they would do their best to place the book into his hands. "You can tell me the circumstances of how you found the book on our way down. But you better drive carefully, we've each got a kid who's counting on us to be there Christmas morning."

Back in the truck they went, making slow but steady progress along the county roads. The plows were thankfully out, and for a few-mile stretch they followed directly behind but far enough back not to get the salt spray, not that it mattered, Brian said, this old truck was barely held together by rust. And as he drove, Nora sitting with white knuckles as they slid a few times, she listened to the story of the book, reading the inscription by Lars Van Diver to his son on the title page, listening intently when Brian told her of the letter from Dan Sullivan to his precious Janey. She couldn't believe how simple it had all been, but how so very heartfelt, with both fathers recognizing the power of these words, the beauty of the illustrations, and wanting to share them with their children and with future generations.

"Brian, this was a gift that Janey's father left her—does Janey know about it?"

He shook his head. "No, she doesn't. Heck, I almost didn't unwrap it, I might have left it for a time when Janey could handle it—emotionally. But curiosity won out. What's key now is Thomas, he's been waiting eighty years to be reunited with a piece of his father. Janey's had a shorter time but no less important loss, and once I explain everything to her . . . I'm sure she would insist that Thomas have the book. She's a generous soul, that one, and I'm lucky to be a part of her world."

"Good, now watch the road," Nora said.

They entered the village of Hudson once again as they had weeks ago on the visit to Mrs. Wilkinson's house on the hill, and unlike that calm day the village was covered in snow. Few people were out and about and Brian easily cruised down Warren Street, neither of them certain what time the train left. Last week it had been a ten thirty departure but that was a weekday; it could be different today . . . earlier.

As Brian turned toward the train station, the next sound they heard was not the one they wanted to hear; the train whistle was wailing in the snowy morning. Whether the conductor was blowing it to announce its imminent arrival or because the train was pulling out of the station, they couldn't be sure.

Into the parking lot they drove, noticing the number of people milling about the platform, some peering north—which to Nora meant the train toward New York was soon approaching. They'd arrived in time. An announcement from the station confirmed this, just as Brian hopped out and went running through the small parking lot intent on finding Thomas. Nora saw him nearly slip, regain his footing at the stairs, and enter the station. She heard the puff of the train as it pulled into the station, saw at least twenty-five people gathering on the platform, all of them with suitcases as well as shopping bags filled with wrapped gifts, last-minute travelers headed toward their holiday celebrations. Her eyes quickly scanned the crowd, finally landing on Thomas's figure. A red tweed hat sat atop his head like a beacon in this snowy storm, Rudolph himself alerting them to his arrival.

"Thomas," she called out. "Wait."

The Amtrak train was coming to a stop, releasing a great hiss of steam into the air. Nora leaped onto the platform, making her way toward her old friend and client, her heart beating as she realized how close they had come to missing him, a minute or two more behind one of those slow plows on the roads might have been all the difference. She came up beside him, her hand against her heart in an effort to calm it down. She was here and so was he.

"My goodness, Ms. Rainer . . ."

She didn't have time to remind him to call her Nora, not now. "Thomas, you can't get on that train," she said.

"Oh, but I must, my dear," he said, his tone heavy.

"Not until you see what we have."

"We?" he asked. "Have you brought young Travis with you?"

"No, me," said Brian, approaching from behind them.

"Brian, whatever are you . . . both of you, doing here?"

The train whistle blew again, a warning shot as the last of the passengers were boarding. A conductor made his way toward them, asking if they were traveling.

"Yes, I am," Thomas said.

"No, we're fine, thank you."

"Brian, I have to make this train," he said.

"There are others, Thomas, there have to be, it's Christmas Eve," he said.

"Just wait until you hear what we have to say," Nora said.

"And if you don't like it, heck, I'll drive you myself."

Nora gave her sidekick a look that said she hoped he wasn't planning on following through on that, not with her and not in the weather, not on a day when family and friends and a tiny village were waiting for them at the Christmas Festival. But of course, they had the trump card, once they presented Thomas with the gift of the book there was no way he would refuse them.

"Whatever could you two be up to?"

"Brian, just show him."

With a wide smile gracing his eager expression, Brian

said, "I'd be happy to," and that's when, just as he had done with Nora, he presented the box to Thomas. The old man looked up from behind thick, mist-coated eyeglasses, first at Brian, then at Nora, finally resting them on the box. The whistle blew once again as the chug of the train distracted them. The doors had closed and the train began to ease out of the station.

"Go ahead, Thomas, open it," Nora said.

He did as she asked, his frail hands fumbling with the lid. Unsteady fingers dug beneath the tissue paper, Brian assisting him by taking hold of the box. When finally Thomas pulled out the antique book, Nora felt her heart swell with an uncontrollable wash of emotion, joy and sorrow and surprise, and that was just her. She could only imagine the range of feelings inside Thomas, disbelief perhaps the most likely, followed by wonder and surprise and a tug at his heart that transformed him from an eighty-five-year-old man to the wide-eyed boy of five.

"Is it . . . ?" Thomas asked.

Nora felt his gaze on her, and she just nodded.

Brian said, "Here, let me show you."

He opened the front cover to the title page, displaying the inscription.

"Papa," Thomas said, his voice more of a wail, one filled with the joy of discovery and the remembrance of loss. "Where . . . where . . . oh Nora, you found it. . . . I didn't even think it was possible anymore, not when you gave me that reproduction. You never stopped, did you?"

"I didn't, and I have a story to tell you about that. But all credit goes to Brian."

"Thomas, come back to Linden Corners, celebrate Christmas Eve with us and be a part of the festival," Brian said. "With this book in your hands, how can you refuse?"

Thomas was silent a moment, leaving Nora nervous

about his answer. What if, after all she and Brian had done, if he refused, and even if he did what did it matter? As she had said, Thomas had his own destiny and it had been aboard that departed train, intent on taking him down along the river's edge to wherever in the world he wished to venture, his reasons private. Now, his journey had been delayed, his story was incomplete.

"I cannot, Brian," Thomas finally said amidst the falling snow, like magic dust unable to transform his will to theirs. "I made a promise, I would read this book on Christmas Eve."

"And you will, to the children of the village," Brian said.

"This promise I made is to another," he said.

"Thomas, please help me understand," Brian said. "I want to help you."

Again, silence washed over Thomas, closing his eyes as though through the power of his mind he was being taken somewhere else, something he wanted to be but couldn't yet. Nora saw him weakening, his lips moving, as though words were formulating, a secret he'd held close to his heart finally finding voice.

"My wife," he said. "My beautiful, lovely Missy."

Now it was the two of them who were silenced. She'd had no idea, she hadn't even known that Thomas was married. Too many questions peppered her mind, none of which she felt she had the right to ask of him. She wouldn't even know where to start, what to say. Thankfully, Brian spoke for them both, and when he did, she knew he was right.

"Thomas, come home for the festival," he said, "and then I promise—and I know how you feel about keeping promises—I will get you to your wife's side. Whether we have to drive all night, you'll have your Christmas holiday with her."

Nora realized that wasn't enough, she remembered the

request Thomas had made that first day at A Doll's Attic. He needed the book not for Christmas Day but the Eve, and here it was, nearly eleven hours old already.

"No, Brian, we need to get him there today," she said.

"Nora, I can't ask you to do that . . . either of you," Thomas said. "Who am I but an old man, I should have known not to expect that all my of wishes would be granted on Christmas. I'm no longer that five-year-old boy, foolishly filled with empty hope as his father heads off to a war he'd never return from. Life is real, wishes are just hopeful ideas you toss to the wind."

"That's what you think," Brian said.

And without another word of protest, Brian led Thomas back to the truck. Nora stopped to gaze at her surroundings, at the historic train station and at the flowing river just yards away, and for a moment she recalled the paintings she had seen inside the Casey Museum, not just those of Santa in the green suit, not just those that recorded the building of the windmill, but those of the land that enveloped them. She heard Nicholas Casey's words about the ever-changing beauty of the seasons, what made each unique. Alex Casey's theory of how they came and went and came back again, living out their cycle on an endless loop, only to return with the same vigor, the same power, always the same time, always next year. Here they were in a place of transience, she could easily hop the next train and let it whisk her wherever, the same for the river, a boat and forceful currents that would transport her far, far away. Both of them modes of transportation seen as windows to the past; everyone was always in such a hurry, driving and flying, flinging themselves into the wind rather than taking a moment and letting their hopes soar first, soar higher.

She let out a heavy sigh, saw her breath as frosty mist before her. She had sacrificed so much coming home to Linden Corners, doing so for herself and for her son, and while she could imagine sharing such wonderful times with her mother, never in her dreams had she imagined a world filled with windmills and wishes, of dreams and desires, of heavy hearts and a thing called hope. Her world might have grown smaller in coming to this tiny town, but somehow she had learned how much larger the heart could grow, and it was this that fueled her now, as Brian called out to her.

"Nora, you coming with us, or are you going to stand there counting snowflakes?"

"I'm coming," she said.

"Good, because we've got one more thing to take care of," he said.

"That's where you're wrong, Brian Duncan Just Passing Through," she replied, happy to have her own holiday surprise tucked away in the back of her mind, ready now to be opened up to this world. "We have two things, and don't they always look better in twos?"

The curious look on Brian's face said it all: Hadn't he heard those words somewhere before?

Making her way back to the warmth of the truck, she settled in next to Thomas, who sat between her and Brian. For the three of them, their worlds had collided, their hopes were forever entwined, and soon, too, would their Christmas traditions.

CHAPTER 20

BRIAN

What he saw spread out before him, he could very well have been stepping inside a postcard, and on the reverse side he would find the hokey sentiment written in a friendly scrawl: "Wish You Were Here," but in truth for Brian Duncan, sometimes called the Windmill Man and often Just Passing Through, he was glad he was right where he was, Linden Corners. Thankful that this was real life and he was witness to all that was unfolding in this village, a rare place on earth indeed. With its rainbow of shiny ornaments, the elegant pageantry, the glow of white light that permeated all throughout the village, he marveled over how busily productive the residents of the village had been while he and Nora had been off convincing Thomas to return. His thought turned to how fortunate Mark and Sara were, not just to have found each other, but to be able to exchange their vows in such a sacred, lovingly created scene, and then realized that he was the lucky one. Not only to be a part of the grandeur of the day, but having played a significant role in what was soon to transpire.

Time had advanced to three fifty-five in the afternoon on Christmas Eve, five minutes to go before the Linden Corners

Christmas Festival would formally commence. He stood on the snowy steps of the gazebo, a nervous Mark Ravens at his side—or rather, he at the groom's side—warming his hands. The snow had stopped falling around noon, the wind dying down, too, and so what was left was a crisp, cold day where tree branches were coated with a few delicate inches of powder, the sidewalks white and virtually untouched, leaving the entire village covered in a blanket of white. Maybe not a postcard after all, perhaps a snow globe that had settled after being shook, all was calm and peaceful.

"Thought despite the cold you'd be dripping with nervous sweat," Brian said.

"Nah, not when I've got a best man that I can count on to defeat even a snowstorm and a loss of power, not to mention the best girl in the world, what's to worry about? Like I said, maybe all I'll do is show up," Mark said. "Really, Brian, the entire village looks amazing . . . I don't think Linden Corners has ever . . . well, it just glows, seriously, that's the only word I can come up with. Don't get me wrong, the windmill would have been a beautiful setting, and I probably cursed it when I said you could blow its circuits . . ."

"Don't think about it, Chuck did his best, but the windmill remains dark."

"Can't say that about the village square," Mark said.

And indeed, you couldn't. Wrapped around the tall pine trees that lined the edges of Memorial Park were strings of white light, and dangling from their branches were numerous ornaments that introduced the small village to the greater world; Travis and Janey and Bradley and a ragtag team of others had spent the morning adorning the sticky needles with glass, silver, and porcelain ornaments, all of them from around the globe, purchased by a woman who had taken to the wind as soon as she could fly, sending back home treasures that had tales of their own, into the hearts of parents who could only dream of all their daughter saw.

Mary Wilkinson might have steered clear of small-town America, but it was her travels that were dotted all over it now, sparkling against a smattering of stars that had fallen from the sky she so took to. At Janey's insistence, silver tinsel had been gently tossed across the many branches, each of them a tiny mirror that reflected the joyous smiles of those gathered.

But what struck at Brian's heart the most were the lights that lined the edge of the park and all down the street, from George's Tavern down to A Doll's Attic, by the Five O' and lining the lot of Marla and Darla's Trading Post and Ackroyd's Hardware Emporium, an endless line of glowing luminaries that flickered in the wind. How this feat had been accomplished in such record time, all while the storm raged, Brian couldn't guess. Small votive candles, encased by a white paper bag and secured to the ground by a handful of sand in the bottom of the bag, only a strong wind could knock them over or silence their glare, and thankfully, for now, all was quiet.

Chairs also lined the village square, set upon a green matting over hard-packed snow. All of them faced the gazebo, where the ceremony would take place, and the pathway leading up to its steps had been cleared of fresh snow. It, too, glowed with the luminaries, creating a swatch of light between which Sara would walk. Half the town seemed to have turned out already, with others arriving by the minute, everyone bundled up against the cold but somehow warmed by the celebration about to take place. All of them were settling into seats, waiting for the festivities to begin. In the front row, Brian could see Gerta, and at her side was a friend she had just met this afternoon, Katherine Wilkinson, who was still gazing around the trees at her own memories of Christmas; it had been Nora's idea to ask her to join them, and it had been the right decision. Sitting behind them, the gang from The Edge, Elsie and Myra and even

Jack, who looked wide awake and attentive. Sitting alone, in his own world, was a rail-thin, pale-faced Richie Ravens, Mark's uncle and the proprietor of the Solemn Nights Motel. Richie, a bit of a recluse, rarely attended village events, so it was extra special to see him here for his nephew's wedding. Marla and Darla were there, of course, they were the opposite of Richie, as they never missed a celebration, and unless Brian was mistaken they were taking turns toasting the night with a flask; hey, whatever to keep them warm. At their sides, a pair of golden retrievers, whom he had come to know as Buster and Baxter. Around the corner, he could see a yellow school bus, and he knew inside were all the children of the village who would make up the parade of lights, keeping warm until it was time for their entrance.

A quick check of his watch again, Brian saw the hands reach four on the nose, and like his cue had been sent out on those reliable currents of the wind, a sudden whistle could be heard floating through the air, growing louder as it neared. Mark turned to Brian, wonder written across his face, and said, "What is that?"

"I believe it's called an entrance," Brian said.

With a murmur of excitement spreading amidst the guests, all heads turned back toward Main Street just as a blazing red fire truck came barreling down. Bright and gleaming against the white line of lights situated on the side of the road, the truck finally came to a rest in front of the village square; the siren wailed once more, the twirling red light casting its own contrast against the white blanket of snow. From the passenger side of the truck, out stepped Nora, and then reaching inside, she helped down a man unsteady on his feet, still pushing her away in an act of newfound strength. The sight before Brian was strikingly familiar, taking him back to his childhood when Santa would ride in on the fire engine while the luminaries glowed all around them, but a detail was noticeably different here, as

it should be. This was Linden Corners, where they celebrated with their own traditions. Even those they were just
establishing today. Because there was Santa Claus, Saint
Nick himself, his outfit causing a stir among the assembled
residents. Because, of course, he was wearing a thick green
suit, fluffy white ruffles lining its edge, a black-buckled belt
around the paunchy middle; the only red in evidence was on
his cheeks, rosy from not just the cold but the excitement
that pumped from within.

He let out a holiday roar of "ho, ho, ho," and made his
way up toward the gazebo. Nora held his arm, and when
Brian's eyes made contact with them both he couldn't help
but smile as wide as he thought possible. They matched his
smile, tooth for exposed tooth, until they made their way
into the dazzling light of the gazebo, Santa taking a seat in a
plush, wing-backed chair they had found inside A Doll's
Attic. Already situated beside him was a sack full of toys, all
colorfully wrapped in the shiniest of paper, silver and gold,
blue and red. Also inside the gazebo was Father Burton, who
just gave Santa a happy nod. As Brian laughed at the presence of both men, the two of them representing two sides to
faith and hope, he turned back just in time to see Bradley
and Cynthia settled into their seats beside Gerta, shaking
hands with Katherine. He acknowledged them with a slight
nod, noting how strange his friend looked without baby Jake
in her arms.

And then he turned his attention to the edge of the park,
where a procession of light was making its way down the
sidewalk, row after row, and then more rows. Candles flickered and shadows walked among them as the solemn chorus
of "O, Come, All Ye Faithful" filled the falling night sky,
sounds from heaven. As the children's parade made its way
up the wide pathway, luminaries dictating their way, he stole
a look at Nora, who had settled in beside her mother. They
shared a look of mutual satisfaction, not just at having

Thomas here dressed as the Santa of his childhood, but at the chance at sharing a part of their childhood again, too. Because leading the children's parade were Janey Sullivan on one side, Travis Rainer on the other side, she in her crushed red velvet dress beneath her coat, he in dark pants and white shirt, his tie a vibrant green, and while he might have been carrying the largest of the candles, held high in his strong arms on a golden pole, it was Janey who captured Brian's heart and those of everyone around. In her arms, she cradled baby Jake, the young tyke celebrating his first-ever Christmas and in the lead role, to boot. Father Burton's influence here, Santa was fine, but let's not forget, as he put it, "the reason for the season."

As the children's parade marched into their designated area, their evensong came to an end, just as a string quartet set up behind the gazebo started up. The crowd looked around, the residents buzzing about what they had witnessed already, what was still to come, and in truth they didn't have long to wait. It was getting colder with each passing minute, and so without any further pomp, the wedding of Mark Ravens and Sara Joyner began in full. From atop the fire truck the siren blew again, drowned out by the eager *whoop-whoop* of Martha Martinson as she led her friend, coworker, and surrogate daughter down from the inside of the truck. They came to the edge of Memorial Park, where lives of the fallen were celebrated in remembrance, where lessons of the past were learned on a daily basis, where futures were planned. As the string quartet started up with the sounds of the wedding march, Martha began to process along the path, eventually coming to a stop opposite Brian.

"So, kid, you finally got that date with me," she said.

"And to the altar, all in one day," Brian added.

They both had to stifle a laugh, Father Burton trying to discourage them with a wary glance. Then Sara began her procession forward, her face a mix of anticipated fear and overwhelming joy. She moved hesitantly along the path of golden light, her dress of ivory and lace, her shoulders warm courtesy of a soft white stole, reflecting off the glowing luminaries, off the glistening tinsel of the trees, from the natural beam of her own smile. At last she came to the steps of the gazebo, Mark stepping down to take her hand, guide her up the four steps and into the roofed enclosure of the round gazebo. All around her were more white lights, hanging from the roof, and from the latticed ceiling. Attached to a red and green string that twirled in the air was another of Mary Wilkinson's ornaments, this one a glass orb that inside contained an old-style windmill, and unlike the one that stood lonely and darkened just miles away in an open field of snow and encroaching moonlight, this windmill's sails turned under a bath of flickering light. Sara got her wish after all, to be married under the glow of the spinning windmill.

"Oh Mark, it's so beautiful," she said.

"A subject you know all too well, my love," Mark said.

Brian stole a loving look over at Janey, and the easy way with which she smiled back at him nearly melted his heart, could have melted the snow all around him if given half a chance. How lucky he was, to have found her and to be blessed with her sunny spirit day in, day out, filling his world with a love more rare than the wind on a calm night. As he turned back to the gazebo, his eyes settled upon Nora. She was placid, focused, watching the events unfold before her, but Brian imagined her mind was miles away, perhaps time stripping away the years to her own wedding day, when she, too, had been filled with hope. Today was a new beginning for Mark and Sara, but for Nora it was no doubt a reminder of promises made, promises broken. Brian knew something about such betrayals, too, so he offered her a supportive nod when their eyes met, receiving one back in return. While some nosy folks in town might see them as a couple someday when their lives were free of complication, when things like holidays and celebrations were in hibernation, he knew, deep down, that Nora Rainer and Brian Duncan were friends, just as she had asked, and he was more than happy with such status. In the short time he had known her, she had taught him much, and she had helped him, too . . . well, he need only to gaze upon Thomas Van Diver dressed in his green Santa suit to know the power of like-minded individuals achieving the impossible together.

But even as the wedding progressed, as prayers were offered up to the heavens, and vows were exchanged and then sealed with a tender kiss, Brian knew that the festival was far from over. There was much still to come on a night when the world expected an array of gifts to fill lives with joy, yet what Brian was most looking forward to was something more powerful. Not receiving, not giving, and so as the best man, with the newlyweds seated on a bench inside the gazebo, with all the town watching and waiting, as a light dusting of snow began to fall from the sky, Brian Duncan stood beneath the spinning windmill ornament and announced that a special treat awaited them all, "for all the kids, as well as for the kid in all of us."

And that's when Thomas Van Diver took from his sack of toys a thin, hardcover volume, opening it up with a slight squeak from age, the other hand pushing his glasses atop the bridge of his nose. Brian stood beside him to assist if needed, having transformed himself from best man to helpful elf faster than the revolution of the windmill's sails. After a quick check of his green-suited Santa, all systems were good to go. Thomas cleared his throat, the only sound in all of Linden Corners, and, with a crowd of children gathered on a blanket inside the gazebo and countless others gathered on steps and in the field around them, he began to read. . . .

"Twas the night before Christmas. . . ."

The village of Linden Corners listened rapt with attention, even Buster and Baxter, who lay quietly, almost sensing the reverence that spread through Memorial Park, through-out the entire village. Brian, too, listened, even as his gaze fell elsewhere, far down Main Street and back toward the farmhouse, and in his mind he saw a flash of light, as though the windmill had suddenly burst back to life, vibrant once more against its former black backdrop. Perhaps it was only in his hopeful dreams, or perhaps it was true. Regardless, he knew that his world was filled with an energy powered by something more than electricity, love in its many forms swirled all around them, sweeping across the land like in an all-encompassing wind. Yes, Annie was here, he thought, and she wasn't alone. George, too, and maybe Dan Sullivan and maybe even Lisbeth and Lars Van Diver, Mary Wilkin-son and her father, Chester, and perhaps even the artist, Alexander Casey, and Philip Duncan, a brother who had first taught Brian the meaning of Christmas. They all hadn't come just for a visit, because like life itself they arrived with a purpose, carrying with them mysteries that could only be understood in the world in which they thrived.

"When are you going to be back?"

"Before you wake up in the morning," Brian said. "Just after Santa's visit."

Janey Sullivan scrunched up her freckled nose, just like she always managed to do when she didn't understand or just plain didn't like something. "Are you sure about that, Dad? I mean, your track record with Christmas morning isn't exactly stellar."

Brian laughed. "Guess I didn't have to get you a dic-tionary for Christmas," he said.

"So I'll stay at Cynthia's then, right?"

"Uh, no, not tonight, sweetie," Brian said.

"Why not?" she said, disappointment in her voice.

"Sometimes, sweetie, you have to allow families to have

their special moments together. This is Cynthia and Bradley's first Christmas with Jake, so we should let them establish some new traditions of their own that Jake will remember for the rest of his life. Like you have, like I have, and now like we both have. So let's leave them some privacy; and don't worry, we'll see them later in the day tomorrow, we have to—we have gifts for them all. By the way, you did a beautiful job tonight with Jake, I barely heard a peep out of him."

"Jake and I, we've got a really strong bond, he listens to me," Janey said. "But if I'm not staying at the Knights, where am I staying?"

"With Gerta, of course," Brian said. "And Travis."

"And Nora?"

"No, actually, Nora is coming with me."

"So, you do like her," Janey said.

Brian just ruffled the little girl's hair; she was always looking for motives behind every little moment. "Can we leave that discussion to another time? Right now she and I have to keep a promise we made."

"Helping Thomas?"

"Yes."

"That's a good thing, Brian."

"Well, thank you, Janey, I hope so," he said. "And you know, your understanding of why I need to do this, it's just the best Christmas gift you could give. To me, and to Thomas."

"I liked the book he read, it had such pretty pictures," Janey said. "Now I get why Thomas wore a green suit tonight, weird as it was."

A short pang of regret hit Brian in the gut, knowing the book's ownership was somewhat in doubt. Not that Janey knew anything about its existence beyond Thomas's possession of it, but had she known the book was a gift to her from her father—the last gift she would ever receive from him and that it had been up in the attic all this time, he wasn't quite sure how she would react. The parallel of the two fathers and their final gifts to their children hit too close to home. So for now, what she didn't know wouldn't hurt her. Christmas Day would be all about her, but for now, Christmas Eve, the promise lay with him and Nora fulfilling the dreams of an old man who had come to town in hopes of finding his past, succeeding beyond his wildest imagination. He was ready now to say good-bye in the only way he knew how.

It was seven o'clock when Brian and Nora and Thomas said good night, all of them back at Gerta's house for a quick cup of hot chocolate or coffee, anything to keep them going on this exhausting, long day. As the families exchanged hugs and assurances they would see each other in the morning, the three of them made their way toward Brian's truck.

"Not a chance I'm getting in that thing, not tonight," Nora said. "Fifteen-minute trips here and there are fine, but not a three-hour journey on snowy roads."

"What do you suggest?" Brian asked.

Nora pulled her keys from her coat pocket and tossed them at Brian. "You've so been wanting to drive my sporty little car ever since you rear-ended it on Halloween. Even though I still suspect you were the one who wasn't paying attention to where he was going that day, that's how much you liked my car. So here's your chance, Windmill Man, get behind the wheel of my red Mustang and take us into the wind."

"Like Rudolph himself," Brian said, happily.

They headed out of Gerta's driveway and down the road toward Main Street, eventually working their way west toward the Thruway, but before they even left Linden Corners they found a good-luck charm riding alongside them. In the open field near the village borders, there stood an old-style windmill, and not only were its sails turning in the gentle wind, it was all aglow with a powerful glow of white light. And even after it disappeared from the rearview mirror, its power fueled them onward, headed as they were into the darkness and into a night filled with sudden uncertainty. Brian was still unsure of what awaited them on the other side of this journey, but he put his trust in Thomas, just as the man had done with him.

There were mysteries still to uncover.

CHAPTER 21

THOMAS

He had shared the story of his life with so few people, but now, on the eve of his eighty-fifth birthday, Thomas found himself wondering why he had maintained such a tight aura of privacy for all these years, more the past few months. His world had been a small one to begin with, just he and his parents in a big farmhouse on a piece of land dotted by an old windmill, and then one day it grew smaller still, just he and his mother, the larger world having swallowed his father and in turn a piece of Thomas he would never recover. Even when they went to live with his maternal grandparents, the boy with the big name had kept to himself, quiet and studious. Was it any wonder he had grown up to be a college literature professor, immersed in stories told to and written in the past? He was never happier than when lost amidst endless stacks of other people's lives. Until the day he had met her, and she had opened up one part of himself he thought was closed forever.

His heart.

Her name was Melissa Dinegar, yet to him and him alone she was his "Missy," and from the moment their hands had touched upon the same volume in the school library—a gilt-edged, leather-bound edition of Miguel Cervantes's *Don Quixote,* he knew his life had shifted to a new axis. They shared a nervous laugh and each tried to offer the other the book, and when Thomas admitted with a sheepish grin that, "I've already read it," the woman with the dazzling smile and the sorrowful eyes he would come to call Missy said, "Me, too, three times. There's something about Quixote's fanciful lunacy that continues to appeal to me, the way he sees enemies when it's only windmills he is fighting."

"Tilting," Thomas had said to her, "the phrase in the text is tilting at windmills," and he said it again now, to Brian and Nora, his story flowing out of him with images of literary allusion making it all seem like a fairy tale. "Something I felt I did, too, always battling against enemies I could never see, and when in college I read the misadventures of Quixote and Sancho, it was like Cervantes himself was talking to me. I could picture the windmill, of course, and why not? I had been born under one's shadow, and even though Linden Corners was far from my life, it was never gone from my mind. For much of my youth, that Christmas memory defined me and so when it came to starting anew with Missy at my side, I knew there was only one way to close out the past. We were married, like Mark and Sara tonight, on Christmas Eve."

For the past two hours, the three of them had journeyed in near darkness, with only the headlights of the Mustang guiding their way. Few other cars were on the road, and why would they be, this was a night in which to travel the sky by sleigh, powered not by six-horse engines but by eight magical, flying reindeer—nine, if you were to believe another fanciful, magical tale of overcoming adversity. Brian concentrated on the road, Nora sat with her head turned, focused on Thomas's face, encouraging him to keep telling his story. The way they both looked at him, with such comfort settled within their giving eyes, he held nothing back, letting go his tight grip on his controlled life. How good it felt to share his life, and not just with anybody. With these two, two souls who had given so much of themselves to provide him his dreams.

"And so she agreed to marry you on Christmas Eve?" Nora asked.

"Just a few of us, my mother and a friend, under a star-lit sky, where Missy and I exchanged our vows. Not unlike tonight—without the fire engine, of course," he said, his face glowing with the memory of that long-ago night. He spoke of the way her hand had felt in his, their connection unlike anything he had ever felt, her kiss when they were pronounced man and wife as thrilling a feeling as any, sweeter than any strawberry pie. "We never had any children, not in all those years together, and I suppose neither of us ever questioned it—sure, we wondered why our little world continued to grow ever smaller, but we left our lives up to the fates, as it had seemed they were in control from the very beginning anyway. We lived a lovely life together, we traveled and we taught—she at the elementary level, trying to instill in students a good study ethic, me at the college level trying to undo all the bad habits from the middle years—and we made a good team. The best team. We traveled and we celebrated the joy of having found each other each and every Christmas, and I was determined that this year would be no different. No, that's not exactly true." He paused, holding the book in his grasp, still unbelieving that after the mistake of eighty years ago, leaving it behind in the attic, that it was once again in his possession. He had gained something, even as he stood to lose something more precious.

"Perhaps our Christmas Eve wedding was a way for us to mark all our celebrations in a short period of time—as you know, I am a Christmas baby, and Missy was born on New Year's. So in the span of two weeks we could dispense with all yearly celebrations, then spend the rest of our days doing as we wished without the burden of gifts. That's how in sync

Missy and I were, how much she knew me, and I her. She need only look deep into my eyes to know what I was thinking, and indeed last Christmas she saw something new. Neither of us was getting any younger, that's what she said, and so she urged me to finally search for the book—'before it's too late, Tommy.' Did I tell you that she called me Tommy? I never thought of myself as anyone but Thomas, straitlaced, thoughtful. But that's how much another person can change you, can claim you . . . Tommy and Missy, childlike names in adults who had never given rest to a lost past."

"She was the woman," Nora finally said.

"What woman is that?" Thomas asked.

"The woman Elliot mentioned," she said. "He told me of this woman who had called him asking about the Casey edition of *Twas,* but she never identified herself . . . oh, last summer or so, wouldn't you say, Brian? She inquired about the antique edition."

"He said six months ago," Brian said.

Thomas smiled. "That would be my Missy."

"Elliot said he never heard from her again," Nora said. "What happened?"

"That, my dear," Thomas said, "is what you're about to find out."

"And soon," Brian added. "We just hit New York."

The view was different from that of the train rides he had taken the past months, as Brian eased them over to the East Side of Manhattan. Thomas could see the tight look on Brian's face, almost as though he knew in which direction to drive but his body was resisting it for some reason. He knew Brian had lived here once upon a time, but Thomas didn't know the details and as he'd said before, we all have stories within us, we tell them when the time is right. Tonight, the tale belonged to Thomas, and more so to his beloved Missy, and he felt his heart beat with fresh anticipation. For so long he had imagined this night when they came together in wedded harmony, neither of them knowing what the future held, not beyond the next minute or hour, day or coming year. Now somehow here he was, ninety minutes from the clock forcing his eighty-fifth year upon him and he didn't know how he'd gotten so old, much less how his Missy had landed in her condition. One day you wake to sunshine, then you blink and the rain has begun to fall . . . or in the case of Linden Corners, the snow.

Only a light snow was falling over the city, the skyline bright against dark clouds.

Brian swept the car off the exit ramp of the FDR drive, making his way toward the Upper East Side. Thomas directed him at Ninety-sixth Street, and it was almost like he didn't need to, Brian's instincts taking over, on the ramp and onto the turn to the usually busy thoroughfare, tonight nearly empty as the city that never slept dozed. Down Second Avenue they drove, looking past buildings where lights dotted balconies that rose far into the sky, at businesses that were shutting down for the night; at Ninetieth Street, a vendor of Christmas trees was packing up the few remaining unsold trees. Christmas Day was just a short while away, plans were made, decorations in place. All that waited the world were gifts to be opened.

Thomas directed them to First Avenue and Seventy-eighth Street, Brian easily finding a parking spot along the street; only a major holiday would afford him such a lucky privilege. As Thomas made his way onto the street with the aid of Nora, Brian came around to join them. He looked up, all around him, let out a heavy sigh.

"You okay, Brian?"

"I lived here . . . not far from here. For many years before Linden Corners came calling."

Nora came up to him. "You miss it?"

A cab drove by, honked its horn at another.

Brian laughed. "Not at all."

Before they took a step toward the building on the corner named the Melton Home for the Aged, all three of them stopped. Thomas clutched the book again, ensuring it was still with him. Still real. As he went toward the entrance, he saw both Brian and Nora remain in place.

"Thomas, I think this is as far as we go, the rest of the night . . . it's yours."

Brian looked at Nora, who agreed, although with a bit of reluctance.

Thomas knew it couldn't end like this, he couldn't leave the two of them on the street, not after the story he had told. It had no ending. "Nonsense, you've come this far, I can't just send you back to Linden Corners now." He smiled broadly, as though he had truly just opened up his world. "Brian Duncan, Nora Rainer, come upstairs and meet my Missy."

So they followed him into the tastefully decorated lobby, where an eight-foot Christmas tree glistened in the corner; all three of them were greeted warmly by the staff inside the nursing home, were guided toward the elevator. Up to the seventh floor they went, the doors opening up and allowing them a chance to step out. Thomas walked with determined strides down to the very end of the hall, not even stopping to say hello to the nurses on duty; it was a skeletal staff tonight anyway, so they arrived at the room without even being noticed. Thomas wasn't sure of the visiting hours for guests, but rules were his least concern now.

He opened the door to a near-darkened room, a lone night-light throwing off a soft glow upon the quiet figure lying in the bed. A machine beeped, air seeped out with a gentle hiss. Making his way beside her, he leaned down and kissed her forehead.

"Happy anniversary, my dear," he said in hushed tones

that somehow held joy. A fresh tear trickled down his cheek. "And merry Christmas."

Taking up his usual seat beside her bed, he set the book down on the table and reached for her hand. His warmth spread to her cool touch, and he believed he could feel her blood pulse anew beneath her sallow skin. Her eyes were closed, as they always were; she hadn't opened them in months, not since the first stroke had silenced her. Yet he still clung to the hope that she could hear him, that with each visit to her side he kept her living that much longer. He felt the touch of hands upon his brittle shoulders, looked up to see Nora. Brian was next to her, and the expression of sorrow on his face made Thomas wonder if this was evoking some other memory within him. Was he recalling Annie, the woman he and that sweet Janey had lost? Had he been selfish in bringing Brian here, Nora, too? She was not without loss, her father a couple of summers ago. She should be home with her son, and Brian with his daughter, not with an old man with only the past to cling to.

"I'm sorry," Thomas said.

"No, no," Nora said, "it's us who are sorry. For what you've had to endure, and alone."

"Such is my nature, for as long as I could remember, it was me, and then me and Missy."

"That's no longer true," Brian said. "You have us, you have Linden Corners."

"Ah yes, Linden Corners. It was Missy's idea to go back, though of course the plan was for us both to live there, that was . . . until the first stroke. She couldn't survive on her own, and so once I decided to follow through with her idea of finding my childhood again, I knew she had to be as close to me as possible. This was the best facility I could find within easy travel," Thomas said. "Well, since you're here, allow me to make some introductions."

So he did, Missy Van Diver quiet as Brian, then Nora said hello.

Thomas smiled as new connections were made, a strong bond made stronger by a world created by the windmill. Yes, he had seen it glowing once again when they left town, and he felt he could feel its power now, reminding him of the boy who used to run like the wind down the hill, that boy being himself, and then he thought of the young girl who embraced the same magic, how on this night when she should have been with her family she was alone, and it was his fault. He had wanted so badly to be with his Missy, he had selfishly forgotten that other people had loved ones to be with.

"Brian, Nora, I think this is where our stories must come to an end," he said. "I have one last promise to keep to my wife, and you have promises of your own. Christmas Day is here, the clock has just struck midnight, and hours away sleep your children, both of whom are still filled with the wonder of Christmas morning, and so I urge you . . . please, go be with them. I will be fine. This night has held so many unexpected surprises already, playing Santa to the children of Linden Corners and being a part of another Christmas Eve wedding . . . and most of all, sharing with everyone my memory of this book . . . one I treasured when my father presented it to me . . . one I tossed away in anger against the world, without regard to how I would one day feel. Hang on to what's precious in this world, just as I am doing here. I have my Missy. You, Nora, you have Travis and he needs you, even as he claims to how grown he is. And Brian, that sweet piece of preciousness that is Janey Sullivan, how lucky you are, you and she and that old home that has shared so many memories, you have so many more to make. The windmill that spun back before I was a child and continues to do so, bridges generations as it seeks out the link between past, present, and yes, future, keep its spirit alive. So go and share your holidays, and I will see you soon . . . I promise. You blessed an old man with so much, with today, and with the hope of tomorrow, but mostly," and then he paused to pick up the antique edition of *The Night before Christmas or A Visit from Saint Nicholas,* then said, "but mostly, what you gave me was what I was seeking all along. The past."

Nora kissed Thomas on his cheek. "Happy birthday, Thomas."

"Merry Christmas, Thomas," Brian added.

And as Brian Duncan and Nora Rainer made their way toward the door, Thomas stole a look back at them and the twinkle that was in his eyes was not unlike another gentle soul who traveled on a cold night such as this, following the path of stars and spreading the magic that is the gift of life.

Then, with the book in his trembling hand, he turned to the woman who loved Christmas and who loved him, and he began to read and he didn't finish until he turned the last page and, with a kiss to her lips, said, "Happy Christmas to all, and to all a good night."

EPILOGUE
TOMORROW

*Just as nobody knows the future, nobody need fear the past.
So the only choice left was to live in the present, with a guiding light called hope leading you through your days. That's
how I see it, my dear, but of course that's hardly news, not to
you. You who know me so well.*

*Speaking of hope, let me tell you about the place I've
found . . . or is that rediscovered? A sense of promise lives
here, inside unfulfilled dreams of unwritten tomorrows. Powered by love and family and by the wintery whims of the
wind, we called this magical little village Linden Corners.
It's a place that some are born to and never leave, while
newcomers accidentally stumble upon its borders, soon
charmed by its welcoming sense of community. And others,
like me, return to the land after many years away, looking
for something that may no longer exist.*

*But that's getting ahead of myself. To understand then,
you need to know about now.*

*So much has happened since the night and subsequent
morning we shared, when snow fell from the sky and bathed
the city in its crystalline glow. Christmas Eve came and*

went, our anniversary, my birthday, Christmas Day, which I must tell you about. And now, it is just hours before you turn another year, a new one for the world, but in truth, what about you? Missy, my dear, do you live inside there, listening to my stories? There's one more to tell, listen carefully. It's about this fellow named Brian Duncan, he's a smart one, quite cunning in his heartfelt way, because even with all he accomplished for the Christmas Festival, and that was a lot, it was Christmas morning where his goodness was truly felt.

He's a giving soul, but on this day he realized just what he had received.

It began when Brian and Nora returned to Linden Corners in the early morning hours.

"Brian, you did it again!"

Brian was asleep on the sofa inside the farmhouse; the fire had burned out, leaving only orange embers and the colored light reflecting off the tree. He had carried young Janey home at three o'clock that morning, she'd barely stirred when he'd brought her home and tucked her beneath her warm blankets. He'd fallen asleep, too, on the sofa, forgetting to set gifts under the tree, and while Janey, poking at his shoulder to wake him, thought he had forgotten . . . again, Brian knew better. He had a plan; oh, this man, he is always thinking up something, and usually for the better of others.

"I did not," he said. "This time, it's on purpose."

"Not accidentally on purpose?"

"No, Janey, that was last year."

So the man she called Dad urged her to get into her warm pajamas and winter clothes, and he did the same, the two of them venturing outside and down the hill, she in the red sled, he pulling the frayed string until it snapped and she went sailing down the snowy hill until coming to a rest beside the *base of the windmill. Yes, the lights were still lit, repaired by some magic trick by Chuck Ackroyd, though it was hardly necessary on this sunlight morning. The windmill had a glow all its own, no doubt inspired by Janey's presence. Brian opened up the door to the windmill, and the two them scrambled up the winding staircase to the second floor, and that's when Brian pulled out two simple, square packages.*

"I know there are more gifts to be opened, back at the farmhouse, for you and for me, those can wait," he told her, "but these . . . they cannot."

They were wrapped in brightly colored paper, snowmen and Santa (in red suit) patterns all over, not that you could discern them after she tore at them with an eagerness that belongs only to the youth. He asked her to be careful, and that's when Janey's eyes grew wide with tears, because, after all, she's a smart girl and she remembers last Christmas and the loving gift he had given her and now she knew what these gifts were . . . yet she confessed that she had no idea what names would possibly be on them. Not until she opened the first and read the name "Dan," in silver glitter letters on a shiny ball of blue glass; and not until she opened the second and read the name "Annie," again, silver glitter spelling out its name, and this one . . . it was golden, and it blazed with light when the sun's reflection hit it just right. Brian tells of how speechless Janey was, a rare feat for her, he had said with a laugh. Her hug lasted almost as long as the time they had spent together as a team . . . no, a family.

When at last she broke from her embrace and the two of them had wiped away tears, they trekked back through the snow, and after waving toward the windmill and receiving back a giant wave from the four hands that spun on its axis, Brian helped Janey find the perfect place on the tree for them, near her own name ornament, and for as long as the tree remained up that season, the names Dan, Annie, and

Janey hovered near each other; Brian's was not far away, either.

That's the start of Christmas, my dear.

But it wasn't over yet.

Gerta Connors was hosting a Christmas feast that night, and her daughter Nora was sitting beside the fire with a glass of red wine in her hands, still musing over the generous gifts they had received that day. Her boy, Travis, was that much closer to being a teenager, and like all kids his age his life revolved around electronics, toys that made beeps and whistles and other sounds, games that landed him in virtual worlds that, as far as I'm concerned, my dear, pale in comparison to what we have here. He also received a science kit about the weather, since he'd taken such an interest in all things about the sky since coming to Linden Corners. Nora, as promised, had been determined to give the boy without a father the best Christmas she could.

And so when Brian and Janey arrived late afternoon to partake in the holiday spirit with their good friends, it was Nora herself who greeted them with an almost childlike enthusiasm, heightened when she presented Brian and Janey with not just one gift but three. Gerta grinned and Travis jumped around even though he knew as well as Janey what was inside those presents. And when Janey opened up the first, and Brian the second, and together tearing apart the paper to reveal the third, both of them easily fell silent. Like the wind had knocked out their own sails, and if that's not a metaphor for the moment, my dear, well, nothing could be. They were staring at three picture frames, all poster size, and each of them represented a stage of the windmill as it had been built, by, of all people, my ancestors.

"Where did you find these?" Brian asked with a sense of wonder.

"You might have tracked down Thomas's book," Nora said, "but I found the original artwork, and someday I'll take you there."

What Nora had tracked down was the original art to my beautiful Saint Nicholas treasure, so close up in the Berkshire Mountains, where the illustrator once lived and where his family still honors his work. The past, it's alive everywhere, here with us and in a house up in the hills near the Hudson River, and on the walls of the farmhouse, that's where Brian has hung those fine illustrations of the windmill. Nora had promised us all a visit to the Casey Museum, the proprietor Nicholas has invited us all to see firsthand the works of art produced by the man who gave life to the Santa in the green suit, and it is a day I look forward to, as it will no doubt be the last time my eyes fall upon such an image.

Even an old man is not without his surprises.

Let me tell you of the final gift.

It was two days after Christmas when I walked my old man shuffle into George's Tavern and found Brian Duncan behind the bar, washing the glasses in time-honored tradition. He said he'd learned how to get all the spots out, a technique perfected by a man named George Connors, who had been Gerta's husband and Nora's father. He passed awhile back, but not before striking a bond between himself and Brian, his first in Linden Corners. One thing ol' George failed to teach the newcomer was how to make a Manhattan.

"I told you, Brian, just wave the vermouth over the glass."

But I drank the one he'd prepared for me anyway, and when it was finished I went about my business. A package accompanied me, but I would leave without it.

"Here, this is for you. Actually, for both of you, can't forget that irrepressible Janey," I told him. My hands were shaking and it could have been because I'm so old but most *likely it was because I was letting go of the one thing I'd come back to Linden Corners to find. My past.*

"What's this?" he asked.

"There's no need to open it, not today," I said. "All it lacks is the letter written by the young girl's father."

Brian did his best to try and give back the present, but that's the thing about gifts, once they leave your possession they are no longer yours to hold on to, that's what I told him. And when he further protested, I told him that I had long ago accepted the past for what it was, I had lived a long, good life and toward its end I had been given such an unexpected surprise in the book. I confessed that I had originally considered it all a pipe dream, pushed on me by a loving wife who wished to see me come to terms, finally, with my loss. Perhaps she was right, I'd never properly said good-bye to my father, I didn't get to hug him one last time or tell him I loved him one more time, I didn't get to sit on his lap and hear him tell me that story again. But Janey can experience the joy I felt over and over again, and as you read it to her, Brian, she'll know in her heart that it came as a gift from another man who loved her so unconditionally.

"Give it to her next Christmas, make the discovery among Dan Sullivan's things all over again," I said, "let her know that life can continue to surprise her each and every day. That's certainly a lesson I take from this, and I have both you and Nora to thank for that."

The mention of Nora caused a reaction in Brian that suddenly had him staring down at the floor, as though he'd dropped something. When I pushed him about it, he hesitated before revealing to me that upon their return to Linden Corners, he had pulled the red Mustang into her driveway, and as the snow fell on their shoulders and a chill seeped beneath their coats, Brian leaned in and kissed her, telling me the moment was not unlike the time she had done the same, in his driveway. This time, though, what was different was there was no windmill to get between them, and Brian said that after they parted, Nora had given him this curious look.

"What was that for?" she asked him.

"Just consider us even," Brian said with a wide grin.

Such is the dance of friends who may be finding themselves growing closer, but how it ends up is for another time. As we've said, all stories have their moment to be told, and for now, Christmas is what has driven us, those we remember from our childhoods, those we wish to share with loved ones, those we wish to establish with new friends.

Before I left the tavern, Brian asked about you, my dear, and I informed him that all was unchanged, you were here but not. Yes, a new year is fast approaching. Back in my new home of Linden Corners, a New Year's celebration is taking place at the farmhouse, with Brian hosting an assortment of friends and neighbors, Cynthia and Bradley, who had been blessed with a child this year; Gerta and Nora, Travis, too; and lastly, the newlyweds, Mark and Sara, a young couple just starting out on this journey called life together.

When I am not here, where will I go? To the village square, of course, Memorial Park, walking behind the gazebo and to the series of stones that honor those we lost. But as much as my eighty-five-year-old self is drawing fingers through the engraved letters of one Lars Van Diver, it is the five-year-old boy inside me who can be found back at the farmhouse. In my dream it is Christmas Eve again, and I am running down the hill toward the windmill; the wind is strong and it picks up even more, almost lifting me into the air and when I land I find standing by its base the man dressed in green, and his smile invites me toward him. No, he is not Saint Nick, it is my father and I welcome him home.

"Come, Papa, read me that story again," I ask.

But when I blink I am back at the memorial, his name is there.

He never came home, and at last I am at peace with it.

I can let go.

Yes, my dear, I can let go of many things.

I am holding your hand, and I feel I always will, even as you grow cold.

Stories have their time and place, just as our lives do. They have their beginnings, their endings. Your time, my dear, it is now. I am fine, but know that I will never forget you. Life journeys onward, led by the constant revolutions of a windmill that gives power to a place you should only be so lucky to stumble upon, a place you won't be just passing through.

Just as seen in the paintings that now hang inside the farmhouse, seasons came and seasons went, until countless years had passed and the men who had crafted her, labored in the hot sun to build the magnificent windmill, were like the wind itself, blown into the past, into the memories we coin as history. The past is a good place to remember, but it's the present we must cling to, it's all we have to inspire the hope of the future.

The snow again continues to fall all across the land, blanketing the tiny village in its deep winter coat, almost as though wiping away any trace of yesteryear, starting fresh. A new year has arrived, my dear, yet all around this special world called Linden Corners it is somehow still Christmas, and, as Papa once wrote at the end of his letters to us during the war, "Yours, now, forever, and always." The same could be said of the snow, it wasn't yet July.

A Note About
Twas the Night before Christmas

The antique reproduction that is featured in this story exists. It was published in 1988 by the children's imprint Philomel Books, now owned by the Penguin Group. I am familiar with it because I worked at Philomel at the time as the publisher's assistant, and her excitement about having the chance to bring the work back into print was infectious. Santa Claus in the green suit obviously stuck with me.

The original edition was indeed published by McLoughlin Brothers in 1888, with beautiful illustrations by the English artist William Roger Snow (1834–1907). For the purposes of my story, this is where fact needed to become fiction. I changed the name of the artist (my apologies) to the fictitious Alexander Casey, as it was necessary for Nora to continue to track—and find—the artist's family and gain information about the original artwork.

There is lore about Clement Clarke Moore not being the actual author, and the story told by Elliot the antiquarian bookseller is well documented. But that hasn't stopped hundreds of editions of the book giving full credit for the text to Moore, as I have done in my story as well.

Return to Linden Corners in Joseph Pittman's inspiring
new novel:

THE MEMORY TREE

Turn the page for a special excerpt.

A Kensington trade paperback on sale now.

$\mathscr{P}$ROLOGUE

Clocks turn even when you're not looking, the sun rises and falls as the passing days move gently into the quiet of night, and so time effortlessly glides by, unseen but ever present. For those with little to look forward to in life, time can drag on till it seems the earth has stood still, while for others the endless rotations of its axis move far too quickly, leaving them with a sense of time running out, always planning, seldom living. Time is universal, yet it represents so many things to so many, and while it can be enigmatic, even mysterious, it also represents one of the few constants in the universe. What no one has in common with time is how much of it they have.

In reality, the world marches on, and before anyone realizes it, time has flown by on the currents of the wind, with another day, month, and year having elapsed, leaving us all a little older, perhaps a bit wiser. And always wondering, Where has the time flown?

Sometimes people anticipate the arrival of a certain day, a birthday or anniversary, a trip that will take them to the far reaches of the earth, feeling it will never come. And then suddenly it's gone, whisked away by time's inevitable advancement, leaving in its wake those things called memo-

ries. Sometimes people wish time would grind to a standstill, allowing them to forever treasure a moment so hard to catch, like witnessing a falling star, the first bloom of love, a long-planned wedding, only to realize that time is a part of life no one can lay claim to—its hold on us strong, our grip, at best, tenuous.

Time is always present, but it's remembered in the past, thought about for the future.

"Remember that time . . ."

"Time will tell."

Time means everything and yet it ultimately means nothing, leaving a place like the small village known as Linden Corners somewhere between yesterday and tomorrow. For eager kids down at Linden Corners Middle School, a year of studies can feel like forever; for anxious adults in the simple act of waiting for a cup of coffee down at Martha's Five O'Clock Diner, time can come to mean impatience; and for the elderly folks down at Edgestone Retirement Center, who have seen their lives fall behind them, time taunts like an enemy. Even the iconic, majestic windmill that looms over this countryside knows of time's unstoppable dance, its spinning sails silently recording every step.

But then come those special times of year when folks dream of better lives. Holidays are like time-outs from the rigors of daily life, filling out days with Memorial Day picnics and Fourth of July fireworks, these events like time caught in a bottle. At Thanksgiving, we take time for our families and ourselves, giving thanks for all we have, all we share. And then of course there's Christmas, which stretches the notion of time to extremes, for it is not just a single day amidst a cold month, but something joyfully referred to as Christmastime, a time built on a giving spirit, on tradition. And what is tradition but time told in reverse.

Only one thing in this world can halt the passage of time.

Only one thing in this world can transport you to another time and another world.

That thing is called a dream.

For one wide-eyed girl in Linden Corners, she with freckles on her usually scrunched-up nose, dreams were sometimes all she could cling to.

Shutters clattered against the old farmhouse as the wind took shape on dark currents. A willowy shadow emerged, sweeping in through the open window, washing over the sleeping figure in the bed. Instead of blocking the moonlight that flowed through lace curtains, the figure was cast in a golden glow. From the small bed, the little girl stirred, although if truth be told—and why not? didn't nights call for honesty?—she couldn't be called little anymore. She had reached double digits, a whole ten years old for just over a month now. Independence, always a trait that ran rampant inside her, had recently begun to assert itself on the outside. So much so that she didn't need to be tucked in anymore, to be babied, and she didn't need to sleep with a night-light anymore. Janey Sullivan was growing up.

But the elapsed time couldn't change everything.

She had memories, even at her tender age.

The moonlight glinted in her eyes and she opened them, green twinkles in the darkness.

For a curious moment, her tired mind was unsure where she was and she reached for her constant companion, a purple frog that remained with her despite another birthday, despite this supposed streak of independence. At night she still sought comfort from a friend made from stuffing, a friend that had never uttered a single word but had seen her through days—and nights—way darker than this one. Nights when not even the moon visited. Then, popping up, elbow on *her pillow, she looked at the shadow on the wall and saw it smile.*

How did it know to do that? How did such a gesture manage to soothe her?

"Mama?" she suddenly asked.

"Yes, Janey, it's me."

The shadow morphed into something more concrete, light hitting it. Yes, there she was, Annie Sullivan, her body floating like something crafted from the heavens, vibrant in the starlit night. The young girl felt warmth spread over her. She tossed back the blankets, and even as the wind howled against the side of the old farmhouse, calming heat continued to surge around her. She couldn't remember ever feeling so warm, not even on those cold nights when Brian had to light a fire in the fireplace and they sat beside its flame sipping hot chocolate—with tiny marshmallows—while orange embers burned and he invented silly stories of a girl who could ride the wind. She would giggle at times, scrunch her nose with doubt at others. Those were special times, the best. At least, the best she could remember since her mother had gone to sleep at a secret place only she knew. Beads of sweat formed on her brow now, and as a drop found its way to a blinking eye, she wiped it away.

The vision—if that's what it was—remained.

"Come with me, Janey. Let me show you."

"Show me what?"

"What it was."

Why was she speaking in riddles? Janey almost giggled.

"What what was?"

"Our life, from before you could remember."

A hand suddenly stretched out toward her, and Janey felt its pull even without touch.

This woman before her, whether real, conjured from her imagination, or perhaps locked somewhere in between, spun her dreams. And while the girl named Janey would follow her anywhere, there was only one possible destination for them both. They were headed where their lives remained connected, forever bonded.

The windmill.

Across the open field they journeyed, down the hill, which tonight was a swirling carpet of fallen leaves and dying grass. Yes, it was windy on this warm autumn night, and the sails of the giant windmill spun like they were producing gleaming straw. But once they had gained entry inside the tower, magically not needing to turn a key or to open the door, the windows remained closed and no one would be letting down their spun golden locks.

Annie had loved coming to the windmill to paint her dreams on canvases, only to close them in a drawer. Never thinking to show them, never thinking her talent commanded attention. Yet several hung now inside the homes of Linden Corners—in the farmhouse and on Gerta Connors' living room wall, just above the mantel. But Annie had mostly come here to contemplate life and all she had been given, all she had lost. Now it was Janey's turn to rely on the windmill's power, some days more so than on the reassuring presence of Brian Duncan. He was real, always dependable, but sometimes Janey enjoyed living out the dream inside her mind.

"Mama, why have you brought me here?"

"What do you see?"

"Why are you answering my question with a question?"

"Because, Janey, sometimes when you listen you hear your own answers."

Janey didn't know what to think of her wisdom; it sounded far too grown-up for her to understand. But then she gazed about the inside of the windmill, her feet taking her one step closer to the iron staircase that curled upward to the second floor. Janey made a dash for it suddenly, almost as though a gust of wind had taken her. When she arrived there, Annie was already waiting.

"How did you do that?"

"The world in which I live, we think of a place, we're there."

"Is that how you keep an eye on me?"

"Both of them," the glowing Annie said, her smile giving light to the narrow room.

Janey gazed up at her mother, recognizing her features, the way her eyes sparkled. The worry she had often seen inside them was gone, replaced by something that sent a wave of relief Janey's way. Her mother was forever at peace. Janey instinctively reached out her hand and felt it pass through the translucent figure before her. Again, warmth spread through her, even as on the nearby window frost suddenly appeared like spiderwebs along its edges. The pattern of snowflakes was left frozen against the glass, leaving Janey wondering how that could have happened.

"Mama, did you do that?"

"Peer through the window, Janey, and tell me what you see."

"I'll see outside, the big hill, and the farmhouse where we live."

"Look again, but this time close your eyes first."

"When you close your eyes, you can't see anything."

Annie cupped the young girl's chin, her touch electric. "Of all the people I've met, you, my sweet Janey, know that when you close your eyes you can see the world as you wish it."

Janey would trust her mother to tell the truth. Didn't she know them all now, traveling to places beyond the world? Which is maybe just where they'd gone now, because as Janey leaned in close to the window, she could no longer see familiar sights, least among them the farmhouse she called home. But she wasn't afraid, not in the presence of her mother. So she did as asked; she closed her eyes and imme-diately she saw sparkles of light dance inside her mind. Those sparkles soon took shape, stars of varied colors. She saw red and green and blue and gold, and they shone like or-naments, and when she opened her eyes she saw that all those lights dotted a tree that seemed to tower toward the sky.

"Mama, it's a Christmas tree," Janey said, wide-eyed. "But how . . ."

"Just watch, Janey."

More images appeared, brightly wrapped presents under-neath the tree, strands of fallen tinsel atop them, aglow from the lights of the tree. It was beautiful, just like those she and Brian had decorated the last two Christmases. Janey had a sense this tree was not one of them, but one from another time. When she spun around to ask Annie, Janey Sullivan found that she was alone inside the windmill.

"Mama?" she asked, a bit nervously.

There came no answer, and Janey, wondering if she was soon to wake from this all-too-real dream, considered clos-ing her eyes again, wishing to be home, safely tucked in her bed with her purple frog clasped tightly in her arms. Her feet, though, wouldn't move, so Janey peered again through the window, seeing the sails of the windmill pass by, as though aiding in turning back the clock. As one of the lat-ticed sails disappeared and allowed a clear view, Janey saw an image melt into the frame, the figure not quite solid. Janey blinked, and then there she was, her mother, part of that Christmas scene she had watched develop before her very eyes.

"Mama," she said, the word breathless.

Annie was moving inside the farmhouse living room, a cup of coffee warming her hands. Wrapped in a snug robe, she settled on the floor near a crackling fireplace, sneaking peaks at the gifts placed under the tree. A smile lit her face as much as did the warm glow of the fire, but neither was a match for the glow when she gazed up and saw another figure before her. It was a man Janey knew but didn't remember, handsome in his matching robe, and in his strong arms he cradled a little girl. It was this little person who elicited such a glow from her mother.

"Oh my," Janey stated with wonder. "That baby . . . that's me."

The man, whose name was Dan Sullivan and who was the father she'd known only from photographs, placed the sleeping baby in his wife's arms. She held her tight against her body, kissing her exposed forehead. Janey had recent experience being around babies, their neighbors Cynthia and Bradley allowing her to help out with baby Jake, so she knew that this infant version of herself was a newborn, or just beyond. Two months, she thought, her birthday being October and this scene before her obviously Christmas.

She realized that unfolding before her was her first-ever Christmas.

This was Christmas of the past.

How had time managed to take her there? Was it because of the power of the windmill, of its sails and the strong wind coming off the land? She placed a hand upon the window, felt the cold of a winter long since passed. Inside the windmill she was still warm, almost feverish, yet just beyond the glass lived a wonderland of snow and ice and the joy of a holiday Janey had come to embrace despite the recent tragedies that set her apart from her classmates. She had no mother and she had no father, but she had Brian, whom she called Dad, and together with the residents of her home of Linden Corners, she'd seen the joy Christmas could bring to all.

But this story that was breathing before her, it was about one family.

A family that back then lived for a tomorrow filled with dreams.

Dreams, the girl named Janey Sullivan knew, didn't always come true.

But on this magical day they did, as Dan and Annie exchanged gifts, their laughter filling their home, their love for each other apparent. Janey watched as her father opened a box and grimaced at the sight of shirts and ties, even though she had seen many pictures of him wearing such clothes. He'd been a businessman, like Bradley, the two of them friends. She watched as Annie opened a cardboard box and withdrew, with a wow of exclamation, a ceramic Christmas tree. Janey pointed her finger, the window stopping her. She knew that piece; they still had it stored upstairs in the attic, taking it out for Christmastime. What she didn't know was when her mother had received it, nor did she realize it had been a gift from her husband. Janey smiled as the two of them kissed, a loving sight that Janey couldn't ever remember seeing.

"I love you, Dan Sullivan," Annie said.

"I love you, Annie Sullivan," he said in response.

And then they looked down at their bundle of joy, kissed her cheek.

"And we love you, precious Janey Sullivan."

Janey felt her heart lurch inside her chest, felt it thunder with emotion.

She didn't cry; she just continued to watch. Curious to see what was to come next.

There had to be a reason her mama had taken her here to share their Christmas.

Dan reached under the tree and pulled out a small, square package.

"What is this?" Annie asked.

"It's not for you . . . well, not really."

"Dan Sullivan, what have you done?"

"I'd have Janey open it . . ."

"Should we wait until she can, perhaps next Christmas? Will it spoil?"

He laughed, the sound deep and masculine. "Are you sure you can wait?"

Dan Sullivan must have known his wife well, since, with little Janey still cradled in her arm and beginning to fuss, she slid a fingernail beneath the wrapping. When she struggled with the tape, Dan took hold of Janey and together father and daughter watched as Annie opened the box and removed from it . . .

"Oh, Dan, you remembered . . ."

Janey didn't hear the rest of her mother's statement, her excitement filling the windmill.

"My frog!" Janey exclaimed. "That's my purple frog!"

Her voice reverberated inside the empty windmill and then inside her mind. That was when she closed her eyes and awoke in the utter darkness of her room, the wind still howling at the old farmhouse, the images of yesteryear gone.

"Mama?" she asked the night.

But it was as if Annie hadn't been there, even though Janey was convinced she had been.

She got up out of bed, gazed out the window to see if the magic from inside the windmill would transfer here, to her home and to the room in which she felt most secure. But all she saw was the early rise of tomorrow over the horizon, just beyond where the windmill loomed, its sails turning forward.

Not backward.

She slept, and then hours later, Janey felt a chill seep into her bones, her little body grabbing at the pillow, hands fruitlessly grabbing at blankets. She stirred, woke, popped up.

She was in bed, the blankets pushed all the way to the edge of the bed. Grabbing for the comforter, she snuggled beneath it and sought out warmth she no longer felt.

"Mama?" she asked the empty room.

There was no answer other than the light of morning sneaking in through the window. It should have warmed her, but a chill had swept over the land sometime during the night. She felt tired, as though her sleep had been interrupted, even if she couldn't remember why. She looked out the window and saw the first flakes of snow she'd seen since last winter.

Then she reached under the pillow and sought out her steady companion, a stuffed purple frog that had seen better days. She might be ten years old, but that meant so too was he. He'd been a gift on her first Christmas, when she'd been barely two months old. Wait a minute, *she thought, looking down at the frog's silent, sewed grin,* how do I know that? And why a stuffed frog? After all these years, she still didn't know its significance. Either she'd never thought to ask, or her mother had told her and she'd forgotten.

Unlikely, that second scenario.

All she knew was that the frog had always been there, constant but unnamed. Back when she was old enough to understand the idea of naming things, she'd refused to give the frog one. People with names only disappeared, like her father had, a man with the name Dan.

Many things were uncertain for Janey Sullivan, most of all her future.

For now, though, on this morning when she felt the first chill of the season, she knew one thing was certain: Christmas was coming.

Acknowledgments

My thanks to the entire publishing gang at Kensington Books, including Laurie Parkin, Martin Biro, Vida Engstrand, and of course, Audrey LaFehr.

Thanks also to the staff at Broadway's Circle in the Square Theatre, who endured near daily updates on the book's progress.

Final appreciation goes to the following: Rosemary Pittman, Peggy Menter, Sarah Menter, Eduardo Vazquez. And lastly, Gerard Pittman, whose spirit rode the wind with me all during the writing of this novel. He, too, loved his Manhattans.